A Little
London
Scandal

Miranda Emmerson

4th ESTATE · London

4th Estate
An imprint of HarperCollins*Publishers*
1 London Bridge Street
London SE1 9GF

www.4thEstate.co.uk

HarperCollins*Publishers*
1st Floor, Watermarque Building, Ringsend Road
Dublin 4, Ireland

First published in Great Britain in 2020 by 4th Estate
This 4th Estate paperback edition published in 2021

1

A catalogue record for this book is
available from the British Library

ISBN 978-0-00-824436-1

Printed and bound in Great Britain by
CPI Group (UK) Ltd, Croydon

MIX
Paper from
responsible sources
FSC™ C007454

This book is produced from independently certified FSC™ paper
to ensure responsible forest management.

For more information visit: www.harpercollins.co.uk/green

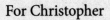
For Christopher

Contents

Prologue

Charlie dressed in the hall of his squat in Clerkenwell. He didn't like to do his hair in front of the others. These were men who lifted wallets, placed bets or moved goods for a handful of shillings a night; they didn't know his world. Instead, he stood in the light filtering through the speckled glass of the front door and greased the curls of his blond hair into a flat wave.

He would be glad to get out of the house. It had smelled for days now of fried tripe and onions; it seemed to cling to the walls. Everything he ate tasted old. He closed the door softly behind him; did not shout goodbye.

He skirted Gray's Inn, eating a packet of crisps as he walked. Then a KitKat. He polished his teeth with his tongue. He could smell the cologne, sweat and cigarettes on the skin of men as he passed. At Piccadilly Circus, he shuffled onto a ledge cut into the side of an arch and cooled his back against the stone.

He had bought something the weekend before – to calm his nerves – and now he took one of them and stowed the others in the pocket of his jeans. The first time he had taken anything it had been with a man called Luke. They had split a small bag and lain in the grass so long that it had grown damp around them in the morning hours. Charlie had kissed Luke and Luke had told his stories about working on the boats out of Liverpool and the crazy nights he had had in Amsterdam and Rotterdam and Calais. Luke had known how to impress a boy with worldliness and Charlie – knowing his place, knowing his age – was still willing to be impressed.

Charlie slipped down from the ledge, crossed the road and stood under Eros. There was a certain kind of man who, without fail, would take the time – whatever else it was that they were doing together – to tell Charlie that the man with wings was in fact Anteros and not Eros. And every time, Charlie would make sure to look grateful for this completely new piece of information. The supplicant bits, the politeness – those he could do well, for those were in his nature. He knew not to disagree with a well-spoken man. He knew to allow his country accent to show through.

He watched from the wrong side of the road as other young men were picked up from the tube exit beside the chemist, and disappeared into the crowds. North into Soho. South towards Pall Mall. He crossed the road, then watched things pick up outside the exits to the west and south.

He felt dark descend with some relief. Now he moved more easily, walking in the centre of the pavement. Leaning on the railings and watching the light play on the water from the fountain. He arched his back, stretched his arms above his head, ran his hands over his hair. He could not seem to catch an eye tonight.

He moved closer to the Regent Street exit. Charlie didn't like to trust the stairs to the north. Too close to the gentlemen's lavatories; too close to the risk of pretty policemen and arrest.

He trotted down into a white-tiled tunnel, still full of passengers. Further along, the shop windows were displaying summer tartan on lines of white plastic girls. Charlie found himself buffeted by men in fawn and grey; ladies in coloured nylon, going home. No one, he realised, could see him in this crush. The walls rang with voices and the clatter of feet. Announcements echoed up from the escalators and tunnels below. Somewhere a guard was shouting for people to 'Mind your step!' He spotted Saj, an Indian cockney he'd shared a cone of chips with once, deep in conversation with a friend, sitting on the steps back up to the road. Charlie doubled back and towards them. But before he got that far, he noticed a lone man, silhouetted against the light from the street, standing on the stairs above him. Charlie looked up. Smiled.

They looked at each other for a moment. Charlie's smile grew a little broader.

And then the sounds began to fracture. Charlie became aware of a whistling from behind him, somewhere in the tunnels. He turned and, as he did so, he saw from the corner of his eye, the man from the stairs disappearing upwards. He thought he saw Saj stand and run.

Charlie's body reacted before his brain fully understood what was happening. He started to charge upwards, rocked first on one side and then the other by bodies, running up beside him. As people passed him on the stairs, Charlie could see that the charge had sucked in theatregoers and tourists, that the whistling, and the shouting – staccato, almost hysterical, the words bent out of shape – had frightened everyone and not just the men it was designed to stir. He fell more than once, knees skidding painfully on the edges of the steps; then tumbled into the street, where he looked desperately around him, to find where the police stood in the crowd.

All along the edges of the pavement, police cars and windowless vans drew into place, forming a barrier between the mass of bodies and the roadways to the east and north. Charlie glanced in the direction of the first exit. More police cars. More vans. He staggered for a few seconds, unsure of which way to run. He saw a uniformed officer chasing three young men around the corner and into Regent Street. He thought he felt a hand on his arm. South was closest. He pushed through the crowd, discounting the women but staring in horror at every man's face he passed, unable to tell who was a policeman and who wasn't.

He charged at the people in front of him, spinning bodies out of his way. Staggered across the mouth of Piccadilly. The deeper dark of Lower Regent Street swallowed him. He heard running. Charlie looked behind him, back towards the lights of the circus, and saw an array of people – mostly men – sprinting, some disappearing into doorways or down basement steps. He caught a flash of boys he knew from the circus. Boys in denim. Men in pale suits scattering. His feet hit the pavement hard. His legs stretched beneath him.

He faltered at Pall Mall, shocked by the flash of a bus, and then ran on. There were railings across the road, beyond the great white buildings. He could hear men – a man, perhaps – just a few steps behind him. His hands found the cold iron – the edge of a garden. He climbed the railings.

Somewhere, behind the trees, men were singing. Charlie's heart battered against his chest. He fumbled in his pocket for the little packet of pills. He almost wondered if he could ask for help, but as the first sound left his mouth a hand reached across his face. And now he couldn't breathe.

You Can't Always Get
What You Want

Earlier that day, Anna Treadway, standing in the wings of The Galaxy Theatre, listened to the actors say their lines; the pace and the music of it all. Bertie was taking his long speech a bit too fast. It was a matinee – a hot Saturday matinee at that – and Bertie spoke with the restlessness of a man already thinking about how he was going to get through his evening performance. The auditorium sweated as one – like some vast coach party packed into an Italianate sauna. The actors streamed sweat over their panstick and soaked their costumes stiff with salt: costumes that Anna would then have to try and freshen before the next performance. She watched how the actors pulled surreptitiously at their clothing; or turned upstage to wipe the sweat out of their eyes.

From the audience, and Anna had sat in enough audiences to know this, the players – beautifully dressed, shining white under the lights – seemed almost godlike. An audience member could no more imagine speaking to these creatures than they could imagine running up onto the stage and touching them as they moved. But in the wings they looked small. Their steps tentative. Anna could see the way their fingers played silently on tables and chair backs when they weren't speaking. She heard the pauses in the pattern of the scene that had not been there the day before – because someone was stumbling on their lines or the person before them hadn't reached their spot.

'Maybe the new boy will freshen it up,' Bertie said, as he unbuttoned his waistcoat and jacket in the semi-darkness of the wings. Anna gathered the pieces of clothing from him as he shed them one by one. The wings had an intimacy to them, but it was not romantic in nature. The intimacy was born of shared secrets, of seeing what the audience could not. Knowing how the machinery worked or knowing that there was a machine at all.

'I don't think the actors are the problem,' Anna whispered back. 'The circle are half asleep. You can see the tops of their heads.'

She caught Bertie's sharp expression. 'Don't tell me that!' he said.

'It's the heat,' Anna whispered. 'They'll perk up when autumn hits.'

'Autumn is a long way off.'

'The evening,' Anna tried. 'The evening will be better.'

Bertie shot her a dry smile. 'That's what we all tell ourselves, isn't it?'

* * *

Nik Christou, meanwhile, was wandering, slow-footed, up the Walworth Road. He had drunk a bottle of beer with friends on Camberwell Green and now, not having change enough for the 68, he was walking into town to see if there was any food to be had before he started work. The Walworth Road was one of those strange London thoroughfares, Nik thought, the ones which you start to walk down and then realise after a quarter of an hour have no actual end. The ones which stretch beyond a reasonable length and start to make the walker feel as if he's going mad. The squeezed faces of the shops on the Commercial Road; the smug miles of Kensington High Street; the stony castles of the Cromwell Road. Nik had walked home – in darkness and in light – down all these roads and thought to himself how crazy it was that London should exist at all, when it had obviously grown too large for any normal person to understand or manage. Like a thousand villages joined together by mistake.

Nik liked to notice mistakes in things. He loved to sit in the pictures and watch the same film over and over again. Thinking about the people in it and if it all made sense. If the guilty were guilty and the innocent, innocent. He worried that the Banks children should not have been left alone with their scatty mother and their Victorian dad. They seemed brighter and more capable than either of the idiots they'd been born to, so why did Mary Poppins leave them to their fate? He looked at Paul in *Barefoot in the Park* and wondered how anyone as alive as Jane Fonda could have chosen such a corpse of a husband. Of course she wasn't happy: she was never going to be happy. Not in two years and not in twenty. She was going to have a baby, stop brushing her hair, and one day find herself on the steps of some building crying for what could have been her life. Time and again the pictures told you something was a happy ending when it was nothing of the kind. Alfie! Smug and selfish, ruining people's lives with only the slightest twinge of guilt. He should have been drowned at the end of the film. Run over by a bus. Stabbed in passing by that smooth abortionist.

Nik was just imagining Rosa Klebb skewering Bond – f—ing Bond, selfish piece of shit – that other ruiner of lives, when he arrived at Elephant and Castle. It was only when an older woman stopped and stared at him in the street that he realised he'd been speaking aloud.

He stopped and gazed steadily at the lady in her ragged house-coat. She looked away first and Nik walked on.

* * *

The Alabora Coffee House was open already for post-work ham and eggs. Anna eased open the door and looked around the empty tables.

'Ottmar?' she called.

There were footsteps in a passage beyond the kitchen and then a low cry.

'Oh my … You scared me! Rachel is not here and I just stepped out the back because … you know …' Ottmar smiled sheepishly. Anna smiled back.

'Safe or interesting?' he asked her. 'For tea? I have pide if you'd like …'

'Interesting,' she said. 'Always interesting.'

Ottmar went back into the kitchen and turned on the burners.

'I'm going to check the mail,' Anna called and slipped quietly back out of the cafe and opened the front door to the right, the one that led first to Ottmar's flat and then, above that, to hers, and lastly to the home of her manager at the theatre, Leonard, and his boyfriend Benji, who did something clever in the city and wore suits from Savile Row.

Anna Treadway lived on Neal Street. Two doors up from the coriander and lamb scents of the Punjab Indian restaurant. Two minutes north of Ellen Keeley the barrow maker and the raucous chatter of boys and vegetable sellers who gathered in the road. Five minutes from Covent Garden itself, where cabbages arrived in their hundreds on horse-drawn carts, only to delay three tonnes of potatoes driven in by truck from the fields of Kent. The only way, Anna had decided, for the incomer to try and understand London was to learn your own square mile of it and then decide that this was, in fact, the whole world. So, Anna had her neighbourhood. Covent Garden for raspberries and carrots – even at five in the morning. Seven Dials for rags – shift dresses and corduroy skirts and a hundred shades of polyester blouse. Monmouth Street for coffee bars – so many coffee bars – musicians and actors and students out on dates. The city thought itself a monument to pleasure, but its citizens knew better. What London sold was not pleasure itself but the promise of it. People came and they brought their hunger with them.

Turkish, but wearing the pale grey mackintosh of England, the Alabora Coffee House was an incomer as well. Tiled mirrors and dark coffee in little glasses. Omelettes alongside kebabs on the lunchtime menu. Once upon a time Anna had been a waitress here, a little beloved of Ottmar, friendly with his customers. When she had escaped into the theatre, Anna had imagined that nothing could be more exciting than to lose yourself in storytelling and bright lights. The fact that the theatre now glowed a little dimmer was, perhaps, more a sign of her years than any fault of the world she spent her afternoons and evenings in. She had a good mind, had been talked of as Oxford material once upon a time, but somewhere along the way she had got lost, or been thrown overboard – she wasn't sure which – and the story of her life would change in her own mind from day to day. Into this confusion had come – just lately – someone else to tell her stories to. For she had fallen in love with a man called Aloysius Weathers: someone with an equally keen mind, but a firmer grip upon his own trajectory. Aloysius – Louis to close friends – had catapulted himself from Jamaica to England to act as an accountant for jazz and ska clubs. Somewhere along the way, in the middle of a strange, discomforting winter, they had met. And had liked each other too much not to take the risk.

On the mat, behind the front door to the flats, lay a letter for her. She opened it and carried it back into the cafe.

Ottmar had laid a place at the tables next to the hatch so they could talk. A glass of water was waiting, cutlery and some home-made Turkish delight in a dish. Anna ate the little orange cubes and read the letter twice to herself.

'How is he?' Ottmar asked.

'I think he must be terribly sad, but he doesn't say so. I'm not sure how he'd even begin to say he was in grief. Mostly he talks about solicitors. Solicitors and trying to execute the will.' Aloysius had been rung by his sister Clemence in May to tell him that his mother had had a heart attack and had been installed in one of the large hospitals in Kingston. Aloysius had flown out within days only to realise that he was losing his last remaining parent and much was expected of him. Aloysius wrote to Anna – sometimes only a few lines when he was overwhelmed – and Anna tried to be as good in return. Mostly they paid for the expense of airmail, their letters flying between Jamaica and England in little more than a day; letters by boat took too long, and there was an urgency in what they had to say.

She read the letter again, slowly when she came to the parts about him missing her or loving her or imagining that she could feel him holding her hand. Ottmar brought her little flatbread boats filled with mince and spinach, a bowl of homemade yoghurt on the side. The kind of thing he didn't always bother with for his normal customers.

Anna dolloped yoghurt onto the edge of the pide and then cut them into pieces. The spinach and mince were peppery against the sweetness of the yoghurt. She scooped large forkfuls into her mouth

9

before the yoghurt grew too thin and ran away. Ottmar sat at the end of the table and watched her eat.

'I don't know what it's like to lose a parent,' Anna said. 'Not really.' She did not see her parents and she knew that Ottmar knew this. But, as with all painful spots in her life or his, he would try and stay away.

'The odd thing,' Ottmar said, 'is that it never really goes away. I still miss my mother. I'd like to cook her something. I never cooked when I was in Cyprus.'

'Because she did ...'

Ottmar shrugged. 'It was her job. And I wouldn't have taken it away from her.'

Anna looked at the broken boats in their sea of mince and yoghurt. 'Do you think she's still ... I don't know ...' She wanted to point to the plate but it seemed rude to suggest his mother was contained in a half-eaten pile of bread and spinach. So, instead, she pointed to the blue walls and the tiles. 'Do you think she's in here?' she asked Ottmar.

Ottmar made a face and sat back in his chair. He pointed a finger at Anna's supper. 'No. I think she's in there.'

Anna laughed.

'They stay, you know,' Ottmar told her. 'All the people we lose. We carry them with us. Not actually them ... My sister has a version of my mother and that will be her version ... But, you know what I mean? Everyone who goes away ... sometimes the going away makes them even stronger. When my mother died she became so large in my head ... so loud ... It's like the voice – I wondered this – it's like maybe we say "soul" when really we mean "voice". There is the voice of the person when you actually know them. And then there's the voice of the person when they leave ... That's when the voice takes on a life of its own. A certainty. These days, my mother is very, very certain.'

He smiled at Anna, wiped his hands on his trousers and stood.

'Coffee,' he said and left for the kitchen.

On her way back out to the theatre she found Nik Christou on his way in. As was his custom, Nik wore a pale beige trench coat draping off his shoulders, despite the heat of things. He looked unusually striking, and Anna found herself trying to peer at him discreetly to judge if … yes, he was wearing eyeliner.

'Ottmar told me you offered to teach him mushy peas,' Anna said, by way of a hello.

'I did,' Nik agreed, wrinkling his nose in thought. He spoke with a Lancashire accent. 'But he didn't seem that keen. I'm actually quite good at mushy peas.'

'Hidden skills,' Anna said and Nik looked at her for a moment, obviously trying to judge if this was a dig at what he did.

'All this talk about flamboyance …' Nik said.

'I don't think …' Anna started. 'I didn't mean …'

But Nik continued. 'Some days every single thing around me says stay at home; meet a man and stay at home and shutter up the windows, bolt the doors. Keep the whole world out. And do you know – do you know – what it takes to walk out of my front door some mornings? To face down that hatred? Like a fucking samurai. That's what this man said to me. This Home Counties chap with his grey three-piece and his silky tie. Like fucking samurais, we are. Like fucking samurais – in our armour, with our faces curled because that is how we have to meet the world. And I can flick my coat, and I can oil my hair but when I leave my house I am still a fucking samurai.'

Anna thought about this. She thought about her clothes and her make-up – not that she really wore it. She didn't feel like a fucking samurai. She felt exposed. Even in her high necks and low hemlines and sensible shoes, she still felt like a samurai who'd had his armour nicked.

'I only meant,' she tried apologetically, 'that some of us can't even cook.'

Nik gave her a tight smile and disappeared inside.

At the theatre, the first part of the evening performance ran mostly as expected. Anna dressed her actors, carried their clothes, made cups of lemon tea and honey drinks for sore throats. Now she was on her way to see Penny, who would be on in fourteen minutes and needed a quick change in twenty-five. Anna gave a knock at the dressing-room door and then, receiving no reply, stuck her head around.

Penny was lying down on a sofa, shielded by a fake Chinese screen which had once been part of a set.

'Asleep?' Anna asked.

The feet on the sofa twitched. Anna went in and briefly ran her hands over the next three changes, counting the pieces on the rack.

'Did I ever tell you about Nell?' a voice asked from behind the screen and then, without waiting for a reply: 'Friend of mine. Bit wild. Always a ball of nervous misery. She got Miss Julie. Just the stand-in first of all …' Anna could hear the sounds of Penny dragging herself up. 'And then she takes over. Garrick. Huge deal. Suddenly she's got a better agent. But she's terrified.' Penny emerged from behind the screen in her dressing gown and knickers, a corset half clipped and half loose around her waist. 'So, she has to calm herself down and she's asking round the cast. Older members. All of that. What d'you do?'

Anna pulled boots and a camisole and a tweed dress off the rack. 'What *do* you do?' she asked obediently.

Penny thrust a hand into her robe with great enthusiasm and mouthed, 'You relax yourself.'

Anna stood, weighed down with the clothes and thought her way round this. 'Oh good God, were you just …'

'No!' Penny said. 'Not me – Nell. But once she started, she couldn't stop. Every night she just got more and more tense, but also more and more nervous, and then – of course – it would take longer and longer. Physio, they called it. "Nell has to do her exercises from the physio".'

Anna's eyes opened wider. 'They knew? Everybody knew?'

'You can't keep a secret in a company. Not for months and months. The dressers would walk in on her. The wig people. The stage manager. It was taking all her time.'

'That's …' Anna laughed. 'That's shocking. Didn't she mind? Everyone knowing she was … you know …'

'Better that than drying onstage …' Penny said. ''Course, after a while it stopped working. She was just so tense. Nothing would relax her.' She pulled off her gown and pushed her bust into the top of the corset.

Anna dropped the dress and boots on a chair and eased the camisole over Penny's outstretched arms. 'But was she okay? Could she still do it? Remember the lines?'

Penny made a face. 'Couldn't do it. Lost her nerve. I think she put so much faith in relaxing herself that it became a sort of talisman. She lost the talisman so she believed she couldn't act. That she'd fail. Go to pieces. And she did. She dried. Lost chunks of scenes. And this is *Miss Julie*. You can't lose half an hour of it. Who's going to get it back? Her co-star, who was – of course – much more powerful than she, had her fired.'

'No!' Anna was genuinely shaken.

'Works in a flower shop in Brentford, now.' Penny stared at Anna. 'God … it's like some sort of awful morality tale about why you should never touch yourself.'

'I mean …' Anna started. 'I would draw the line at work.'

'Mmm,' Penny said. 'I suppose most people would.'

Anna buttoned Penny's dress over her underclothes. Six minutes to go.

'Do you get scared?' Anna asked.

Penny turned towards the door. 'I'm scared of everything,' she said. 'Scared of the stage, scared of drying, scared of not being any good, scared of not working, scared of losing it, scared of ageing, scared of being hated.' She pushed the dressing-room door open before her. 'But I do it anyway.'

* * *

Nik smoked and thought and watched the lights move on the signs at Piccadilly. He started to cross the road and paused by the statue to take in the groups on every corner. The usual group of boys on the step of the all-night Boots. An assortment of guys near each of the exits. Some men in suits passed through, mainly from the south, making their way up from Pall Mall and the clubs. There were young people passing through from Leicester Square. The Wimpy bar was full, mostly with teenagers, though Nik thought he spotted a group of bleary-eyed American tourists in sports coats sitting in a line in the window, a large camera propped on the counter in front of them.

He had just finished rolling a cigarette when his eye was caught by a man moving slowly past him about fifteen feet away. Nik glanced up and then looked away. He knew him.

Nik tore a strip of card from his pack of papers and rolled a little roach for the cigarette. Then he packed his smoking things away.

The man he knew stood now by the rearing horses at the top of Haymarket, looking away. Nik put the cigarette in his mouth and made as if to walk down Haymarket, patting at his pockets for a match. He passed the man and started slowly towards the Odeon.

He waited for the lights, halfway down the road. On the other side, his man took over, heading north and then down Orange Street, a dark little road which ran below Leicester Square. As they came towards the church, the man turned left and Nik followed after him, turning again a minute later, twisting around the Reference Library and into the semi-darkness of an alley.

The feet in front of him stopped. Nik stopped too. The man in front of him coughed, so Nik risked it: 'Hello.'

'Hello,' the man said back.

Nik walked down the alleyway, brushing the walls so he didn't walk into them and staring at the little light from his cigarette. When he could see the man, the dim expression of his nose and mouth, he took a final taste and ground the cigarette under his heel. He felt for the man's belt, found the buckle and undid it. Then he knelt, gingerly, on the ground he could not see.

'Okay?' Nik asked, pausing for a second.

'Uh-huh,' the man said.

Nik took him in his mouth.

When the man was finished, Nik brushed his face with his hands and helped to rebutton the fly he could feel in front of his face. Then he braced himself on the wall, stood and waited for a hand to find him with some money. He heard the rattling of coins in pockets, heard the man searching for something.

'Can we go closer to the light?' the man whispered.

They walked softly along the alleyway and closer to the corner where the light broke through in shafts. The man found his wallet and counted notes from it and Nik found his pouch of tobacco to make another smoke. They had done the same thing, different places but the same thing, ten times before. The man had never offered his name but he was well dressed. He wore a ring on the third finger of his left hand. He never offered information about himself but he always paid a little extra than was asked for.

'Can I ask you something?' Nik said.

The man glanced up at him, just for a second. 'Depends what it is.'

'You seen *Alfie*? The film …'

This stopped the man for a second, then he went back to finding change in his various pockets. 'I saw the play,' the man said. 'Then the film. Why?'

'What d'you make of him? Are we meant to like him? You know, because he's pretty or because he's Michael Caine?'

The man handed Nik two £1 notes and thirteen shillings, several shillings more than Nik usually asked for mouth. He smiled at Nik, obviously puzzled by the turn of the conversation. 'I went and saw it in the theatre. And I think I thought that he was charming. And then … after a while I thought that he was the most dangerous man I could imagine. But then, the odd thing is, I saw it again … on film. And there he was again. And I knew the story. But I was charmed by him. Again. Even though I knew where it was going. Which made me – afterwards – feel rather stupid. As if I couldn't be trusted with people. Do you know what I mean?'

'Like you were one of his girls? And you couldn't see how dangerous he was.'

The man smiled. 'Well,' he said. 'Maybe. Maybe that's the point of it. How easily we allow ourselves to be deceived.'

Nik nodded. Then he pocketed the money and walked out the way he'd come in. He finished rolling his cigarette on Orange Street and began to smoke it, half watching the alleyways to see when his man left. But his man did not emerge. And after five minutes Nik found himself heading back towards the circus.

Hovering at Eye Level

Anna had a quiet thirty minutes before the interval when she would take herself to the green room, sit on a sofa and drink instant coffee. Her mind drifted to Aloysius and all the things he wasn't telling her. All the hard moments and the grief. All the things she would see if she was there with him but could not feel through the paper he wrote on.

Her thoughts were interrupted by stomping on the stairs and then Bertie was there, come to make himself a drink in his break.

'How are they now?' she asked, mostly out of politeness.

'Bit dead. And there's an irritating cougher in one of the boxes. Waits for a pause before a punchline and then launches into their hacking.'

'Bastard,' Anna said.

'Indeed,' Bertie agreed. 'Big bloody bastards, the lot of them. D'you know who's in tonight?'

'No.'

'That MP. That Richard Wallis.'

'Who's Richard Wallis?' Anna asked.

'The one who was arrested. For the boy in Golden Square. Had to resign his post …'

Anna shook her head.

'Penny's been friends with the wife for years. Very pleased with herself they're in. "Do you think he did it?" I asked her. Not the right thing to say at all!' Bertie laughed to himself.

'Did what, though?'

'Two winters ago …' Bertie began. 'There's a party, so the papers say. Labour MPs mostly, people of that ilk, in a flat on Golden

16

Square. That night they find a boy – a prostitute – battered and half dead outside. Wallis man gets arrested. He was a junior minister in some department. Home affairs or justice. Something embarrassing to the high ups. Anyway ... Big political stink. But it never goes to trial. He disappears and I think most people thought he'd give it up. But no. He stands again – in Peckham. Keeps his seat. Brazens it all out. And he's still with the wife.'

'Oh,' Anna said. 'Yes. Okay. I think I know. I just ... I didn't follow it. Didn't really know who he was. But if he didn't do it ...'

'Who says he didn't do it?' Bertie said. 'It didn't go to trial. That's something else altogether. That's money.'

'Do you think?'

Bertie looked at her. 'If there are enough men standing round you ... If they have your back ... How often does anyone in Parliament go to prison for anything? Profumo sneaks away from all the mess. Galbraith's writing letters to a Russian spy and nobody even touches him for it. There're so many walls around these men – walls and barbed wire ... There's practically an infantry of little boys – all standing to attention, ready to be sacrificed.'

Anna thought about this. She wondered who the boys were in this analogy. 'Still, though ...' she said at last. 'It's not as if Penny's friends with him, in particular. And we can't help who our girlfriends marry ... Women can be odd about that sort of thing. And men so hard to read.'

She saw Bertie looking at her. He wasn't married. Didn't seem to be divorced. She'd probably said the wrong thing without meaning to.

'I'm going to go and sort out that suit of yours,' she said and took the chance to run away upstairs.

* * *

Nik stood in the off-licence on Panton Street doing maths. If he bought the smallest bottle of gin that would be 15 shillings. He could take twenty minutes to himself, try to pick up someone else and he'd be even for rent tomorrow back at home. His share of rent was £1

17

6 shillings, but he hadn't bought any food for the house in days. He needed the best part of a pound for bread, tea, milk, jam and maybe some ham and cheese. So, that was £1 6 shillings for next week's rent. Plus 15 shillings for gin. £1 for food. Seven shillings for a small pouch of tobacco. Another shilling for papers. Three pounds 9 shillings in all. He didn't even have £3.

The girl behind the counter had painted thick black lines above her lashes. Her nails were green. Her chest strained against the white nylon shirt she wore. The black lines from her eyes were snaking down the creases at the side of her face, bleeding in the heat. She turned the pages of the *Daily Mirror* with careful fingers, her eyes flickering around the field of type. Nik watched her breathe.

One more customer, Nik thought; something that paid well and he'd knock off until next week. He bought the little bottle of gin, stowed it in his coat and walked out and onto Haymarket.

Nik sat for a while on a park bench in the quiet and the green of St James's Square. The roofs of houses all around him clustered with pigeons. Nik found himself watching them and then tracing a small brown bird which flew from tree to tree above his head.

When the man walked towards him, Nik had a flash of recognition. The slim snakeskin suit. American band T-shirt. The man's hair was long and shiny, cut in an expert fashion, in the way only rich young women and successful musicians could afford. Nik had seen his picture on the wall of the pub at the end of Wardour Street. In a band photo in the window of a men's clothiers. He could not remember his name.

The man stopped in the centre of the square, and turned slightly on his heel. He had been looking at Nik but now he looked away. Nik put the top back on the bottle of gin and slid it away from view. He ran his tongue over his teeth. He looked around him but there were few people in the square at this point in the evening. A couple of elderly men, leaning together and talking. Some kids in black clothes and make-up sitting on the grass and rolling what was probably a joint. Nik stood. And as he stood, the man with the long hair started to walk away again, off to the western side and its little gate.

Nik dragged his fingers through his hair. Five pounds, he thought. Don't ask for too little.

The man with the shining hair walked quickly along King Street, dipping his head when a girl, walking towards him on the pavement, seemed to recognise him and began to speak. He jogged past her and she closed her mouth. Nik jogged a little and passed her too; as invisible as the pretty man had been conspicuous. The man in front turned a corner.

This was not Nik's world at all. Rolls-Royces, Jaguars and Bentleys were parked up on the edges of the pavement. They passed an auction house, then a window with 'Antiquarian Books' painted across it in gold and black letters. Nik was used to knowing the routes out of places. Used to knowing where to run. But he had lost his bearings.

Turning right now and down an alleyway. 'Mason's Yard', the sign said. Darker still and then out – just for a moment – into light. As Nik stood and blinked, the man was disappearing into the mouth of a passage in the far corner of the square. In the passage a large metal door stood open, held by a hand – the only part of the man that Nik could see. Nik clasped the edge of the door and peered inside, but the man in front of him was already disappearing up a flight of wooden stairs that twisted away into the dark above. Nik followed but when he got to the top of the stairs the man was nowhere to be seen.

He stood in a corridor, lined with posters of musicians, of festivals and Isle of Wight happenings. Painted doors, purple, red and green, led off into rooms marked 'Tech' and 'Dressing Room' and 'Manager'. The door nearest Nik was painted orange and had a single stick figure of a man painted on the outside. Gents. There was a thumping from the floor below as if music was being played at a loud and steady rhythm.

As Nik stood there, the door marked 'Dressing Room' was flung open. For a second, he caught a glimpse of mirrors, tables lined with bottles and brushes and plates and make-up, and the half-seen reflection of men in underwear. The man in the snakeskin suit nodded towards the orange door.

The gents was a small, white-tiled room, hung with pornographic pictures of women, naked, legs spread wide. Nik stared for a moment at an extremely lush crop of pubic hair that happened to be hovering at eye level. Then the man entered and locked the door behind them. He was older than Nik, late twenties. Possibly even thirty. He seemed hot, flushed, a little unsure.

'How much?' he asked.

Nik took a second to breathe and finesse his prices. 'Five pounds for oral or hand. Seven pounds for anal. Ten for half an hour, whatever you want.'

The young man straightened up and nodded. He looked at Nik and then he looked at himself in the mirror.

'You okay?' Nik asked.

The man nodded. He took off the jacket of his suit and hung it on the back of the door. Then he unbuttoned his fly and pulled his shirt out of the waistband of his trousers.

'Can you tell me what you want?' Nik asked.

The man gestured to the floor beside the toilet. 'Get down on your knees.'

Nik carefully put the lid down on the toilet. 'Are we agreed on the price?' he asked. The man seemed both to be very nervous but also intent on being in charge.

'Kneel down,' the man said.

'Can you pay me first?'

The man in snakeskin stared at him. His fly was open. He was hard. Nik's hand trembled slightly so he pushed it into the pocket of his coat. 'I need you to pay me,' he said again.

The man shook his head. 'You don't do this to other people,' he said.

Nik steadied his breathing. 'I do the first time. We don't know each other.' He felt the incongruity of it. He in his jeans and his shirt, his trench coat and his heavy shoes. This other man, this man that young women on the street could name, stripped nearly bare and yet somehow imagining that Nik was – what? – flattered to be in this position.

The man shuffled round and felt in the inside of his jacket pocket. He pulled out his wallet and took from it a £20 note. Then he returned the wallet to its place and turned back towards Nik, holding out the piece of paper. 'You take this and shut up.'

Nik reached out a hand, took the note, folded it and put it into the coin pocket of his jeans. Then he removed his coat, unbuttoned his jeans and crouched down on the tiled floor of the little bathroom.

* * *

In the post-show world of the green room, the atmosphere was generally convivial. The actors sat and waited for their friends. The technical crew who had finished early stopped to deposit teacups and say goodnight. Sometimes a bottle of wine was opened. Sometimes a bottle of whisky. Saturday night performances meant no show on Sunday; meant lie-ins and late nights and the slow exhalation of another week passed.

Anna paused, her handbag on her arm, leaning one knee on the side of the sofa, wondering if she should wait and say goodnight to Leonard.

There were voices on the stairs and now visitors emerged. Dick from the stage door leading a wealthily clad young couple, her in purple suiting and him in slim, matte grey. Business, Anna thought. Or banking.

'Well, she was always so bold at university,' the woman was saying. 'And we were always a bit in awe. She had a confidence about her, on the stage. Beyond what any of us felt at nineteen. Just keeping yourself stocked with soup and bread seems impossible at that age. But she knew what she wanted.'

Dick crossed to the sink and started to uncork a bottle of white wine. Leonard appeared at Anna's shoulder and walked past her, towards the new arrivals. He was a man of around fifty, with olive skin, dark eyes and wiry brown hair beginning to turn grey. He wore tight brown cords and a beige shirt which hung open at the cuffs and neck, giving him an appearance of managed loucheness. 'Leonard Fleet. I'm the company manager for *Lady Angkatell's Secret*. Who are you here for?'

'Penny,' the young woman said. 'I've been promising to come and life's been mad and really, between work and children, we barely leave the house. Well, no, I mean ... I barely leave the house. Richard's more of an office boy.'

The Wallises, Anna thought. Of course, this was them.

Richard smiled dryly at Leonard. 'Apparently I'm a boy.'

Leonard smiled back. 'Whatever she says. Isn't that the way?'

'To stay married? Well, yes. It is, isn't it?'

'I'm a bachelor myself,' Leonard noted, accepting a glass of wine from Dick.

'Not found the right girl yet? Or maybe you like your freedom ...' said the wife, and shot a bashful grin at Leonard, signalling she meant no harm.

Leonard drank his warm white wine. 'The right girl has been elusive,' he agreed, and the husband turned his back on them and went to look at the framed photographs from past productions.

'He won't know who anyone is,' the wife confided to Leonard. 'I'm the theatre buff. I'm the one who went to every *Saint Joan*, every *Henry V*. Richard likes whatever the wireless has to throw at him at ten to twelve.'

Anna noticed that Leonard seemed not entirely to be listening. Rather, he was watching Richard Wallis out of the corner of his eye. The rest of the wardrobe department slowly filtered in and stood in a gaggle by the stairs, chatting. Bertie appeared next and crossed to Anna, giving her a rather meaningful look.

Seemingly unaware of the various tensions around her husband, the wife ploughed on. 'It was the theatre that made me love literature, more than novels. Because I'd read Shakespeare, I wanted to see what else there was. I asked my French teacher and she gave me *Tartuffe*. I never understood why London was so slow to do French plays, or German plays, or Spanish.'

'Well ...' Leonard said, dragging himself back into the conversation. 'There are an awful lot of plays in English.'

'There are,' the wife agreed. 'But are they all that good?'

'Are you attacking our native culture again, darling?' her husband asked, his voice amused. 'Because I think we agreed that stays behind closed doors.'

'Richard did PPE, I did French,' the wife continued. 'He thinks he knows how we should run the world. I just want people to think in other languages.'

Anna watched the woman carefully. She had a nice face, soft and round; youthful, Anna thought, grey eyes blinking with interest when she listened. But she was a little too manicured. Dark bobbed hair glistening under the lights as she moved carefully in her clean, pressed suit and heels. Anna liked the kind of women who wore jeans; who cut their hair like men; who dressed as if they wanted only to please themselves. She wanted to be like them one day. When she was properly grown up. And not only thirty-two. Anna listened to Mrs Wallis's back and forth with Leonard. She had a brain, that much was clear. So why was she with him?

'To be fair, quite a number of the English struggle to think in their own language,' Leonard was saying.

'It's not even that ...' the wife went on.

'Merrian ...' her husband said in a quiet voice. 'Shall we just wait for Penny?'

'No. But it's important,' Merrian told Leonard. 'French has words for things that we can't even properly translate. *Dépaysement* is un-countrying, the feeling of being out of your country, out of comfort. Another language is fresh eyes. It's a reminder that things are not settled or fixed. The world was not made for English.'

Merrian's husband looked over at Leonard and they shared a smile. Merrian's face fell a little.

'I know,' she said. 'It's a hobby horse. I'm too long at home.' She took her glass of wine and went to look at pictures on another wall.

'Who's that?' the husband asked, pointing to a shot of an animated woman gesturing towards the camera.

'Peggy Ashcroft. Miss Madrigal in *The Chalk Garden*,' Leonard told him.

Merrian spoke, but this time she didn't turn. 'It won't mean anything to him,' she said. 'But I saw her play Hester Collyer in

The Deep Blue Sea and I felt like my heart was breaking. So much sadness.'

'Too much,' Leonard said, darkly.

The other members of the company were filtering in now. The green room quickly filled to busting. Anna hovered, watching the Wallises. Leonard was touring the edges of the room with Richard Wallis, telling him who everybody was and what they were playing.

Bertie came and joined them, dressed in his post-show uniform: chinos and a shirt and his green safari jacket. He was a little sensitive about his weight so he liked to do the belt up snug around the middle. Anna suspected that it made him feel younger.

Anna could see Bertie watching the Wallises, and flashed a grin across the room. He moved closer to her and whispered in her ear: 'It's compulsive, isn't it?'

'It really is.'

'What do you make of her?'

'Clever.'

'Silver spoon?'

'Can't tell,' Anna said.

'Why's Leonard sticking to the man?'

Anna looked at Bertie. 'Probably for the same reason we're both watching him. Scandal!'

Bertie laughed softly and looked at his watch. 'It's getting on for eleven. I should be going home.'

'Me too. Give it another minute, though.'

Bertie smiled and gave Anna a wink. Then he shifted to another sofa to better watch the wife.

In a shiver of exclamations, Penny arrived on the scene and kissed Merrian many times. Anna could hear a lot of 'wonderful's and 'well done's. Leonard and the Wallis husband hovered on the edge of all the cooing.

Anna knew that she should go home. But now the little room was rammed with more than forty people and there was barely passage to the stairs at all. Somewhere in the mix she could hear Bertie and one of the other actors complaining, and the crush of people slowly started to filter out into the corridor and towards the stairs.

Anna shuffled slowly alongside all the rest. Then finally found herself standing next to the Wallis wife as they were pinioned for a moment at the top of the stairs.

'It was very good,' Merrian said to Anna, obviously believing that Anna was another actress and that she should say this to everyone involved.

'Yes,' Anna said. She had rehearsed her response to this many times. 'It's a fun evening.'

'Fun to play in, I'd think,' Merrian said.

'Well, I'm not an actress.'

'Oh. I'm so sorry. I just assumed. Were you watching?' Merrian asked.

'I'm a dresser,' Anna explained. 'I dress Lisa, Maeve, Penny and Bertie.'

'Oh,' Merrian said and nodded vacantly. 'Well, that must be fun as well. All the lovely frocks!' And she looked around for someone else to talk to.

The crowd of theatre people came to a halt again one flight short of the ground floor and then stood there, apparently unable to proceed. Anna could see the Wallises jammed in front of her, along with Leonard, Bertie, Penny and about half the company. Autograph hunters, she thought, or else someone is trying to move some enormous piece of set through one of the doors.

'I think, if you don't mind, I might just slip away for an hour. Quick drink at the Hellenic,' Richard Wallis was saying to his wife.

Merrian did not reply but turned instead to Penny and said in a jovial tone, 'I think my husband has run out of things to say to us.'

'It's really fine,' Penny assured them both. 'You're under no obligation.'

'It's nothing grand. It's just that I'm on a committee trying to deal with oversight for the Concorde,' Mr Wallis said. 'You know, the transatlantic aeroplane, and everything's rather … tense at the moment.'

'All the men in Richard's circle just love to redesign the world,' Merrian said. 'Over Scotch. His club is like a great crèche.'

'A friend of mine once said that universities were just holding pens for the unnaturally clever,' Leonard put in. 'Perhaps gentlemen's clubs are closets for the overly design-conscious.' He paused. 'Somewhere where they can imagine themselves as gods on Mount Olympus. Only it's a map of Britain on the table, not the world.'

'Look, does anyone know why we're all standing here?' came Bertie's voice.

'Okay! Could whoever is doing whatever outside the stage door be moved along, please?' Leonard shouted to the crowd of technicians and stage hands in front of them.

'Well, I think it must be lovely to have a club and everyone's just jealous,' Penny said to Richard Wallis. 'Go and have a drink and talk about all the fancy jet planes in the world. Where's the harm in that!'

Anna watched Mr Wallis give Penny a milk-coloured smile of gratitude.

* * *

When the man from the band had finished and left the little toilet, Nik crouched on the floor for a minute or so, getting himself together. He re-dressed, checked his jeans for the £20 note and then went to the door to see if the way was clear for him to leave. But now he could hear many voices and a lot of laughing and he realised that the men from the dressing room must have come out into the hall. He kept the door bolted and laid his head against the wood.

The men's voices echoed outside.

'Like the one in Liverpool?' one of them was saying.

'Amazing!' another voice said.

'And it went down to the end!'

'They'd have let us go all night.'

'D'you remember?'

'Yeah!'

'And at the end Pete came forward?'

'She was a dirty birdie. Could have split her right in two.'

'And he just kept playing and playing and I'm thinking the management'll soon come on and kick us off.'

26

'And the girl with yellow in her hair!'

'And Marianne was screaming at him …'

'Filthy pig! Yer filthy Irish pig!'

'Hooked the bass line right …'

'And Danny was on his knees!'

'On his knees with brown stuff bubbling.'

'And the dirty bitch with pink trousers.'

'You could see her tits …'

'Her nipples!'

'You could see her bloody tits …'

'Right up on the stage.'

'Jesus!'

'Like she was coming on the roof of a train!'

'And Danny said …'

'And Danny said!'

'And Danny said …'

'Sit on my face!'

'Oh my god!'

'The slut.'

'The slut!'

Nik's head was spinning. For a long, slow moment at the beginning, he had thought that they were talking about him. He could hear the voice of the man in the snakeskin suit, in amongst it all, with the 'slut's and the 'coming' and the whoops of manly solidarity. What a bunch of absolute arseholes, Nik thought. And then: I'm trapped in this lavatory and how am I going to get out?

The Un-Nightliness of
Summer Nights in London

The Hellenic gentlemen's club stood on the corner of Pall Mall and Waterloo Place. It smelled like old wood and stone. Richard thought about this whenever he stood in the main entrance. It literally smelled of the thing it was. Not money or power or connections made over cigars. Stone. Wood. Polish. Metal. A building immune to the culture that swam inside it.

Richard smiled to himself. Culture. Like a yoghurt. Like old milk. He walked through to the smoking room, swinging his arms at his sides. *I am swimming in old milk.*

Angus sat by a window, his legs crossed, a *Telegraph* discarded on his knee. He seemed to be watching the lights out in the darkness.

'How are the other microbes this evening?' Richard asked.

Angus looked up. His face betrayed very little. 'The man from St Andrews has a birthday and there are a lot of people being loud on the terrace.'

Richard sat down across from him. 'How ghastly,' he said, in a tone that seemed to mock the words he spoke.

Angus looked steadily at him. 'It is ghastly. It's one of those evenings that makes me wish we had somewhere else to go. Why are people like that allowed in here?'

'We're people like that,' Richard pointed out.

'On election night. Sometimes. For an hour. The rest of the time we behave like adults.'

'I had to sit through a play this evening,' Richard said, feeling it was the right moment to change the subject.

'How bad was it?'

Richard thought about this. 'I don't know,' he said at last. 'I wasn't listening to any of the words.'

A waiter passed and Angus ordered them both drinks. He always paid for Richard. And Richard always felt slightly belittled by the gesture.

'I'm surprised you haven't gone home,' Richard told him. 'What's there to stay for? They'll be caterwauling here all night.'

Angus looked at him sternly. But he did not answer the question.

'Henry?' Richard asked.

'Somewhere in the garden making everyone feel loved.'

'It's funny,' Richard said. 'You watch him doing it to other people but when it's you ...'

'His sun shines very brightly,' Angus said. 'Lit by a million pounds.'

They both smiled at once.

* * *

Merrian sat in the driving seat, staring at the red light in front of her at Trafalgar Square. She felt warm and drunk and relaxed and bruised all at once. Life-sick. Just a little. And terribly tired.

She watched a crowd of young women in bright boots and small dresses cross in front of her. She heard the edge of their accents. Their desperately loud non-U-ness. The girls who had not been conditioned out of the habit of 'lounge' and 'toilet'. She wondered if she could smell them. All Tigress knock-off perfume and yesterday's knickers. Her hands tightened on the wheel.

The lights moved to green; she released the handbrake and the clutch. The car creaked slowly around the bend and she felt a little free of London. Leaving now, she thought. Shaking off the centre. Dulwich wasn't London. Dulwich was a tree-lined anywhere. It was the bits of Reading that her parents had dreamed of living in. It was quiet streets and white faces and children in clean uniform. Her parents loved that she lived there. And she loved it too. And was embarrassed by it. And didn't want to let it go.

* * *

Anna walked home down a busy Charing Cross Road. The men in the entrance of the Cafe 101 – Saturday night shirts, dark jeans – smoking and drinking espresso, calling to the women.

'I can smell you, girl.'

You can't smell me, she thought.

Cambridge Circus now. *The Sound of* bloody *Music* still rumbling on. 'It's not all blind horses and Brecht,' she could hear Leonard snapping back at her, somewhere in the velvet interior of her head. Shaftesbury Avenue. A fug of petrol fumes, unpleasant on the tongue in the warm air.

She wrote to Louis in her head, knowing the words were as much for her as they were for him. *I love you*. Didn't people know they spoke these words to comfort themselves? I love. I feel love. I have you. I am keeping you. I am not alone.

I wish I was there, she would start.

Or maybe something more direct: *Are you a different shape, Louis? Do you feel changed?*

I am scared that you won't come home. That in a time of grief people need their real families and their real homes.

It is hot here. London smells.

What am I meant to say to you, my darling?

What was she meant to say? And did it even matter? Wasn't the fact that she wrote something on those little pages the thing that really mattered? She could write 'fish' a thousand times and he would still know that she was thinking of him.

Fish. Fish. Fish.

* * *

Richard had thought he would leave after a single drink, but the drinks had left him weary and he was in no rush to stumble into his dark bedroom and lie down beside his snoring wife. Instead, he smoked a little with Angus and tried to wake up enough to stay until midnight.

'They'll have to go eventually,' Angus said, as the shouting and singing from the garden forced its way into the room.

Richard's face crumpled. 'I wish someone from the club would have a word.'

Angus smiled. 'Breathe, Mr Wallis. Breathe.'

* * *

Ten minutes after the unseen band emerged into the hallway to trap Nik in the little bathroom, they'd been called downstairs by someone shouting, 'Fifteen-minute call! Can I have everyone by the stage!'

Nik gave things a couple of minutes and then tried to picture his way out. There was a flight of stairs that twisted round. No windows and no light when he'd come in, but maybe there'd be a light on for the band. And then a door to the passage outside, though he couldn't know if it would open. He quietly unlatched the toilet door and stepped out into the hall.

The stairway, when he found it, was dark, as was the hall below. He had one hand on the banister and a foot on the second step when voices came from the ground floor.

'Have they come yet?'

'No. But they will and you're going to have to shift the gear.'

Nik crept backwards and through the open door marked 'Manager'. There was no light on in there; no jacket on the chair by the desk; no lingering smell of fags. He sensed the room had been empty for some time. Voices on the stairs now. Someone running. A door banged in the corridor.

He stood in the dark of the room and listened. Who would he say he was if he was caught? A fan, was the obvious answer. Would they believe him? Would they call the police? He'd been beaten by the police before now. He'd been detained. He'd been spat at and kicked in the groin until he cried.

He had grown smart. Older men had made him smart – had taught him. This job had been a mistake, but then every tenth job was, in some way or another. He'd make it out.

He stood in the semi-darkness. Time passed. The door stood open a crack, giving him enough light with which to read the walls.

The Revolution of Rock	**Emperor Rosko & Full Supporting Programme**	Shaftesbury Avenue, London – *The Electric String Band*	*Zoot Sims & Ottilie Patterson*
*The Byrds *Them *Charles Dickens	Axis, Bold as Love AND ALL STAR COMPANY	*ABC Belfast* **ON THE STAGE** *Saturday, 16th July*	**GERRY** *& the Pacemakers*
THE FOUNDATIONS and THE FLIRTATIONS	ᵉENGELBERT ᵒHUMPERDINCK And THE HOLLIES	The Fabulous **WALKER BROTHERS**	New Exciting Sound of 60s **TROGGS**
Capitol **CARDIFF** September 1965	**Cat Stevens** And Other Exciting New Sounds	The 'Pop' **Music Event** of the Year!	**BEACH BOYS** *Lulu – David and Jonathan*

It was one of the smartest things Nik had ever seen: he wanted to live in a room covered with music posters, but all he could do right now was read the words. Someone in the room next to him kept moving. Walking, coughing, sighing.

Time moved. Though he wasn't sure how fast. There was a little window in the room but it was dark now. It had still been light – just – when the man had picked him up. Half past nine maybe, so now it must be well after ten. Maybe even getting on for eleven. He took a little drink from the bottle in his pocket. He started to roll a cigarette and then thought better of it.

The floor below him thumped. The boards in the building seemed to hum. There was a gig going on. Guitars, he thought. And drums.

But there was silence on his floor now. No more walking in the room next door. Nik crept out into the corridor and onto the stairs. He moved as soundlessly as he could in the darkness, feeling with his feet and his hands. The staircase turned and turned again. He felt the end of the banister and put his hands out into darkness. He had to move across the space now and find the inside of the door to the outside world. His eyes had adjusted. There were outlines, deeper patches of black.

The lights blazed on above his head. He couldn't see. He was blind and in his blindness he was reaching out in front of him. There were voices very close. He found the banister again. Stairs – he could see them now. He started to run back up them and too late – a whole half a second too late – he realised he should have run the other way.

Nik ran, knowing that he was making too much noise and stumbled through the doorway and back into the hall above.

There were lights on everywhere now. 'Hey!' he heard behind him.

He reached for the manager's door but he misjudged, pushed it closed instead of open and then fell against it.

An arm reached round him from behind and caught him at the waist. He was pulled backwards and thrown onto the floor, his hand crushed beneath him. People were swearing. Instinctively, Nik hid his face with his arm.

'You were stealing,' he heard a man say. 'You were in here stealing!'

Nik looked at the man from over his arm – his long beard and dark clothes made him look like an angry hippie. Then he looked across the line of other faces that crowded in on him. There was a singer with dark hair, whose face had been on magazine covers. A red-haired man. The man who had bought him, in his snakeskin suit. His brain couldn't cope with all the faces.

'I'm sorry,' he said.

'What?' the angry hippie asked.

'I'm sorry,' Nik said, louder. 'I didn't steal. You can check. I'm just a fan. I wanted something from the band.'

He looked forlornly up at them.

'He's lying,' the angry hippie said, unmoved.

Nik looked at the man who had bought him, in his American band T-shirt, and though he should have known better than to try, he pleaded with his eyes.

The group fell silent for a few seconds and then Nik saw – too late, always too late – that at least one of the man's band mates had seen the look he was giving Nik and the one Nik gave him back.

Nik felt the mistake in his bones.

The man in the snakeskin suit reached down towards Nik and pulled him upright by the collar of his coat. Nik didn't see what happened next but he felt the wall. He cried out and then someone hit him and he closed his eyes and waited for it to be over.

* * *

Anna let herself into her silent flat and put on the living-room light. Her flatmate, Kelly, would not be back from working in the clubs until nearly two. Anna rather liked this little stretch of time. Half eleven until two. When she had the whole flat to herself and could take midnight baths or lie in her underwear in the living room just reading books or listening to the radio.

She stripped off her damp black shirt. Unhooked the waistband of her trousers. Peeled off her socks. The windows had no curtains. She watched the traffic on Shaftesbury Avenue go past, the buses nearly at the right height to catch her looking back: there in her underwear, sweaty and unkempt. She didn't know when she'd stopped caring so much what people thought of her, she only knew that it was slipping away. All that dreadful self-consciousness, dying at her feet.

Perhaps it was meeting Aloysius. Perhaps it was the awfulness of Lanny's disappearance. Lanny had been her actress two years before. An American movie star, making a name for herself in the West End with the main part in *The Field of Stars*. But she had disappeared one night after the performance, and Anna had gone plunging after her. It had been a winter of baptisms. Meeting Louis in the clubs, seeing him beaten by the police, following Lanny into places she had not known existed. Losing faith in some things; gaining faith in others.

Anna watched another bus go past her window. She felt the sweat drying on her skin. She unclipped her bra and threw it onto the arm of the sofa. Bliss. She spread her arms wide; stretched the creases out of her. The naked samurai. Another bus went past.

Anna turned on the radio – found Radio Caroline – and settled her cooling body into the depths of the sofa. A delicious numbness descended upon her, there in the darkness, with the flashing and pulsing of the lights in the street reflected on the white walls above her.

* * *

Nik didn't know what time it was. He thought he might have blacked out, for a while, on the floor of the hall. He remembered someone kicking him in the stomach and that had roused him. He remembered it being over. He remembered hands, dragging at him under his arms and pulling him down the stairs. He remembered the smoky, sharp smell of the air as the door to the alley had been pulled open. He remembered trying to put his hands out in front of him as he fell towards the pavement.

It was warm, too warm for this time of the evening. And the sticky atmosphere – the un-nightliness of summer nights in London – made him feel rather sick. He had stumbled down one alley, and then another, and turned a corner, only to find himself in St James's Square gardens once again. Nik walked to a bench and sat down. He reached into his pocket for the bottle of gin but it was gone. He felt for his pouch of tobacco and that was still there. He attempted to roll a smoke but his bruised fingers could not pinch the paper straight or tight. He made, instead, a loose cigarette – fat in the middle, like a sweetie – and smoked the airy and disappointing thing without a roach.

When he'd first come to the city he had slept in parks. It had been the autumn after he had turned fifteen, and he remembered how the benches had still felt warm at half past nine. As the night crept on, cold had travelled down from the sky, its fingers peeling at his skin. Hour after hour he'd lie awake. In time-free black. Not ever knowing how long it was until morning.

Sometimes he would doubt himself. Think that he wasn't in Green Park at all. Or in Kensington Gardens. Or by the Serpentine. His brain would tell itself he was back home. At Ashton Gardens or Moor Park. Or walking by the water on the Ribble estuary.

All those things he'd done. Those moments. The corners of his life where he'd turned this way or that. Leaving home; getting on the train to London. The first evening when he had spoken to another boy at Piccadilly. Made his first introductions, looking for a room. These memories, this map, seemed thin at night. Like the pattern of it all might tear right through and he'd be Nik in Preston or Nik in Blackpool or Nik in anyplace, the words on the edges of the streets not meaning much at all.

He wondered if it was midnight. He felt for the £20 note in the pocket of his jeans. Still there.

Nik walked out of the square, in the direction that he thought would lead to Piccadilly. But he found, instead, after turning and then turning again, that he was further south, on a pavement of Pall Mall.

He walked east, with the idea of catching a night bus from Haymarket. But at the corner of Pall Mall and Waterloo Place he paused for a moment, listening to the screaming of a man from somewhere in the darkness. The man was wailing and crying. He sounded old, unhinged. Nik did not move. This wasn't for him to deal with. Some other good Samaritan would have to walk towards that sound.

'Hey! Stop!' The shouts came out of the darkness and now there was a pounding of feet on stones. Nik turned away, signalling that this was not his problem and waited for a taxi to cross in front of him before he made his escape.

The policeman took him by surprise. Hurtling into him, either by design or by mistake, Nik could not tell which. They fell together. Half on the kerb, half in the road – the policeman panicking under his breath and dragging them both out of the way of traffic.

Nik tried to sit up but the man was straddling him. Crushing his hips, battering at his arms.

'What …?' Nik asked. Unable to find the words to follow this.

Monday Morning, Hot and Tired

They had found the boy in the gardens. Waterloo Gardens. A stretch of green, lined with bushes and high trees, which looked like a railed-in park or square, but really served as a back garden for some of the clubs along Pall Mall.

Detective Sergeant Hayes sat, sweating in his nylon shirt and fastened tie, listening to the details of the morning's post mortem. Charlie or Charles was thought to be the first name, according to some boys on the street, but his last name was a mystery. No fixed abode, they thought. Rent. Somewhere between sixteen and nineteen was their best guess. Somewhat malnourished. Signs of some abuse. Old bruises, abrasions to the groin. Three of his ribs had been broken and his hand fractured soon before or during death. He had been found, face down in the earth, half hidden beneath the bushes at the edge of Waterloo Gardens. Just inside the railings that separated the green space from the quiet street outside.

There was earth in Charlie's mouth and nose. He had been smothered, or possibly crushed until he could no longer breathe, lying face down in the soil. There were signs pointing to asphyxiation but also cardiac arrest – heart attack; it was thought that the first might have prompted the second.

They'd arrested a lad – rent as well. Nikos Christou. He'd been spotted on the corner of Waterloo Place and Pall Mall just minutes after the body had been seen through the railings. A homeless man, a derelict, had guided a policeman to the spot where he thought two men had gone in. The man had said he'd heard noises. Perhaps a little yell.

Christou had been found with a £20 note in the pocket of his jeans. His face and body had, as Saturday night turned into Sunday morning, displayed more and more bruises – signs of a recent alter-cation. He had protested his innocence. They all did. But officers believed strongly that Charlie's death pointed to a mugging and a fight between two street boys. A vicious act of violence, possibly made worse by the amount of alcohol that Mr Christou seemed to have consumed that evening.

CID were taking the lead on the murder but they had three officers from Vice assisting with the rent-boy angle of the thing. Detective Sergeant Hayes had been fourteen months in Vice. He had been sent there from CID as punishment for making a fool of himself, when, two years before, he had borrowed a police car only to drive hundreds of miles out of his jurisdiction following a miss-ing person who had then taken her own life. In his defence, and he had had to defend himself many times, he had just been left by his wife and daughter, and his judgement had been somewhat impaired. But Hayes' show of weakness, his mental vulnerability, did not play well in the Metropolitan Police. Officers faced worse shocks in their day-to-day duties. And breakdowns were what you had when you were off duty or on your hols. He'd been signed off work for five months after the incident and, frankly, no one had expected him to return. Everyone seemed to know it was only a matter of time before he resigned or somehow went off the rails again.

Hayes knew all this. But he didn't really know what to do about it. He had approached this strange new world of Vice – the drugs and the sex work and the trade in human bodies – with the kind of grinding competence that made him hard to fault. But he couldn't banter. His dirty jokes would have seemed tame in the mouth of a twelve-year-old. He'd never physically hurt a suspect and he refused – uncomfortably and with an enormous amount of embarrassment – to take bribes. Every day he was a policeman and every day he somehow failed at being a policeman.

He sat now with a cluster of colleagues and listened to the CID inspector's assessment of the case so far.

'He's not the biggest lad, this Nikos. Five foot seven and slim ... but wiry,' Inspector Kite told them. 'But then it wasn't necessarily a crime of strength. If he'd got the lad face down and got on top of him, Charlie would have been at a disadvantage.'

'Why Waterloo Gardens, sir?' someone asked. 'Aren't their gates locked? It's private land.'

'As Vice will be able to tell you, there was a raid on Piccadilly Circus tube station at about half past eleven on Saturday evening. Eighteen arrests were made but many potential and possible offenders fled the scene. We're working on the theory that this Charlie ran south at around the same time as Nikos and that Nikos knew or discovered that Charlie had been well paid earlier in the evening. Some of the officers from the raid pursued a group of men down Lower Regent Street – it's possible that Nikos and Charlie climbed the railings of the gardens looking for somewhere to hide. That would also explain why Charlie was found in the bushes in an area of the garden that is particularly overgrown and shadowed.'

Kite puffed out his cheeks and read over his notes.

'We've conducted two interviews with Christou already and we've been in court this morning so we can hold him for another forty-five hours or so before we have to decide whether to charge. Needless to say it would be nice to have a confession, but these things take time. We've got a decent number of bodies at our disposal given that we've got both Vice and CID working on this. I'm not worried about getting a conviction. I think it's mostly a case of working together and getting all our ducks in a row.' He looked up at the officers with a broad grin. 'If you'll pardon the cliché.'

Detective Sergeant Williams raised his hand. 'Any prior convictions, sir? Against Christou?'

Kite opened a file on the table in front of him. 'There are. Give me a moment. We've got a Nikos Christou of no fixed address bound over for vagrancy in August of 1964 and then again in January of 1965. We've got one charge of solicitation in September 1965, and then another for solicitation, no other charges, eight months later.'

'Did he serve time, sir?' Williams asked.

'We're still looking at all of this. I've got a handwritten note on the files telling me that he was held for eight months on remand from September 1965 until April of 1966. He was released after the trial due to time served. No notes on what happened in April but he obviously went straight back to his old ways. I mean, I think we have to ask whether the spell inside introduced this lad to a more violent outlook on the world. Because we all know this, and it's most unfortunate, but that does happen.'

Hayes raised his hand. 'Sorry if I missed this, sir, but how old is Mr Christou?'

'Going by the date of birth on the records from the charge and trial … er … Mr Christou is currently nineteen years old.'

'Thank you, sir,' Hayes said.

Kite looked at Hayes. 'We haven't got much out of him in interview. He's pretty much blanking us. Complaining of pain. Asking for doctors. He hasn't told us anything. He hasn't even admitted to knowing this Charlie. Or to being at the raid. We had wondered whether a different kind of interview …' Kite trailed off and studied Hayes.

'Sir?' Hayes said. 'An interview with Vice?' He paused. 'Concerning some lesser charges …?'

Kite smiled. 'Exactly my thought. We think this Nikos might benefit from a soft handling.'

There was sniggering around the room. Hayes ignored the insinuation.

* * *

Nik was marched to an interview room for the sixth time in two days. Was it two days? He honestly wasn't sure. There hadn't been a stretch of hours with lights out since he'd arrived in this place. He was convinced that a humming followed him from cell to room. The electricity – perhaps a generator – somewhere in the police station. He found himself searching for it … And there it was. An insistent low hum. Now that he'd found it, he tried to tune it out.

The man who entered looked to be in his thirties. He was dressed in a brown suit, a pale beige tie over his white shirt. Nik stared at the tie and took a moment to notice what a sad and colourless choice the man had made. The policeman smiled at Nik as soon as he entered the room. He had a long, pale, boyish face and above it, red hair, which sat high on his forehead. A little sign of age.

'Hello Nikos. I'm Detective Sergeant Barnaby Hayes. I belong to one of the Vice units of the Metropolitan Police. Up to this point, as I'm sure you'll be aware, you've been interviewed by CID. This isn't quite the same thing as you've been doing up to now. Think of it as a side-interview, as it were. A quick chat, since you're here. We wanted to talk to you about the work you do and some of the men you might have come into contact with on Saturday night. Nothing to be scared about. Very routine. Before we start … Would you like a cup of tea?'

'No. Um … Yes. Could I have a cup of tea?'

The policeman smiled encouragingly. 'Sugar?'

'Two. Yes. Can I ask you something?' Nik said.

'Of course. Go ahead.'

'Have I been charged with something? Have I been charged with assault? With solicitation? I don't know what's going on.' This wasn't the first time Nik had asked these questions, but half the time no one would answer him and the other half the answers that he was given were evasive or contradicted other things that he'd been told.

'Well … I'm actually not here to talk about the main complaint.'

'They think I killed someone. A boy. Called Charles or Charlie. They've interviewed me five times. And I keep telling them … They're telling me I killed a boy in Waterloo Gardens when I was nowhere near Waterloo. I was north of the river. All evening. I don't know if they have a witness, but then no one's come to look at me. And I didn't even know this boy. I don't know who he was. They say he was – you know – on the game. But how do they know? Because no one explains anything to me.' Nik, in his frustration, stood. It was so hard always to be sitting, always to be so bloody passive. 'Both times I've asked them … They've sat me down and I've asked them, "Please. Tell me what the evidence is? Did someone see someone who looked like me? Did this boy have my name, my number in his pocket?" Because they're talking about a £20 note. And I did have a

£20 note, but it was mine. How could it have belonged to this Charlie? Or maybe it did. Maybe it did belong to Charlie – earlier in the day or the week. We all touch money all the time. I'd only had the note an hour or two; it could have come from anywhere. But they're saying that I fought him for it, that I hit him. That he hit me. That all the bruises – that's where they came from. That I broke two of his ribs. But I've never broken anyone's ribs – not in my life. I don't understand. And no one will explain it to me. Will you explain to me? Because I can't tell you what really happened or where I was if I don't know what I'm meant to have done or when I'm meant to have done it.'

The man with the red hair gave him a tight, apologetic smile. He held out a hand and it hovered nears Nik's. 'Nikos – can you just take a breath for me? And sit down? Please. Sit back down for me. Breathe. I'm going to get us sorted out with tea. Okay?'

'Are you going to tell me?'

'This isn't a formal interview, Nikos.'

'What is it, then?'

'It's a chat.'

'I didn't hurt anyone.'

The policeman shook his head. 'We don't even have to talk about that. I'm just here today to talk about your working relationships and about this weekend past. Charlie this or Charlie that – it doesn't come into it.'

'Are you releasing me? I don't understand. Do I talk to you and then I'm allowed to go?'

'Not in my power, I'm afraid. But there's nothing sinister here. Tea. Chat. We can make it a lot simpler than anything that went on on Sunday.'

'Is it Monday today?'

'Yes. Monday morning. About half eleven. Are you meant to be somewhere?' the policeman asked.

'No. No. It's just that I lost track. I wasn't well on Saturday night. Sick. And then there were lights on all the time. I feel like I lost a night somewhere. Sorry. Sorry. I know I'm talking a lot. I'll stop in a minute.' Nik stood again, he couldn't stop himself; his legs told him to run, he ached to run. He bit his hand to stop himself from speaking. 'I'm nervous,' he told the policeman through a mouthful of flesh.

'I know you are.'

'I can't seem to calm down. I don't suppose you've got some aspirin? I've had a headache for two days and it's so hard to think. I asked them yesterday and they kept saying "after the interview", "after the interview". And then no one brought me anything.' Nik felt tears welling. He couldn't think why at first and then he knew. The man's sympathy, it was getting to him. This man felt sorry for him so now he felt sorry for himself.

'Okay. Nikos. Sit down for me. Just keep that seat. I'm going to go and fetch those teas and I think I have some aspirin on my desk.'

'Thank you. Sergeant …'

'It's fine. Just sit for me, Nikos. Take a breath.'

The policeman with red hair disappeared through the door. Nik slumped on the chair and rested his head on his folded arms. His heart thundered.

'Okay! Here we go,' Hayes announced, reappearing after a couple of minutes with a mug and a small brown bottle. 'Tea for you. Two sugars. Bit milky. Hope that's okay. And a bottle of aspirin. Now, I'm not allowed to hand these over. But if you take two now, then I'll ask the duty sergeant to drop another two in for you later this evening. To help you sleep. Would that be good?'

'That's very kind of you. Thank you. Sergeant … Um … I'm sorry …' Nik could not for the life of him remember what the man was called.

'Hayes. It's fine. You've got a lot to think about. I'm Detective Sergeant Hayes. Can I ask something? Nikos Christou. That's an unusual name.'

'Actually, it's Nik. I mean, I am called Nikos. I just prefer Nik.'

'Of course – my apologies. Nik it is. Do your parents live here, Nik? In England? Maybe up north? It's just I notice an accent …'

'Well. Dad's Greek. Mum as well. Came from Greece. In '48, I think.'

'To London?'

'Manchester. Liverpool, first. He was a sailor. Came in and out of Liverpool and things weren't great at home so one summer he stayed. Brought Mum over. Fish and chip shop. Learned it all. Cooking and all that. And we ended up in St Annes. Down the coast from Blackpool.'

'Selling fish and chips?' Hayes asked, smiling in a show of evident but seemingly good-natured amusement.

'Yeah. I can chop. I can batter. Clean out a fryer ...'

'But you didn't stay?'

'No.'

'According to the birth date in the files, you're nineteen. Is that right?'

'Yeah.'

'And you've been in London ... four years?'

'You've got all my records, then?' Nik's mind started to race through all the things that might be written down about him.

'We have, Nik. We have. You've been in jail. Eight months or thereabouts.'

'Yeah.'

'Wormwood Scrubs?'

'Feltham.'

'Of course. You were under eighteen ... I'm going to ask you one or two questions, Nik. They're about the weekend but not about the boy or Waterloo Gardens or anything like that. Okay?' Hayes removed a notebook and pencil tentatively from the breast pocket of his jacket.

Nik drank some of the tea and swallowed two aspirin. He was calmer now but only because the part of him that was raging had grown smaller. He closed his eyes for a moment. At least this man didn't seem ready to beat him or shout at him. 'Okay,' he said, quietly.

'I just want you to talk me through Saturday. Just ... all the other stuff. Forget about what happens at midnight. Just things like, you wake up, you have some breakfast. Do you get up early, Nik?'

'Not really. Not on Saturdays. After ten at least. Between ten and twelve. Sorry ... What's this got to do with anything?'

'It's just boring police procedural stuff. London streets. Details of this and that. Try and be positive, okay? Look at it this way: if you didn't hurt Charlie, then all the other stuff … All the other stuff might help.' Nik watched Hayes write his full name – Nikos Christou – at the top of a sheet of paper.

'Are you talking about an alibi?' Nik asked.

'I don't know. Do you have an alibi?'

Nik couldn't hide the frustration in his voice. 'An alibi for when? I don't know when this happened.'

Hayes gave a small smile and shook his head. 'Okay, that's fine. Let's go back again. Walk me through it. Get up at lunchtime – something to eat?'

'Heel of the bread. Toasted. We were out of butter.'

'We?' Hayes asked.

'I live with three other men. Two-floor flat. In Brixton. Three bedrooms and a sofa, so we all get a room. No sharing. Nothing like that. We each buy our own food but we sometimes share the bread, the butter, jam …'

'And then?'

'I went and met a friend on Camberwell Green.'

'Is this work, Nik?' Hayes asked.

'No. Not work. It was three in the afternoon. I've got a friend of mine lives just north of there and he's always out on sunny afternoons. Him and some people from his block. Camberwell Green's their garden. You know? So they'll go and sunbathe. So, I walked up to Camberwell Green and I went and sat on the grass with him. And we had a bottle of beer. 'Cause he'd brought a few from home. But I couldn't return the favour, so I only had one.'

'Why couldn't you return the favour? Were you out of funds?'

'I was. Yeah. So we had a bottle and I stayed there for a bit and talked. And they'd brought a radio out. It was nice. Very, you know, relaxed.'

'Okay. So, you're with your friends at Camberwell … Where next?' Hayes made careful notes. Nik could see the names of streets. Time periods in brackets.

'About half five, they were thinking about going home, or maybe getting supper. But I wasn't really up for that so I started walking up. You know …'

'The Walworth Road?'

'Yeah. Up past Elephant and Castle. It takes an hour or so to get to Waterloo. And then I crossed the river, and carried on up towards Piccadilly.'

'So, you arrived at Piccadilly at, what, seven? Quarter to?'

'Yeah. Except, no – I hadn't had anything to eat yet. And there's a couple of places. There's just some places where they're … You know … they know me. So when I got to Aldwych I cut up, through Covent Garden. Because there's a place on Neal Street. And the guy there … I don't like to take advantage … But he's nice. And he'll give you something. Like, if he's made it and it isn't going well. I'm in there every couple of weeks or so and he'll give me a plate of something. And I get to sit down. And there's coffee.' Nik felt a twinge of self-pity, thinking of the safety of the Alabora.

'Okay. So, you go for something to eat on Neal Street. What time?'

'Between seven and eight? Around that. I don't have a watch but it was light for a while longer afterwards.'

'Okay, so you have something to eat at …?'

'Alabora Coffee House. And then I left there – maybe between eight and nine – and I went towards Piccadilly.'

'Alabora. Okay.' Hayes thought to himself. 'Yes. I know where you mean …'

Nik watched Hayes' reaction. Did that matter? That he had mentioned the Alabora? He knew not to mention his men. He knew not to mention the names or details of other boys. But Ottmar, surely Ottmar was safe from the police? 'Will he be in trouble? I don't want to get anyone in trouble …'

'For feeding you? No. Feeding someone is not against the law. And it's up to him if he takes money. I mean … I'm sorry, I have to ask this, but have you at any time conducted your work on the premises?'

Nik almost choked on his tea. 'No! Oh my good God. No! Have you seen the place? It's tiny. I mean … I just … No, that's not the kind of place it is at all.'

'Okay. Thank you, Nik. You're doing well. Do you want another cup?'

'No. I'm fine. Just waiting for the aspirin to work.'

Hayes turned to a fresh page in his notebook. Nik had seen him fill three already. 'So, you leave the coffee house by nine o'clock and then …'

'I went up to Piccadilly. But I didn't get that far. I mean, I did. I got to Eros but then … I don't know. I just stopped and had a smoke. And then I met a friend, and we headed back towards Leicester Square. And I was by Leicester Square instead from a bit before nine to a bit after. I think. I don't know.'

'Okay. Good. So, you're by Leicester Square. With your friend. And then you go back to Piccadilly?'

'No. Um … there's an off-licence on Panton Street. I went in there. I bought something. I remember the girl because she had green fingernails. She had a white blouse and black eyeliner. Do you think she'd remember me?' Nik didn't mind in the slightest if he pulled some girl into the investigation. She was – like Ottmar, he hoped – immune.

'I don't know,' Hayes said, his face creased in thought. 'What time do you think you went in there?'

'Between nine and nine thirty. Probably. Does that help?' Nik felt himself a little lighter suddenly. 'Does that give me an alibi? If she remembers me?'

'I don't know. What did you buy?'

'Gin. A half-bottle. Gordon's. It was on special offer. Cheaper than normal. She might remember me if I saw her again. Mightn't she? Don't you think?'

'So, you're in an off-licence and you buy some gin and then …'

'I went and sat in St James's Square gardens. And it was still light. So it can't have been ten yet.'

'That's good,' Hayes said. 'Right. It's nearly ten and you're in St James's Square. Do you stay there?'

'Only for a little while. Then …'

'Then what?'

48

Nik blinked in confusion. The experience of trying to be completely honest about most of the evening without mentioning anything about his men was more than a little confusing. Of course, he'd had these conversations before, but not when he'd been up for two days, was covered in bruises; when his head throbbed and the hum followed him. It was getting harder and harder to keep track of what bits he should be honest about and how he should cover over the things he didn't want to say. 'Um … nothing,' Nik said, knowing how unimpressive this sounded. 'I went up to Piccadilly.'

'You went up to Piccadilly? A bit before ten?'

'Yeah. I kind of sat on the step and had a chat. I smoked some cigarettes. I was outside Boots … I remember that.'

'A chat with whom?'

'Just one of the lads. No-one important. Couldn't even tell you his name.'

'But you remember the incident?'

'Sorry?' Nik said, genuinely nonplussed. Was this the crime they were talking about now?

'You'll have seen the commotion. At half eleven …'

'Er …'

'The incident. Involving the police …'

'Oh … The accident? Was there an accident?' Nik racked his brain for what had been suggested to him in other interviews.

'Not an accident … No.'

Nik had no idea what it was he was meant to be saying here. He tried to give Hayes his most honest and guileless smile. 'I mean, I might have stepped away to stretch my legs.'

'And no one mentioned it when you got back? You were sitting with other young men, weren't you? On the step of the chemist.'

Nik kept smiling hopefully at Hayes. 'Yes. I'm sorry. I'm not sure. The circus gets busy on a Saturday.'

'So, you were sitting on the steps of Boots, thinking your thoughts, and you failed to notice the vast plain-clothes police raid that took place at a number of locations in the tunnels around Piccadilly Circus tube station? The arrival of vans to take the arrested men away? The sudden disappearance – and I have been at raids like this – the sudden disappearance of many men, young and old, from the vicinity? You sat there and you saw … nothing.'

Oh good God, Nik thought. Someone else had mentioned a raid. Back in the first interview. Maybe more than once. Had he been in the raid? they'd asked. No, he'd told them. I wasn't at the raid. 'No! I … um …'

'Nik, what's the point in lying to me?'

'I'm not lying!'

'Where did you get the money for the gin?'

'What?'

'At Camberwell Green you have no money for beer and yet after you've hung out with your friend at Leicester Square you buy half a bottle of gin. You claim to be at Piccadilly but you don't see a police raid? Where are the bruises from? Where did the twenty-pound note come from? We're not idiots, Nik.'

'I know you're not. I know …'

'You were at work. We both know that. You saw a man between eating supper and going to the off-licence. Yes? Is that right? Is that where the money came from?'

Nik's heart sank. The nice policeman with the red hair was just like all the rest of them. 'I don't know his name.'

'Okay,' Hayes said. 'Could you identify him again? If you had to?'

'I'd rather not. He's not a part of this. He hasn't done anything wrong.'

'You cannot legally have sexual intercourse with any man. Nor can he. Even when the law changes you'll still be too young. And you were in a public place!'

'But we didn't have intercourse!' Nik tried.

'Well, you did something … Didn't you? How much did he give you?'

'Two pounds, thirteen shillings.' Nik was just too tired to lie about anything apart from the most sensitive details. He had to keep some of it the truth or he'd never remember for the next time.

'And this man in the coffee house? The one who gives you food. Would he remember you?'

'Yes! He would. He knows me. He knows my name.' Nik sent up a silent prayer that no shame would accrue to Ottmar over this.

'And what about the £20 note? What happened after St James's Square? You went with someone? You fought with someone? You stole it from someone?'

'I didn't steal it. I was given it.'

'By whom.'

Nik thought about the man in the snakeskin suit. The one whose picture hung in a window on Carnaby Street. Even if Nik did not value him, even if he did not like him, he could not name him. It wasn't only that it was the right thing never to name another man; but his earnings, his reputation were built upon the idea of discretion. Bring down another man's career and his name would be like dirt. He had wondered over the course of the past two days if somebody might step in, might save him from what was happening. But the man in the snakeskin suit would not be sympathetic to his plight. He would not sacrifice himself to save a boy he felt nothing for. Nik shook his head and gazed at Hayes, his face full of apology. 'I don't know his name! Honestly! I swear to you. I do not know his name ...' At least that was a kind of truth.

*　*　*

They were rehearsing in a new actor for Edward Carmine. The production had now been running for so long – nearly twenty months – that they were starting to lose actors whose original contracts had run out. Jerry Newsom had walked straight into the cast after finishing RADA earlier in June. And, thus, there were morning calls for all the cast and crew that Monday and Tuesday, as they dressed and teched the new arrival into place.

Anna sat drinking tea in the green room with half the cast, Leonard and the other dressers. The younger actresses, Maeve, Lisa and Penny, sat together – as was their wont – joking slyly about everything that happened around them, in a code that was very much their own. The men, meanwhile, had taken over the largest and comfiest sofa and were killing time tormenting the only

Liverpool supporter over his team's failure to finish in the top four. The dressers were formulating a plan to descend on Kath's fiancé's house at the weekend to watch the start of Wimbledon in colour. In the midst of all the babble, Anna squatted on a coffee table next to Leonard and listened out for instructions being relayed from the stage. The director was wringing the life out of everyone down there, going over and over Jerry's entrance.

'I thought this was meant to be a dress rehearsal,' said Colm, staring pointedly at Leonard. 'That's what the notice said. He's re-blocking the bloody thing in full dress. Why is he doing that, Leonard? Why?'

Leonard paused to think about this. 'Because he's an arsehole, Colm,' he said at last. Which made everyone laugh.

'I know Jerry seems nice enough,' Anna could hear Penny saying, 'but he's much too young. They've made him up to within an inch of his life, tortured his hair, put him in those terrible glasses. Whereas they could just have employed somebody over the age of thirty-five.'

'Men of forty make me feel physically sick,' Maeve said, dryly. 'I don't even like to see them walking from a distance.'

'He's got no stage experience,' Leonard butted in. 'RADA's all well and good on paper, but you can't just shovel someone straight onto a thousand-seater stage and expect they'll be able to do it all.'

'Do you have any sway with management?' Penny asked him.

'Absolutely none,' Leonard pointed out. 'And he's a very pretty boy and they think he'll do television. Might even pick up some telly work while he's doing this.'

'It's always about someone somewhere wanting to nob us,' Penny said and swung one leg over another. 'All just members of the fuck circus; everyone of us a clown.'

Bertie came in from the stage-side entrance and made a face at the assembled cast.

'Bloody hellfire,' he said and leaned against the nearest wall. He was streaming sweat and he'd unbuttoned his waistcoat and his jacket.

'Tea, Bertie?' Anna asked, standing with care, and picking her way to the kitchenette to make him a cup. Bertie shuffled through the others and stood beside her, fanning himself with an old programme which lay on the draining board.

'How is he?' Anna asked.

Bertie looked at her and said, almost apologetically, 'Not very good.'

'Oh …'

Bertie shook his head. 'He'll get better.' He gave a mirthless laugh. 'He has to get better.'

Anna poured the milk and handed him the cup. She nodded at his undone fronts, wondering if his suit had been properly cleaned or was still stiff from last week's run. 'Is it just unwearable?'

Bertie looked down at his protruding tummy and made a face to himself. 'No. It's not your fault.' He smiled at her sadly. 'Heat and too much cake, sweetheart.'

Anna felt sorry now that she'd drawn attention to it. 'We all need cake, Bertie.'

'I think you'll find, Anna, that cake is for the young.'

In the distance, the assembled company heard the director call loudly to start again from the top of the scene. There was a shuddering exhalation. Bertie handed his undrunk cup of tea back to Anna and with a quiet 'Bollocks' walked back down towards the wings.

* * *

Of course, Hayes knew the Alabora. He'd been here before. In the weeks after the actress had gone missing as he chased the ghost of her across London. He'd met the owner, his wife and daughter – Turks. The daughter had been arrested, out late in the snow, improperly attired. And the mother had made the most awful fuss about it all. Had screamed and shouted and embarrassed everyone concerned.

Hayes felt a twinge as he walked through the door. He had sat here, in this man's cafe, on a chill morning after Orla had left him. And the owner had talked and talked and all Hayes had been able to think about was that his wife and daughter had left home and he didn't know where they'd gone.

The cafe was even hotter than the street outside. He found himself blinking away the sweat in his eyes and running his fingers across his brow to stem the flow.

He saw the owner immediately. That large man in the white apron, standing at the hatch talking to a waitress with two plates of ham and eggs. Hayes waited to be noticed.

'Please! Sit anywhere!' the man called to him and then went back to talking to the waitress.

Hayes looked for a table near to the kitchen, but the one just to his right was taken by a middle-aged man with dark eyes and an emerald shirt and a good-looking young woman who …

'Anna!'

The young woman looked up. He had not meant to use her first name.

'Sergeant Hayes?'

'Detective Sergeant. Not that it really matters.'

The young woman's eyes narrowed slightly. She gave him a polite nod. Hayes held his breath. Following on hard from the first pleasure of recognition came the memory of how he had humiliated himself in front of her. Prostrated himself. Cried. He took a moment to get beyond the memory. 'I need to talk to Mr Alabora,' he told her, adopting his most business-like tone.

'I'm sure he'll find a minute when he can,' she said and went back to talking to the man across the table from her.

'I'm sorry about your friend,' Hayes said.

Anna looked up at him, a little bewildered.

'Miss Green,' Hayes said. 'Lanny. It was all horribly unfortunate.'

Anna nodded and looked rather blank. 'Yes,' she said. 'It was.' Then, after a pause, she said with a small frown, 'I'm sorry about your wife.'

The man across the table from Miss Treadway took this in with rapt attention.

'Thank you,' Hayes said and then didn't know what else to say. 'It was a sad year,' he tried.

'What was a sad year?' the man across the table asked. But Hayes did not answer. He looked across to the man in the kitchen.

'Excuse me?' Hayes said. 'Mr Alabora? It's Detective Sergeant Hayes. We've met before.'

A Fantasy of Falling

Anna Treadway stood on the island at Piccadilly Circus and tried to understand the pattern of people on the streets around her. It was half past nine, the very end of rush hour, and the buses and cars packed themselves thickly between the sets of lights. She had walked here from her flat without really thinking what she would do when she arrived. Perhaps she thought she would see Nik, though she had never looked out for him round here. In fact, in the normal course of events, she would have been embarrassed to spot him on the street at all. At the Alabora, she could make small talk with him on an equal footing. She could pretend that she didn't know how he earned his money.

She had listened as Hayes questioned Ottmar for nearly half an hour the previous night. How did he know Nik? What sort of boy was he? Had he attempted immorality on the premises? Had he mentioned being in debt, having money troubles? How long had he stayed on Saturday night? Saturday night ... she had seen Nik on Saturday night. In his coat and his eyeliner, balking at her silly comment about mushy peas. And she had felt sorry for him. And stung by his sharp tongue. When Ottmar had asked Hayes what had happened to prompt all these questions, Hayes could only say that it was very serious, 'very grave indeed'. After he left, Ottmar and Leonard had joined her in exclaiming at the oddness of the visit. Had Nik been hurt? Or, worse, had he been killed? Leonard had read reports in the paper of a young man found killed in the garden of a gentlemen's club. Had this, in fact, been Nik? Anna had watched tears run down Ottmar's cheeks. For herself, she felt only cold.

The uncertainty followed her to bed. It woke up next to her.

She stood at Piccadilly and looked for his face, but though she could see many young men, Nik was not one of them. Anna crossed the road and paused near the place Leonard had told her about, the entrance to the tube where the young men often stood. Feeling only a little sick with fright, she approached a man with sandy hair. Dressed in a moddish way, drainpipe jeans and a dark shirt, he perched on the edge of the railings that ran around the steps to the tube.

'I'm so sorry,' she began. 'This is probably going to sound silly. But it's about a man called Nik.'

* * *

Merrian Wallis rinsed the plates and stacked them carefully in a lopsided pyramid. She heard a creaking of the boards. She listened to the house. The house made sounds. It created ripples and tensions around her as she moved through it.

She took ham, butter and cheese from the refrigerator; flour, salt and onions from the pantry and began to make a pie. She watched her fingers grasp the white of the onion, the knife move cleanly inside the flesh. She thought about how instinctively she protected herself from the blade. How instinctively she caught herself at the kerb to any road. How carefully she guarded her body from all harm. Sometimes, just sometimes, she would have liked to let the knife slip or feel not just the wind of the car but its bumper and its shell. She had a fantasy of falling. She imagined herself lying pale in bed. The children on chairs beside her. Richard bent over, his face grey with the strain of worry.

'I'm fine,' she'd tell them, in a voice soft and weak. Her daughter would stretch out her little hand. 'I'll be okay,' Merrian would say and then close her eyes. She could feel their eyes on her, even now, here in the kitchen. She watched her own hands chopping the butter into blocks, sieving the flour. She brushed hair behind her ear so she might have flour on her face if somebody called her to the door.

She turned the oven on to hear the company of its roar. She touched her hand against the chopping board, the knives, the frying pan. Cold, sharp, hot. Sometimes, in the long silence of the day, she came to believe that she was a part of the house itself, or that the house had emanated from her. The cooker had grown from her womb, the table from her hips, her eyes had made the light above her head.

She started. The phone was ringing in the hall.

'Wallis residence. Good afternoon.'

'Is that Mrs Wallis?'

'It is.'

'Mrs Wallis, my name is Simon Hartford and I write for the *News of the World*. Would you happen to have a comment for us on the murder of the rent boy in Waterloo Gardens on Sunday morning?'

'Sorry. What?'

'The murder of the rent boy in the early hours of Sunday morning. In Waterloo Gardens. The gardens of the club of which your husband is a member.'

'I … What are you expecting me to comment on? The murder? I think murder is dreadful.'

'Mrs Wallis, we'll be running a story this coming Sunday about the deaths of rent boys in upmarket locations in central London. There have been several in the past few years. This boy at the weekend. Vincent Mar …'

'Vincent Mar wasn't murdered.'

'Well. No. Attempted murder, then.'

'You're trying to tie my husband to this case?'

'Not really. Just pointing out the relationship between various cases and locations. I wondered if you had any thoughts on this. I thought it would be polite to ring. As a matter of courtesy.'

'Courtesy?'

'Your husband's name will make an appearance in the feature. Possibly more than once.'

'Linked with Vincent Mar?'

'He was arrested on suspicion of attempted murder.'

'But the charges were all dropped! You can't … This has nothing to do with Vincent Mar!'

'How can you know that? Do you know who killed this lad? Who tried to kill Mar?'

'This is … spurious and unfair. You are persecuting my husband when he's done nothing wrong.'

'It is the business of a free press to investigate, and that's all we're doing. Reporting. Investigating. Letting the general public decide for themselves.'

'You're trying to link one crime with another based on the fact the victims were both prostitutes. Prostitutes, for God's sake. Do you know what a dangerous profession that is? Of course prostitutes get killed. I mean, it's awful, but it isn't exactly unexpected.'

'Where was your husband on Saturday night?'

'He was at the theatre. With me and about eight hundred other people.'

'Lovely. What did you see?'

'*Lady Angkatell's Secret* … at The Galaxy. A friend of mine is in it. We went to the theatre. And then we came home.'

'You came straight home?'

'We had a drink and then we came home.'

'And your husband didn't go to his club?'

'No!'

'I see. Well, that's very fortunate for him. Isn't it?'

'Nobody apart from you has suggested that he's connected. Nobody but you has thought to link these things at all. I don't … I don't know how you do your job.' She was about to cry and then that would sound in her voice, so instead, Merrian pushed the receiver back into its cradle.

The onions were burning in the kitchen. She walked back in, turned off the gas and dropped the whole sizzling lot into the sink; pan and all.

* * *

Anna stood at the reception of the police station and rang the silver bell once. The duty sergeant appeared through a little door with a glass of water in one hand and a clutch of files in the other.

'Can I help, miss?'

'I was after Detective Sergeant Hayes. He knows me. Anna Treadway. Is he in? Can I have a word?'

'I can go and ask,' the duty sergeant said and disappeared again.

Anna went and took a seat on one of the benches. After a couple of minutes, Hayes appeared at a side door.

'Hello,' he said. 'Do you want to step through for a minute?'

Anna followed him through some double doors and down a corridor painted pastel blue and white. Then up some stairs, the walls of which were covered with notices of police training courses, the need for expense reports, and other Metropolitan Police ephemera. Hayes led her to his office and held open the door. Anna planted herself in a seat to the side of his desk.

'So,' she said, as he sat down opposite her. 'Nik. Has he been charged with something?'

'Maybe,' Hayes said. 'Sorry. Why?'

'Because you were in asking Ottmar about him yesterday and we were really worried. We couldn't imagine what had happened. So this morning I walked down to Piccadilly and a young man there said Nik's been in custody since Saturday. Accused of murder.'

'Sunday morning,' Hayes agreed. 'He has. But … I can't really discuss that with you. Unless … Do you have some additional evidence? Did you see him on Saturday?'

'I did as a matter of fact. I saw him as I was leaving the Alabora and he was going in.'

'What time was this?' Hayes asked.

'A bit before seven, probably. I have to be in the theatre by seven at the latest.'

'And did you speak to him?'

'Yes,' Anna said. 'We talked about mushy peas and samurais and … well, that was about it. I often see him, as it happens. He's in every week or so. Chatting away to Ottmar. Eating all the spare cake.'

'Right,' Hayes said. He opened his pad and noted down the timings. He looked at the sentences he'd written and sighed. 'I mean, that's very interesting and thank you for telling me but I'm afraid that's several hours before the crime occurred and it doesn't provide

Nik with any kind of alibi.' He looked up at Anna. She glared back at him severely.

'Have you met Nik?' she asked.

'I have met Nik,' Hayes said.

'Did he strike you as a kid who might kill someone?'

Hayes shook his head. 'I wouldn't have called him a kid. He's been out there four years.'

'Yes, but you've met him.'

'I have.'

'You've met him,' she said again.

'Miss Treadway, people who kill people are often likeable. They have friends. And pets. And mothers.'

'Do you know what the man at Piccadilly said?' Anna tried.

'No.'

'He said – he was there on Saturday night, when the police … you know – anyway, he said that everyone had been talking about it, comparing what happened, what they saw, and when Charlie ran down Lower Regent Street – during the raid – other people said he wasn't alone.'

'Wait … what? Who have you been talking to?'

'You know … the young men. By the tube station. I went and asked someone …' Anna trailed off because Hayes was looking at her incredulously.

'What men are these?'

'You know …' Anna did not like the word rent. 'The men. Nik's friends. You must have talked to them. Some of them knew Charlie …'

'How do you know Charlie's name?'

Anna looked at Hayes. 'I don't think his murder is any kind of a state secret. Haven't you talked to these boys?'

'I'm Vice. I'm not CID any more. I'm not looking into the killing. You really shouldn't either, you know … This is sensitive. It matters.'

'I know it matters. And I know it's sensitive. And, of course, this isn't really my world. But you're worried about Charlie and I'm worried about Nik. We're on slightly different tracks.'

'Nik hasn't been charged,' Hayes told her. 'He's currently just under arrest.'

'Has he seen a solicitor?'

'He doesn't have any money, Miss Treadway.'

'I thought he could get one appointed.'

'Yes. If and when he's charged, and if and when the Crown Prosecution Service decides that he'll stand trial, there is a system to get him a representative.'

'Well, that's leaving it a bit late. By that time he'll be in prison.'

'He's been in prison before, Miss Treadway. I'm sure he'll cope.'

Anna sat more upright. 'When was he in prison?'

Hayes looked at her. 'How well do you know this man?'

Anna thought about this. 'He's an acquaintance. A friendly acquaintance. He's a kind of friend ... Look – I know him. I saw him and we were talking about mushy peas. He'd offered to teach Ottmar to cook them. And I noticed he was wearing make-up.' Anna smiled. 'And he made a joke – well, it wasn't really a joke – he said something about needing to be a samurai. But it wasn't violent. He wasn't violent. It was more ... you know that coat he wears ... have you seen it? This long beige mackintosh, too big for him. He's only slight, really. He meant, I think he meant, that the make-up and the coat, that all of it was to make him brave. Because he was exposed, vulnerable. Like this Charlie. All of them ... all those boys. We all see them. We all see how exposed they are. Don't you? In your job? Don't you look at them and think that?'

'You need to give this a few days,' Hayes said. 'Maybe nothing will happen. Maybe he'll be released.'

Anna pushed her handbag onto her arm and stood. She straightened her top while she thought about how she might leave things.

'Of course you know,' she said at last and quite pointedly, 'who was at the theatre that evening ...'

She moved to the door and then paused. She could use her inner actress when she wanted to.

Hayes looked at her, all creased bemusement. 'No. Go on.'

'Richard Wallis. The MP. He was at the theatre that night. And he has a club. He went for a drink there. I know because I stood next to his wife when he told her he was going. And do you know which club he belongs to?'

Hayes was silent for a moment. 'You're going to say the Hellenic. Aren't you?'

Anna didn't say anything. She held his gaze for about half a minute and then she walked purposefully from the room.

* * *

Hayes listened to Anna Treadway walking down the hall and then the stairs. The sound of her shoes a gentle and self-satisfied clack-clack-clack.

'Bugger,' he said to himself, aloud. He thought about Nik. Certainly the boy seemed nice enough. Bright enough. But Hayes tried his best not to pay attention to the likeability of those he arrested. Every part of the machinery was gearing up to charge Nik with murder. They had a motive, an opportunity, examples of poor character. The boy had no alibi. The girl in the off-licence had not remembered him. The Alabora man had, but that was far too early in the evening to help anyone. Nik had, presumably, turned a trick or two between supper and the buying of the gin, and again between then and midnight. But he would not give details of these encounters and he had told Hayes that at quarter to twelve, at the moment when they believed the murder had taken place, he had been sitting in St James's Square gardens. In the darkness. Nursing bruises from an altercation that he could give no details of.

Hayes called Williams in CID.

'Robert, can I ask you something?'

'Go on.'

'It's about Nik Christou—'

Hayes did not get to finish the thought. 'Charged,' Williams said. 'We've got him. Couldn't produce an alibi, a defence. I mean he hasn't admitted it, but I think he hasn't really faced up to the fact that we've got him yet.'

'Right,' Hayes said. 'Okay. I ... Yes. I spoke with him yesterday and he couldn't provide an alibi for me. I told Kite, but ... I don't know ...'

'Doesn't matter now,' Williams said tersely. 'I'd be surprised if we didn't get a conviction on this one. It feels very tight. And the jury won't like the rent bit. Previous conviction. Four years outside the law. I'm almost wondering if he'll put up a defence at all.'

'Yes,' Hayes said. And then he held his breath for a moment. 'You know the club … the one the body was found outside. In the gardens of … Did the men there – I assume it was open – did the men there give you anything useful? I seem to remember Kite saying no witnesses, except maybe a vagrant …'

'Vagrant's gone. We can't find him. Club didn't give us anything firm, but I'm not sure they even knew what happened. First they knew of it, apparently, was a policeman standing in their lobby with his grubby shoes, apologising and asking if he could use their garden for a crime scene! Toffs didn't have a clue. Completely oblivious. Bloody typical, if you ask me. Can't see what's under their own noses.'

'You wouldn't remember who the officer was, would you? The one who found the body?'

'It was Pilling. At West End Central. That was your old station, wasn't it? Seems a bit young and dewy-eyed to me, but he obviously did his best on the night. Rent boy in a gentlemen's club – all the makings of a messy one – but it seems he kept it as clean as he could.'

* * *

Merrian sat for a while in the hall and watched the dust motes move in the shadow of the stained glass above the door. She felt calm when she sat in darkness. When the house was still, when she was alone, no one could get at her. She rather wished that she could pull the phone connection out of the wall but she knew that she would fret then and put it back. What if her mother needed her? The children? What if someone couldn't get through and they told Richard and he was angry? Alone in the house she never knew quite to whom her time belonged.

She watched a shadow drift through the garden – watched it through the rumpled glass – and mail dropped through the letter-box. Merrian read the names from her place on the stairs. Richard Wallis. Rt. Hon. Richard Wallis MP. Not any longer, Merrian thought. Maybe never again. A backbencher forever. She worked her big toe through a hole in her stocking, tearing the material around it, and watched the ladder run a little way up her foot.

She stood, dusted her behind, and went to phone her husband.

It was Angus who picked up; Richard hardly ever answered his own phone.

'Richard Wallis's office. How can we help?'

'A journalist phoned me.' Merrian did not need to tell him who it was.

'Really?'

'About a boy who was murdered in Waterloo Gardens.'

'Ah.'

'You know about it, then?'

'I heard.' Angus was as forthcoming as ever.

'Does Richard know?'

'I would imagine so.'

'Can I speak with him?'

'He's in session,' Angus said. Richard was always in session when she rang.

'They're running a piece on Sunday. His name's in it. *News of the World*.'

'Well ...' Angus said. 'Bother.'

'He asked me what happened on Saturday night. What *did* happen on Saturday night? Were you there when the boy was killed?'

'Of course not. I knew nothing about it until the papers picked it up.'

'I think he came home at one. Or one thirty. I don't really know.'

'What did you tell the journalist?'

'I lied.'

'You lied?'

'I lied. He asked me what Richard did and I said we had a drink after the theatre and came home. I didn't say anything about Richard going off.'

'Why did you say anything at all?' Angus's tone was severe.

'Because I was trying to prove to him that Richard couldn't be involved.'

'But we don't speak to the press. Do we? Not without me being there. Not without it being arranged. And never to the *News of the* bloody *World*. What were you thinking?'

'I was trying to disprove what he was saying. I thought if I could put him off maybe he'd dump Richard from the story.'

'Oh for God's sake …' Merrian shut her eyes and waited for the conversation to be over. Angus sighed deeply on the other end of the phone. 'Anything else that I should know?' he asked her.

'No. I don't think so. Only that.'

Angus didn't answer but she could hear him breathing.

'Will you tell him I called?' she asked.

'Always,' Angus said, and the line went dead.

* * *

Detective Sergeant Hayes looped twice around the block, mulling over the possible repercussions of talking to an officer he did not know. He had not the easy charm of some others in his field. Members of the public mistook his awkwardness for gravitas, propriety. But other officers looked at Hayes and internally rolled their eyes. It had been one thing when he still sounded Irish, before he changed his name from Brennan to Barnaby and launched his voice into the warm waters of the near Home Counties. But he was still an outsider, even now. He walked, his head up, into West End Central.

'How can I help, Detective Sergeant Hayes?' the female constable on the desk asked him.

'I was after … Pilling. Police Constable Pilling. Could I have a quiet word if he's around?'

'I'll go and see, sir. He might have gone off shift.' And with that the constable disappeared through the back door.

A couple of minutes later, a round constable who looked to be in his late twenties appeared at the door to the offices and smiled.

Hayes explained that he only wanted a quick word and Pilling took him behind the counter and showed him into the common room, with its padded benches and old armchairs. A radio in the corner played band music. Pilling trotted over and turned it off.

'Sorry, sir.' He spoke in soft east London tones.

'Hayes. And don't be sorry. You were there, then, when the body was found?'

Pilling took a seat on one of the benches and Hayes sat opposite him. Pilling looked rather fearful and Hayes reached forward to wave a placatory hand at him. 'You're not in any trouble. I'm just dealing with the same suspect and trying to compare details.'

'I gave a statement,' Pilling said. 'Two. Short and long. Did I leave something out?'

'No!' Hayes said, hoping that it wouldn't be obvious that he hadn't been given Pilling's statements. 'No. I just need, from the standpoint of Vice, to take you through it once more. This isn't even a statement. It's a chat. Nothing to be scared about.'

Pilling flashed him a hopeful smile.

'So …' Hayes began, drawing out his notepad and pencil. 'You were on patrol? Talk me through it. Eleven onwards. Earlier, if you like.'

'I was patrolling, ten 'til two – Saturday night shift. All the normal stuff. A few drunks; few lost lambs; some vagrants in the park; noisy kids. We go to Lower Regent Street, Piccadilly, Leicester Square, Trafalgar Square, the Mall, round to St James's again. That's the loop. There was a raid on the station, up at Piccadilly. About eleven thirty, I think …'

Hayes nodded. 'You weren't at the raid?'

'No. No. I was patrolling and I had another officer with me. PC Shaw – but he'd come back off sick leave and … er … Sorry. He wasn't well … you know … in the tummy department.'

Hayes smiled. 'I see.'

'So, he needed to find a place to … you know … But the toilets at Piccadilly weren't the best place to be. Not at half eleven. And we'd just walked up from the Mall and Shaw was hopping around and I said, "Don't be silly. Just go back to the station and come back when you're … feeling better." So he did. He went off and I walked up the steps towards Regent Street because we'd agreed that I'd do a couple of turns around Pall Mall while I waited, on account of it being better lit. So, I was walking past that big statue, just by Carlton House Terrace.'

'The Duke of York?'

'Sorry?'

'The statue of the Duke of York? On the column?'

'Is that who that is? I never know … Sorry, sir. Okay, I was by the Duke of York—Wait! As in "he had ten thousand men"?'

Hayes laughed. 'I think so. Yes.'

'Oh my God,' Pilling said, delighted. 'I *have* heard of him. How weird. Like seeing Bo Peep in Trafalgar Square. Okay. Blimey. I wondered why he had that enormous column all to himself. I'll take the wife. We've never heard of half these men on posts …'

'Do you think …?' Hayes asked gently.

'I'm sorry. Yes. So I was walking past the statue. And you know, you've got the big road in front of you going north. And then the gardens with their railings to the right and to the left. So, I thought I could hear voices in the gardens, nothing loud though. No shouting. Then someone came stumbling along the road: a homeless man, elderly. Or maybe not elderly, I don't know. It's so hard to tell with them. Older, though. Grey in the hair. Beard. Bit shorter than me. Five foot six, no more than that. He reeked of alcohol. Everything else as well, but he'd been drinking. He saw me. Looked frightened as anything, and I thought, okay, I know the score, you're going to run away now. But he didn't. He looked at me and said: "There're men climbing into that garden." And I looked at the railings – he was standing by Waterloo Gardens, round the back of the Hellenic – but there was no one on the railings. I listened and there were voices from inside the gardens but they were far away and they sounded … normal. Men talking. Bit of a sing-song, maybe. Nothing panicked.'

Pilling paused for breath and cast a careful glance at Hayes. Hayes smiled approvingly, his pencil poised above his pad.

'So I asked him, "Do you mean there were men breaking in?" "Sneaking in!" he said, and his voice was unsteady – you know how

68

it gets when they're drunk. "Maybe robbers but what if … murderers?" Honestly, at this point, sir, I didn't think much of it. Nearly told him to take himself to bed. But we were right there, so I said to him, "Let's walk the railings and see what we can find. You tell me if you see the men from before. What did they look like?" And he told me that the one he saw most clearly was a young lad. Jeans and T-shirt. Teenager type of thing. But then he didn't want to go and look with me. He was scared and … jabbering, frankly. His stuff was round the edge of the British Academy and he wanted to go and get it and move into one of the parks. So I told him I'd go and get his stuff with him if he'd do a quick walk down the railings with me and show me where it happened. He agreed. He was lagging behind me and I was trying to peer over but the gardens were full of trees and bushes round the edge: to give the men in the club some privacy, I suppose. Anyway, I could see a group of gents – thirties, forties, I reckon – in suits, through the trees and on the lawn. And then there was another group, older men in three-pieces, smoking, on some benches. But I could only see bits of them. No one looked upset. It was all very agreeable. You know?'

Pilling rubbed his nose and took a breath.

'Then the old man screamed. Not a loud scream. Just this cry. Absolutely horrible and my tummy went over. You know?'

Hayes nodded.

'And I bent down,' continued Pilling, 'and there was his shoe. Legs. One of them straight, one of them bent, and he was lying face down but I couldn't see the top of him at all. He was half covered up by bushes. I didn't even know for sure he was dead. Except … you know … the stillness of him. And the old man had his arms round himself and he was curling up like a kid who's seen a dead cat. And I was trying to haul him up because I couldn't do anything that side of the railings and I knew I was going to have to go into that club. Into that garden. And ask them …'

Pilling cast his eyes to the ceiling. 'And now *that's* making me feel sick. But there you go. What you going to do? So it took me a minute or so but I got the old man to stand up and I was leading him back towards the corner because, of course, if I let go of him he was going to make a run for it so now I was thinking, oh my God, I've got to drag this misery into that palace of gold and get them to show me the garden and what am I going to do with the old man? Stick him in the billiards room and hand him a cue? Not likely. But then, I don't know who heard it first, but the old man was looking north up Waterloo Place and I looked too and there was a young boy, jeans, T-shirt, just like the old man said. He was pale as a ghost, looked properly unwell, and he looked towards us for a minute but then he turned. And I could see he was about to have it away. So I dropped the old man and I went after him. Running like I don't know what 'cause I had this feeling: this boy really doesn't want to be seen. And I crashed right into him, 'cause I was going that fast and I forgot to slow down. And then I sat on him. Right down on him. And, of course, this is Nikos Christou, not that I knew that then.'

'And what about your old man?'

'Gone. Vanished. Knew he would. I was with Christou thirty minutes. And he'd completely lost his cool. Crying. Asking for a doctor. Telling me he was in pain and I had to let him go. He was making such a fuss … I had to get someone to help me ring for help with the arrest and I was trying to watch what was going on around the railings but by the time I got this Christou safely in custody, it was after one in the morning and the old man had gone. No sign of his stuff or anything.'

'You looked for him …'

'Of course!' Pilling looked at Hayes with wide eyes. 'We looked for him. We did dozens of turns round the parks and all the favourite benches and the squares. No sign.'

'But he's your witness.'

'Not unless we find him, he's not. Look, I mean, it's not great, but it is what it is. I can attest to the man's description. And we found Christou with twenty pounds in his pocket, obviously scared of being caught. No alibi. Matches the general description. The Charlie lad had no money on him. Few pennies in his jeans.'

'This Christou …' Hayes started. 'Wasn't he wearing a coat … a mackintosh? Was he wearing it when you saw him on the Saturday?'

'Um ...' Pilling thought about this. 'I believe there was a coat. Yes.'

'But your old man didn't mention a coat. Could your man really have seen the T-shirt and the jeans underneath it?'

'Well ... I only ever got the one description. He said he'd seen two men. So the one he described might have been Charlie.'

'But ... if that's the case then you have no description at all for the possible assailant. And Nik Christou's been charged. He's actually been charged with this ...'

Pilling's face flushed as he sat there. He pushed himself further back on his seat, virtually hugging the wall. 'Maybe they just gave him a lot of ciggies,' he said, and shrugged.

Hayes looked at him.

'Like, you know, when you're trying to clear up eight burglaries,' Pilling said, 'but the guy in the room will only agree to one so you give him a pack for everything extra you can put on the sheet ...' Pilling trailed off. 'I mean ... I was joking, sir. Obviously, it wasn't ciggies ...'

Hayes closed his notebook. 'One more thing,' he said. 'The club. Were they helpful? They must have let you into the garden.'

'We, um ... The garden was rather full. So we let the club have a quiet word with all the men to ask if they'd seen or heard anything. And the club did make a list of who was there. But we waited for the members to go home, sir. The men from CID, they waited in the bar until they'd all gone home. It was easier to deal with the body once they'd left.'

Hayes gave Pilling a long look.

'None of them had seen anything, sir. The men had gone over the fence but this Charles guy, he'd either been dead as he went over or strangled in the trees. No one knew anything about it.'

Hayes breathed heavily, no longer bothering to hide his frustration. 'Someone told me Richard Wallis was in the club at the time. You remember Wallis? He was arrested for an attack in '65.'

Pilling shook his head. 'I didn't see the list, sir. I handled it. But I was more making sure it got to a superior officer. And Christou fitted the description.'

'The description that might just have been of Charlie? That description?'

Pilling looked at Hayes and chewed on his lip.

'Who dealt with the body? Who collected evidence? Do you remember?'

'DS Hench, he was doing the evidence. I don't know about the body.'

Hayes nodded.

'You know,' Pilling said, 'it wasn't an easy thing and we just tried to make the best of it.'

Hayes shut his eyes.

A Million Children – Victims of
a War They Will Not Stop

It was different from Feltham, the look of things, the smell of things. At least Nik thought it was. He had tried to forget the last time he'd been inside. He was confused by the smell of food. It drifted through the corridors and wings for hours, filling the whole prison with odd smells from five in the morning until six at night. Porridge; burnt milk; vegetable water, tangy with cabbage; cooked onions; something indistinct which smelled like luncheon meat; potatoes boiling; a fetid smell of gravy – the sour notes telling you how bad it was going to taste. Nik felt nauseous from the moment he woke up until the lights went out at seven, and he lay on his bed worrying about the night instead.

Other people had hated the smell of his dad's fish and chip shop. The girls who came to work in the summertime moaned about how it ruined their stockings, making them smell when they went out on dates. How the grease got into their hair and they could not wash it out. But Nik loved it. He had a younger brother called Dennis who would sit under the counter, beneath the till and away from the fryers, and read his Noddy books over and over again. That's how Nik thought of him. *Noddy. The Magic Faraway Tree. Five on Treasure Island.* His mother, who spoke so quietly outside the shop to hide her accent, would go to Lytham Library when they sold off the damaged books every July and buy everything with the name Blyton on it. So many books came back to live with them that Nik's father had to build Dennis a shelf to carry all the books he owned and would not give away.

Nik could bone and batter fish; peel and slice potatoes at the rate of a hundred an hour. He made mushy peas with his mother in the little kitchen behind the main counter. He loved the sharp smell of the vinegar, the feeling of the bags of salt as he hefted them and filled the pots, the noise it made as it ran from bag to glass bottle – as comforting to a young boy as so much sand to play with. His father's shop was his own world. Mysterious and enticing to the other boys at school. Nik lived on as many chips as he wanted, they said. Chips and battered sausages and never lettuce for tea. Of course, the truth of the matter was that his mother would no more have let her boys live on battered sausages than on sweets. Every afternoon Maria would make them luncheon meat and cucumber sandwiches and pack them in wax paper with an apple each for the good of their teeth. Chips were what his father gave him. The scrag ends of the batch. The crunchy parts. The cuts of fish so small that the custom-ers would have complained. While Maria sat in the chair in the back kitchen, her feet up on the kitchen steps, and dozed at nine at night, Nik would eat his second supper – his 'little snack of something' as his father called it.

He would wink at Nik. 'I'm investing in you,' he told him. 'You're the family business and I'm filling you up.'

School was not the easiest thing. Nik was good at football but he didn't concentrate in class. He found every day to be a little spell of prison. The kind of prison that a nine-year-old imagines. The rooms of the school seemed to exist in a permanent grey light. Trapped within those walls there was a pallor which filtered through the words that every adult spoke. The endless lessons on spelling and punctuation. The recitation of the times tables. Nik would do his best for fifteen minutes and then he would dream and draw and play football in his head. No boy could be expected to keep sharp in so dull a place. He did not need school. And school had made it clear that they did not need him.

He did not take the exam at eleven. Instead he went up to the Technical and started there, with a group of boys made bold by age and the change in status. If primary school had been grey, then the Technical was bright white. A whirl of woodwork in giant work-shops and soldering in metalwork cabins, built out in the muddy space where a rugby field had once lain. Lunch and general science;

cookery in kitchen halls so long that Nik could not see the end of them. The boys screamed and ran pell-mell at breaktime, playing impromptu games of British Bulldog and cricket with pieces sneaked out of the gym hall. You could be punched in the chest for walking with your head down, kicked for handing homework in when others did not. Nik was once held down and punched in both eyes – one at a time – for being a 'fucking wog'. He thought of Dennis, little Dennis, with his books and his hushed concentration, being pushed and beaten every day at half past ten.

'Put him in for the exam,' he told Maria. 'He won't like it at the Tech. It's not right for him.'

And Maria looked at her son, at the bruises on his wrist, and said nothing.

First form. Second form. The beatings got worse in third. The boys were bigger, the angry children seemed only to grow angrier with time. Nik walked through the school, hearing the names at his back and never reacting. He made himself deaf and blind. They called him 'wog' and 'faggot', 'spic' and 'shit'. Sometimes the insults were specific to who he was and sometimes he could have been anyone.

He no longer worked every day in the shop. Some nights he stayed home. He claimed he had homework. But it was something else. He had lost the habit of talking to his father. Three years of hiding the awfulness of school had taken their toll on his ability to speak. His mouth thronged with things he could not say. Some nights he wanted to scream in his parents' faces, to cover them in the hot bile of everything he was being made to endure. His anger came out in shortness with his father. In conversations where Nik snapped and barked instead of listened. Nik watched his father – slowly, very slowly – withdraw from him in return. No longer asking him to stay late in the shop; letting him find the scrags of chips for himself; giving up on his little boy just as his little boy was giving up on him.

Sometimes the boys from school would come into the shop, would order chips from his father and then laugh in groups – at the sight of Constantin, at his subservience. The words that the summer girls used about the shop – greasy, greasy – became a part of what was rotten at his family's core. There was something unsavoury about the Christous; something dirty and unclean.

* * *

Anna sat alone at home, trying to make her way through *The Magus* for a second time. In the moments she was reading it, everything seemed to slip down quite easily. But in the aftermath her mind got confused and tried to insert bits which perhaps hadn't been in there at all. There were gaps and passes in the information. Jumps which made no sense and which Anna's brain wanted to smooth over or fill in. And now she was thinking of Louis and she realised that she had read an entire page without taking in any of the meaning.

She put the book down and thought about taking her clothes to the launderette. She was getting dangerously low on everything. But before she was forced to corral her money and dive into the smelly basket of discarded tops and socks and knickers, the phone rang and rescued her from work.

'Hello,' she said, thinking for a moment that it might be Aloysius, who, having broken his lifetime habit of financial parsimony, had decided to call long distance.

'Miss Treadway?' It was Hayes. Very much not her Aloysius. 'It's Detective Sergeant Hayes. Mr Alabora gave me your number. I hope you don't mind. I felt … I felt that I had to ring. Just out of decency. I certainly didn't mean to mislead you. Please don't think that. In fact – you see – I didn't know. That your friend had been charged. Just around the time we met yesterday. But I hadn't yet been told.'

'They charged him?' Anna asked. 'Nik? Are you serious? They charged him with murder?'

'Yes. I'm afraid so. I was listening when you came … I just didn't want you to think … I wasn't there to give you a stock response. Or to tidy you away.'

'No,' said Anna.

'I … forgive me … I wanted to just touch on something you said before you left. You told me that Mr Wallis was at the Hellenic on Saturday night.'

'I heard him tell his wife that he was going there at quarter to eleven. I mean, that was about the time he had the conversation. I don't know what happened afterwards.'

'And you said that the boys on the street told you they had seen this Charles going south … after the raid … with a second man?'

'A young man told me that. Detective Sergeant Hayes?'

'Yes, Miss Treadway.'

'Is something bothering you?'

'Yes. It is. I mean …' Hayes seemed to give up on his thought. There was a silence at the other end of the line.

'Do you have some doubts about the charge?' Anna tried.

'I don't know,' Hayes said. 'I wish … I wish that time had not been so restricted.'

Anna knew that the kind thing, the useful thing, would be to put the man out of his misery. But she was annoyed at Hayes.

He had behaved badly, unkindly, to Aloysius all that time ago when they first met. And he had tried to make a pass at her, a clumsy and inappropriate pass, that rankled with her still. She searched inside herself to see what she felt about him now. And she found, as she had noticed in other circumstances, that time had blunted her strong feelings. That what had been anger was now something more like annoyance. And what had been disgust had become a sort of weariness. The strange and concertinaed mania of those few cold days: Aloysius there and Lanny missing and everything spiralling around them. It was hard to think that anyone had been their ordinary selves.

'I am free this afternoon,' Anna said, a spot of tension in her voice. 'If you had doubts … If you wanted to speak to someone who might have seen something … I could meet you at Piccadilly, late afternoon, four or five. I could try and introduce you to the man I spoke to. Though – and I do mean this very seriously – I won't do it if there are going to be arrests. You can't use this—'

Hayes interrupted. 'I wouldn't. I understand. No one will trust me if I just start arresting them. This would only be to ask about Charlie. Nothing else.'

'Well. Okay,' Anna said. 'As long as we're clear …'

'Yes,' Hayes agreed. 'Quite clear.'

* * *

It was Benjamin who talked the most at breakfast. At school they were learning about the Federation of Saudi Arabia and he wanted to lecture everyone on all the important facts he had gleaned the day before.

Richard Wallis spread his toast thick with marmalade and tried to read the newspaper under the table. Merrian cut an apple into pieces and placed it carefully on Frances's plate, as the girl ignored her and – like her father – attempted to read a magazine that was hiding in her lap.

'Prince al-Badr is a modernist and as such he prefers to stay a part of the Federation, rather than to slide backwards and become another dusty nowhere,' Benjamin was saying, in what his mother liked to call his 'thirty-five-year-old voice'.

Richard looked up briefly and met Benjamin's eye. 'You do realise we're about to lose it. I don't know why the school persists in teaching this. Ever since the start of the Aden crisis our days have been numbered. We don't have the strength. We don't have the allies. In a couple of years, it'll belong to someone else.'

'That's not what Mr Hollister said,' Benjamin pointed out.

'Does Mr Hollister read the newspapers or does he read the textbooks?' Richard asked. 'Because in the case of the empire, the first is of more use than the second.'

'I thought you didn't like the newspapers,' his daughter said, surprising everyone with the revelation that she was listening at all.

Richard looked at Merrian and Merrian stepped in. 'Your father doesn't like the newspapers,' she said. 'But neither is he much of a fan of textbooks. Except maths. And some of the sciences. They're generally fairly accurate.'

'What's inaccurate about the history books?' Benjamin asked, obviously offended by the idea that his school might be getting anything so disastrously wrong.

'Everything,' Richard said. 'For a start, they claim to be full of facts.'

'They are full of facts!' This was Frances, who was now equally insulted.

'Your history books are one version of events, written by people from one country and one point of view,' Richard Wallis pointed out. 'There is historical evidence. There are dates. But how you interpret things is not a matter of fact but … conjecture. And for reasons which have never become clear to me, they only start teaching you that if you make it as far as university – and perhaps not even then.'

Frances looked at her mother, possibly expecting her to correct some great wrong their father was doing to the honour of their schools.

Merrian made an apologetic face. 'Most of school is learning to parrot. Keeping in line. Remembering all the right things.' She picked up a piece of apple and waved it hopefully in front of Frances. Her daughter took it and slammed it back onto the plate.

'Then why do you make us go?' Frances asked.

Merrian smiled at her daughter and was silent for a moment. She stared into the middle distance but all she could come up with was, 'Convention?'

'They look after you for free,' Richard pointed out.

'And they probably won't let you go to university unless you've also been to school,' Merrian said.

'Maths!' Richard said. 'They teach maths perfectly well.'

'And friends,' Merrian said. 'Friends are important.'

Merrian watched Frances stare at her brother across the table. They shared a look of disgust. Oh dear, Merrian thought. Honesty with children often worked much better in theory than in practice.

While the children were upstairs pretending to do their teeth, Merrian cleared the table of plates and buttery knives. Richard was normally gone by now. But today he lingered. She watched him as she cleared. He seemed to be reading the newspaper but he'd had it open at the same page for half an hour.

'There's going to be a story in the paper,' he said, without looking up.

'I know,' Merrian said, her voice full of sympathy.

'On Sunday, I believe. And it'll probably be horrible. I don't want you to read it.'

'I wouldn't read it,' Merrian assured him.

'I'm worried about Benjamin,' Richard said, still avoiding eye contact with her. 'Last time this happened he was still at the junior and they shield the kids there from stuff like that. I have a feeling that someone will see it and someone will say something and I have no idea whether we should warn them.' He folded the newspaper into a square on his lap.

'Do you want me to have a word with Benjamin? Before next week?'

'I don't know. Should I do it?' Richard asked, obviously hoping she would not say yes. 'You're better with him, you know. You'll feel your way through it ...' He paused.

'It's okay,' Merrian said. 'I'll think of something. I'll ... Yes. Okay. That's fine.'

Richard nodded and she carried the stack of plates into the kitchen. Alone there, running the water, Merrian felt guilty at the way they had spoken to the children. It was unfair to teach Benjamin and Frances to respect school and then mock them for their orthodoxy.

It was so easy, as an adult, to use your power – your worldliness – against your children. To feel superior because they were there and didn't know. Such a small daily victory and so easily won. Once upon a time they had been generous with their knowledge, she and Richard. They had wanted to use all that knowledge to beautify the world. To show everyone around them that these things were achievable. That we could all be better.

* * *

Anna had just reached the top of Haymarket. It was nearly five o'clock and the roads along her way were thick with traffic. But as she turned towards the circus she could see that something strange was happening to the cars and buses at Piccadilly. They seemed to have stopped, paused in the middle of their manoeuvring, in an odd configuration. The sound of a great cheer came from Regent Street. Anna ran through the stilled traffic and onto the island where the statue of Eros stood. Fifteen police officers, looking barely old enough to have left home, walked in a line across the road. The women who came afterwards – and at first they seemed all to be women – were of a grandmotherly kind of age, handbags perched on crooked wrists. Sensible nylon day dresses buttoned to the neck. A few young women marched to the sides, pushing babies in prams and strolling chairs. Just behind this first group Anna thought she could discern male faces, a cluster of banners and placards, written in black marker or sewn like the banners of the miners and guilds which she had seen growing up.

'Out!' came the call.

And 'Out!' the rest replied.

'Out!' they cried and 'Out!' came back in greater number.

'We Are Ashamed' read the placard of one older woman in a raspberry-coloured summer suit.

Behind her came 'Americans in Britain Call for an End to the Vietnam War' and 'Start Negotiating Now!'

'Students of the London School of Economics' walked beneath a wealth of placards, all of which proclaimed who they were and where they were currently studying.

'The Federation of Young Socialists' had stitched their banner with the face of an egg-headed and misshapen Lenin.

'A Million Children – Victims of a War They Will Not Stop' was surrounded by daisies and poppies, each flower crying petals across the words beneath.

Anna climbed the steps on the pedestal of Eros to get a better look. It was not that protest was so very rare, in the past year or two Anna had seen more than a dozen demonstrations protesting against the war, it was more that the sight of the march itself was incongruous. Human bodies, human faces – real, irregular and un-made-up – in place of the carefully engineered lines of cars and taxis. Chatter and shouting where there should have been the sound of engines and squealing brakes. The streets of London were not designed for these people and this purpose. London was a place where hundreds of years and great amounts of money had been spent on the curation of fine buildings; the application of wealth to raw materials. No normal person – plain and solid, a little grubby from their breakfast – could compete with the refinement of the city's façade. The human slid quickly off the skin of London, like rain from the gun flap of an oilskin coat. Anna realised, only quite slowly, that Hayes was standing next to her watching the same stream of people.

'Were you at the raid on Saturday night?' Anna asked him. There was something in the strangeness of the situation that made a plain 'hello' seem too trite.

'I wasn't. I'd worked seventy hours the week before and Kite told me to take the whole weekend. But I've been at others. Some of the boys on the street … I mean, I'm in Vice. I will have arrested some of them. Or they'll have seen me here.'

Anna nodded and Hayes went on: 'I thought perhaps you could talk to them first. Introduce yourself: friend of Nik. Explain that I'm investigating that night and trying to understand what might have happened. To Charlie. Emphasise that we're doing this for Charlie. I'm not here to arrest them. Just to ask some questions.'

Anna straightened out her clothes and dragged her fingers through her hair, which was a little damp with sweat. 'Right,' she said. 'Okay.' And she crossed the road towards Boots.

Anna waited for a minute or two on the pavement outside the chemist, pretending to fiddle with the strap of her handbag, carefully taking in who was around her and judging whether she recognised any of them. She couldn't see any of the young men she'd spoken to before. There was a dark-haired boy standing near the steps who looked familiar but to whom she had never spoken.

'Hello,' Anna said, approaching the young man with a light step. 'Can I ask you a very quick question?'

The young man looked at her with a degree of puzzlement. 'Is it about God?' he asked.

'No,' Anna said. 'Not really. Not God.'

'Are you selling things, though? Because I don't have any money.'

Anna laughed. 'No! Not selling things. I was going to ask you a question on behalf of a friend of mine.'

'What friend?'

'Nik,' she said. 'I'm a friend of Nik's.'

He stared at her for a few moments. 'I don't know Nik,' he said. 'Sorry.'

'I was here a couple of days ago,' Anna said. 'And I spoke with a tall young man. Dark blond hair. He knew Nik. He helped me with some other things. I don't suppose ...'

'He's not here now,' the young man said. 'Not Nik. Not this other man. I don't know who that is.'

Anna glanced very briefly towards Hayes, who was half hidden behind the pedestal of Eros.

'Can I be really honest with you?' Anna tried.

'Don't know,' the young man said. 'Can you?'

'Yes. Yes, I can.' Anna squared her shoulders. 'There is a young man called Nik. You're probably aware of him. He's been arrested because of Charlie. Yes?' She watched the young man, but his face gave nothing away. 'He's actually been charged now. Charged with ... with what happened. And I don't think ... I think there's been a mistake. I think the police sped through things and Nik was just an easy arrest.' Anna saw the young man's eyes flicker. 'Because that's the way things work. They've pounced on Nik and there's no reason. No reason that makes any sense. And that's why I'm talking to people. And why I've turned up here and I know I don't really fit in but someone has to ask the questions.'

Anna watched the young man's face soften slightly.

'Because that's the other thing,' she went on. 'I can walk into a police station and have someone speak to me, someone listen to me. And they won't treat me the way that they treat Nik. The way even that they might treat you. I know someone. A policeman. And I'm going to ask you something. Something that's going to sound a bit insane. But I would like you to talk to this policeman. He won't arrest you. You have my word ... But no one will talk to him, you see. Because of ... all the reasons. And they can't investigate what really happened to Charlie if no one will tell them what they know.'

She stopped and left a space for the young man to speak. And the young man looked at Anna and then down at her bag and he slowly put out one hand.

'Can you pay me?' he asked in a quiet voice.

'Sorry?' Anna said, and clutched her handbag.

'If you pay me I can introduce you to people who knew Nik. And Charlie. Not now. They're not here yet. But later. When they get down here. If you come back, I can introduce you.'

His hand still hovered in front of him. Anna cautiously opened her handbag. She had no idea if this was sensible. Did one pay prostitutes because they promised to do things later?

'Er …' she said. 'I have … Wait. I can give you fifteen shillings.'

The boy nodded at her. Anna scooped up all the coins in her purse and deposited them in his outstretched hand.

'What time is it?' he asked her.

'I don't know.' She looked around for a clock and found one over Lillywhites. 'Quarter past five.'

The boy nodded. 'Come back and see me after six. I'll be here.' And with that he turned, cradling the money in his hands, and walked into Boots without a backward glance.

* * *

Nik lay on his bed after exercise time, turning things over in his mind. The men who lined themselves along the galleries of the prison; the men who occupied the corners of the recreation yard; the men who watched you in the queue at lunch and dinner … with a great and sudden lurch Nik knew he was back at the Technical again. First Feltham and then here. The Technical was a place that seemed always to reoccur.

There had been a boy called Ian, Ian Huxley, who stood out amongst the bullies of the school for having something sharp about his style. Where the Gareths and Johns, Raymonds and Kenneths, Richards and Dereks, only hit you, Ian Huxley would take you in. He could feel the vulnerability of others. He could sense the places where he could get beneath your skin. In the early years, he had, like many of the others, played with the word 'wog'. Nik had walked past him and heard it echo down the corridors. He had sat in class and heard it hissed behind his back. He never flinched, never reacted.

In the third form, things changed. The occasional 'faggot' had been thrown at him since he'd arrived in school. Nik knew that he was tall for his age and thin, that he looked sometimes delicate, and he ascribed the use of the word to the way he looked. But in the spring term of third form, Ian Huxley took hold of the accusation and made it something else. He would pass Nik's desk and casually write the word in the margin of the paper he was working on. He would take an ink pen and write it on his school bag as he showered. By fourth form, Huxley had started to follow Nik into the communal showers and stand beside him, speaking the word slowly and deliberately just beneath the sound of the running water. In Nik's dreams, Huxley would come to him, speaking the word over and over, a great stream of accusation, so that the last syllable merged into the first and vice versa.

Huxley spoke and Nik listened. And didn't listen. And denied it to himself. And underneath it all there ran another sound. The long-felt stirrings of love, of desire, that had no place being heard in the same space as that hateful word.

Hayes Under Eros

Anna and Hayes went to the Wimpy bar for cups of tea and to wait for the time to pass. Anna felt embarrassed that she had handed over all her money to a man who could well now disappear. But Hayes seemed impressed that she'd got anywhere at all.

Anna chose a table near the window and she and Hayes sat opposite each other, cradling off-white china cups. The Wimpy bar was loud with teenagers, flirting and sharing coarse jokes, and Anna realised too late that she might have misjudged the milieu of the place. The atmosphere at Anna and Hayes' table became rather tight.

'Obviously, I'm not saying that Richard Wallis … I'm not saying that I have any knowledge. As such. Because it's …' Anna searched for the right words and then, dropping her voice down low, 'It's a very big thing to accuse someone of.'

'You can't think of it that way,' Hayes said. 'If you think of it that way no one would ever accuse anyone. We'd all just walk away.'

They sat in silence for a moment. Then Hayes said, 'They told them there was an animal.' He blinked at the surface of his tea.

'Sorry?'

'At the Hellenic. I went to speak to the constable and he told me that the people who ran the club had had to clear the garden before the police could go in and deal properly with the body of the boy.'

'Yes …'

'So, I rang the Hellenic this morning and I asked them about the list of people from that night. Who'd made it, how they'd made it. Not really my job to be asking but they weren't to know one police sergeant from another. And they told me that the list had been made 'discreetly, by members of staff who can readily identify the members and would not need to ask'. And then I asked them if they had explained to their members what had happened and with a kind of laugh the man at the end of the phone told me, "Goodness no, we told them an animal had got in over the fence."'

Anna thought about this. 'Sometimes that whole world turns out to be exactly what you thought it would and still it's just a bit shocking.'

Hayes ladled some sugar into his teacup. 'The thing is, Miss Treadway, that's exactly what they would say about the working classes. Everybody's life is shocking to somebody. And once you find the shocking parts they seem to smother all the normal things. The secret is to see the shocking part for what it is – one little part of something larger. It's when a whole life – or a whole world – is made up of shocking parts, that's when you need to worry.'

Anna looked at Hayes, at the way his hair sat a little further back on his head. He looked a different man than the one she remembered from two years ago. A little less good-looking; more roundly human.

'Has being a policeman made you sanguine?' she asked. 'Or were you sanguine to begin with?'

Hayes smiled, a bit abashed. 'I used to believe in things, Miss Treadway—'

'Anna,' she interrupted.

'Thank you. Anna. I believed in things like morality – very much, morality. Also love … and sacrifice. I became a policeman because I wanted to serve. I wouldn't have made a good soldier – there isn't enough fight in me. And I think I felt too restless to make it to the priesthood.' He paused and looked up at her.

Anna smiled, realising he'd let his religion slip out. 'Go on,' she said.

'I went into all of this thinking that I understood the building blocks of making a good life. You find your calling. You find a future wife. You earn. You serve. You live your best idea of morality. It was clear. As I laid it out in my head. But, of course …'

'Police work was harder?'

'At the risk of sounding soft: police work was … shocking. Horrible, grotesque, messy. I had no idea …' Hayes smiled again.

'I thought I could cope with it all. And I thought I'd fit in. I was wrong. On both counts.' Hayes sat and seemed to contemplate that for a few seconds. 'And once one part of my life came apart. Everything else started to collapse as well. That's the state you saw me in, when we first met. You found me sunk.'

'I'm sorry,' Anna said. 'Though sinking can happen to the best of us. You seem much more held together now, if that helps.'

'Thank you. I am. I've learned things. I went very low for a while but I think I got back up.'

'I'm pleased,' Anna told him, thinking that, despite all her misgivings about Hayes and the job he did and the person he had been, that she actually meant it. Her mind veered back to the case at hand. 'Why were the charges dropped?'

'What charges?'

'The charges against Richard Wallis. In the Vincent Mar case. He was never prosecuted.'

'Well, as I remember it – and I was mostly distracted by your Miss Green – Richard Wallis's name was on rental documents for a flat on Golden Square. Richard Wallis was not usually resident at that address, it was occupied more often by one of his staff, but he was there that night. Himself and the man who lived in the flat. Mar was found about twenty yards away from the steps up to the main door to those flats. And the man who called the police, he told the officers which flats had had their lights on when he found the boy. So the police went and interviewed everyone in that part of the square, but they paid special attention to the flats where someone had been there and awake when the crime was committed. Now, I don't entirely understand how they came to take Richard Wallis in so quickly but Vincent Mar was known to the officers as rent and Wallis was found in a flat with another man when he had a family home less than an hour away in south London and a wife and two young kids.'

'Was that it though?' Anna asked. 'Was that the connection?'

'I seem to remember that one of the neighbours had thought there was a party happening in the Wallis flat earlier in the evening. Music, maybe some guests. But, yes – it wasn't very much. However,

I do remember this: all those officers on that case, they were convinced, absolutely convinced, that Wallis had done it. And if not him, then the other man in the flat. They were just waiting for Mar to wake up and identify him.'

'But …'

'But Mar didn't wake up. I mean, it was weeks, and even when he did, he didn't remember anything about the assault. And all the time it was in and out of the papers. And the government leaning on the Chief Inspector not to embarrass them. Lots of angry phone calls. The way some people tell it they pounced on Wallis in a panic, trying to placate the papers. And then they unpounced in an equal panic, trying to placate the government. And no one can tell if the real embarrassment is that they let a guilty man walk free or that the whole thing was done in such a rush. It's that pressure for a solution: people seem to think it's what drives us, it's the thing that gets results. But half the time it just messes everything up. Thinking that human events are like a maths problem and if we can only pin down the right number then everything will somehow work out well.'

* * *

The Easter holiday of 1964 had brought a little respite. Nik worked extra hours in the fish and chip shop in return for the promise of ten shillings to buy records on the last weekend. Dennis sat beneath the counter and read his Blyton. Nik dipped the fish and chopped the potatoes and made the mushy peas. On the last Saturday before Nik returned to school, Constantin handed his son the ten-shilling note and kissed him on the head.

'Go, while they're open,' he told Nik. 'And take Dennis, he's barely seen the sky all week.'

Nik and Dennis walked south along the front and turned right into town, Dennis bouncing along beside Nik and listing all the twists and turns of *The Castle of Adventure*. As they approached the shops, Dennis could see a crowd of boys filling the pavement. Ian Huxley stood outside the cafe by the station, with other fourth-formers, his gang from school. Nik put a hand on Dennis's shoulder and started to walk faster, head up. When they got to the little group, Nik's pace drove him and Dennis through the middle of them and he heard only laughter in his wake.

But in the record shop Nik could not concentrate. He allowed Dennis to bring him things and to choose two records – 'Day-O' and 'Rock-a-Billy' – from the little stacks in front of them.

'Den,' Nik said to his brother. 'The boys out there. They're from the Tech. Barmpot, all of them. Don't mind anything they say.' Dennis nodded and smiled at him and clutched the little bag with the new discs.

Outside, Huxley and his friends had spread across the pavement. Nik took Dennis by the shoulders and tried to steer him through their midst. He heard the word. Huxley spoke the word as they drew close. Nik did not react. They walked towards a gap between the boys. But now the boys moved and made themselves into a fence, hands on the shoulders of the boys next to them.

Nik seized the bag of records and took Dennis's hand. ''Scuse me!' he said, loudly, thinking of how an adult might handle it. One of Huxley's friends – Jonathan – reached out, caught the records out of his hands and threw the bag and its contents into the path of the traffic.

Nik heard the records break beneath the wheels of a car. The boys stood in silence for a minute and then Huxley and his friends stood aside and let Nik and Dennis pass.

They did not tell their father about the records. Instead, at Nik's prompting, they told him they had saved the money for another day.

On the first day of the summer term, Nik took a paper bag from home and went hunting in the grass verges on the way to school for dog mess. When he found some, he wrapped the foul stinking mush in the bag and carried it into the halls as discreetly as he could manage. In the cloakrooms, he went looking for Huxley's bag but found only his spare blazer hanging on a peg. With his jumper pulled up to protect his nose, Nik spread, as best he could, the dog mess all over the lining of the jacket, its sleeves, the insides of the pockets. He even smeared some on the badge of the school, oblite-rating the stupid red sword and the crown beneath it.

Nik had assumed that because he never went to teachers with complaints of other boys' behaviour that the same would be true of Huxley. It was not.

At two o'clock he was called to the office of Mr Wilkins, the deputy headmaster. Mr Wilkins explained that Ian Huxley had complained to their form teacher of vandalism and bullying. And that, as it turned out, Nik had been seen by a second-former befouling Huxley's spare blazer. Mr Wilkins sat and Nik stood, and the man explained in a weary manner that he could not be bothered to beat him but that his father had been called and Nik had been expelled from the Technical school for an act of 'unforgivable filthiness and moral degeneracy'. Nik tried to open his mouth to tell Mr Wilkins the reason, but instead his throat filled with pain and all that came were tears. He was sent to wait in the main lobby for Constantin to arrive. Constantin did not come.

Three o'clock passed. Then four o'clock. The other boys went home and the school secretary told Nik to fetch his things and go and wait on the pavement. Nik waited by the wall of the school. He watched the last of the teachers leave. The sky started to darken. Nik picked up his things and walked to his father's shop on the seafront. It was closed. It was never closed on a Monday.

Nik walked with trepidation towards his house. There were lights in the upstairs windows and in the lounge. He stood on the doorstep for a few minutes and then he rang the bell. He could hear footsteps in the hall. He waited. Out of the corner of his eye he could see Dennis by the lounge curtains peering out at him. He thought he could hear his mother crying. He knocked. Someone closed the lounge curtains and he could no longer see inside. Nik sat on the little wall between the garden and the street and stared up at the house. Upstairs, an unseen hand closed the bedroom curtains.

Nik waited on the wall, not knowing what to do. After the street lamps on the main stretch went out he went round into the back garden and found the back-door key under a flower pot. He let himself into the silent house. He crept upstairs and into the room he shared with Dennis. He heard his brother sit up in bed.

'Nik!' Dennis whispered in the darkness.

'Yes.'

'You've been expelled!'

'I know,' Nik said. 'Why won't they let me in?'

'Mum keeps crying. And Dad keeps saying he doesn't know you. He can't imagine anyone doing such a dirty thing.'

'I'm freezing outside. I need to come to bed,' Nik told him and started to take off his uniform and search for his pyjamas.

There were voices in the room next to theirs. A light went on. Nik heard his mother's voice. Then his father was in the corridor. 'No!' his father was shouting. He turned on the light in his children's room. Nik stared at Constantin. His father did not speak. Constantin waved a finger at Nik. It shook.

'No!' he said again.

Nik stood there in his underpants and vest. He felt all the anger of his fifteen years and all the fear of childhood joined together.

Constantin stared at him, enraged. 'We did not let you in!'

Nik looked to his brother, but Dennis crawled beneath the sheet. Nik opened the drawers of the dresser and took out winter trousers, a jumper, a shirt and socks. Waiting for his father to stop him, he dressed in as many warm clothes as he could find. Then he crept back downstairs and found his shoes. Constantin stood at the top of the stairs and watched him, as Nik let himself out of the back door and put the key back under the flower pot. He went and sat on the wall of the house again. The hours dragged on.

The next morning the house seemed to wake up late. The curtains were not pulled until after eight. Dennis came out onto the doorstep, took one look at his brother and then ran past him and off in the direction of his school. Nik waited for his parents to come out or to appear at the windows. He tried knocking at the door but no one answered.

Sometime after lunch Nik walked into town and stood at the station looking at a map of routes. Eventually, he climbed on a quiet train to Preston and hid in the little toilet. He did not have the money for a ticket.

* * *

It was after six. Anna left Hayes on the central island and crossed towards the steps of the chemist. The end of the working day had tipped thousands more out of their offices and onto the pavements all around her. Her eyes searched for the young man outside Boots and then in the crowds who stood and shuffled, who wove and crossed her path.

And then she found him. A slim figure sitting hunched against the wall, his head resting on one raised knee. Anna started towards him, wondering for a moment if he'd fallen asleep.

'Excuse me,' Anna called gently, reaching her fingers out towards his shoulder. The boy did not move. Anna touched his shoulder and, when he remained still, she gave it a little shake. Nothing. Anna knelt on the pavement and tried to see the boy's face. It was still, impassive. He seemed to be asleep.

'Excuse me,' she tried. 'It's me again. Can you wake up, please?'

The young man did not stir. Anna looked about her, but with the crowd milling tight around them she could not even see as far as the road, let alone all the way to the island and Hayes under Eros.

'Please wake up,' she hissed at him, her tone no longer solicitous. And then quieter. 'I gave you money.'

'Because you're looking for Nik,' a man's voice rang out behind her. Anna shuffled round on the pavement and there behind her was a tall man in his thirties, in an oddly scholarly outfit of wool jumper and cords. Anna nodded and then realised a moment too late that his statement wasn't quite accurate.

The man in the wool jumper walked closer and leaned against the wall beside them. 'Of course, your mistake was giving him the money in the first place …'

'Yes, I see that. Is he okay? What's he taken?'

The man in the jumper looked quizzically at the younger man. 'Very hard to say. Methadone? Methamphetamine. Would that knock him out? Drugs aren't really my thing, I'm afraid. Not beyond the odd spliff. But that doesn't count now, does it?'

'No,' Anna agreed. 'Not really. How would he have … I gave him money but you can't just buy …'

93

'Scripts. Prescriptions. He'll have a pocket full of them. You buy the scripts from the doctors round here, and then you just need the money to fill them at the chemist.'

'I only gave him fourteen shillings.'

'It must have been enough. Why are you looking for Nik? You're not family, are you?'

'No. Friend. He's been arrested. Did you know that?' The man nodded at her and Anna prised herself off the pavement and stared down at the boy's slumped form. 'I'm so sorry. Do you think he'll be okay?'

The man shrugged and studied her with interest.

'I don't suppose,' Anna tried, 'and I'm sorry if I'm assuming something that I shouldn't be assuming, but I don't suppose you were around Piccadilly last Saturday night? Around the time that Charlie ...' She didn't know how to speak the crime aloud.

The man frowned. 'I was here.'

Anna glanced towards the clock above Lillywhites. It was nearly quarter past six. 'I have a favour to ask you. I'm a friend of Nik's. But I'm also a friend of a man who works for the Met. And I think that both of us ... well, all of us, really ...'

'What are you asking?'

Anna took a second. 'Would you be willing to talk to me – and a policeman – about Nik and Charlie. Because I don't think Nik hurt anyone. And we solemnly swear that this isn't some kind of covert trap. He doesn't want to arrest anyone or anything like that. It's just about Nik. And Charlie. And trying to find the truth of what actually happened.'

The man gestured with his head to the roads north of the circus. 'Shall we talk somewhere quieter?'

'Yes,' Anna said. 'Oh yes. Thank you!' And with that she turned and tried to find Hayes between the heads and the buses and the passing cabs. Anna raised her hand and waved but in the end it took her standing by the railings and jumping up and down to cut through the coloured noise of the circus. Hayes spotted her bouncing figure and stood and, turning back towards the man in jumper and cords, Anna noticed that an expression of slight disbelief registered on his face.

94

'Not exactly discreet, are you?' he said.

'I can be discreet,' Anna replied. 'I just didn't manage it that time.'

'Tony,' the tall man said and held out a hand.

'Anna,' she told him and shook his hand warmly. 'And the man coming now is Barnaby. Though, obviously, he goes by other names.'

'Barnaby's fine,' Tony told her. And with that he turned and headed north, across the road, and towards Shaftesbury Avenue.

Anna looked round to see Hayes was following and then she turned and hurried after Tony. He moved decisively onto the wide, theatre-lined road. Past the great grinning black and white faces on the billboards at the front of the Globe Theatre and then on, and left at the Queen's Theatre and up Wardour Street. Hayes was now in step beside her and Anna tried to explain to him who Tony was and where she thought they might be going.

Tony turned and turned again, sometimes nodding to other men he saw in passing. He slowed on Berwick Street and glanced over his shoulder to check that they were still with him. He nodded to Hayes, then indicated a pair of steamed windows to their right. The sign above the door read: 'Coffee Pot'.

Tony held the door for them and they settled themselves at a booth near the window. The Coffee Pot smelled of cigarette smoke and roasting beans. Beside it, a sweet tang of cannabis hung in the air. Above the tables the walls were decorated by an array of violently cubist paintings. A silver coffee machine steamed and hissed on the counter and beside it glass platters sat piled high with glazed buns and madeleines. Anna watched Hayes pick up a plastic-covered menu as he tried not to meet the eye of any of the other clientele.

'Are we eating something?' Hayes asked. It seemed he was not going to introduce himself to Tony.

'There are cakes by the coffee machine,' Tony pointed out.

Hayes nodded. 'I'll buy,' he told them. And then he made his way to the counter where a young woman in a green overall was washing down the doors of the cupboards.

Tony got up almost immediately and went to talk to a man who sat in the booth behind them. Anna played with the clasp of her handbag and tried to take in who the other customers were. At a table across the room sat a group of young men in suit jackets and leather jackets. They were smoking and talking and an array of empty coffee cups was strewn about the table. One of them, who looked as if he might be two races – Indian and white – wore black eyeliner in long curling lines. His T-shirt had been cut and torn to expose parts of his chest and Anna found herself briefly gazing at the colour of the skin beneath the cloth. She remembered herself and looked away. The bottoms of her thighs were sticking to the leatherette. She unpeeled herself painfully and pulled her skirt down lower.

Tony came back to the table and took a seat across from Anna. 'Just quieting the troops,' he said. Hayes carried over their cups of coffee and a little pile of madeleines. He sat down next to Anna.

Tony looked at both of them. 'She gave me assurances but feel free to repeat them.'

Hayes spoke softly, staring mostly at the coffee in front of him on the table. 'This is about Charlie. Also about the charging of Nik Christou. It isn't a fishing expedition connected with your work. You have my word.'

Tony nodded. 'I'd met Charlie, you know. In passing.'

'Do you know his surname?' Hayes asked.

Tony stared at him. 'Do you still not know who he was?' he asked. 'Have you not told his parents?'

Hayes shook his head. Tony made a face and drank some of his coffee.

'You know Nik as well, don't you?' Anna said.

Tony nodded. 'I do. Nik's been around years. He's bright, you know. Sharp. More of a grown-up than a lot of them.'

'He's nineteen,' Hayes pointed out.

'That's not what I meant.' Tony frowned for a second. 'Most of the boys there are boys. Of course they are. But they're also …' Tony searched for the word. 'They're stuck. Because they're not kids. No one's going to look after them as though they are. But they're not adults. People don't want to hire them for proper jobs. What do we think of teenagers? Loud? Stupid? Graceless? And the ones who didn't finish school? They're criminals. They're scum.'

Hayes said nothing.

'He's not violent, is he?' Anna said, 'Nik. It's the last thing anyone can imagine him being ...'

Tony shook his head. 'He's got his head screwed on. He has a place to live. He's not addicted. He's one of the sane ones. The okay ones. The ones you don't have to worry about. He's not vindictive. The boys in the tube on the night of the raid ... the ones who didn't get taken in ... they said Charlie had been standing near someone on the steps down into the tube. He was standing near to another man when it started and Charlie came shooting up those stairs and ran down Lower Regent Street. Well, the punter ran down to Lower Regent Street too. I mean, a lot of them did. It was the natural direction to head for. Anyway, this punter. You see ... It wasn't Nik. It was some other man.'

'Do you think we could get more of a description?' Hayes asked.

'It would depend on the terms,' Tony said. 'No arrests. No taking people in.'

'I'm not arresting anyone for giving information,' Hayes said, sounding a little annoyed. 'I might need to take a statement. But that's different.'

'And you can't ask him to do it for nothing,' Tony said. 'You have to give him something. He's sticking his neck out ...'

Anna could feel Hayes go tense beside her. 'Okay. Yes. If I get a description.'

Tony stood and looked behind him, into the centre of the cafe. The young Indian-looking man in the torn T-shirt stood up and walked over to their table.

'Yeah?' the young man asked softly, looking at Tony.

Tony sat again and nodded. 'No arrests. No nothing. And he'll give you something for it.' The young man slipped into the seat beside him.

Hayes pulled off his jacket and laid it in his lap. The sides of his face ran with sweat. 'Three pounds,' he said. 'It's what I've got. But I need a proper description.'

The young man in the slashed T-shirt nodded. 'Okay. Fine. I'm Saj.' He reached out and shook Anna's hand. He didn't bother to do

97

the same with Hayes. 'I hear you're a friend of Nik's,' he told her. 'So … you know … thanks.' He spoke with a broad East End accent.

Anna smiled. 'Did you see the man, Saj? The one with Charlie on Saturday night?'

'I did. But it was in little bits. 'Cause I was deeper down the stairs and when it started, it was just chaos. We hadn't even seen Nik that night. Which I remember because he was normally there on a Saturday, at least for a bit. But just before the raid started I was talking to another guy, we were sitting on the bottom step.' He smiled. 'Annoying people, 'cause it's a crush after the theatres get out and we could hear everyone tutting behind our backs. Anyway, I looked up when I first heard the shouts. And there was Charlie – just standing at the bottom of the steps, below an older guy – and he looked around him when the shouting started and then he just bolted.'

Saj had been staring at the table but now he risked a quick glance up towards Anna.

'These two policemen,' Saj went on, 'they were in normal clothes but you could tell what they were from the way they moved – they came running down towards us. And there were customers, you know, tube passengers and they were going this way and that because they didn't know what the hell was happening. And this man in a suit – passenger, punter, I don't know – fell right over Peter, who's the guy I was talking to on the steps. And I couldn't leave him so I was trying to pull him up and he was tangled in this sprawling fella. And then I looked up to see how close they were and that's when I saw the back of the older guy, disappearing up the top of the steps.'

'And you saw this man run down to Lower Regent Street? Towards Pall Mall?'

'No. No. Because we were further down. That was another guy – don't know his name, he's new. He'd run south already but he was just crouching in this doorway, in the dark down Lower Regent Street. But he saw Charlie run past, down towards Pall Mall and another man just behind him. Running, panicked, looking behind him, so not a copper.'

'But what did he look like?' Hayes asked. 'This man on the steps.'

'I didn't look at him properly. He was picking Charlie up so I didn't really bother to think much about it. He was older than twenties. I'd say forty, maybe, or fifty. Not elderly. Nicely dressed. Neat jacket. Middle-aged. But ... honestly ... that's pretty much everyone we see.'

Hayes had pulled a little notebook out of his pocket and was writing this all down. 'Can you give me more of a description?' he asked. 'Anything?'

Saj closed his eyes. 'I know he was a white man. I'd have noticed if he weren't. Mid-colour clothes. Like, not a black suit. I feel like he was wearing summer clothes, but smart. Like a beige or brown suit ...'

'Could it have been a grey suit?' Anna asked, thinking back to Richard Wallis.

'I don't think it was grey.' Saj opened his eyes; he looked downcast. 'I don't know. Not bright white, not really dark, that's all I'm sure of. Don't remember his hair standing out. Not light blond and probably not black. But I saw him from below. I didn't know to pay attention.' He stared at Anna for a few moments and then his eyes seemed to fill. He looked away.

'It's okay,' Anna told him. 'You're doing your best.'

Saj shook his head. 'Charlie. I didn't think to pay attention to him. You think you'll be arrested. You know that sometime someone's going to get beaten up. You don't think anyone'll kill you.' He looked at Anna. 'I don't think Charlie thought that someone would ... you know.'

'I'm sorry,' Hayes said. 'I didn't realise you were friends.'

Saj shook his head. 'I wish I'd been his friend. I only talked to him properly just once. Before Christmas. There was this horrible night. Pissing it down. It was so cold. I didn't have enough to buy anything so he bought us a cone of chips from a cafe. We sat and ate them under one of the arches. We had a laugh. Told stories. He was sweet. Funny ... He'd grown up on this farm. Wiltshire maybe? Think it was there. Horses, they bred. And his dad rode. He'd wanted to be a jockey and he'd ridden the – what d'you call them? Ponies. He'd learned to ride the ponies – help kids have rides and stuff at the weekend – and he'd muck out the horses. Loved them … Went on about them like they were his cats or something. But he got diagnosed with a bad heart. I don't remember the details. Hole? Or beating wrong? I don't know. So they put a stop to it – couldn't be a jockey. I remember that … I remember thinking about him – big, tall bugger he was – and thinking: you're just built wrong for jockeying. You'd need to ride giraffes.' Saj smiled. 'It's weird, isn't it? The things that matter but you don't think it at the time. After they said he died I just kept finding myself back on that step. You know? I want to tell him. I want to warn him. I want to tell him to go home.' Tears were leaking out of Saj's eyes and he rubbed his face clean. 'Sorry. Stupid boy – me, not him …'

Hayes reached into his pocket and quietly placed three £1 notes on the table. Saj didn't acknowledge the money. He just stared ahead of him.

'Thank you,' Tony said quietly and nodded to show Anna and Hayes that it was time to leave.

Unpicking the Mistakes

There had been so many moments, in those first few days after leaving home, when Nik thought he could see a way back. He had boarded the train to Preston without a ticket, figuring that at least he knew the town centre and would sit somewhere and figure out what he was going to do and how he was going to talk to his father. And he had nearly made it all the way to Preston, sitting in an almost empty carriage and gazing out of the window, when the inspector arrived at the glass door and asked to see his ticket.

Nik searched in his pockets, trying to pass off his panic as a kind of genuine desperation. He expected the conductor to tut and move on but instead the man sent him to stand in the guard's chamber at the end of the carriage and when they got to Preston Nik was marched into the office of the station master.

'Well, you'll just have to buy a ticket, won't you?' the man said to him. 'Where's your wallet?'

'I don't have a wallet,' Nik told him. 'I'm fifteen.'

'Well, where's your dad, then? He can buy a ticket.'

'He's back home in St Annes but we've had a row.' Nik sat on a chair in the corner and scratched at his knees.

'Number?' the station master said.

'20483. Constantin Christou. That's … his name.'

The station master dialled the number and waited.

'Hello?' he started. 'Mr Christou. My name is Henry Cabbot. I'm the station master at Preston and we have your son here … Yes. Well, yes. He didn't buy a ticket … Yes. Rode the train to Preston. No ticket and no money … Mr Christou, no, the thing is … Mr Christou? Mr Christou?' The station master hung up the phone.

'Your father put the phone down on me,' he told Nik. 'He sounded furious. I don't think he's coming to get you.' Nik covered his face with his hands. The station master shooed him out of the station telling him not to do it again.

Nik walked up to Fishergate and into the middle of town. He'd always rather liked Preston. It had beautiful buildings and a friendly, homely feel to it. But now he wanted nothing more than a cup of tea and he had no way of getting one. He stood on the pavement in the quiet bustle of a weekday morning, failing to comprehend what on earth was really happening. He should have asked the station master for a ticket home. But then, of course, he'd had no money.

He thought perhaps he might apologise to his father. Perhaps if he got him a gift … No. He would have to get himself unexpelled. But he didn't know how to do this either. He walked until he spotted a Woolworths and then loped round the aisles unobserved for half an hour, turning over in his mind how he might convince the school to take him back.

'Christou!'

Nik couldn't make sense, at first, of the word that was being shouted at him.

'Christou! What in the name of heaven are you doing in here?' Nik turned and came face to face with the metalwork master, Mr Jones. The man was carrying a planter full of bulbs and a miniature watering can. He was quite pink in the face.

'Christou! You're not even in uniform.'

'I've been expelled, sir,' Nik told Mr Jones.

'Expelled? For what?'

'Putting dog mess in Huxley's blazer, sir. Sorry, sir.'

Mr Jones clutched his hyacinths to his chest. 'Why would you do that? You're not one of the stupider ones.'

'No, sir. He was being very mean to me, sir. Very … cruel, sir.'

'Huxley was being cruel to you?' Mr Jones seemed as surprised by everything that Nik said as he had been by spotting the boy in the first place.

'It's been going on for years, sir. And it's not just me. He does it to lots of the boys. Punches us, sir. Takes our things.'

'And you think it appropriate to stand here telling tales? What's wrong with you, Christou? Rise above it, you idiot. What did you want to get yourself expelled for?'

'I didn't, sir. I didn't want. I want to go back …'

'Back!' Mr Jones almost shouted the word and a pair of old ladies carrying boxes of flesh-coloured tights stopped and stared at them both. 'They'll not have you back. What the hell is wrong with you? Once you're gone, you're gone.' And Mr Jones started to walk away towards the tills.

Nik immediately set off after him, trying to catch him up. 'I know, sir. It's just that I've never been in proper trouble, sir. Barely even detention, sir. Never the cane. And now they've expelled me and I just thought …'

Mr Jones turned on Nik. 'No!' he said decisively, as if Nik had assaulted his dignity. 'No! You don't get to treat the school like that and just come back. We don't need boys like you.' And with that he turned his back on Nik and thumped his purchases down onto the counter. The lady at the till in Woolworths gave him a gently horrified stare and Nik retreated, returning to walk the streets.

At half past three he found a quarter of a fish paste sandwich wrapped in paper in a bin in Moor Park and ate it hungrily. A close inspection of other bins, when no passers-by were looking, revealed some crusts of bread, a half-eaten apple and a toffee stuck to the inside of a paper bag. Nik tried to drink the water from the Serpentine lake, but it tasted strange – bitter and gritty and not like water from the tap at all. After he had eaten, Nik lay down in the grass, under one of the trees that surrounded the lake, and slept.

When he woke it was twilight and he was no nearer knowing how to get back home. He walked until he found a phone box on the Blackpool Road and tried to make a reverse-charge call to the family shop but his father would not accept the charges. Nik returned to the park and found a quiet spot away from the paths where the grass grew thickly enough to make a pillow. He slept.

Later that night, confused in the dark, he woke because something was pulling at his leg. He kicked out and heard a cry, then something grabbed at his other foot and a moment later was gone. He stood, feeling the damp grass soak through the bottoms of his socks. Someone had stolen his shoes.

* * *

It was nearly quarter past seven when Anna finally ran through the stage door and up the stairs to Bertie's dressing room. The call would come for beginners at any minute and she had no idea what state he was in.

She shouted her 'Sorry!' at Dick as she ran past him, genuinely wondering if she could get sacked for being this late on a performance day. She barged through Bertie's door to find the poor man bent nearly double, struggling to get his first jacket either on or off.

'Oh good God … Bertie. I'm so sorry.'

'They came and did my wig,' Bertie said, trying to straighten up. 'But I don't think my make-up's fit to be seen and I've somehow managed to get tangled in this bloody thing.'

Anna dropped her handbag and helped him out of the twisted jacket. Bertie stood, sweating, and tugged at his clothes. Anna reached a hand out to pull his shirt straight and Bertie stiffened and stepped out of her way. She saw him blush. Of course, he must know that he'd put on a few pounds, and actors were scared of things like that, even men. She pretended nothing had happened, shook out the jacket in her hands and then held it up for Bertie to ease himself into. Bertie carefully buttoned a single button and Anna fetched the panstick and the powder from the dressing table. Together, they eased the strands of the wig back into place and then Anna blotted Bertie and they both tensed a little as Dick's voice on the tannoy called for 'Beginners!'

'I'm really sorry, Bertie,' Anna said.

Bertie shook his head, and she thought for a moment that he was properly disappointed in her, but he managed a very small smile and told her: 'These things happen, love. None of us is perfect.'

Anna accepted the kindness and then ran from his dressing room to Maeve's to see what state she was in. After the performance had started, Dick brought Anna a postcard – showing a brightly coloured Montego Bay – which had arrived at the stage door covered in tiny ink-pen letters.

Monday, 3 July

Darling,
This is a beach. I am not allowed to go
to it. I spend my days writing letters
and trying to remember how
everything works here. In the evening
I drink too much beer and end up
sitting in the garden on my own.

Clemence is rather taken with
Marjorie's nephew who is a 'radical' –
Clemence's word – in Kingston
politics. If nothing else, it has
distracted her.

Write to me. Please.
All my love, Louis x

Miss Anna Treadway
84b, Neal Street
London
W1

Yes, Anna thought. Of course. I haven't written in days. But then everything suddenly seemed too complicated. After the performance, Anna stood and unstuck Bertie's hairpiece, using a sharp-smelling liquid to melt the thick, clear glue which pulled at his skin and the wisps of his hair.

Bertie was playing music, as he often did. *The Magic Flute* on the cream portable player he kept in the corner beside his books and old papers. Anna liked standing in the semi-dark, late in the evening, listening to the Mozart. She found it more relaxing than Penny's Radio Luxembourg and all the endless guitar-playing and jangling that entailed. Instead, Papageno sang his delicate and precise bird calls and made the whole room sound like a flower-strewn glade.

Bertie had the crossword spread out on the dressing table in front of him but he hadn't written anything since Anna had started to unglue him five minutes ago.

'Do you think,' he asked her, 'that people feel most for other people when sadness is involved?'

Anna thought about this, and levered off another inch of hairpiece, pushing her fingers deep under the wig and across Bertie's scalp. 'I don't follow,' she said.

'Someone once told me that happiness makes us stupid. Inwardlooking. We become kind – empathetic – when we're in a state of grief. Sadness brings out the best in us.'

They were both silent for a minute. 'But,' Anna said at last, 'sadness can make people cruel. It can make people lash out and say awful things. I think happiness can make us gentle.'

Bertie watched her in the mirror. 'I think when we're happy we don't spend a lot of time looking at other people and really trying to understand their happiness. But when you lose someone ... when you're in grief ... don't you look at other people in grief and really think about what they're going through? That's how we work, isn't it? Sadness makes us think – about ourselves and then about other people. Happiness is the opposite of thinking.'

Anna had freed the front eight inches of hairpiece and began to peel Bertie's head like an awkward satsuma. 'Yes. Okay. I see that. One of you has to be in grief. One of you has to be suffering. Because if you're both okay, you don't really think about each other.'

Bertie nodded, as much as he could manage with large parts of his skin still adhering to the rubber cap of his wig. 'No one comes to this play to think,' he said. 'Everyone on the stage is basically okay. All the suffering is muffled. You go to *Hamlet* to think. Or *King Lear*. *Death of a Salesman*, even. You go to understand a person in distress. It opens you out.'

Anna smiled at Bertie in the mirror. 'You're sick of this play. Aren't you?'

Bertie's face remained impassive. 'I don't mind so much. It's only work. I'm grateful to have somewhere to go every day.' He looked down at the table in front of him. 'There was a time ... when my father died. I felt as if the skin had been lifted right off me. I could feel everything. Took me years to regrow that skin. Years to make patches over it.'

Anna stood with Bertie's wig in her hands and then smoothed it gently over the mannequin head which sat beside him by the mirror. 'And then here I come, pulling it all off again!' she said, by way of a joke. But she seemed to have misjudged Bertie's mood and she could feel, in the quiver of his shoulders, how he withdrew from her.

'Shall we get you out of these clothes?' Anna asked Bertie, knowing how much of a mother she sounded at these moments.

Bertie stood, awkwardly, gripping the chair. He staggered to his feet, seeming twenty years older than he really was.

He stood with his back to the little window and allowed Anna to unbutton his jacket and his waistcoat. The buttons of the former straining in their buttonholes, rebelling against the extra girth.

'Bertie?' Anna asked gently. 'Would you like me to ask Susan to have a look at the jacket for you?' She didn't want to use the words 'let it out'.

Bertie breathed deeply and then he started to cry. Absolutely silently and without looking at Anna, the tears flowed slowly down his cheeks and dripped onto the front of his shirt.

'Oh goodness, Bertie,' Anna said. 'I didn't mean anything by that. I'm so sorry. I said a stupid thing.'

Bertie shook his head. 'That isn't why I'm crying.' He pulled a handkerchief out of his pocket and blew his nose. 'It does need a tweak. You can ask Susan if you like.' He blew his nose and then wiped his face with his hands. The panstick and the mascara spread out over his cheeks. 'I'm sorry,' he said. 'Don't mind me.'

'Are you sure it wasn't me?' Anna asked. 'I really didn't mean anything by it ...'

Bertie shook his head violently. 'Not you. Not you at all. I reminded myself of something sad and I should remember not to do that at work.' He forced a smile. 'No one wants to see a man cry at work, now, do they?'

Anna shrugged. 'Penny told me a story about a friend of hers who used to pleasure herself as a pre-performance ritual. And everybody knew about it. Open secret. If that's allowed, then crying is basically nothing …'

Bertie laughed. 'Oh God, Anna. Theatres.'

'I know.'

'Do we shock you?'

'I'm relatively unshockable,' Anna pointed out. 'And the bit of me that was shockable has been reconditioned by five years in this place.'

'Lead stomachs, steel minds and loose knickers,' Bertie said.

Anna wrinkled her brow.

'I once had a dresser called Arnold. Bit of a queen. You know the type. And he always told me: lead stomachs, steel minds and loose knickers were the three things you needed to survive in theatre. I think he said it because it made me blush. But, then, we're all more shockable when we're young.'

When Anna got home she took out her writing things, determined not to let Louis down, if only in this one way.

Louis,

So much has happened here and I thought at first to protect you from it. But I don't know how long you'll be away …

You know Nik? The boy in the mackintosh we see at the Alabora … He was arrested because one of the young men from the circus was killed. It's terribly upsetting. I can't properly explain. I don't think they have any real evidence. He was just walking home and happened to walk down the wrong street.

I went and spoke to some of the men at the circus. No one thinks he did it. You've met him – he's clever and sharp but hardly a bully or a thug. He seems so young to me. I've been asking around to see if someone will help him. Because someone must. He doesn't seem to have any family.

Sympathy is such an inadequate response, isn't it? I feel sorry for Nik. And I know that that's probably a bit naive – who am I to think I know that world? But all the same. He's virtually a child. And I don't know how the best of us would cope with the police and the courts and all of that – let alone some half-homeless child, without the money or education to fend them off. Listen to me! Am I terribly patronising? Goodness knows, if Nik were here he'd probably tell me to f—k off. But he isn't. So I shan't.

Bravery and all that …
Anna xxx

* * *

Hayes had not been left unmoved by Saj or Tony's words. He could see that Charlie's death was very sad to those who'd loved him. His family especially, wherever they were. He was more bothered by the failures in the investigation than by any details of the men themselves. The men, if he was honest, made him somewhat uneasy. But he could see that there was a mother without her son and he felt – when he allowed himself to feel – the dark unsettling reality of not knowing where your child was in the world.

So, the evening of the trip to the circus, Hayes stayed late and phoned a couple of stations in Wiltshire. Just to ask – a long lead, but there it was – if they had a missing teenager called Charlie on their books.

At the first station, they were sure they hadn't. But at the second Hayes was told to ring back in the morning as there was nobody around to get into that filing cabinet.

When Hayes got in at quarter past nine the next morning a detective sergeant from CID called Falls was sitting in the chair across from his desk.

'We got a call earlier from Swindon. Wanted more details of the boy we were looking for. They had your name,' he said.

'Oh,' Hayes said, thinking through the possible lies that he could tell and then resolving to avoid as many of them as he could. 'I'll tell you what that is. As part of work, I fell into conversation with a couple of lads yesterday. Very upset about Charlie. Had known him in passing. They happened to give me the Wiltshire lead. And – not wanting to waste your time because you know what those lads can be like – I gave them a quick ring. To see if there was anything in it.'

Falls stared at him. 'This is our case. You're meant to pass the information on to us. We have no problem with you sticking your fingers into unsavoury pies. But information about the murder comes to us. You know that. You used to do it yourself ...'

'I did,' Hayes said.

Falls stood up and made for the door. 'The gaffer wants you to know that he's more than a little pissed off. It's our case. You know that. Anything you know, you come to us first.' And he walked out of the room.

Hayes thought about the man seen with Charlie on the stairs. It was the kind of thing he could potentially learn at any time. So, there wasn't necessarily a problem with keeping it to himself for a day or two. In his heart of hearts, he knew that questioning CID's case meant trouble. He put it out of his mind and drew towards him the files for the possible raid on a brothel, planned for the week after next.

* * *

Nik hadn't thought of himself as homeless. Not at first. Not that first week in the park in Preston. Even though he had slept outside, even though he now had no shoes, when he thought of his situation he just assumed he was having a catastrophically bad day. Obviously, his situation was not permanent. He would eventually be going home.

His second day in Preston dawned bright and clear. He hung his socks on the back of a bench to dry them of dew. He tried to drink pond water again and managed to keep a little down. The warmth of the morning made him sleepy after a fitful night and he slept again, under a tree, and woke not knowing what time it was. He went to find his socks, but they were not on the bench where he had left them. He thought he could spot one of them, floating in the middle of the duck pond. Kids, he thought, his stomach sinking. The kind of thing that boys from his school would have done. He pulled his trousers lower to try and hide the fact that his feet were now bare and went for a walk in the streets around Moor Park.

In a road just to the south there stood a tall and imposing church with three spires and a stained-glass window so big it could have belonged to a cathedral. Nik stood in front of the glass-covered noticeboard and read about the charitable groups who worked there. There was a session for the destitute every Wednesday between ten and twelve, with small donations of food available for the most in need. Today was Wednesday but as Nik stared up at the clock above him he registered that it was already ten to two. He wondered about knocking on the door. It was a Catholic church from what he could tell, and his parents were Greek Orthodox, but since neither of them went to church he wasn't quite sure what he was meant to be.

Nik sank onto the little wall that separated the church from the pavement. The sun was hot on his face, too hot for the clothes he had put on in the cold of night. He thought of calling home again. He thought of how he could get his mother on the line.

Nik had vaguely become aware of a man standing across the road from him and now, as he glanced up, he realised that the man was staring at him. The man crossed the road.

'Were you after the session this morning?' he asked, in a broad Lancashire accent. He was a man of thirty or forty, Nik thought, but dressed in jeans and a shirt like you would get from an army surplus shop.

'Maybe,' Nik said. 'I don't know.'

'I know the priest,' the man went on. 'Though you'll probably not get hold of him right now. Do you need something to eat?'

Nik could not bring himself to nod. It was too shameful.

'Look,' the man said. 'Not to be rude but I can see you're having a bit of a time. I might have some shoes you could borrow. Are you interested?'

Nik's chest felt tight. He was being talked to like something he wasn't. Like an adult. He nodded at the man.

'Lovely,' the man said to him. 'I'm Harry. My flat's round the corner. I could make you a cup of tea. I might even find a sandwich.'

Nik followed the man without speaking and in a couple of minutes they had come to a cream-coloured terraced house and the man was letting them into a downstairs flat through a door with peeling paint. He gestured for Nik to go into the living room and he went off to boil a kettle. Nik settled himself on a slightly torn settee which was decorated with big brown flowers. The room smelled of old tobacco and the side table was littered with fag ends in ashtrays and empty bottles of beer.

Harry brought Nik a cup of tea in a china mug and took away some of the old beer bottles. Then he went into the bedroom to look for old clothes. The tea was deliciously hot and sweet, full of sugar and creamy with milk. It was the loveliest thing Nik could remember tasting. He felt another wave of tiredness pass over him.

Harry came back with a pair of old black boots, tied with muddy laces. 'What size are you, then?'

'Eight. Around that anyway,' Nik told him.

'I think these are nines, but if you put some socks on inside them they'll stay on fine. They were my army boots so they've seen a bit of the world. Not that I'm sentimental. I never wear them now. Would you like them?' he asked and Nik nodded gratefully.

Harry disappeared again and found Nik some old socks and then they sat together in the living room and Harry told Nik all about his time in North Africa during the war and the time he'd been stationed in the mountains and seen monkeys playing in a waterfall and a wildcat that looked something like a lion. He told Nik about the motorbikes they'd ridden on the edge of the desert and then the time he'd slept under the stars on the sand and how cold they'd got because they didn't know they needed a tent.

'It was cold this morning,' Nik agreed and then, when Harry looked at him, realised that he had given something away.

Harry told Nik about playing football with the local Arabs even though neither side could speak a word of the other's language. He told Nik about the ladies who walked with their husbands early in the morning in long blue and brown veils. He told Nik about the six years he'd spent in the army after the war and how bored he had sometimes been, and at other times how scared. He made Nik a cheese sandwich with lots of butter and then gave him sugar biscuits from a packet. At times, the food and the warmth almost overwhelmed Nik and his eyes would start to close.

Harry insisted that he sleep on the sofa, just for one night. He said it was too much for Nik to do two nights out of doors without a cover. Nik agreed and Harry made the sofa up into a bed.

The Real Thing. Absolutely.

The woman on the doorstep didn't look like she was selling religion. Too short a skirt. But neither did she look like she was selling mops. There was something faintly student-like about her. Like someone from an art college. Probably from an art college, Merrian thought.

'Can I help?' she said. 'Only I'm in the middle of some cooking and I have washing to hang up.'

'Yes. Sorry. I know this is all quite unannounced. My name's Anna. I don't suppose you remember me? I'm a dresser at The Galaxy. We met when you visited your friend.'

'Oh! Oh yes, I'm sorry. Forgive me. Mind somewhere else entirely.'

'No, really,' the young woman said. 'I'm out of context and we only met for a moment. Can I ask you something? I promise I'll make it quick.'

Merrian hovered on the doorstep. 'I have soup on the stove. I should go and stir it,' she said, looking over her shoulder, as if to indicate the veracity of the claim by marking the direction in which the soup might be found.

'I'll follow you,' the woman said brightly. 'But I won't stay. I honestly only need two minutes.'

'Okay then,' Merrian said and led the way through the large hall and back to a little kitchen that overlooked a large lawn with a playhouse and a rope swing hanging from a tree. The woman, Anna, nodded at the window.

'Nice garden for children,' she said.

'Thank you. Yes. We're very lucky.' Merrian filled a kettle and lit a ring on the hob.

'Is that for me?' Anna asked. 'You really don't have to.'

'I'll boil it and then if you want some it'll be there waiting,' Merrian said and absentmindedly punched the large white lump of dough on the chopping board with her right hand.

'What are you making?' Anna asked.

'Bread. To go with the soup,' Merrian said. 'Was it something about Penny?'

'Oh. Penny. No, actually not. It's about the night you came to the theatre. Something happened the night you came to the theatre.'

Merrian moved to the chopping board and started to turn the dough around on the flour, being very careful to touch it gently. She waited for Anna to speak again.

'A very sad thing happened. And a friend of mine … he's been blamed for it. Which is dreadful because really he's a very gentle man. But, of course, the police can't be expected to take that on trust.'

Merrian started to fold the dough and squeeze it between her fingers. 'No. No, they can't. Sometimes – of course – we think we know people, but really we only know a little part of them. Not meaning anything in particular about your friend.'

'Of course not,' Anna said.

'Of course not,' Merrian agreed.

'It's just that I believe there is a tiny chance … no, I'm playing it down … I believe that there's a chance your husband might have seen something that would exonerate him.'

'Do you think?' Merrian asked. 'What could he have seen?'

'Well, I remember … You know that we all got held up on the stairs going down to the stage door?'

'Of course.' Merrian folded the dough over and then turned and folded it again.

'And you remember you were talking to Penny about going for a drink? I'm sorry. This is going to sound like I was eavesdropping but we were just in that big group and I heard.'

'No. It's fine,' Merrian said.

'And your husband said he was going to his club. The Hellenic. I think he used that name. And, you see, the Hellenic … that's where it happened.'

Merrian paused and pressed her hand into the top of the dough. It left a long, slim print of her fingers, splayed a little open. She looked at her fingers and then at the partner of that hand embedded in the ridges of the dough. 'Mmm,' she said, in response to Anna's question and smiled faintly.

'Of course I haven't told you what happened,' Anna pointed out, in a gentle tone.

Merrian thought about this as she replayed their conversation. 'No,' she said at last, 'You haven't. What was it?'

'A young man was murdered. In Waterloo Gardens. Do you know where that is?'

The kettle had started to rattle on the stove. Merrian moved to the hob and shut off all the burners. 'Do you want tea …? Now that it's boiled.'

'I will. If you don't mind.'

Merrian opened a cupboard and found mugs, a spotted teapot and a small blue jug with the word 'Verona' painted on one side. She fetched milk from the fridge and tea from a caddy on the window-sill, covered with pictures of golden elephants.

'Have you been to Verona?' Anna's voice behind her asked. Apparently, the subject had moved on.

'Honeymoon,' Merrian said and spooned tea into the pot.

'Is it lovely?'

Merrian thought about Verona. The bleached colours, all the alleyways with their shadows in the evening. The smell of the square as night fell. The lights above their head. 'It is, actually,' she said. 'Not a cliché at all. It was beautiful.' She swirled water in the pot, but glanced over her shoulder at the woman's face. 'If you ever get a chance to go … It doesn't disappoint. There are the houses just like you imagine. Even as a little child I had that image in my head … Lamb's *Tales from Shakespeare*. Did you read them?'

'Yes.'

'It's all there. Just like you think it's going to be. The real thing. Absolutely …' She trailed off, transferring the tea things to the counter beside Anna. 'We'll give it a couple of minutes,' she said, nodding to the pot.

'Waterloo Gardens,' Anna said. 'Does it ring a bell with you? I find most people think they're next to Waterloo.'

'Are they not?'

'No. They're this green space round the back of the clubs … sort of behind Pall Mall. They look like a park but they're locked – iron railings round the outside. They're rather beautiful.'

'No. I don't know them. I don't think I've ever been inside.'

'Well, no, you wouldn't have. No woman allowed in. Clubs.'

Merrian poured milk into the cups. 'There's a ladies' annexe,' she said. 'On the side or underneath. I think we made a joke about that.'

'Underneath what?'

'The Hellenic. You're allowed to take ladies to dinner, but Richard never did. It's not really my scene. Not his either. Not really. I suppose we all like a bit of pomp.'

'But he's a member?'

'Oh, yes … Not always done to be Labour and to go to places – he tends to keep it a bit quiet. Of course, if you're Liberal or Tory, the world's your oyster.'

'Quite,' Anna said and smiled.

'No, we … um … we had friends from university. Not Labour Party, really. Some of them are members at these places. So Richard got invited. And he loved the libraries and the quiet …'

'And the feeling that you're somewhere a bit special …' Anna said.

'Like the House of Commons,' Merrian agreed. 'It's the honour, isn't it? Like going to Oxford. Did you go …? University?'

Merrian watched as Anna shook her head and glanced down at her hands. A faux pas. Of course. The woman was a dresser.

'You'll probably think this is silly,' Merrian said. 'But there's this thing … I don't know what it's like for boys from Eton, but if you're grammar school and then you arrive at Oxford … You stand in these buildings, the Sheldonian, the Radcliffe Camera, and you look around you and of course, part of you is thinking about all the people who have been there before you: Oscar Wilde and Isaac Newton. But you're also thinking about all the people who will never get inside. That's the moment, you see. The moment you begin to slip.'

'How so?'

'You fall in love with being special. And it doesn't matter what your political beliefs are. You fall in love with being special and it changes you. I'm making myself sound awful, aren't I?'

'No. I think you're being honest,' the young woman said and reached out for her cup of tea.

Merrian thought for a moment. 'There's a fine line, isn't there? Between confidence and self-aggrandisement. Richard took our son up to Oxford one weekend. To listen to a concert. That's what he said.'

Anna smiled. 'But he knew …'

'Of course he did. He wanted that moment, that moment when Benjamin would say: I want this too. Then, of course, it isn't our fault any more. We can still be good socialists. We haven't told Benjamin he has to go to Oxford. It was Benjamin who said it, Benjamin who wanted it. We just took him to a concert.'

Merrian could see Anna's eyes travelling around the kitchen walls – taking in the wonky oil of Stonehenge, Frances's certificates for ballet and oboe, the cluster of social invitations pinned to the board – and suddenly she saw herself, the ridiculousness of her claims to an intellectual life. She felt her face grow red, so she turned the dough again.

'Do you think your husband might have seen something that evening? Do you think it's worth asking the question? I mean, I know it's horrible to be tangled up in anything like this …'

Merrian could feel the dough stiffening under her hands. She made herself stop. 'Um. Are you aware …' She didn't finish the question but she did look up.

Anna's face looked stricken; perhaps she was embarrassed for both of them.

'You are aware …' Merrian said.

'Of the thing two winters ago? I'm sorry. I wasn't going to mention it.'

'A lot of people know. I mean, I think in my head it's only thousands. That's how I cope with it. But millions would be closer.' She couldn't find the words.

Now Anna was holding up both her hands. 'I didn't come here to accuse you of anything or to make you feel bad. I'm sure you love your husband. And – for my part – I care for my friend. And I'm upset for him because he's lost in that system. And it's scary ...' She tailed off and stared anxiously at Merrian, who nodded.

'The system is scary,' Merrian agreed.

'It is.'

'And you don't think you'll be on that side,' Merrian added.

'No one does,' Anna said, nodding and smiling sympathetically.

Merrian paused and thought for a moment. 'But the young man arrested was a prostitute. It's not as if he'd never ...' She stopped herself. Because of course, she'd told this Anna that she knew nothing of the case.

She studied the young woman, but her face betrayed no surprise, only a kind of friendly interest. Merrian changed tack. 'You're probably judging me.' She laughed. 'A degree from a good university and I'm making bread.'

Anna shook her head.

'The young women in the party, the activists ... they pity me. Not a very good advertisement for feminism.'

'Do you have to be an advertisement?' Anna asked.

'Yes,' Merrian said, rather more sharply than she'd meant to. 'Yes. Of course I do.' She turned towards the window, blocking the young woman from sight, and rinsed her teacup in the sink. 'Look ... I do know about the case. I read about it in the paper. Of course I thought of my husband. But, equally, I knew that he'd come home to me after his drink.' Now the admission was made she turned back towards Anna. 'I'm sorry your friend's been pounced on. And maybe he didn't do it at all. But if that's the case it will probably come out at trial. Richard came home to me. By one. And he isn't violent. Or malicious. Or particularly angry. I've hardly ever seen him riled. And you know a person. Don't you? When you've been married to them thirteen years. You just *know* them.'

She stopped but Anna did not speak.

'I'm not a weak woman.' Merrian dried her hands on her apron. 'I know the domesticity makes me seem ... But I'm not stupid and

I'm not naive. Richard believes in things. He has that sensibility. That essential goodness. You know what I'm trying to say ... Clever men with principles and heart, they're the men you marry. Aren't they?'

Anna smiled.

'And they don't walk out onto dark streets and bludgeon people, smother people, stab people. They just don't. Those actions, they belong to other people ... people from terrible homes and awful childhoods. People who don't know any better or who've had it done to them. People like my husband don't kill. They have everything. Success. An income and a family. No one throws away those things.'

Merrian sank into silence. And suddenly she wanted this woman out with real urgency. Out of her kitchen and her home. 'I'm afraid, Anna, that I have to go and pick up my children in a minute.'

They moved to the hall and towards the door, Merrian following Anna closely.

'Mrs Wallis,' Anna said. 'Just before I go. Your husband came home, at one. And he didn't say anything ...?'

Merrian opened the front door and held it tightly. 'What was there to say?' She hesitated. 'He went for a drink. At his club. With friends. Lots of witnesses, I dare say. He got a taxi home. He was probably through the door before the terrible event even happened. It was proximity. That was all it was. Proximity and shitty luck.'

The young woman's eyes widened momentarily. She opened her mouth but seemed to hesitate. Merrian flashed a very brief smile – as warm as she could make it – and closed the door.

For a while she sat on the stairs in the cool of the hall and tried to recall the conversation. The shutting of the door, the swearing, had felt wonderful in the moment but now she was filled with a wretched, spreading shame.

She climbed the stairs and walked to the back of the house, to a sunny yellow room with a wallpaper of birds on a vine. She lay down on her stomach on the carpet and for a moment her fingers worked at the red tufts, examining the dirt which lurked there. Then she rolled onto her back and pushed herself beneath the wooden bed. She had first done this two years ago, when Frances had lost a doll's shoe – a little blue, buckled thing – which they had searched for but never found.

Above Merrian's head was a web of springs holding a pink flowered mattress. And between the springs and the mattress was an object wrapped in a clean blue duster. And inside the clean blue duster was a book. A book with leather sides and a brown ribbon bookmark.

Merrian reached up into the space between the rows of tensioned wire and plucked at the corner of the small blue package. It came free in her hand. She lay in the quiet, dusty stillness holding the book. Then she slipped it carefully back between the springs.

* * *

Hayes picked up the phone with some trepidation. He could think of no clever excuse as to why he should be asking questions about the murder in Waterloo Gardens. He was Vice. He'd had his shot. He'd talked to the boy and extracted a few details and now Christou had been charged and that was that. He dialled a number and was put through to the service at Central and then to the right department.

'Detective Sergeant Hench?' he asked, hopefully.

A deep voice replied, 'It is.'

'Um. Detective Sergeant Hayes. You don't know me. We overlapped briefly at Central. Constable Pilling pointed me in your direction.'

'What can I do you for?' the voice asked him.

'You evidence-gathered in Waterloo Gardens, I'm told.'

'I did.' The voice seemed to be growing somewhat colder.

'I'm in the middle of an investigation,' Hayes said. 'Looking at sales of methamphetamine and similar around Piccadilly and Leicester Square. Forgive me going out on a limb, but you didn't find anything like that on or around the dead young man, did you?'

There was silence at the other end of the phone. Hench sighed. 'He had pills found near him. I couldn't tell you what. Give me a minute. I've got the report … Bear with me.'

Hayes heard the phone laid down and the sound of drawers being pulled open and then slammed.

'Got it, got it …' the voice faded back in. 'I only did the evidence-gathering. The inspector got the toxicology report. Came back after they charged the other lad anyway.'

'Can you give me a quick description?' Hayes tried. 'The gist of it?'

'Okay. Wait. In the immediate vicinity of the body there was a spoon – I've noted possibility of use as drug paraphernalia. However, it was extremely dirty and honestly it looked as if it'd been dropped and forgotten about. There was a silver chain, quite discoloured. Two brandy glasses, fairly clean, knocked over under a bush. Couple of sheets from the inside of a newspaper. *Daily Express*. Blown in off the pavement, I'd reckon. About fifty cigarette and cigar butts, place was littered with them. Then I've got – assuming this is what you're after – a small plastic bag found by the body containing five pills. Small, they were – less than a quarter of an inch from memory – and white. No marks or lines on them. And I believe he had a few pence on him. Less than a shilling's worth. But that was in his pockets. I mean, it was dark and we had a lot of torches but it was tough searching in all the shrubbery and whatnot.'

'Thank you,' Hayes said, a little stunned by the avalanche of new information. 'Let me check I've got this down right. The spoon, you would say it was old, dropped before that night?'

'That'd be my best guess. Very dirty and discoloured. Dropped by someone from the club, I'm assuming.'

'Okay. Great. The newspaper – did it have that day's date on it?'

'Blimey. Couldn't say. I took it in, just in case. No, I think it had a trial report about the Stones. There was a big picture of Keith Richards. But if it was a trial report, it's at least two weeks old. It was quite crumpled. Not clean. My hunch is that it was rubbish.'

'Brandy glasses: those were clean?'

'They were, but a bit like the teaspoons, my thought was they'd been left by club members. I know that when we arrived there were cups and saucers sitting on benches on the lawn. Wine glasses, tall glasses propped up in the grass. They're mucky pups, the rich.'

Hayes laughed. 'So I hear. So: recent, but discarded. Like the spoon.'

'I'd say so,' Hench told him. 'Is any of this remotely drugs connected?'

'Oh, it is. It is!' Hayes told him and then immediately moved on before Hench could ask how or why. 'Cigarette butts. Silver chain. Been there a while?'

'That's how it looked. Very discoloured. Earth stuck between the links,' Hench confirmed.

'And the five pills in the packet – type unknown.'

'It'll be in the toxicology write-up,' Hench told him. 'Do you want me to ask the inspector if you can have the report?'

Hayes thought about this. Was it more dangerous to say no or yes? He couldn't risk making contact with the inspector. Inspectors questioned things, remembered things.

'Err …' Hayes said. 'Not yet. I'm following up one or two extra leads from that night. Tell you what, I'll be back in touch anon. Let's just leave it there.'

* * *

The morning after Nik's first night on Harry's sofa, his host made them both fried eggs with bread and butter. He didn't have a phone in the house, he said. But he could probably lend Nik something for a phone box only he didn't have any change on him right now. Nik asked, shyly, if Harry could perhaps lend him the money for the train or the bus home to St Annes and Harry seemed a bit embarrassed and offended, explaining that he didn't live on much himself, not since his discharge from the army and jobs being how they were right now … Nik apologised and was grateful when Harry seemed in no rush for him to leave. He had boots and socks, but still nowhere to go. He'd been away from home three days.

In the afternoon, Harry went to sign on at the dole and Nik decided that when he came back he'd ask again about some money for a phone call. But he didn't get the chance because Harry came back buzzing about a friend he hadn't seen for ages who he'd met outside the labour exchange and who was looking for people to employ in Blackpool.

'Do you think he'll give you a job?' Nik asked, delighted at Harry's sudden turn in fortune.

'It's better than that,' Harry said, his eyes shining. 'He said we could both go up there and he might be able to sort us out. He's even going to give us a lift – tomorrow. Are you up for that?'

Nik thought about this. He didn't want a job in Blackpool. He wanted to go home to St Annes and have a cuddle with his brother.

'I don't know, Harry,' he told him. 'I didn't really want this to be a long-term thing and … look … I don't even know my National Insurance number.'

Harry looked at him. 'Okay. Well, then – we'll keep you off the books. Cash in hand. It's better!'

Nik didn't know what to say. He didn't want any kind of odd new reality. But he couldn't be rude. Couldn't antagonise Harry, not when he was being so kind.

Harry was watching his face. 'Look. Okay. Don't worry. Why don't we both sleep on it and tomorrow, if you want to, you can come up to Blackpool and just chat or drink tea. You don't have to do anything you don't want to.' He nodded at him seriously.

'Okay,' Nik said, relieved. 'Thanks. Thanks for understanding.'

And Harry gave him a big smile and went off to pick them up some fish and chips for a signing-on-day treat.

It was odd for Nik to eat someone else's fish and chips. His family never went away in the holidays – that's when his dad made most of his money. So he'd only ever eaten the fish he battered himself. The fish from Harry's chippy seemed a bit firmer, maybe even a bit fresher than the kind they bought, but the chips were hard in the middle and too quickly cooked on the outside. Nik felt a twinge of pride that he and his dad could do something better than these other people.

After tea, Harry told more stories about his time in the army. He told Nik about secret runs into cities to find illegal drink or to buy someone a visit to a brothel. He talked about the other boys losing their virginity to women who knew four dozen ways to pleasure a man.

'Did you go?' Nik asked Harry, his eyes rather wide.

Harry thought about this. 'It wasn't really my thing,' he said. Then Harry stood up and came and sat beside Nik on the settee. He put his hand lightly on Nik's knee and looked at him. 'Do you know what I mean?'

Nik felt his heart begin to speed. He had no idea what to do. Of course he knew within himself that he fancied men. But this was not a fact that he had voiced to any other person. And now here was Harry, this much older man, and he seemed to know – to know without them ever having discussed it.

After about a minute Harry took Nik's hand and he placed it over the crotch of his trousers. Nik could feel that Harry seemed to be hard underneath. Nik felt his breath waver and almost stop. He wanted to pull his hand away but he couldn't make the muscles of his arms contract. Instead he sat perfectly still, barely breathing, and waited for Harry to stop touching him.

Harry pressed Nik's hand more firmly down onto him and then after another minute he released him. Harry stood and nodded towards the blanket and the pillow piled into the corner of the living room.

'Sleep well,' he said, quite casually. And then left to make his way to bed.

Remember You Are Precious

Thursday, 6 July

Darling girl,

There is nothing inadequate about sympathy. I think there is a kind of English sneeriness about it. My mother would say that it's because none of you properly goes to church! At least some of you do, but I'm not convinced that many of you listen. I'm being judgemental – aren't I? It's being back at home.

Sympathy is the best bit of who we are. Never apologise. Until Nik actually tells you to f—k off, I think you're quite within your rights to do your bit.

I'll tell the truth, I'm almost jealous. 'Where is my Anna?' I sometimes think. Not because I'm annoyed that you're not here. Don't hear reproach. But only because I have ever so slightly forgotten how to go about my life without you. Clemence only cries – and when I try to tell her that I am grieving also, she tells me that she is grieving more because she stayed and saw Mother all the time and didn't run away to England to pretend to be a white man.

Be brave and kind, but please, stay safe. Piccadilly Circus is not the kindest of places – drugs and thuggery and all the rest of it …

Thinking of you an unhelpful amount. Remember you are precious.

Your Louis xxx

* * *

126

'Benjamin?'

'I'm reading.'

'I know. But you're miles off finishing and I just need a bit of a word.'

'Can't it wait?'

'Not really.'

Merrian walked all the way into Benjamin's room and closed the door softly behind her. Benjamin slung his book down on the bedside table and sat up against the headboard. Merrian sat herself down on the end of his bed and pulled her legs up in front of her.

'Listen,' she said. 'This is a bit delicate and I'm not sure that Frances could quite handle it. Or that she even needs to know. So this is just you and me. Okay?'

Benjamin leaned forward on the bed. He was a lanky boy with a long, expressive face and a lot of dark hair which curled around his ears. 'Are you ill?' he asked, suddenly alert to what might be happening here. 'Is it Grandma?'

Merrian reached out a hand and touched his knee. 'No! No! No one's ill. No one's died. It isn't like that. Really. It's just a bit grown up.'

'Okay,' Benjamin said and pulled his legs around him to mirror hers.

'Do you remember, a couple of years ago, there was a fuss one winter around Daddy and Daddy was even taken into a police station for a little while?'

'Of course I remember that,' Benjamin said quite sharply, surprising Merrian with the tone of his voice. She remembered working so hard to keep the children from ever being aware of her husband's problems.

'Okay. Are you aware of what he was accused of?'

'Yes. He was accused of hitting a man late at night in London. But he didn't do it.'

'Yes. That's right. The man got hurt and then he didn't wake up for a very long time and because Daddy had been at a flat near to him they suspected Daddy for a little bit. Okay. Well, on Saturday night, you know that me and Dad went to the theatre, to see Penny in that show. Well, after the theatre Daddy went to his club for a drink and I drove home. Right … now the thing is that – and it's very, very sad – but a young man who was pretty much living on the streets and wasn't having a very good time of things, he died. This is very sad, Benjamin … but this man died, that night, Saturday, when we'd been out. And they found him early in the morning near the club that Daddy goes to. And the police haven't been here. No one has accused Daddy of anything. But there's a horrible paper, one of those gossipy rags that publish at the weekend, and they're going to publish a story on Sunday saying that Daddy might have been connected because of the thing that happened before.'

Benjamin looked at her and for a while he didn't speak. Then his face creased deeply and he said, 'But the police aren't going to arrest him, are they?'

'No, darling. No one proper thinks Daddy has anything to do with this at all. And there was someone else arrested for it. Another young man. Very troubled, like the first one. They think they had a fight over some money. Nothing to do with Daddy, of course. Just an odd coincidence.'

'Why are you telling me?'

'Because last time this all came up – the man who got hurt a couple of years ago – you were at the junior school and you weren't really aware of the papers. Not the kind of papers who print this mean stuff. But you're at the big school now and, although I very much doubt that many parents will take the *News of the World* at the kind of school we've sent you to, it is just possible that a boy will read it and decide to say a mean thing. And Daddy and I, we thought it might be better if you were warned in advance. I mean, it probably won't happen, Ben. But if it does …'

Benjamin nodded and stared at his feet. 'If it does, what do I say?'

'Well …' Merrian said, thinking this through only now. 'I suppose you could just ignore it and walk away. Or you could tell the boy that the paper is a very bad paper because it prints a lot of things that are untrue. And that part of being a grown-up is learning that you can't believe everything just because it's been printed out for you.'

Benjamin nodded slowly. 'Is that it, then?' he said. 'Dad was at his club and the man was found nearby. Is that really all the evidence they have for accusing him?'

Merrian thought about this for a long half-minute. 'Yes,' she said. 'That's all the evidence they have. Silly, isn't it?'

And Benjamin nodded and smiled at her and she squeezed his knee with her hand and told him to go back to reading his book.

* * *

The new actor in the company, Jerry, was not terribly good – but he was funny. He had a small, boyish face and lots of brown spiky hair. He delighted in entertaining the younger actresses in the bar after the performance and even treated everyone in the cast to drinks one night in the Garrick Arms, just along the road from the theatre.

'Where's he getting all the money from?' Anna asked Leonard after Jerry had produced a half of lager for her and a whisky for Leonard.

'Daddy's a banker,' Leonard sang quietly into her ear. 'All the money in the world.'

'Oh,' Anna said. 'Well. There you go.'

She sat and listened thoughtfully while Jerry regaled the shorter-skirted cast members with riotous tales of his time at RADA. How his girlfriend of the time had accidentally cut her knee open while entering for a scene during a performance of *Peer Gynt*.

'Absolutely grim!' Jerry announced with great glee. 'Blood gushing down her leg and making big dark splashes all over the stage. We were being marked on every performance so of course she just carried on. Her parents were in that night and after about three minutes of Minnie spilling blood all over the place her mother appeared below the footlights with a handkerchief and tried to truss her up each time she passed. Course, Minnie was having none of it, and just kicked wildly in her mum's direction whenever she had to pass. Audience were completely horrified – you could hear the groaning – and everyone on the stage was trying so hard not to laugh. God, it was awful!'

One of the young actresses opened her mouth to speak but she didn't get the chance, for Jerry ploughed on.

'Not as bad, though, as the time my friend Nolly decided we'd have a competition to see who could get mystery words into the text of *Tamburlaine*. It was fifteen points for penguin; ten for colonoscopy; and five for vulva. We never managed colonoscopy. Surprisingly hard word to smuggle into anything.'

Leonard finished his drink and left, so Anna shuffled along the bench and sat by Penny, Maeve and Bertie instead. Penny lifted up her right hand and rubbed her fingers together, indicating money.

Anna smiled. 'Lots,' she said quietly.

'Mmmm,' Penny said. 'It oozes. When I was up at university we would get asked for drinks in the nice colleges sometimes. Always by boys and all because … well … you know. And at these parties you would meet these very confident young men simply brimming with joie de vivre. And you would speak to them for a while – and one always supposes with people like that that they'll be bright, to have made it to the university.'

Bertie blinked at her. 'Well, they must be. You went to Oxford, didn't you?'

Penny smiled tightly. 'Most of them, Bertie, most of them were bright enough. A few of them were properly brilliant – or at least they seemed to be. But now and then you would come across a real idiot. Someone who genuinely seemed not to have read any books. Someone who could barely make conversation.'

'Jerry's not an idiot,' Maeve put in.

'No,' Penny said. 'But he's not very good at acting. Is he?' And she sipped her drink.

Bertie had his *Times* out on the table, folded over to the cross-word, and now and then he would fill in another answer as they sat and listened to Jerry perform his set. 'Belgian hare?' Bertie said now and then bit back the words. 'Sorry. Don't mind me.'

Maeve smiled at him. 'I don't have the knack,' she said. 'Someone told me you have to learn the trick of them. Did your dad teach you?'

Bertie shook his head. 'Dad? No. Not really a reader … My sergeant did them. In Egypt. Old copies of the paper. We had these long day watches and we did the crossword … He did the crossword. Taught me how. We didn't take a paper in our house, growing up.'

Anna tended to forget that men like Bertie had been in the war. No, not quite true – she tended to downgrade it. To her, being in the war meant Europe, the continent. It meant France and Germany and Poland. When you left and who survived. The English version of being in the war had become a sort of B-movie cliché to her. Lots of stoic chaps in khaki waiting to get back to bacon and warm beer. They never talked about it, anyway. Not compared to when she was growing up. Somewhere along the way it had all got edited out.

Anna looked at Bertie and tried to imagine him young and slim and scared. 'Were you out there the whole six years?' she asked.

'Five,' Bertie said. 'Wasn't sent until nearly the end of '40.'

'Were you acting then?' Penny asked. 'When you got sent?'

Bertie bowed his head. It seemed this line of questioning made him shy. 'I did the wages in a factory. When the war started gearing up we shifted into making supplies for the army. I thought perhaps they wouldn't send me. Because I worked somewhere useful. But … no. It didn't work like that.'

'When did you go to drama school then?' Maeve asked.

'After the war. Bristol Old Vic. A few of us went. I got a scholarship.' Bertie smiled to himself.

'Were your parents proud?' Maeve asked him.

Bertie's expression melted. 'Never saw me act,' he said. 'Not what they called a proper job.'

Maeve reached across the table and laid a hand on top of Bertie's. She left it there for half a minute and they all turned back to listen to Jerry tell his tales.

* * *

The night Harry touched Nik and made him put his hand on him, Nik couldn't sleep. He had just started to feel that Harry's flat was a place of refuge but now that sense was being pulled down all around him. Nik felt an extraordinary weight of dread. How did Harry know? No one knew about him. Huxley had called him that word but Nik had told himself that was not because Huxley knew. He just saw the effect that that word had on Nik and then he kept on going.

When Huxley had called him a faggot, Nik had taken all his feelings about that word, all his difficult and ambiguous feelings, and he had placed them very far outside himself and very far away. Huxley would call him that word and Nik would feel an absolute horror at the closeness of that word to him. And then later – in a quiet class or on the way home from school – he would reach inside himself and scoop up all the pain with his two hands and throw it into the long grass as he passed or down a drain or into a rotting garden on the bad side of the estate. You had to get it out of you or else you couldn't walk, or speak, or climb the stairs to bed.

Completely separate to all of that was the way he felt about other boys. The way he could feel the most extraordinary warmth inside of him when he was attracted to someone. The way that someone could become very clear to him, very vivid. This oddly and intensely and insanely wonderful feeling belonged in an entirely different place to all the disgust that he dropped upon the verges and the hollows of St Annes. But the oddly and intensely and insanely wonderful feeling was private. Any fool could see that it wasn't to be shared with anyone. It happened and it happened just for Nik.

So, when Harry placed a hand on Nik, he did not know: was it the disgust or the joy that Harry saw in him? And if Harry could see it, could everyone else see it as well?

Nik was still thinking about this when the light started to spill around the curtain. When Harry came downstairs and made them each a cup of tea.

'Harry?' Nik said. 'If I promise to pay you back, could I please have some money to make a phone call to my parents?'

Harry's face wrinkled. And he said, 'I'm sorry. I spent all my change at the chippy. Can it wait until later on?'

And Nik said of course it could and then sat and wondered if Harry was going to try and touch him again. At ten, Harry said he had to go out and that he'd be back later to chat about going up to Blackpool for the job. Nik agreed, but when Harry was gone he put the door of the flat on the latch and walked, in Harry's socks and shoes, to the payphone by the park to try a reverse-charge call.

There was no answer at his house. And no answer at the shop. Dennis would be in school and his parents must be out, somewhere. He nearly made a reverse-charge call to the Technical but he couldn't think what he would say, even if they accepted the charges. He rang the operator again and tried both numbers for a second time. No answer. He walked back to Harry's flat.

Just before twelve, Nik was sitting in the kitchen of the little flat. He was eating a dry piece of toast since he had felt odd about taking a slice of bread without asking and he felt butter would compound the offence. There was a terrible racket out in the street, a blaring and a beeping. He ignored it for a little while and then it started to make his skin itch and he went into the front room to see what was going on. Outside the house, a large blue Rover sat. Harry was in the passenger seat, and another man of about fifty, with longish grey hair, was sitting at the wheel, pressing away on the horn and smoking and laughing along with Harry. Nik stepped out of the door of the flat and Harry shouted to him.

'There's a job for you in Blackpool if you want it!'

Nik did not want a job in Blackpool, but Blackpool wasn't very far from home and he wondered if they might give him a lift to St Annes on the way back. He climbed into the car.

The driver's name was Patrick and he was extremely jolly and quite loud. He couldn't take Nik to St Annes just now but of course there might be a chance if they all came back together later on. They'd just see how it went. Patrick played the radio at full blast and smoked constantly, along with Harry. They talked about football and who might start the season at Preston North End. Nik tuned out and watched the world go by. Constantin did not own a car and Nik found it quietly thrilling to speed along the roads in your own seat, with an uninterrupted view of all the world.

They arrived in Blackpool in time for lunch and Patrick bought them each a bag of chips on the front. These chips, Nik thought, were actually very well done. Thick and fluffy and rich at the edges from the oil, not overcooked at all. He picked a couple apart and examined them, but when Harry caught him scrutinising the chips, Nik was too embarrassed to explain. Afterwards they left Patrick on the front and went to meet Harry's friend in a pool hall. Harry bought Nik a bottle of Coke, though he first offered him half a beer and Nik declined. He had never drunk more than a sip of alcohol and didn't know how he'd handle half a pint. Harry's friend was much quieter than Patrick. His name was Kingsley and he seemed to have a room to himself at the end of the main pool hall. He wasn't playing pool, as such, though a couple of young men with pool cues were sitting at a little table in the corner and chatting over a beer. Nik understood, without anyone pointing this out, that these men were friends or followers of Kingsley.

Nik was invited to sit, and Harry and Kingsley talked for a while. Then Nik was called over to talk to them.

'So,' Harry said, 'Kingsley thinks he can put some work my way in Blackpool. On a Friday and Saturday. Maybe other days, we don't know yet. And that's brilliant, isn't it?' He beamed at Nik and Nik nodded eagerly.

'And I explained to Kingsley that you were having a rough time of it. And he was very sympathetic because he knows how things are at the minute. Tough times and all that.'

Kingsley stared at the table and nodded.

'And he has offered to advance you money in return for some work. Because he understands that you're in a bit of a bind.'

Nik nodded again. Immediately he was thinking of his train fare home and how close he might be to it right now.

'And I also told him that I hadn't asked you for anything for the shoes or the socks or the bed or the food …' Harry left that hanging in the air and Nik leaped in immediately.

'Oh, of course. Of course, I'd want to give you something. As soon as I have some money. I don't need much at all for me. You can have all the rest.' And Harry gave Nik a long and appreciative smile.

Kingsley reached into his pocket and produced three £1 notes. 'This is money for three days' work,' he told Nik quietly. 'And I can advance you this. But I would need for you to do some work for me tonight. As a gesture of goodwill.'

Nik looked from Harry to Kingsley. 'Of course,' he said. 'Of course, I will. And I will give two pounds to Harry to thank him for the shoes.'

Harry smiled again and pocketed two of the three £1 notes. 'Good lad,' he said.

'Take the other pound,' Kingsley told Nik, 'Then we'll get you started upstairs.'

Nik nodded and pushed the £1 note deep into the pocket of his winter trousers. 'Thank you,' he said, nearly on the edge of tears. 'Thank you so very much.'

*　*　*

Darling Louis,

*I'm thinking of you. All the time. And trying to be brave …
And sympathetic.*

*Darling – Nik was charged with the murder of the young man.
Honestly, it's terrible. There's nothing even to link Nik to him,
except for the fact that they both do the same job.*

*Do you remember, at the same time we met, a story in the
papers about a rent boy hit on the head in Golden Square?
There was an MP – Labour, Richard Wallis – arrested for it
but never charged. The poor boy who's just been killed was
found in the garden of the club this man goes to. And he was
there that evening. His wife went to university with Penny, so
I've actually met her. I went to their house. Just on the off
chance, to ask about Nik. There was an invitation on a
noticeboard. A gala, this Sunday. I couldn't help reading the
details. I've half a mind to turn up there in my good black
frock and surprise them both. Well, him at least.*

*I'm going to be the worst kind of coward and send this surface
mail and then you won't get it until the gala has come and
gone and either I'll have made a terrible fool of myself or I
won't!*

*I send you all of my love, your A, always and patient (and
impatient but still always) xxxx*

You Love Me Like a Hurricane

Richard Wallis stood in the front hall of his house, gazing into space, waiting for Merrian.

He had had to order the *News of the World* especially from their normal shop on the high street. If there was something horrible to be read about himself he would do it in his own home. He had woken early – half past five, he thought – and sat in the kitchen, drinking strong coffee and waiting for the papers to arrive at half past eight.

No article. He had scanned every page, then read every word in detail, searching with his finger for a sign of his name or a mention of the club or Vincent Mar. And when he had finished searching the *News of the World* he had searched the *Sunday Telegraph* and the *Sunday Times*, the *Sunday Mirror* and the *Observer*, thinking that perhaps his shame had been diverted. That his disgrace waited for him on some other page, in some previously agreeable newspaper. Merrian had kept the children out of the way, had taken them eggs and soldiers in bed, had let him search every column, every sentence.

Nothing.

She appeared now at the top of the stairs, wearing a long red dress, with beads on the bodice and layers to the skirt. Her eyes were lined in black. She had put on lipstick.

He offered her a nervous smile. 'Beautiful.'

She stood on the stairs and looked at him. 'Thank you.'

* * *

Anna arrived early at the entrance to Kensington Gardens. It was only seven in the evening and the park was still full of picnickers and sunseekers, behaving as if it were the middle of the afternoon.

There were little girls in swimsuits and towelling dresses running and rollerskating on the paths. A group of men – some of them in suits – had improvised a game of cricket with jumpers, tree branches and walking sticks for wickets. Three generations of Indian ladies, the youngest a cluster of toddlers at their mothers' knees, were gathered on a tartan picnic blanket in their saris eating sandwiches and tomatoes out of Tupperware. The temperature had dropped from the highs of the afternoon and hovered around the mid-seventies. It was still too warm for the black nylon, floor-length gown that Anna wore, and she attracted more than a few glances as she walked along the paths towards the pond. All around her women were sunbathing in bikinis or lying with their skirts pulled up to the tops of their thighs, trying to give their legs a bit of colour. Men lounged on towels or the shirts they'd taken off their backs. And spotted between these examples of firm youth were circles of deckchairs holding the middle-aged and the elderly, in crimplene dresses and grey Sta-Prest trousers – hankies and battered sun hats on their heads.

She didn't remember exactly how the invitation had described the venue – she'd worked hard only to read it when Mrs Wallis wasn't looking at her – but she remembered something about the Round Pond, so it was bound to be somewhere near there. She remembered the words dinner and charity auction, boating and champagne. 8 p.m. arrival and carriages at midnight. She had decided to wait until the boating started and then go and stand beside the dock and gently insinuate herself into the party's midst. It was a vague plan, but then, as she kept comforting herself, there was nothing to lose if she didn't pull it off, only a little bit of pride.

The Round Pond was oddly named for it was not a pond so much as a lake, and not really round at all but rectangular with edges that curved like those of a tea tray. There was a marquee on the far side, looking a little like a white circus tent, with a kind of turret at its highest point, and a Union flag flying from a flagpole. Anna circled the lake with casual slowness and noticed with delight that the marquee did not seem to be fenced off in any way.

A group of men down by the edge of the pond were setting up a temporary landing stage, and on a path nearby a truck was delivering a dozen brightly coloured pedalos, which Anna eyed with some alarm. So much for boating, then. Everyone would see her lace-up Oxfords if she had to sit with her feet up. She briefly cursed her giant feet – no woman that she knew had feet big enough to lend her shoes.

Round and round the pond Anna walked, growing warmer and moister in her dress. She began to spot other overdressed people picking their way through the rows of deckchairs and the naked flesh. Ladies in sparkly peacock- and salmon-coloured evening dresses. Jackets on shoulders, beads glinting in the sunlight. Velvet bags and gold brooches and lots and lots of pearls. All the men wore tuxedos, as stiff-looking and unblemished as army uniforms. Anna took a handkerchief, Aloysius's handkerchief, from her handbag and tried to mop her face and neck.

She had been hanging back from the marquee itself for at least fifteen minutes and now she saw, with a sinking heart, that a line of string fencing had been erected to either side of it, blocking off the path she walked on and allowing only one entrance to the patch of grass where the party lay. The guests she watched pulled invitations from their breast pockets and showed them to the tuxedoed host at the entrance. Each invitation was checked and a note made in a little notepad that the host carried with him.

She had no invitation.

She saw, from a distance, Mr and Mrs Wallis arrive together and make their way in. There was a flood of people at what Anna supposed was eight o'clock and then it slowed a little. After a while, the man with the little pad left the empty entrance and went inside the marquee. Anna saw her chance and started towards the gap in the string fence but before she could get there, she saw a young man with dark red hair in a tuxedo jogging around the edge of the pond and she slowed, uncertain of what to do.

The man saw her and slowed too. 'Late as well?' he asked. 'Aren't we dreadful!' In a tone that implied he did not think he was dreadful at all.

The man with the notepad reappeared and hurried towards the young man in black, who produced an invitation from his breast pocket and walked inside the enclosure.

'Are you coming in, madam?' the man with the notepad asked.

'Waiting for my date,' Anna said, unsure how to bluff this one out. The man looked at his watch and made a face.

* * *

The tiny windows meant that the cells stayed cool even in summer. Well. No. Cool was not the word for it. There was a coldness and a dampness in the air. A scything smell of mould that you could taste on the back of your tongue.

Nik lay on the bed, his stomach in spasms. This morning a man had taken him by the back of the head and smashed his face into some wire fencing that ran along the side of the walkway. Then the man had walked on as if nothing unusual had happened.

A boy with shaggy brown hair and a long, beautiful face had found him some time later and taken him to the nearest shower room to clean his face.

'Head down, don't go out, don't speak to anyone,' he'd told Nik. 'If anyone wants something from you – food, tobacco, toothpaste, doesn't matter what it is – hand it over. Don't listen to anyone who tells you to stand your ground. You're remand, aren't you? Me too.'

'I was in Feltham before,' Nik said.

'Were you?' the young man said, brightening. 'Oh, well that's okay. You'll be fine.'

Nik looked up at him. 'I'm not sure that's how it works.'

* * *

Time seemed to pass very slowly. Anna breathed the air and felt her chances slipping away. At length, a few guests started to come out and stand in the space between the marquee and the pond. Waiters appeared from inside, holding trays filled with glasses of champagne. Two men in tuxedos started to push the pedalos into the pond by the landing stage.

She paced in the stretch of grass behind the marquee and wondered if she should wait for the gala to be over and try to meet the Wallises coming out. Anna crossed behind the back of the marquee for the fiftieth time and then stopped as she heard a shout.

'Escaped already?'

She looked round. A middle-aged man with a moustache was leaning over the string fence and calling to her.

'I'm sorry?' she said.

'Boating not your thing?' He grinned at her. He had a Yorkshire accent, his face was rather flushed and he was smoking a cigarette.

'Not exactly,' Anna said, maintaining her distance. What on earth did he want chatting her up over a fence? Men were so awkward.

'You're missing all the champagne,' he called to her, undeterred by her refusal to close the gap between them.

Anna considered the fact that the host might hear him shouting and come over. She edged a little closer to the fence. 'My date didn't turn up,' she said. 'I'm meant to be inside. I was the plus one. But he isn't here.'

'And you've been standing out there all this time?' the man asked. 'It's nearly nine.'

'He's probably just late,' Anna said. 'I'll give him hell when he gets here.'

'Don't be silly!' the man cried. 'Come inside. I don't have a plus one – I'll just say that you're my guest. And when your boy turns up we'll both have a shout at him.'

This wasn't what she'd imagined at all. And the man did seem rather keen on her. But it was undoubtedly her way in. 'Thank you,' she called. 'That's very kind!' And set off for the entrance.

The man with the notepad looked most suspicious when the moustached gentleman, who seemed to be called Gerald, explained that she was his plus one and was joining him a little late. But he smiled and nodded her through all the same.

Gerald took Anna's arm, rather too enthusiastically for her liking, and led her over to a waiter where he got them both a glass of champagne.

'Here's to late men, patient women and their rescuers,' he said, evidently pleased with his toast. Anna clinked glasses.

'It's ever so kind of you. All the same, I'm sure he'll come.'

'Well, till then you can be my date,' the man said. 'Pedalo?'

'I really can't in this dress, but do go ahead,' Anna said, smiling tautly.

'No. No. We'll find something for both of us,' Gerald said to her. 'Let's see what people are up to inside. There's a band, you know.'

He took her arm again and led her into the marquee which was filled with large circular tables covered in white tablecloths, lots of silverware, glasses and floral bouquets. In one corner a group of waiters were starting to serve the first course. There must have been close to a hundred people inside. A few were dancing in front of the band which played Cliff Richard numbers in the style of a lounge-y seaside ballroom.

'Shall we?' said Gerald, but he wasn't looking at her, nor did he wait for a reply. Instead he grasped her hand firmly and drew her through the tables and out onto the dance floor. They deposited their glasses and Anna's bag on a nearby table.

'He might get here any minute,' Anna tried.

'One dance,' Gerald said. 'A little thank you for the rescue?'

Anna unwillingly raised her right hand and he took it and led her in a strange semi-waltz, to the strains of 'Bachelor Boy'. He danced rather too close and breathed on her face a lot when he spoke.

'Labour Party?' Gerald asked.

'Sorry?'

'Is he from the party? This late man of yours.'

'Oh. No. Not, actually. Why would you ask?'

''Cause it's all Labour in here tonight. Few Liberals in the corner. Chairwoman's married to the undersecretary at the Foreign Office and he sold most of the tickets. So it's Labour to the gills. I thought you'd know.'

'No. Not really. Are you in the party then?'

'GMB. We got some tickets as a thank you for a favour we did them. But there must be fifty MPs in here tonight. Bet the Tories would love to drop a bomb on us right now.'

Anna laughed, despite herself.

'You've got a nice laugh,' Gerald told her. 'What's he do then? This man of yours.'

'Oh. Um … he's an accountant,' Anna said, unable to think quickly of another job.

'Do they have left-wing accountants?' Gerald asked.

'I think so,' Anna said. 'My one leans that way. Most of the time. I think.'

'But he provides,' Gerald said. 'That's the main thing, eh?'

Anna knew that she was meant to let this pass. She knew it. 'Actually, I support myself,' she told him, with a slightly icy smile.

'You one of those feminists?' Gerald asked, a dose of amusement in his voice.

'Yes. I'm fairly sure I am,' Anna told him and suddenly Gerald let go of her hand and made a hard grab at her waist. Anna pulled away.

They stared at each other for a moment, confused and frozen on the dance floor.

'What are you doing?' she asked him.

Gerald took a step towards her. 'I was trying to see if you had a sense of humour,' he said and made another grab at her waist.

Anna stumbled backwards again and the couples around them stopped dancing.

'Jesus,' Gerald said, all humour gone from his voice. 'I was only trying to tickle you. It's not like I was going to bloody rape you.'

Anna was aware of the women on the dance floor looking at her, waiting to see what she would do. She folded her arms across herself and stepped back a little further. 'It's just that my date will be here any minute and he wouldn't …' She worked hard to stay calm. 'He'd be upset, you see. I didn't mean to offend anyone.'

Gerald's face was flushed an even deeper red than it had been by drink. He looked around him at the men and their wives.

'Can't take a bloody joke, can she?' he said, a tremor in his voice.

Anna kept waiting for him to seem calmer, to walk away, but it wasn't happening. There was a silence and Anna looked for a way to leave the dance floor but now people had stood up and were filling the spaces between the tables.

Behind them, the band started playing 'Summer Holiday', either oblivious to the scene on the dance floor or anxious to cover it with music. Gerald took the pocket square from his tuxedo and wiped his streaming face. Anna made a step to one side, a cautious attempt to signal that she was going to leave the floor now. Gerald took a step towards her.

'Come on,' he said, breathing hard and attempting a smile. 'You owe me a dance. You know you do.' He held his hand out to her.

Anna turned away from him and tried to signal with her eyes to the women nearest her that she needed a way through, a way out. None of them moved.

She heard Gerald behind her, his voice quiet. 'Don't be a bitch.'

'Please?' Anna said to the woman standing nearest her, part of the wall of humans blocking her in.

'Bitch!' she heard again. This time the voice was closer.

A woman's voice called loudly on the far side of the dance floor.

'Excuse me!' the voice said. 'Excuse me, please! Trying to get through.'

Anna turned towards the sound of it. She could see Gerald in the periphery of her vision, standing less than ten feet away. She stumbled sideways, her shoe caught on the hem of her dress.

'Excuse me now!' The woman's voice was nearer. 'Anna!'

Anna looked towards the voice in confusion. It was Merrian Wallis, holding the skirts of her red gown up to her knees and picking her way through the mass of bodies and legs of seated guests.

'Anna!' she said again, and Anna nodded.

'I thought it was you!' Merrian said, beaming at her in a most odd and exaggerated way. She swept on, as if the people around them were not watching and everything was quite normal. Then Merrian caught Anna firmly by the elbow. 'I'd been wondering where you'd got to! You must come and say hello to everyone!' And with that she pulled Anna back the way she'd come, happily 'Excuse me'-ing her way through the crowd.

Anna was too stunned by everything that had happened in the previous ten minutes to speak. Instead, Merrian led her through the mass of tables to one where the food had already been served, and Richard Wallis and a group of male friends were clustered to one side, deep in conversation.

Merrian pulled out an empty chair, sat Anna gently in it and handed her a glass of wine that happened to be sitting on the table.

'Drink something,' she said. Anna drank.

Merrian dropped her skirts and sat down next to her.

'Well,' she said. 'What a bastard! I'm only glad I recognised you from so far away. I came to see what was going on and there you were. What a sod.' Her cheeks were flushed and her eyes seemed very bright. 'I appear to have lost my drink.'

Anna finished the glass of white wine she was holding and wondered what she would say when Merrian asked her what she was doing there.

'Lost your date and gained a pig?' Merrian asked and Anna nodded, stunned that it did not occur to the woman that Anna might be here because of them. How naive, she found herself thinking. But how nice as well.

'Thank you,' Anna said to her. 'They wouldn't let me through.' She meant the women; the failure of the men to help was somehow less meaningful.

'Nobody wanted to be shouted at by the stupid man. And people are cowards,' Merrian said. 'Don't think about it. I need another drink.'

Anna started to get up. 'I'll get you one,' she said.

'No,' Merrian told her. 'You stay here. Have a little sit. We've a spare seat. And a spare starter if you'd like it. Can't stand salmon mousse myself. I find the texture unnerving. I'll rustle up more wine. Or champagne. Do you like champagne?'

Anna nodded.

'Good. So do I.' And she left in the direction of a line of waiters near the marquee entrance.

Anna tore apart a bread roll and covered one half of it in the pale pink mousse. It had a sort of clammy wetness and tasted mostly of cream cheese. While she ate she studied the men sitting across the table from her. Richard Wallis was in the centre and beside him was a tall, slim man with dark, bushy hair and very pronounced eyebrows who gesticulated a lot and rapped the table occasionally. Flanking them were two older men of about forty or fifty, one with short-cropped greying hair and the other with a blond mop and blue eyes. She didn't recognise any of them, but then she didn't know what most MPs looked like. Anna angled herself so that she was looking away as she strained to hear the conversation. She could think of no convincing way to introduce herself, not when they were en masse like this. If she could have caught Richard Wallis on his own …

'… into committee and then that's it sunk for ten years …' she managed to catch.

A somewhat portly singer dressed in a white and turquoise tuxedo walked onto the stage and launched himself forcefully into a Richards standard. Anna bucked her head, trying to shake the sound, but the music rode an insistent and uncompromising melodic wave that the fretting of the suits could not compete with.

'… the French just throw money at the thing and Benn's lost interest …' she heard and then the end of the sentence drowned in a stutter of vibrato.

'… Barbara said she wouldn't …'

'Ohhh … Oh – Oh. Oh – Oh!' The mermaid-coloured singer span and cocked a jaunty finger at the dancers on the floor. The microphone squeaked in complaint.

'… but then she does what he says anyway. Makes no bloody sense!' a raised voice maintained before Anna heard it being shushed.

The voices of the men across the table had dropped down. Merrian returned eventually with four champagne flutes gripped in her hands. As she sat, Richard Wallis stretched out a hand towards the drinks but Merrian only gave him a curt: 'They're ours, darling,' and then turned back to Anna.

'All Labour then?' Anna said, tilting her head back towards the men.

'Mostly. Angus was a Liberal but he defected,' Merrian said, indicating the tall man with bushy hair.

'Didn't that annoy his constituency?' Anna asked.

'Oh. No. No constituency. He's a political agent. My husband's Man Friday, as t'were. He runs both our lives.'

'Thank you,' Anna said, accepting a glass of champagne. 'Did I say thank you, before, for rescuing me?'

'You did. And you really shouldn't mention it. Least I could do.' Merrian sat up very straight and knocked back half a glass of champagne. She glanced meaningfully across at the group of men and then, mimicking a man's voice: 'Tony and Barbara. George and Harold. Oh my goodness! You'll never guess what Richard said to Peter!' She dropped back into her normal voice. 'It's like listening to a group of women in a launderette discussing *The Archers*. But less compelling.' She touched Anna's arm for a moment. 'Thank God for champagne,' she said.

Anna smiled. She was delighted to have found a version of Merrian so obviously relaxed and gossipy, but she did not know what would happen if she brought up the subject of the club, or Saturday night, or Mar. All around them waiters were clearing the first course and bringing out the mains. Anna was too late to rescue her bread roll. She finished her latest glass of champagne without really meaning to. Merrian handed her another.

'We're both behaving rather badly,' Merrian said, leaning in towards Anna. 'Because something awful was supposed to happen today and then it didn't. And everyone is very relieved.'

'I see,' Anna nodded. 'Um … Sorry. None of my business. But … what didn't happen?'

Merrian looked at her and frowned. 'Something horrible was going to be written about my husband. Smears. Hateful. But it never came. Nothing. Just dropped away.'

'Oh!' Anna said. 'That's wonderful.' And immediately wondered what exactly the newspapers were going to have said.

'Anyway,' Merrian said, shaking her head hard, 'it's over. Gone. Don't want to think about it.'

A mysterious piece of meat arrived, sitting on a raft of sauté potatoes and topped with a little wheel of orange. Anna gazed across the table at Richard Wallis. There were so many things she wanted to ask.

'Do MPs go to a lot of parties?' Anna tried. 'I thought they mostly worked.'

'Functions. Birthdays. Conferences. Late-night sessions of who knows what. Drinks to hammer out this or that. Old boys' reunions. Charity galas. We're being governed by the inebriated. Quite literally in George Brown's case …' Merrian made a face. She poked at her food, made a face and then pushed the plate into the centre of the table to make more room for the champagne glasses sitting next to her.

Anna grinned. 'Just drinking?'

Merrian looked at her. 'What do you mean?'

Anna mimed smoking a cigarette and rolled her eyes.

'Oh,' Merrian said. 'Oh! I see. Well, probably. But it's hard to get anything done if you're blotto on … whatever. Uppers. Downers. Cocaine. I know he's tried cocaine,' she said in a quieter voice, 'because he told me. But he didn't think it was for him.' Merrian thought about this. 'We're both a bit Middle England.'

Anna smiled. 'Does that make a difference?'

'These things either seem normal or they don't.' Merrian knocked back the rest of her glass. 'No. It's not just that. We each have at least one parent who can remember being working class.' She looked sharply at Anna. 'Do you?'

Anna shook her head. Her parents, though faintly impoverished for much of their lives, were descended from lines of doctors and graduates and writers. Going to university, being a professional, those were just things that you were expected to do. Which was, as Anna thought now, probably the reason she felt so ashamed of her occupations so far.

'There's a memory,' Merrian went on. 'The memory of not know-ing what to do in certain places. The fear of getting it wrong. It infects people, like a cold. Like something worse than a cold. You grow up with it and you become infected with this … nervousness. This hesitation. As if you're waiting to be found out – by your clothes; the way you speak; choosing the wrong wine; speaking too loudly; not knowing how to tip.'

'But Oxford …' Anna said.

'Reminds you that you went to the wrong school and wore the wrong clothes and grew up in the wrong town. 'Oh, you don't ski?'; 'Didn't you think to bring a gift?'; 'Why would you wear those shoes?' On and on. I have a bachelor's in French and a doctorate in humiliation. Shall I get us more drinks?'

'No!' Anna said, fearing that neither of them could take much more. She looked longingly at the plate of food in front of her, wondered if the brown thing might be duck and ate a solitary potato. She wanted to keep the conversation flowing and her attention on Merrian but she was beginning to feel extremely tipsy.

'Oh, God. It's neverending. There's a bloody auction as well,' Merrian said. 'Where are you meant to be sitting?'

Anna stood, alarmed at the change in subject. She didn't want to be found out now. 'Don't worry about that! Shall I see if I can get us another drink? Stay here!' And with that she exited towards the bar.

Her bag. She'd put it down with her drink before Gerald started dancing with her. It must be on one of the tables over by the dance floor. The marquee was full of waiters again, clearing the main course and preparing to bring out dessert. I have nowhere to sit, Anna thought. Do I just stand by the bar? She started to make her way through the tables, keeping one eye out for Gerald and the other for her bag.

Across the room she spotted it, on the edge of a table by the dance floor. She kept her head down and shuffled towards it.

'He turned up then,' someone said. Just below her a man was sitting at the table which her bag was on. It was the young man with dark red hair, the one who'd entered when she'd first lied about her date.

'Yes,' Anna said and smiled at him. 'Just left my bag.' She carried on around and picked it up. She opened it for a minute. It seemed to all be in there.

'I don't think people steal from handbags at these things,' the red-haired man said to her. Anna felt herself blush. 'Mind you,' he went on, 'you never can tell about the staff. Are you going to the bar?' He stood up. 'I thought I'd have a last one myself.'

Anna smiled at him but said nothing. As soon as they were there she'd shake him off.

They were close to the bar when he asked her, 'Did I see you sitting over there with Jones and Wallis and all that? I thought it was you but I couldn't tell.'

'I was at Richard Wallis's table. I know his wife. We were just having a chat. That's all. Not my table.'

'Thought it odd if we ran in the same circles but I'd never seen you.'

'I don't think I'm properly a member of any of these circles,' Anna said and smiled. 'Just a friendly interloper. I work with Mrs Wallis's best friend from university. One of those London things. You know … how you think it's so big but then eventually you meet everyone who knows everyone else and it suddenly feels small.' She was being much too chatty. She would make her excuses in a minute.

'Oh God. That is so true, isn't it? It's so fucking incestuous, this town. Everyone knows everyone else, everyone went to the same schools, same resorts, lives in the same streets. It's a wonder we're not all inbred.' He laughed at his own joke. 'Richard Wallis though. Jesus! The stories I could tell you about … and he looks so mild.'

'Really?' Anna said, immediately a little more sober. 'No, really, do tell. Please?'

The man stood and looked at her and then at the crowd of black-clothed backs at the bar. He sighed. 'I've had enough of this,' he said. 'Other plans. Not to be rude but I'm expected on the other side of the park later tonight. And the pudding looks ghastly.'

'I wouldn't mind a breath of air,' Anna said. 'I've had far too much to drink. Shall I walk with you? Just for a minute. Not to be dreadful or anything, but I would *love* to hear what you had to say about Richard Wallis.'

What's the Matter With You, Rock?

There was a daddy-long-legs in the corner of Nik's cell. It picked its way slowly – for reasons which he could only guess at – from the left-hand corner of the window to the top of the light on the opposite side of the room and then back again.

There was a telly in one of the rec rooms, but it had been smashed two weeks ago and the prisoners had been informed that they couldn't have another one until the next part of the budget was received in the autumn. Nik tried to unpack some lovely memory in all the gloom, but everything stayed tightly shut. He desperately wanted to smoke. He hadn't had a smoke in seven days.

As the night wore on and he tried to sleep, he found that pieces of the past started to spill open, unexpected and vivid, a trail of yolk running from a cracked egg. He saw himself on a beach, sitting on a blanket between his mother and his father. Dennis was little more than a baby and had dug himself a hole, where he sat sieving sand through his fingers. He wondered if it had been a Sunday morning. He wondered why they had not been at the shop. His father stood, he was wearing trousers but no shirt, and started singing, there on the almost empty beach.

Nik could not understand the words – they were all in Greek – but his father sang in great swinging phrases, tunes that sounded half like opera and half like something from a music hall. He lay back on his mother's lap and watched her smile and her hair blow around them both in the wind. Nik felt that embarrassing and familiar feeling – caught between thrill and shame at his father's oddness.

He remembered standing on the edge of the circus, the Coca-Cola sign swirling red, listening to the boys talk. He remembered laughing and hanging onto someone else's shoulders, someone flapping madly with their hands at the pigeons gathering above their head. He remembered feeling that it was the most natural thing in the world that he should be someone different. Someone not like anybody else. Different and exceptional and odd, just like his father.

* * *

Out in the real world, as Anna suddenly thought of it, a man slept alone, half clothed on a towel outside the string enclosure. It was after ten now and the light was gone. Outside the marquee, strings of fairy lights adorned the tented opening – Anna hadn't even noticed these before. The picnickers were gone, so were the children, but many of the younger adults stayed and smoked on the grass, filling the air with scents of tobacco and marijuana.

The red-haired man walked ahead of her at speed and Anna could feel her advantage dropping away in his unwillingness to linger. She raised her skirts and hurried after him. He was heading away from the Round Pond and down to the south side of the park, below the long curving sides of the Serpentine Lake.

'Are you late for a date?' she asked, not knowing how to draw him round again to Wallis without seeming too desperate.

The man stopped dead on the path and felt inside his tuxedo for something. He withdrew a long and very neatly rolled spliff. Then he pulled matches from his trouser pocket and lit it. He took two long drags, blowing the smoke out slowly towards the ground. Then he resumed walking but with a slower pace. Anna wondered what might happen if they passed a policeman.

Here and there a star was visible, the clouds passing quickly over the land. 'I don't know why they don't just ask everyone for £100 and be done with it,' the man said. 'Why the pretence of a party? Cliff Richard!'

Anna smiled. 'Not a follower?'

'Kinks. Animals. Stones are bearable. Beatles are … hippies. Middle class playing working class. So Labour.'

'Not with the party, then?' Anna asked.

'They want to undo everything that's good,' the man said. 'Culture. Beauty. Architecture. We all have to pretend we're equal! Nobody believes we're equal. Do you want some of this?' he asked her, proffering the spliff.

Anna wavered. It wasn't that she'd never smoked. She'd been to seven years of cast parties and first nights and actors' birthdays. She'd been passed weed more often then she could remember. But she'd never properly smoked anything. And though she had attempted to get high a number of times – when surrounded by safe company – the foulness of the act of smoking and her inability to inhale correctly had put her off the whole endeavour. She wasn't the sort of girl to chase highs of any kind, though it had been suggested to her that she should probably, one day, learn how to relax.

'Okay then,' Anna said gamely, emboldened by the large amount of alcohol sloshing round her system. The man passed her the joint and Anna concentrated very hard on trying to smoke as if she knew what she was doing. 'I don't even know your name,' she said.

The man thought about this. 'Nor I yours.' And then stopped abruptly as if to signal that that was the end of that particular part of the conversation.

'There's something odd about the park at night,' she tried, handing the spliff back to him with some relief. 'I always feel as if I'm not really allowed to be here. As soon as it's dark, it becomes something else. Like it doesn't belong to London any more.'

The man peered at her. 'Where do you think we are?'

'Somewhere out of time. I think it's the dark. All the buildings melt away. All the details. You could be anywhere. There was a book when I was a child … About breaking into the garden of a castle at night and sometimes there were dinosaurs and sometimes princesses. Night has that feeling … slipping between time.'

'The wood between the worlds?' the man said. He rolled the spliff between his fingers.

'Exactly.'

'So, if you jumped into the lake …'

'There'd be another reality on the other side,' Anna agreed.

The man took a long, slow drag, then he handed the spliff back to her. He nodded his head towards the burning fragment. 'Wood between the worlds,' he said and Anna smiled.

The old tea rooms emerged out of the darkness and the man decided they should swerve up towards the Serpentine. He waved a hand to indicate that Anna should smoke more, so she did.

'Miles Davis,' she said, thinking at least to steer the conversation onto something a little less fantastical. 'Do you like Miles Davis?'

'Jazz is for people who think they're French.'

'Ska?' she tried.

'Scar?' The man looked at her.

'Ska. It's from Jamaica. They play it in the clubs.'

'Not in any clubs I'd go to.'

He's not very polite, Anna thought. And then wondered if that just meant he was cleverer than her. 'It's quite good,' she told him, through partly gritted teeth. 'Sort of joyful, off-tempo. Resets the thinking.'

'Is that good?'

'Resetting the thinking?' Anna asked. 'Well, yes. Isn't it? Thinking of things afresh. Different eyes.'

'Why would I want different eyes?' the man asked. 'What if they were the eyes of someone stupid?'

'But seeing the world … Other people …' She was getting confused now. 'Other people are important,' she tried.

'Other people are inevitable. It's hardly the same thing.'

'No,' Anna said. 'No. I …' She had the sense that she was going to sleep.

'You've stopped walking,' a voice said. Someone took the spliff from her fingers. Anna tried to focus.

'You're just standing,' the voice said. It sounded irritated.

She wanted to lie down.

'Shall I leave you here?' the voice asked.

'No. Wait,' Anna said. She had to ask him about Miles Davis. No! Not about Miles Davis. About Richard Wallis. 'You said there were stories.'

'Did I? I'm meant to be at the Dorchester.'

154

'Where's the Dorchester?'

'On the other side of the park. I'm going to go now.'

'No. No!' Anna said. She stretched her eyes open and put an arm out towards him, steadied herself against his arm. 'I'm coming. Please. Too. I want to hear.' She didn't know if it was the spliff or the four glasses she had drunk in less than an hour but she didn't feel very cogent.

The man threw the end of the joint on the ground and stubbed it out. He reached inside his tuxedo pocket and brought out a clear plastic bag. From it he shook something which he held in his hand.

'Do you want to wake up?'

'I'm sorry. I really am okay,' Anna said. She tried to let go of his arm but she thought she might fall over, so she grabbed back on.

The man showed her a pill in his hand, smaller than an aspirin.

'It's caffeine. A stimulant,' he said and took it. They were standing so close together that she couldn't properly see his face. Anna focused on the path in front of them and shook her head.

'It's caffeine,' the man said again. He sounded exasperated. 'You know, like the stuff in coffee. I'd buy you a coffee but there's nowhere around here open at this time of night.'

Anna wanted to move but her limbs were not cooperating. The longer they stood here like this, the more she simply wanted to lie down and sleep.

'Okay,' she said. 'Okay.' She held out her hand and he gave her another of the pills from the little bag. Anna peered at it sternly. 'Caffeine?' she checked.

'Just like a strong espresso.'

She crunched down. It tasted sweet.

'Wallis,' she said, trying to clear her head. 'You know him.'

'Well, he's hardly a friend … He runs with a crowd of poofs. God – what am I saying! You're a friend of his wife, aren't you?'

'Oh, yes. But … I mean, I think she knows.' Anna worked on putting one foot in front of the other. They set off slowly down the path together.

'I don't need any shit splashing its way back onto me,' he said.

'To be fair,' Anna tried to laugh, 'I don't know who you are.'

'Mm. Well, he's totally under the spell of his battle-axe wife, the great and powerful Angus.'

'His agent?'

The man laughed. 'Angus pulls all the strings. They were up at Oxford together apparently, only Angus's family live in a castle and Wallis grew up in a semi. Angus was terribly brilliant. PPE at Christchurch, then a DPhil at Cambridge or Harvard or somewhere, whereas Wallis was just one of those grammar-school boys ... there to make up the numbers. Wallis trots his rather pedestrian mind off to the Labour Party. Then Angus ends up doing research at Westminster and there is his former love, working for some ex-miner. So he becomes Wallis's everything, they even have a flat together using Wallis's living allowance once he's made MP.'

'But he's married ...'

The man with red hair looked at her. 'Well, he's not a complete idiot, is he? He had to get elected. Anyway, Wallis – with Angus's help – lands a plum seat; absolutely safe as you like. Peckham, full of the unwashed, so he's in clover. Wallis is much fancied – not in the filthy sense, though who knows – and is made shadow junior at justice. All eyes on Wallis. '64 rolls round. Suddenly, Wilson's in government and Wallis is a junior minister for real. Talked of as future cabinet, all of that. Everyone proclaiming Angus as a political god. But ...'

'But?'

'One year in, Vincent Mar goes down hard, right outside their flat. Oh calamity! And the papers are in on it. No more glittering career for Mr Wallis. Though he did manage to keep his seat. Which is surprising, really. But then the Met bottled it and withdrew all the charges. Never trust a policeman!'

'Blimey,' Anna said. And then, 'How do you know all this?'

The man with red hair treated her to a long, hard look. 'People in politics gossip like fishwives and I know a lot of people in politics.' They curved around the south side of the lake. 'Also,' the man said with a sigh, 'I was at school with Angus. But he was years above me. Never really knew him. Anyway. London. Yes? Constantly running into the same faces, over and over ...'

156

The lamps along the edge of the lake cast a line of moving beacons on the water, and just for a moment Anna watched the reflections slide and break. She did feel more awake now. Almost focused, which was odd given how much she'd had to drink. 'I know I'm being dreadful – and I swear, I won't tell the wife – but Golden Square: do you know what really happened?'

'Yet another party. Someone's birthday. All assignations and dreadful queens getting high.'

'Was that why Vincent Mar was there? He was part of the party?'

'One supposes. Not for me to say.'

'But the Hellenic …'

'Hideously bent.'

'Is it?' Anna asked.

'Academics, liberals, intellectuals … I spend five minutes in the place and I need a bath.' The man laughed to himself. 'Not in there, of course! God, can you imagine!'

'It's really quite chilling,' Anna agreed, treading carefully.

'Isn't it? Come friendly bombs and fall on Waterloo Gardens … God, Betjeman wasn't one of them, was he?'

Anna pretended to think about this. 'I don't know,' she said. 'It's so hard to tell with poets. Do Wallis and Angus still have their parties?'

'You remember the year they got that actor?'

'What actor?'

'In the toilets …'

'Gielgud?'

'Yes, him. That same summer they got a Labour MP as well. Bill Field. Another London one. It's always London MPs, isn't it? Anyway. They got him in the gents at Piccadilly. And first he pleads guilty because no one's yet found out. But then … *News of the World* run a piece on him. Suddenly, he's defending his honour. Even got a Tory MP friend of his to defend him in court – well, that smells to high heaven, doesn't it? But they find him guilty. And that's that for Field. Other MPs take note. They get clever. No more gents' toilets. They won't get away with it. So, now it's members' clubs and flats and private parties. Down and down into the earth …' The man reached into his breast pocket for the little bag. 'D'you want another one?'

'Um … no,' Anna said. She was beginning to have suspicions about who this man was and why he went to so many parties. And then, not wanting to sound too wary, 'If it's caffeine and I have some more, I'll never sleep tonight.'

The man smiled and pointed to the way ahead. Beyond the main road, on a corner over to the left, lay a large, cream-coloured building with ironwork balconies stretching across its front. The lights above the entrance doors glowed yellow-orange and lit a group of men in dark green livery who stood at the top of a little flight of steps, looking as if they were attendants in a play.

'This is where I get off,' he told her.

'Oh, right. Of course. The Dorchester,' Anna said, wondering if there was a way to invite herself inside. She had no name for this man, no address. And he seemed to know more about Richard Wallis than even his close family.

'Are you sure you wouldn't like another one for going on with?' he asked. 'It's no bother. I've got lots. I work absurdly long hours and I couldn't do it without them.'

'I don't know,' Anna said. 'Maybe. Do you know what I *do* need, though? Please don't think me awful. But do you think I could step inside the hotel with you and use the facilities?'

The man laughed. 'Is your nose unpowdered?'

'Horribly so. And it was rather a long walk.'

'Okay,' he said, seeming to fall into an easier pattern with her. He reached out and took her hand. 'You can be my date, but only for the foyer.'

'Much obliged,' Anna told him. 'You are a gentleman.'

Inside the foyer of the Dorchester, everything shone. The floor shone black and white, the walls sang pink, the fittings and the ceiling roses dazzled gold and brass. The counters and desks rang with inlay and varnish. Every bulb was brighter than any bulb had ever been before. The effect, after the deep, calm darkness of the park was startling. Anna's eyes struggled to take it all in. Why were rich people obsessed with shiny surfaces? she wondered. What was inherently glamorous about things that hurt one's eyes? It was like being on the stage during a technical. When the lighting crew turned up all the spots to test them one by one. Oh, she thought. Yes, of course. It's a set. Well, that makes sense.

The tall man with red hair was looking at her, his lips pursed.

'I don't suppose you know where I'm going?' she asked.

The man nodded and gestured to a far corridor. 'The gentlemen's are in that direction. I'd wander that way, if I were you.' He was obviously anxious to go and Anna could not think in this moment of a clever way of delaying him.

'Well, thank you,' she said.

The young man touched his jacket where his breast pocket was. 'Sure I can't leave you with something for the road?' he asked.

'I'll manage,' she smiled at him, and then she made her way through the cavernous entry and along a gold-flocked corridor in the direction he had pointed.

In the bathrooms – a symphony of cream, embossed angels and spotless sinks – she locked herself in a cubicle. She peed and looked through her handbag to check that she had money for a cab or a bus.

The odd thing was that she didn't feel tired. In fact, she felt rather refreshed, as if all that alcohol, the glasses of wine and champagne, had poured right through her and left her brain untouched. She didn't feel drugged, whatever that meant. Just terribly awake.

She washed her hands and tidied her hair in the glass. An older woman came in, petite and well groomed, neatly dressed in a beaded gown and jacket. The woman cast her the smallest of small smiles and adjusted her make-up in front of the mirrors. Anna looked at herself, in her black dress, and then at the tiny lady standing beside her. She wished that she wasn't so tall, so broad in the shoulders. She felt like a giantess. She felt like a man. How blissful it must be to be a man, she thought. And never to have to think of things like this.

She walked out into the foyer and took in the people it contained. There were two or three middle-aged couples talking on the love seats. Two young women in eveningwear, sitting together and searching through a handbag. Three concierges. The men outside the doors. A boy in livery by a set of lifts. Anna made a casual walk towards him, paused and then smiled.

'Can I help you, madam?' he asked her.

159

'I'm so sorry. I feel quite foolish. I came in with my boyfriend but he seems to have gone up to the party without me. Did he go in the lift? Tall man, tuxedo, red hair …' She beamed at him.

'Yes, madam. Yes, he did. On the second floor. The Snellgrove party? It's in Ballroom Two.'

Anna laughed and shook her head. 'I can't believe he went on without me!'

The boy pressed a button to call the lift. He smiled shyly at Anna. She continued to beam back at him.

The lift doors slid open. 'You're too kind,' Anna said.

The hallway on the second floor was gentler than the excesses of the entrance. Cream walls, brass light fittings; almost peaceful. The Dorchester smelled like eucalyptus and hyacinth, Anna thought, though the latter seemed rather a suburban flower for such a place and the bouquets in the vases were of lilies, roses and hydrangeas.

Between the tables and their displays of floral bounty sat plump love seats, covered in ivory and duck-egg satin. Anna felt a momentary desire to sit on one, but she was sure that such a piece of furniture would break under the weight of someone who was not supposed to be there.

A pair of arrows directed her to 'Ballroom 1' in one direction and 'Ballroom 2' in another. But the room when she found it – and it was signed above the door – didn't look like a ballroom at all. Instead there was another corridor and then off it, to the left, a vast room covered with pale blue fleur-de-lys and lots of cream-white panelling. White cloth-covered tables were set with metal trays, most of which held a few glasses of red wine, or a couple of glasses of white. Anna took half a step inside the door and looked around. A group of men in tuxedos were standing at one end, glasses in hand. Anna eyed the trays of wine; a lady in a black dress and white apron smiled at her.

'Drink, madam?' she asked. Anna nodded to the champagne. The lady picked the stem of the glass up gingerly, resting her other hand beneath the base and offered it to Anna as if it were a precious spice. Like myrrh, Anna thought, and accepted it. There was a door in the corner the room, through which music could be heard and lights shone dimly. Anna walked slowly into the blackness of the ballroom proper.

There was a stage at the far end, with a golden curtain streaming behind it and a microphone. At the very side of the stage a dark-haired woman stood in a shining evening dress, her back to the audience. She was drinking a glass of water. Here, as in the marquee, a sea of round white-clothed tables spread out before Anna. There were people in eveningwear seated at the tables, but the lighting was so low, and so many of them were turned towards the stage that she could not see many faces. She took a small sip of champagne and looked around for the red-headed man.

'Oh – oh – oh – sinnerman, where you going to run to?
Sinnerman, where you going to run to?'

Anna turned back to the stage. There stood a diminutive black woman in a magnificent silver-blue gown. She was singing with one hand cupped around the microphone, a look of intensity on her face.

The lady seated closest to Anna, in pearls and a thick brocade dress, smiled and tapped her fingernails on her glass. Beside her, two men leaned close in together and talked over the noise from the stage. Anna could hear them saying 'Charlie Bubbles' and 'smoked it right out of her!' and laughing.

The lady beside her began to sing along with the chanteuse on the stage. 'Please hide me,' she trilled quietly.

Anna felt quite disoriented. As if each new room in this hotel had a language of its own and she hadn't learned any of them.

'Took her up the Bombay passage!' a man to her right cried with delight.

'I can't hide you!' the woman in pearls trilled louder, to cover – Anna imagined – the awfulness of her companion.

The lady on the stage sang with her eyes closed.

'I run to the river, it was boiling.
I run to the sea, it was boiling ...'

Anna was held by the woman's voice. A volcano of pain seemed to bubble there. She was no Nina Simone but she was someone entirely herself. English, for she had an English voice.

A hand plucked at her shoulder and Anna stumbled back.

'What are you doing here?' It was the man with red hair. 'I thought you went to the loo.'

'I did,' Anna said. 'Sorry.'

The lady in pearls had stopped singing along and was looking up at them, evidently shocked by the man's fierce tone.

'Are you invited?' the man asked.

There was nothing to do but brazen it out. 'I might be,' Anna smiled.

The man stood back, temporarily unsure of himself. 'How do you know Lulu?'

Anna raised a glass to him. 'I think we have ascertained that I know everyone.'

The man stared at her, his handsome features twisted in confusion. 'No. You asked me why I was going to the Dorchester. What is this?'

'Nothing terrible,' Anna replied sweetly.

'You're following me,' he said, leaning in towards her.

'I'm really not.' She attempted a laugh but the man grabbed at her arm and caught it angrily. He started to push her forcibly back towards the door. Anna tried to pull away from him, to shake him off.

'Get off me,' she hissed, furious to be touched in such a way.

'Who are you?'

'Absolutely no one,' Anna said. 'No one!'

He let go of her for a moment, then she felt a hand on her back pushing her towards the exit. She stumbled in front of him, clutching her bag and grabbing at her skirts, exposing her laced black shoes. She felt herself almost unbalanced and realised that he had grabbed hold of the back of her dress and was using it to steer her through the rooms. Her drink tipped wildly onto the carpet; she dropped the glass without meaning to. The men in tuxedos were still drinking in their little group. She thought she heard laughter. Anna looked the other way, her face hot with a mixture of embarrassment and anger. She wondered if he would push her all the way out of the hotel itself, but when they arrived at the corridor out onto the main hall, she staggered forward, seemingly untethered, looked round and realised that he was gone.

In the main hallway, two very young women in pastel chiffon gowns sat on one of the love seats, leaning hard in the direction of the little corridor to catch all the drama as it happened. Anna caught their eye for a moment and then looked away.

'Do you want a cigarette?' one of them asked.

Anna attempted to pull herself together. 'Thank you,' she said in a quiet voice. 'I don't smoke.'

'My mother says that Gill is a bastard's bastard. Utterly unsuitable for events that the young will attend,' her friend said.

'Gill?' Anna asked.

'Parents are terribly wealthy,' the one in baby blue confided, in a delighted whisper. And then, 'Not blue blood but not new money either. He can pass. You know? He'll marry someone someday.'

Her friend in yellow honked with laughter. 'You!' she squealed. 'You hope it will be you!'

Anna watched the two girls in quiet astonishment. They had the mannerisms of children but she could see from their dresses – the quiet sheen of the fabric, the fluent lines – that everything they wore had been bought from Chanel or Yves Saint Laurent.

The one in baby blue unclasped her handbag and removed a small plastic bag full of pills. Glancing slightly nervously at Anna, she extended the bag in her direction.

'That's very kind,' Anna said. 'But I think I've had enough.'

* * *

Richard Wallis sat on a bench by the Round Pond and smoked a cigarette in the darkness. Merrian had got terribly drunk and he'd had to put her in a taxi home. He was watching the men from the catering firm pack their crates into a van. Another group were taking down the marquee. There was no light where he sat. He imagined he was invisible, save for the glow of his cigarette.

He'd spent half the evening discussing transport and the cliquey tendencies of the current cabinet until drink had got the better of everyone. Once upon a time he'd been co-authoring a paper on justice reform. Now he was asked his opinion more by way of courtesy. He was still a little staggered by the way in which influence could appear in someone's life. Power, really. And, then, how quickly it could disappear. What he felt now were the ripples of something he used to have. The ministerial him. A version of himself that he had barely had time to accept before it was thrown into a drawer. The further he walked through the shadow of his own life, the less he understood it. He no longer trusted himself to steer the ship. Perhaps he never had.

A Little Time. A Few Mistakes.

Anna spent most of Monday recovering from the Sunday that had gone before, but, come Tuesday, Penny surprised her by diving into the subject as they stood in the wings during the quick change in the second act. Anna was lacing Penny into a velvet evening dress and Penny had to strain her neck to whisper and be heard.

'I didn't know you knew the boy who'd been arrested,' she said.

'Nik?' Anna was thrown by the collision of two worlds. She stopped for a moment and whispered back. 'Yes. He eats in the cafe below my flat. Why?'

'Merrian rang me. She said she'd met you twice in the last week. That you'd asked her about the thing at the club. You never said anything to me ...'

'Don't take it personally,' Anna whispered back. 'I just didn't want to drag you in unnecessarily. It's such a mess.'

She finished fastening Penny into her dress and the actress turned to look at her, their faces only just visible in the darkness at the side of the stage. 'She wants to meet you. Merrian. Tonight or tomorrow.'

'Me?' Anna asked, aware that Penny's cue was fast approaching. 'Why?'

'She needs to ask you something about her husband.' Penny fixed Anna with a look that was at once somewhat scandalised and a little excited. And then she turned, with something of a flourish, and deposited herself into the pool of light onstage.

* * *

Nik had so wrapped and obscured the time in Blackpool – so covered it with brown paper and baking parchment and old news – that he could no longer remember any one day as being distinct from other days. There were moments of absolute fear that he had worked very hard to make unclear, both to his waking and his sleeping self. But mostly what remained of those weeks he had spent living above the pool hall in Blackpool was the terrible loneliness of the days. The hours he had spent trying to understand his way out of things. Trying to understand how to make everything stop around him. The blind panic, which had not felt like panic at all, but more like being a marble rattling around in a wooden, glass-topped maze. Nik could not understand his own direction, not the starting point nor the ending point nor the way to escape. But all the same the faces came and stared in through his glass roof, observing him closely, carefully, dispassionately, angrily. He was watched as one who knew what he was doing, what game it was he played. And yet he did not.

It was on the second time of trying that he had made it out of there. Five in the morning and with no money to his name – for he kept nothing that was earned – he found himself at last upon the streets of Blackpool with no man following him or watching him. With the tower always to the left of him, just above his line of vision, Nik walked along quiet streets lined with hotels and boarding houses faded watercolour pale in the half-light. The Osterley, the Warwick and the Royal; the Kimberley, Bracondale and Sunset Lodge. Milk bottles jammed the doorsteps of the smaller lodgings and the signs at the window invariably read 'No Vacancies' and 'We Are Full'. Nik tried not to look into the darkened windows.

He walked north for a little while and then he turned on his heel and paused for a moment, imagining the line along the coast, the promenade, the walk back to St Annes and his parents' house. He could start walking now and, if he kept a steady course, be standing outside his house by nine o'clock. All this he thought in under half a second. And then he turned and walked to Blackpool South instead, to wait for a busy train to Manchester. All that he wanted, in that moment, was to push his way through the crowds and lose himself.

At first upon the train. And then in the Victorian hubbub of Manchester. Amidst towering buildings and streets thick with traffic and fumes.

As Nik stood, now, on the little landing of the Scrubs, he gazed down at the line of landings, the slim slope of the stairs, the movement of the dark-haired heads on the ground-floor level. Here, then, was another city. A different colour and a different shape but not so very distant from other towns that he had known. It was only a matter of another world to be learned. A little time. A few mistakes.

* * *

The women met in Cafe 101, across the road from The Galaxy, where the windows seemed to be permanently steamed up regardless of the weather outside, and the red leather banquettes carried an undulating and gritty layer of deep brown grease and dirt. Penny bought them all coffee while Anna sat in the booth and waited for Merrian to arrive.

She came late, looking sweaty in a creased yellow dress with large, overblown peonies painted on it. The dress did not match her mood.

'Do you want me to go?' Penny asked.

'No. It's fine. There's nothing you don't know already,' Merrian told her quietly. 'I need to ask ... Sorry, Anna. I know we don't ... And I was frightfully drunk on Sunday ...'

'You were very kind to me,' Anna said. 'Don't feel bad. Whatever it is, none of this is your fault, is it?'

Merrian shook her head. 'I don't know. Not directly.' She lapsed into silence.

'What did you want to ask?' Anna prompted.

Merrian played with her fingers and lowered her voice. 'It's the article. The one that didn't appear. The day you came to see me in Dulwich ... you asked me all about the boy in the gardens. And, of course, I knew. But not because I'd read it in the paper. Because a horrible journalist, called Simon Hartford from the *News of the World*, rang me and told me he was running a story on my husband. About Vincent Mar and this new case and God knows what else.

We took it seriously. I warned my husband. I warned Angus. We even talked to our son about it. But then Sunday came and – as you know – nothing. No story. Richard's relieved, which is all well and good but now I'm wondering why. Why would they pull it? Why wouldn't it appear? And is it because something bigger's coming?'

'Oh,' Anna said. 'I see. Well, I've no idea … I don't really know any journalists.'

'But you're worried about this friend of yours, aren't you?' Merrian said. 'Do you know anything … Is there something that I'm missing – about this? Or even Vincent Mar? I just … I need to know what's coming before it hits.'

Anna's mind tried to reconcile the tenor of this meeting with the strange welter of information she had learned from the man called Gill. Could Richard Wallis be guilty of something and his wife so terribly innocent? And how much did she really know about her husband and his relationships? 'Um … yes,' Anna managed. 'I don't know. I don't really know anything yet. Not for certain. It's all rather confusing.'

'Look,' Merrian said, her face earnest and taut. 'I'm just asking you to warn me. I am asking you – if you discover that my husband was involved, in any of this – I'm asking that you tell me. Warn me. For the children. Will you do that? Please?'

Anna nodded. 'If I find anything out for certain … Yes. Of course. Yes.' She did her best to smile at Merrian. 'I'd want the same.'

* * *

Besides the guards, Nik had barely spoken to another soul in his first week in the Scrubs. There had been the boy with shaggy hair, the one who had taken him to the bathroom to wash his bloody face, but that was about it.

Nik wondered if the state of his face might serve as a beacon for abuse. That he would be jeered at, or laughed at, or hit again just as he would have been at school. He kept his eyes fixed upon the stairs and then the floor. Said only 'Please' and 'Thank you' as he stood in line. By and large, everyone just seemed to ignore him.

He managed to creep away from the exercise yard early and spent most of Monday afternoon lying on his bed in the quiet of the cell. On the Tuesday, the boy with the shaggy hair appeared in front of him in the queue for food. Nik smiled, without really meaning to, at the back of his head but said nothing. After breakfast, as they were carrying back their trays to the main counter, Nik tried to catch the boy's eye and he thought he saw him glance over slightly. But he couldn't be quite sure. Nik looked for him again at lunch and saw him from a distance. But there was no eye contact that time and Nik suspected that the young man was distancing himself.

After lunch, Nik was asked, along with another three inmates, to help rearrange the communal area for game-playing. He shifted tables and spoke quietly, when he had to, to the other men carrying the furniture alongside him. They all seemed much more confident than he, laughing and joking and swearing with a certain amount of panache. As he prepared to go back up to his cell, he caught sight of the young man with shaggy hair making his way down towards the common area. The young man seated himself beside the long table which held the chessboards and the draughts and the backgammon. He seemed to be unpacking a chess set and Nik waited for the area to fill up a little more before he walked back over and pointed to the board.

'I never learned,' he managed. And the young man looked up at him, rather startled and then back at the set.

'We played in school,' the young man told him and Nik tried to imagine the kind of school the young man had gone to.

'I can play backgammon,' Nik tried. He was still standing, waiting to be told to eff off, or for someone else to arrive to play with the young man.

The man glanced around quickly. 'Do you want to play backgammon? I don't mind. I know the rules.'

Together they set up the board, stacking counters in little towers of black and white and finding the dice. They started without further small talk but after a couple of minutes the young man asked him, 'You okay?' And Nik said, 'Yeah,' because it seemed easier than telling the truth.

'You just left then?' the young man said.

'Sorry?'

'School.'

'Oh! No. When I was fifteen. Um … four years now. You?'

'I was in sixth form until last July. And I didn't get my grades. So, I didn't get my place at Exeter. And I was resitting. Maths. Ugh.'

Nik smiled. 'Hated maths.'

The boy smiled back. 'Me too. But I was meant to be an engineer. Or … I don't know. Maybe I'm still going to be an engineer. I'm not really sure how any of this works.'

'Will they take you? Exeter? When you get out?' Nik asked, not knowing if this was a silly question.

The young man laughed. 'I wouldn't think so. And I still don't have my A levels. My dad thinks maybe I'll make it to a poly.' His face fell and he rattled the dice hard inside his fist.

Nik smiled. 'I don't think it should matter how it happens. Poly or whatever. I never got any CSEs. No O levels. Nothing.'

The young man smiled back sympathetically. 'They might let you take something in here. Maybe not CSEs. But maths and English. I've a feeling you're allowed to study something.'

'I don't think I could go back to school,' Nik said. 'Not now. Not after everything.'

The young man hopped his counters along the points. 'I mean … you don't have to. I just think it helps … To make plans.'

Nik wanted to tell the young man that he couldn't make plans because he didn't think he was ever getting out. But he thought that that might tie a kind of sadness to him and he would rather have a friend. All things being equal.

* * *

A young woman's voice sprang into life. 'Good morning. *News of the World*. How can I help?'

Anna took a breath. 'I was after Simon Hartford. He was working on a story about a friend of mine.'

'Can I take a name?'

Anna paused. 'Wolf,' she said. 'Anna Wolf.'

'Thank you, Miss Wolf. I'm going to see if he's at his desk.'

The phone went silent for more than a minute and then the tone at the end changed and a harried male voice answered. 'Hartford. What story is this concerning?'

'Hello. I'm ringing about the boy found in Waterloo Gardens ...' Anna paused to judge the reaction. There was only silence on the end of the phone. She tried again. 'I believe you're writing a piece. Possibly about some MPs. And the club. Is that right?'

'Not exactly,' the man's voice had slowed down considerably. 'You told our receptionist you were friends with people involved.'

'I'm a friend of Nik Christou. The man arrested. I ... also know Merrian Wallis. In passing, as it were. She's the wife—'

Simon Hartford interrupted her. 'I know who she is. Did you have information for me, Miss Wolf?'

'Not exactly,' Anna said. 'Though I did wonder why the story you were working on hadn't appeared yet. I thought perhaps things had widened out. That you were working on something bigger.'

There was another pause at the end of the line. 'The story won't be appearing, Miss Wolf. At least, not anytime soon.'

'Sorry?' Anna said. 'Why would that be?'

The voice when it came again sounded uncertain. 'Editorial make the decisions they make. Apparently, we've moved on.'

'From everything?' Anna asked. 'The whole case? Waterloo Gardens? The historic cases? All of it?'

Anna could sense he was weighing his words. 'We've moved on,' he told her again. 'Sorry. Just one of those things.'

But No One Can Ever See the Bear

Hayes sighed deeply and peeled off his jacket. Anna pretended not to notice that he was sweating straight through his shirt.

'I walked over to the offices,' he told her. 'Very friendly. Offer of cake from the canteen. A quick chat. Asked Rogers about the list. Did he have it around and could I take a look?' Hayes fixed Anna with a pointed stare.

They were standing together under the dense white cage of stone and glass that was the Hellenic gentlemen's club. Like a bear cage, Anna thought, but no one could ever see the bear.

Anna shook her head. The list. The names of everyone present in the club when Charlie had been killed.

'Did you mention the other man on the steps of the tube?' she asked.

Hayes shook his head. 'I start a conversation and they shut me down. I even went to the pub. I never go to the pub.' He paused. 'They've reprimanded me. Not in writing. Not yet. But I got pulled up on it on Friday. Why was I asking? Why was I straying past my remit?'

'I'm sorry,' Anna said. 'I'm like the Angel of Doom, aren't I?'

This, at least, made Hayes laugh. Anna was weighing how much of what she knew should be passed on and how much she should keep to herself. She didn't know what she felt about the gossip of a probable drug dealer in the park. Then there was Merrian. Merrian and her marital woes. What to make of that?

'I'm not sure if I can say how I know this,' Anna started, 'but there was meant to be a story in the *News of the World* on Sunday. About Charlie and the club and Vincent Mar and Labour MPs. I mean, I don't know which bits were going to be in exactly. But it never appeared. It was pulled. That's the bit I actually know. I spoke to the journalist. Editorial decision, he said.'

Hayes stared at her. 'It's all going quiet,' he said. 'I spoke to a man called Hench last week. He was the DS in charge of gathering evidence from the scene. He ran through what was found around the body – I told him it was for a drugs investigation ...' Hayes made a face but ploughed on. 'So, someone – possibly Charlie – had a packet of pills. Five pills. I'm not sure what they were yet because I can't ask for the toxicology report. Anyway ... They also found a teaspoon. But Hench thought they might have been there months, years, I don't know. A silver chain, discoloured, probably old. A couple of pages from the inside of an *Express* – old again; two weeks out of date, Hench thought. Brandy glasses, just left under a bush. Those were clean, so probably recently used. Cigarette butts – but those probably don't mean anything.'

'So, which bits matter?' Anna asked. 'The glasses, the pills?'

'Any of it might matter,' Hayes told her. 'You just don't know. The pills made me wonder about the thing that that boy said in the cafe. About Charlie having a bad heart. Were they for that? Or were they methamphetamine? Did they weaken him in some way?'

'What did the doctors say?' Anna asked.

'In the post mortem? Well, they read us a summary last week but it only said that he'd had a heart attack at roughly the same time as he suffered some kind of asphyxiation. Or smothering. Perhaps the pills don't mean anything in the grand scheme of things. Or maybe they didn't even belong to Charlie. I don't know. My thought now is just to go inside, find a friendly manager and run some of it past him. Not making it too obvious I haven't seen the list ... Who was there? What was found? I don't know what else to ask about at this point. And then just hope he doesn't follow up and ring the station.' He looked at Anna. 'You can't come with me, you know. This is police business.'

'I know,' she said, though she was rather put out all the same.

Hayes walked up the steps and disappeared through the main doors. He was gone about a quarter of an hour, and Anna walked up and down the streets, peering over the railings and into the deserted gardens of the clubs. To an outsider they certainly looked like parks; she could see why someone might be confused into escaping into them.

Hayes plodded back down the steps and came to stand beside her.

'Well?' she asked.

'There was a porter, who seemed to want to be helpful, describing the night in the garden – nothing useful, but he was trying. Then I was passed on to the manager, who immediately asked me why I wasn't working from the list. From that point on, he seemed to lose all confidence in me – kept naming superior officers – then said he'd handed all relevant information to the officers investigating and started to show me out.'

'Oh,' said Anna. 'Damn. What about the porter, though?'

'He told me he was on that night, he'd been there …'

'I don't suppose you could go back in?'

Hayes gave her a slightly withering stare.

'Okay,' she said. 'Maybe not … Well, do you think the porter takes a lunch break or a smoking break? It's worth a try.'

'Maybe,' Hayes said.

'Are you meant to be going back to work?' Anna asked.

Hayes shot her a wry look. 'I worked the weekend. This is my day off.'

'Is that why I'm allowed to be here?' Anna asked.

Hayes shrugged. 'Sometimes I like to have company.'

'Come on,' Anna said. 'Let's look at where he went over.' They walked across the road and down to the south side of the gardens, to Carlton House Terrace, a road shadowed by the Royal Society on one side, and by the trees of the clubs' gardens on the other. Expensive cars were parked along the edge of the road – a deep bronze Jaguar and a low green Aston Martin, shiny like the carapace of an exotic bug. They were standing beside the railings of the club which came almost to Anna's shoulders.

'Look at these,' Anna said. 'Could you get over them? I mean, could you try?'

174

'I'm not climbing into the Hellenic,' Hayes said, sounding horrified. 'Anyway, yes, of course I could climb over the railings. You just put your foot on that bar about two foot up and vault.'

'Well, okay, but not exactly easy, is it?'

'They were running from the raid,' Hayes said. 'They were probably quite scared. And young. And fit.'

'Only Saj said the man on the steps was older. Not young, he thought. Maybe not so fit. And they're not the easiest railings to climb. I'd struggle. Even in trousers. And then they're in the dark. And they'd have to land quietly enough that no one in the gardens would hear them. Ten or twenty men, we think? Some of them only – what – ten or fifteen yards away perhaps ...'

'Well ...' Hayes thought about this. 'The more men there were, the more noise, I'd say. Maybe some music from the inside. The alternative is that you could hear them and some – maybe all – of the men in the garden are lying. But that's ridiculous. I'm not fond of conspiracies at the best of times but why would they all lie? I'd say they'd have been more likely to call the authorities, or at the very least, the manager of the club, and get the trespassers thrown out.'

A man in livery walked out into the garden and glanced towards the patch where they stood. Anna couldn't quite be sure that he saw them, but they drew back into the shadows nonetheless. They walked down towards the statue of the Duke of York and then crossed the road until they were opposite the gardens of the Hellenic – a little too far away to be readily spotted. They took up position behind a large white van and in front of a statue of Field Marshall Lord Clyde, who was being guarded by a lady and a lion.

'Colin Campbell,' Hayes read. 'Ended the Indian Mutiny. He looks like a butterfly collector.'

They both looked up at the man on the plinth. He had curly hair and a lined face and was dressed in a somewhat crumpled fashion with tall boots and what looked to be a satchel. He gazed across the road, towards Waterloo Gardens. Towards the spot where the boy had been found.

Anna dropped her handbag onto the kerb beside the white van and sat down on it. Hayes sank, after an uncertain minute, and sat beside her.

'I was thinking,' Anna said, 'about what you were saying the other day in the Wimpy bar. About not feeling,' she looked at him, 'entirely comfortable being a policeman.'

Hayes' expression wilted.

'I think,' Anna went on, 'you can only be the policeman you are. But that isn't necessarily a bad thing. Where are all the other officers sitting outside this club? Or paying to talk to men in the cafes? You care. And I'm not saying the whole of policing can be like that. Because it's possible that thousands and thousands of idealistic officers might not be the most effective crime-fighting force the world has ever seen. But what if there was no you at all? What if nobody cared?'

Hayes gave her a small smile.

'It is possible,' Anna said, 'to become completely enamoured of all the things you're not good at. I'm guilty of that. I spent years obsessed with all my failures, and my near-failures and all of the times I'd humiliated myself. I'd lie in bed replaying every disaster, over and over again in my head. And if anyone said to me, "But Anna, you're actually very good at x or y ..." I wouldn't even listen to them. Because anything that I could do must be easy. It must be something that anyone in the world could do. I'd lost sight of the idea that I could be really good at anything.'

Hayes looked at her. 'Did you really used to replay disasters in your head?'

'They accounted for the first two hours of every night in bed from the age of seventeen until I was at least twenty-nine. And I think I probably embellished them. I made them worse. If I had dropped someone's favourite cup, then I imagined smashing all the cups. If I had hurt someone's feelings, then I imagined the ways in which I had ruined their life. There was no small mistake that I couldn't imagine into a catastrophe.'

'But why?' Hayes asked. 'Why would you do that?'

'I don't really know,' Anna said. 'Punishment, perhaps? I think I thought that I deserved to suffer. And then I just had to make myself suffer more and more.' Anna suddenly remembered Penny's story about Nell and the pursuit of pre-show relaxation and she felt herself grow red. Not really a story for Mr Hayes.

'Did it never occur to you that the world might treat you kindly because you were a decent person?' Hayes asked.

Anna thought about this. 'No,' she said. 'I thought I was awful but also that I was getting away with something. Anyway, that isn't the point. The point is this: you strike me as someone who is very good at describing all the things that he's bad at.' Hayes laughed. 'And I'm trying to tell you that if poor Charles's mother was here she wouldn't care that the policeman asking questions doesn't get invited to the pub or that he finds crime scenes upsetting. She would just be so relieved that someone cared enough to ask the questions in the first place.'

Hayes nodded. 'Yes,' he said. 'I suppose. Yes. Thank you for saying that.'

'Because we're sitting here,' Anna told him. 'Under these trees. And we can smell the grass and the cars and feel the sun on our skin. And Charlie can't do any of those things.' Her voice dropped lower. 'He has as much right as we do to be here, in this place, swimming in all this warmth. He has exactly as much right as we do to be alive right now. And I can't stop thinking about that. That people talk about him as if he were an exception, because of what he did. But he wasn't an exception. None of us are. Not really.'

They sat in silence for a while. Neither seeming to know how to follow this thought.

Hayes was the first to break the silence. 'Maybe you should join the police,' he said.

Anna smiled. 'I'd be a terrible policewoman,' she told him. 'I wouldn't want to follow half of the rules and I'd question things and … No. But thank you. I appreciate the vote of confidence. I am willing to help though, if you'll let me. Whatever else you think about the mess of things, I am better at being invisible than someone like you. And no one's going to tell me off or threaten my job just because I put my foot in it or ask too much.'

Hayes frowned. 'Are you suggesting …?'

'I talked to the men at Piccadilly,' Anna said.

'Well … yes,' Hayes agreed.

'I'm just saying, if the porter comes out. He hasn't met me before. And I'm unlikely to frighten him. And I can't possibly get you into trouble if I'm the one asking all the questions.'

Hayes looked at her, warily.

'I'll just try,' Anna said lightly. 'You know … maybe. If the opportunity arises.'

They sat together and stared at the entrance to the club. The afternoon had grown oppressively hot and Anna's legs felt heavy. She listened to the birds singing in the trees. It would be rather idyllic if only she was lying on the grass somewhere, staring at the sky. But all the green spaces took on a Gothic air when she thought of the young man lying dead in the bushes. No one was supposed to die in summer.

At length, Anna produced a pack of cards from her bag and attempted to teach Hayes bezique while he watched the entrance of the club and lost three games in a row. Every so often, men in grey and black suits would walk up the steps or leave through the main entrance. But never a porter.

After more than an hour had passed, a young man appeared on the flight of basement stairs which led up to the road at the corner of Waterloo Place and Pall Mall. He wasn't wearing a suit, or a uniform, but simple trousers and shirtsleeves.

'Who's that?' Anna asked Hayes.

'I think it's the porter I talked to. I don't know. He looked different in uniform,' Hayes said, getting to his feet.

Anna crammed the cards and their packet into her bag and they both set off after him, watching as he crossed the road at Pall Mall, and then choosing to cross to the other side of the street, so they could follow him more discreetly.

They wove their way across the circus, trying to keep the porter in their sights. At the north side of Piccadilly, the porter paused and then took Shaftesbury Avenue. Anna wondered for a minute where he could be going. It seemed rather far for a lunch break, but then he turned left down Denman Street and, as she and Hayes hurried to catch him up, they caught just a flash of him disappearing inside a cafe emblazoned with the dark pink words 'New Piccadilly'.

Anna looked at Hayes. She could see the indecision in his face.

'Can I have ten minutes?' she asked him. 'If I'm getting nowhere, I'll come straight out and give you a little wave. If he's eating lunch he should be in there half an hour ...'

Hayes shook his head but he told her, 'Okay. Go on. Be charming.' Anna gave him a broad smile and disappeared inside.

The New Piccadilly was decorated with a kind of crazy modernist flair that wasn't very modern at all, but made Anna think of the 1950s, and places where everything was shaped like a rocket ship in silver and pink. Hanging above the heads of the diners was a vast white horseshoe on which the menu had been written in a curling hand. Spaghetti and chips available together, and escalopes of chicken next to steak and omelette, on a menu that made no sense but sounded delicious nonetheless.

The man they'd followed was having a shouted conversation over the top of a steaming, rattling coffee machine with an older gentleman who seemed to be called Pietro.

Anna hovered by the bar and waited for them to finish. The cafe was stuffed full of little yellow tables and around many of them crowded four or five people, often more than the chairs allowed. Young women sat on men's knees and teenagers crowded to share seats between them. And now it occurred to Anna that there was nowhere for either of them to sit down and perhaps that was why the young man seemed so engrossed in making chit-chat. After a couple of minutes, a group of men in building clothes vacated a table near the door and Anna slid in that direction, waiting for the porter to follow her. She saw him look at the table and then at her and, seeing his indecision, she called across the heads of the diners: 'Do you want to share?'

The man smiled at her and called back: 'If you don't mind.'

'Not at all,' Anna shouted back cheerfully, and slid into the little booth seat. The porter nodded at Pietro and came and joined her at the table.

'Very kind of you,' he said, in an accent that was something European.

'I won't be long,' she told him. 'I'm only having a tea. I just need to sit down somewhere. I've been on my feet all morning.'

'Shop?' he asked her.

'Swann & Edgar,' she agreed, naming a department store just a couple of minutes' walk away. 'I'm in accessories,' she went on, rather enjoying the invention. She would normally just do with being herself, but she had only asked Hayes for ten minutes, and somehow this felt as if it needed easing along. 'We're readying for sale time and it's all go. What about you?'

'Porter. We stand a lot as well. I work in a club – like a gentlemen's club.'

'How swish,' Anna told him. 'I'm Anna, by the way.'

'József,' he told her. The waiter arrived at their table and József ordered himself escalope with spaghetti and chips and a double espresso. Anna ordered herself a pot of tea.

'Is it posh?' Anna asked. 'Your club?'

'Oh,' József laughed. 'You have no idea. They're all rolling. And everything is terribly refined … There are all these rules about how we talk to people, stand near people, dress, make eye contact, don't make eye contact, call them by a name, notice them or don't notice them. It's madness! But the pay is okay. So …'

'I never really thought much about them, to be honest. And then a couple of weeks ago … There's a girl called Marjorie, works in hats, and she was out for her birthday at Piccadilly, walking down to get a night bus and she got caught up in the most almighty row. People screaming and yelling and policemen running about. Just at the bottom of … oh, you know … where that big column is … before you get to the park.'

'Was it by the Duke of York?' József asked. 'The big white clubs down there? Is that where you mean? Because we had a murder.'

'No!' Anna said. 'I think it must … it must be the same thing, mustn't it? Marjorie said a boy had been found. Not a little boy. A …' She dropped her voice. 'A prostitute.'

József leaned over the table and dropped his voice as well. 'Yes. That was my club. And there were all these men out there partying and drinking and then this poor man dead in the trees. It was very scary.'

'It must have been. Did you see him? Before he was killed?'

'I don't think so. Someone told me he was only wearing jeans and a T-shirt and I would have noticed someone dressed like that. But I'd been out there serving drinks. Only a few yards away from where they found him!'

Anna propped her elbows on the table and leaned even further in, so close to József that she could almost feel his breath on her face. 'Do you think it was one of them? The gents? Did someone slip away and do something awful in the bushes?'

József held her gaze for a moment. He was flattered by the intensity of her attentions, she could tell he was. 'Okay. We all talk about this. You can imagine. Because we were in and out of there and here is the thing … There were three groups of them out in the garden that night. There was this group of old teachers and some young man who is going off to Africa to look at vines or something … And then there were these younger men. Banking, yes? Money men, I think they were. They were drinking very, very much and it was someone's birthday and they were all together. And then there was another little group. They were mainly politicians. Maybe banking, a bit, as well. But here's the thing: after the body was found, we all went inside and we were standing in the library, all of us. And the deputy manager, he was there and he was getting us to go round and quickly make notes on who was there so we could let them all go home. But everyone was talking. I mean, we were not meant to but we were. And I talked to all the other lads and they said all the little groups they stuck together. We were constantly in and out. We were bringing them drinks and fetching glasses or finding a light. The little groups, they were moving around but all together. No one remembered anyone missing. Anyone breaking off. So, then I thought maybe they can't have done it. But also, if one of them did, then the others in the group, they must have seen. Or at least been very close.' József shrugged. 'That's just my hunch, though. I mean, who knows?'

Anna thought about this. Could the staff really be so sure that no one had broken away? She decided to change tack while there was still time.

'You know you said about having to remember what everyone likes ... Their drinks ... things like that ... Does that mean you've got it all in your head? So-and-so likes brandy. And this is how they'd drink it ...'

József swivelled his eyes. 'I'm worried that all the useful things will fall out of my ear one day. All the maths and the writing. But I will still know that Lord Ponsonby-Swanfather likes one measure and a half of port.' He laughed.

Anna tried. She tried as best she could. She kept bringing up the brandy but – without revealing who she was or why she was asking – she could not draw him on the brandy glasses. She did manage to get from József that no one took the *Daily Express*. And when she asked about drugs he only laughed and said he was paid never to notice things like that. When she finally emerged from the New Piccadilly she smiled a slightly apologetic smile at Hayes and proceeded to tell him what very little she had learned.

Angels

The young man's name was Max. He was friendly and quiet and seemed to be as happy as Nik to have someone to talk to. They met in the yard and would lean against the wall, talking in the sunshine instead of walking or running or doing pull-ups. One morning Max had been gifted the end of a roll up and waited to share it with Nik, a grit-tasting, burning-lipped moment of shared pleasure.

Nik told Max funny stories from the street without ever mentioning his work. He told him about his family's fish and chip shop and the beaches of the north-west. About trying to catch dabs in the Ribble estuary and swimming off the beach at Lytham in nothing but pants, on warm June evenings when the sparkle of the Irish Sea hid icy guts.

'But you keep swimming,' Nik told him. 'Even when you can't feel your bloody legs, when your feet are aching like a bastard. 'Cause you just keep thinking you can outrun the cold.'

Max told Nik about going to school in Muswell Hill. About watching Spurs play at White Hart Lane and the fear and exhilaration of moving in that crowd of men. The shouting and the singing and the crazy, electric energy of it all. About Saturday afternoons in the Odeon on Fortis Green Road. Watching the same film twice in a row and how when he was a little boy he would still his breathing at the start of every film, believing if he made any noise at all he would break the magic of the place. About the synagogue his father went to on a Saturday and the church his mother went to on a Sunday and how it had taken three years of pleading, from the ages of nine to twelve, before he was allowed to attend neither and worship at the pictures all alone instead.

'We go to the same church!' Nik told him. 'If I've got the money on a Sunday I'll take communion three times.'

'Bless you, my son. Hast thou seen *The Shuttered Room*?'

'I hast not. But I was looking forward to *Bonnie and Clyde*,' Nik countered.

They both stopped.

'Christ,' Max said. 'It was half an ounce. Half a bloody ounce. We were only smoking on the Heath and I was the stupid bugger who picked it up. Wasn't even mine.'

Nik stared at him. 'Why didn't you tell them?'

'I was trying to be noble. It was my best friend's and I thought they'd let us go. When I realised they were going to charge me I tried to tell them but it was too late. They weren't listening.'

'Maybe they'll give you six months and you'll get out for time served,' Nik tried.

'That's what my dad said. There are people in here,' Max dropped his voice, 'who've killed people. Rapists. Armed robbers. It's like being inside someone else's crazy. D'you ever feel like you're living in someone else's fever dream ... and maybe the rules make sense to them but you have nothing that will let you play the game?'

Nik smiled.

'Every other Sunday,' Max went on, 'after she came back from church, my mum would drag me and my dad and my little sister over to her parents for lunch. My grandad, he's a sort of military historian. When I was little he used to take me off into his living room and recreate Agincourt on a chessboard. Aleppo with playing cards. The Battle of Maldon with matchsticks. Years of tactics I sat through. Never understood a bloody thing. I'd just drift off. I know it's important to not be caught in a valley if the other side have archers. Or ... maybe I mean on a hill. None of it stuck! Tanks and aircraft battles and submarines and the Hun and the Cherokee and a thousand years of samurai. My dad says they're worried I'm too Jewish and I don't know how to fight.' Max laughed.

'I knew a man once,' Nik said, 'called us all samurais. All us boys out in London. The ones who knew the streets. I had this coat. God, I loved my coat. And it made me feel so safe. I could sweep around, like an avenging angel. Or a knight. Like I had warpaint on and I could fight anything that came.'

'Yeah. My grandad's always been a bit suspicious of the samurai. Not just 'cause of their colour – though I think that comes into it – but because they knew all this stuff … Tea ceremonies, and how to read, and poetry and art. Found it all a bit fruity, if you know what I mean.'

Nik found himself catching Max's eye, though he hadn't meant to. That was the thing about outside. That was the thing, one of the many things he'd lost. Besides the possibility of staring at the sky for hours or drinking a hot cup of tea, sweet with milk. He had lost the freedom to spend time with people who just knew.

'Do they come and visit you?' he found himself asking Max.

'The family? Yeah. Mum and Dad. Not the grandparents. 'Cause, you know, they haven't told them I'm in here.'

'Bloody hell,' Nik said. 'But you've been in here ages.'

'I know. My parents told them I've been sent to a public school to do resits. They think I'm living in a castle in Scotland taking my maths exams again.'

Nik started to laugh.

'I know!' Max said. 'Fucking families!'

'Fucking families,' Nik agreed.

* * *

The costumier's Morris Angel & Sons lay just north of Anna's little flat, its windows piled with hats and gloves and wigs, Regency bonnets and Tudor hunting caps. Sometimes a mannequin would appear in the window replete in the costume of a medieval queen. Other times there were military uniforms for hire or sale – some of them for film and theatre work, others for actual British Army officers who dressed themselves at Angel's beside the ingenues and charactermen who stood patiently for tailors and seamstresses, offering legs and arms to be assessed and catalogued.

Anna met Bertie on the doorstep of the shop and they were welcomed into the oddly dim interior. Anna went at once to sit on the stairs in the main part of the store, ostensibly to keep out of the way but really because she wanted the best view she could get. On a rail near the doorway hung great swathes of cobalt- and raspberry-coloured velvet dresses, with gold and silver coronets in plastic bags tied to coat hangers, and rows of buttoned boots leaning on the bottom of the rail. Her mind slipped between the costumes and the fragments of information that seemed to crowd around Charlie and his final hours. The man on the steps who may or may not have followed him down St James's Street. The homeless man who'd seen it all and disappeared. The newspapers, the pills and the brandy glasses. All those men in the garden moving about in their little groups like children in a playground. How was it possible that a young man could have been murdered fifteen yards away and no one heard? Unless that meant that they all heard? How many people were hiding what they knew – Anna couldn't even tell …

Her thoughts were interrupted by a tailor coming out from the back, neatly dressed in waistcoat and white shirt, just as if this was Savile Row, and gesturing Bertie towards a clear area of floor, four foot by four foot.

'Let's take some measurements, shall we?' the costumier said.

Bertie held his arms out wide; Anna watched him struggle out of his rather tight-fitting shirt and submit to more measurements. Poor Bertie, he was finding this all a source of humiliation.

'Three suits?' the costumier asked.

'Yes,' Anna called to him. 'Three suits. All three pieces. There's a shooting set in tweed, a dinner suit in black wool, and a Harris tweed as well. Also, a velvet smoking jacket and a pair of pyjamas in paisley cotton. And then at eleven thirty we've got the new cast member Jerry coming in for final fitting for his costumes as well.'

The costumier stared at his notes and then measured around Bertie's girth and over the cotton vest he was wearing. Anna had noticed how the safari jacket had disappeared in the past two weeks. The piles of fruit on Bertie's dressing table had grown bigger. She never saw him eat, only an apple or two between the shows. Poor thing.

'Can I measure underneath the vest? I assume you're not wearing it in performance and it's probably adding an inch,' Anna heard the man ask Bertie. 'You can step into the changing room to undress.'

'I'd rather not.' Bertie was rather pink now and his tone a mixture of fluster and annoyance. The costumier glanced over at Anna and she made an apologetic face and shook her head. He shrugged and measured Bertie once again, over all his underclothes.

* * *

Merrian was in the kitchen when Benjamin let himself in.

She called 'Hello!' to him and went back to trying to form the crust of a chicken pie. Outside, in the hallway, Benjamin threw his school things down with his usual aggravating force.

'Ben …' His mother called to him. A reminder.

'No one's said anything.' He was in the kitchen now.

Merrian turned. He was leaning against the far wall, his arms crossed. She noticed his school blazer was looking tired.

'Sorry?'

'At school. No one's anything-ed at all. Is there something I don't know?'

'Oh,' Merrian said. 'Well … The article never came out. We were told that it would and then absolutely nothing. I mean … it still might. I'm sorry that I scared you.'

Benjamin's face wrinkled. 'Do you think they got better information?'

'Maybe.'

'They thought another boy did it. Someone homeless, you said.'

Merrian nodded. 'Yes. I suppose they must have decided …' Her voice trailed off but she gave him a determined nod.

'So … Do I not have to worry about this any more?'

Merrian wet her hands in the sink and patted the pie crust. Turned away from her son, she called to him over her shoulder, 'I think we should just all hope it goes away.'

'Mum …' She carried on with her work but he called again. 'Mum!'

She crossed to the kitchen table, where she slumped gently into a chair. Benjamin sat down across from her. Merrian could feel his eyes searching her face.

'Is there something else?' Benjamin's voice was quiet.

'It's just a very difficult thing to be happening.'

'I'm fifteen,' he said. 'You can talk to me.'

Merrian gave a gentle laugh. 'You don't have to worry about anything. Daddy can worry about the country. And I get to worry about him and you two—'

Ben interrupted. 'No. But really. I mean it. You can talk to me ...' His expression held so much feeling that Merrian could barely look at him. 'I'm not stupid. And I don't just think about myself ... I know I seem like I do. But if something awful happened, you could tell me and I wouldn't fall apart.'

Merrian had the most terrible and inappropriate desire to confide in her son. She could almost imagine the release of allowing the words to come out. And yet, at the same time, she could not imagine this house and how it would feel if she ever spoke those words within it. She felt for a moment that there had been a slippage between the inside of her head and the outside of the world and wondered if Benjamin could see everything that she knew and everything she felt. She opened her mouth just briefly to see if words would come out unbidden. But there was no sound.

Benjamin took her hand and they sat for several moments just looking at each other.

'Sometimes ... I get very tired,' Merrian said. 'And sometimes you can see that in me.' There were tears in her eyes. And then she was crying. Benjamin got off his chair, knelt down on the floor next to her and leaned his head against her shoulder.

* * *

Anna knew that at some point in all of this she was going to have to speak to Richard Wallis. She didn't like the man. She had built an impression in her head of someone unreliable, someone essentially a liar. Someone who thought he represented the people, but also believed that he could behave in any way he chose. He was cavalier, she had decided. The thought of him made the hair on her arms stand on end.

By ringing around, Anna had ascertained that Wallis held surgery on a Monday at his offices by Peckham Rye. She rang and made an appointment. The lady at the constituency office said they were very busy for this week already but if she couldn't wait she could have a short meeting – last one of the day – at ten to twelve. Anna accepted.

Mr Wallis's office was on the ground floor of a large Victorian house near the corner of Peckham Rye and East Dulwich Road. Inside the wall of the front garden and under a little wooden shelter leaned several wooden painted placards reading 'Vote Labour'; 'Vote Wilson'; 'Five Years to Finish the Job' and 'Wallis for Peckham'.

The door was opened by a man of about twenty, wearing grey suit trousers, braces and a white shirt. 'Hello,' he said. 'Are you Miss Treadway?'

'I am.'

'Please come in.' The young man ushered her into a tiled hall. Along one wall stood a line of dining-room chairs and a little table which was piled high with old copies of the *TLS*, the *New Statesman* and *Private Eye*. 'I believe your appointment is ten to twelve. Bear with us. We're running rather late today.' Anna nodded and sat down. There was no one else waiting, but she could hear voices coming from behind the door at the end of the hall. Anna picked up a copy of the *New Statesman*, then put it down and decided to look at the cartoons in *Private Eye* instead. She hadn't entirely decided what she was going to say.

She didn't live in Wallis's constituency at all, but she would have to pretend she did. What was there to complain about? Prostitution? The more she thought of questions, the more she realised that she didn't know what to ask. 'Did you kill Charlie?' That wouldn't get her anywhere. 'Are you sleeping with your political agent?' Well, what did it matter? She wasn't trying to blackmail the man. Or was she? That's what everyone else did, wasn't it? The Soviet Union. MI5. Newspapers. That's what you did with homosexual men: you blackmailed them.

The door at the end of the hall opened and a dishevelled, middle-aged man was ushered out by a tall, slim man with bushy hair. He looked down the hall at Anna. Anna stared at him for a moment. She'd seen him before, at the gala. Angus. The young man who had shown her in emerged from a room opposite.

'Last of the day,' he called down the hall. 'Miss Anna Treadway.'

Angus held the door of the office open for her and waited. Richard Wallis's office looked to have been an Edwardian dining room once upon a time. There was a large oak desk in the centre, behind which Mr Wallis sat. Along two of the walls stood a selection of filing cabinets. Angus moved to a chair in the far corner and waited for her to take a seat.

'Hello,' Anna said, in her least threatening tones. 'I'm Anna.'

'Hello, Anna,' said Richard Wallis, rising to shake her hand and waiting for her to take her seat. 'I'm Richard Wallis. How can I help you today?'

Anna noticed that he did not introduce his friend. She brushed some imaginary crumbs from her lap. 'I'm worried ...' she said, speaking very slowly to allow herself time to think. 'I'm worried about my neighbours.'

'Okay,' Richard Wallis said. 'Can you tell me a bit more?' He spoke slowly and kindly and Anna found herself slightly taken aback by how normal he seemed, now that he was sitting in front of her.

'They're two men,' she said, warming to her story. 'Not related. And they live together. I think they're a couple.'

Richard Wallis sat back in his chair and looked steadily at her. 'Have they been behaving inappropriately?' he asked. 'In public?'

Anna pretended to think about this. 'No,' she said. 'I'm only guessing they're a couple.'

Richard Wallis nodded. 'What's your concern, Anna?' he asked her.

'Someone put a brick through their window,' she said, watching both Wallis and his friend as she laid each statement in front of them.

Richard Wallis's face furrowed. 'I see. But isn't this a police matter, then? I'm still a little confused. You're visiting me here today because ...?'

Anna was quiet for a few seconds. She could see Angus watching Richard. The further she went, the more she got the feeling that she was not quite blackmailing these men but that what she was doing was something rather unpleasant nonetheless. 'They can't report it,' she said, wishing to release a little of the tension in the room. 'They can't report the brick through the window and I think we all know why. So, I'm here to tell you that it happened. And that I'm not here to get them into trouble. But it's not right, is it?'

Richard Wallis frowned. 'No, Anna ...' he said slowly. 'It's not right.' He fell silent and no one spoke for a few seconds. She realised that he was studying her face.

'Have we met?' he asked.

'I don't think so.'

'Where do you live, Anna?' Angus asked from his place in the corner.

'In Peckham. Just off the high street.'

'Which road?' Angus asked.

Anna's brain span. 'Hawthorn Road,' she tried, plucking the name from the air.

'Hawthorn?' Mr Wallis said. He opened a drawer and drew out an A–Z of London and opened some creased pages near the end. Anna's stomach sank.

'Are you sure you live in our constituency, Miss Treadway?' Angus asked.

'Oh yes!' She fixed Mr Wallis with a smile. 'I voted for you!'

Angus shifted uncomfortably. 'If you're a journalist, Miss Treadway, I think you're meant to tell us ...'

'Oh no! Not a journalist. Not at all. Nothing like that.' She was protesting too much. She fell silent and tried to look relaxed and unalarmed.

Richard Wallis looked up from his A–Z. 'Where *do* I know you from?' he asked, quietly.

'Where *do* you know her from?' Angus asked.

Richard Wallis shook his head at his friend.

'I was at the theatre,' Anna said. 'The night you came to see *Lady Angkatell's Secret*. Your wife knew Penny.'

191

Richard Wallis blinked at her. Angus stood but came no closer.

'You were looking at the pictures and talking to Leonard,' Anna went on. 'And then we all stood on the stairs and you told your wife and Penny that you wanted to go for a drink at the Hellenic.' Angus was moving towards her now. 'So you would have walked down there, I reckon, at about eleven. You might even have gone through Piccadilly.'

Richard Wallis's face creased further. 'What do you want?' he asked her.

'I'm not accusing anyone of anything,' Anna said.

Angus was standing close to her now. 'Of course not,' he said. 'What could you possibly accuse Richard of?'

'Nothing,' Anna repeated. 'I was only wondering if you had seen something? If you knew the young man ... Charlie ... His name was Charlie. He came from Wiltshire. Grew up on a farm.' She tried to engage Richard Wallis with a smile but he only looked bemused.

'You *are* a journalist,' Angus said. 'It's completely unethical to come and see Mr Wallis in this way ...' He moved to the door and opened it. 'Please leave.'

'If you saw something in the garden ...' Anna tried, still fixing Richard Wallis with her stare. He opened his mouth and closed it again. 'There's a young man in prison who has done nothing wrong,' she said.

Angus drummed his fingers on the door. 'We've asked you to leave.'

'Please,' Anna tried again. 'I will leave ... only I have one question. Just a very small question.' She was backing slowly towards the door, buying herself a few more sentences inside the room. 'What were you drinking that night, Mr Wallis?'

Richard Wallis looked utterly confused.

'Drinking?' he asked. And then the man at the door put his fingertips firmly on Anna's shoulder and pushed her out into the hall. The door shut with a thump and it took a minute before her legs were able to carry her away.

* * *

There had been a time, maybe eight weeks in the autumn of 1964, when Nik had tried to call his mother. His time in Manchester had been short and rather painful. He'd been offered a place to stay by a man he had met outside the station. But after the first few days of sleeping on a sofa in a large squat with six other men, Nik had discovered that he was expected to pay the man for staying in this place, by one means or another. He had acquiesced once, but the situation he found himself in seemed so similar to the one he had escaped in Blackpool that he left the next afternoon. Still with no money to his name, Nik made the journey from Manchester to London in stages, hiding in toilets on quiet trains to go from Manchester to Crewe and Crewe to Tamworth and Tamworth to Milton Keynes and from there onwards to London.

On his arrival in London, he had slept rough for nearly two months, seeing nights on a park bench as infinitely preferable to an unsafe house or squat. He remembered getting ill continually, picking up every cough and summer cold around and how the boys he had met in the parks had joked with him that these were London germs and northern boys were no match for them. It was a boy in one of the parks, Green Park it had been, who had explained to Nik that his best bet was to look after himself and offer himself out from somewhere central, making sure to keep all of his money. There'd be trouble, he explained, from pimps who'd want to take him over. And from older men who would steal his money, especially when he was cold and tired at the end of the night and trying to go home. But selling himself on the street would mean that he had an income, and with an income you could get a room in a house, a proper room, not one where you had to sell yourself whenever the landlord wanted it. The secret, the boy said – and Nik thought his name might have been Lachlan, though he could have misremembered this – the secret, the boy said, was not to make yourself too vulnerable with taking drugs, or working when you were too tired to run, or working every night so you got conspicuous, so people felt that you were hogging all the trade. You needed to have your wits about you, and the wits of three more men besides. You needed to be a warrior, a Royal Marine, you needed to grow metal instead of skin. 'Skin rubs off too soon,' he said.

Nik heeded his advice, he did, even though he never saw the boy again and started to wonder what had become of him. He didn't want to sell himself, he didn't know how much to charge, he didn't want to go down alleys or into rooms in houses that he did not know. But he did want freedom. At least, he thought he wanted it.

After a week in London he called his mum. Three o'clock on a Tuesday, when his dad would have gone to the restaurant and she'd be still at home. He called her with money he had earned by sucking someone off the night before. He had had to put a night's sleep between that and picking up the phone.

He put the coins in and – in his imagination – he heard the sound of the phone ringing in his house in St Annes. Someone picked up.

'Hello?' they said. It was Maria.

He opened his mouth. No words came out.

'Nik?' his mother said. 'Is that you?'

Nik drew in breath to tell her yes.

'Nikos?' he heard his mother say. He heard the pain in her voice. 'Nikos?'

'I'm sorry!' he screamed, silently, in his head. He was hot with shame. He could barely hold the phone.

'Nikos?'

He leaned against the cool glass of the box and tried to breathe.

Two weeks later, he tried again. He remembered the shame of the last time. He steeled himself to it. He walked around St James's Park six or seven times before he even made the call. He went to a phone box in sight of a tree he loved. A weeping willow, on the very edge of the park. He looked at the curve of it. The wind-blown leaves lying on the grass below. He dialled the number for home.

'Hello?' the voice came. 'Christou house.'

It was his father. He put down the phone.

As September turned into October, he tried again to call them. That last month in London had felt like a year. He'd gone from charging ten shillings a time to knowing that you had to charge at least £2 to make ends meet. He'd learned that sometimes he had to walk away. What pretty policemen looked like. That some of the boys who sold themselves were like him and some preferred girls –

but there was no money to be made in liking girls. He'd learned that there were safe places, known places: coffee shops, pubs, clubs, rooms in clubs, places where everyone was near enough like you and you could speak as you found. He had found that London wasn't like St Annes. That he didn't have to feel so terribly lonely because there were hundreds like him – thousands, he reckoned. Boys on park benches, boys who had to beg, boys who couldn't or wouldn't go home, every flavour of man who liked men – young and old and working class and posh. There were black boys and boys from India and Jewish boys and boys from every part of the world, so many accents and strange names that he felt a fool half the time and kept his mouth shut and his ears open. He was scared and sharp and full of amazement at how much bigger the world was than he had ever imagined.

He was starting to ask around, starting to find out about places to stay. He'd had a couple of weeks in someone's room while they were inside for soliciting. His cough had cleared up and he'd slept long and deeply now that he was safe. He was a hundred times older than he had been in spring. He was a man now. His virginity, barely remembered. Blackpool, barely thought of.

He called home. He imagined the cream phone ringing in the hall. He wasn't the same person, he knew that now.

A break in the sound, then a fumble, breathlessness – she had run from somewhere. 'Yes?' his mother said. 'Hello?'

Nik breathed. He heard her, so close.

'It's okay,' he said, quieter than he had meant to.

'Nik?' his mother called, loud in his ear, harsh, he held the receiver away from him. 'Nikos? Is that you? Talk—'

He hung up. He couldn't do it. He felt so calm, here on this day, in this place. And her so loud, so full of chaos. He could not open that door. He didn't have the strength.

* * *

Richard was not a member of the Colony Club. He found the whole place vulgar. Loud and crowded and full of people who wanted to be seen. Richard didn't want to be seen. He thought perhaps he wanted to be heard. He had been thrilled to stand up and speak for the first time in the House of Commons. He'd felt a warm, consuming pride when he was asked to address a trades' union meeting or student group. He could not quite get over the idea that he had become someone who was worth listening to.

No, it had been Henry's idea to meet in a place like this. The Hellenic was rather out of bounds while all the nastiness was rumbling on. And the Colony was light on policemen and heavy on drunk artists and writers who did not bother themselves with the private lives of backbench MPs. It was after eight and Richard imagined that Henry would be up there by now. He didn't want to walk in and be humiliated by the dreadful woman at the bar. The owner, Muriel. Who could peel the dignity from your sides as if you were a banana.

Richard took off his jacket and headed up the stairs. The smell of tobacco and sweat started before he'd even opened the upstairs door. Richard felt himself yearning for the cool stone of better places. He walked into noise.

There was a large Jewish-looking individual at the piano playing something unmelodic. Richard tried not to make eye contact with any of the acolytes who surrounded him. Henry would be somewhere tucked away. He walked experimentally to his left and peered around a pillar.

'You a member?' someone called to him.

'Henry Deauville!' Richard shouted, towards the crowd of backs at the bar. 'I mean … I'm not him. I'm meeting him.'

'Henry Deauville?' Now it was a woman's voice. Richard's eyes struggled to find a face and there she was. In turquoise and navy swirls, and badly smudged red lipstick. 'What kind of a name's that then, Mary?'

There was a pause and Richard looked desperately around himself. A young coloured couple were kissing against a pillar to his right, the woman's hand reaching beneath the man's shirt.

'Henry Deauville? He's a member, Muriel,' a voice called back. A barman, Richard thought. 'Not one of our regulars, but still …'

'What have I done wrong now?' Henry Deauville appeared beside Richard. 'Man goes for an innocent piss …'

'How d'you find the lavs, then?' Muriel asked, with a certain sharpness.

'Full to the brim with human happiness.' Henry gave Muriel a slow, confident smile.

Muriel laughed, but she was watching Richard still. 'Buy some fucking drinks,' she told the men. 'We're not here to keep your cocks warm.'

Henry ordered a glass of Scotch and another of brandy and guided Richard to a table in the far corner, where Angus sat, swilling his Black & White in a very Angus-y manner. He looked up at Richard as they arrived at the table. There didn't seem to be a need to speak.

'Cheers!' Henry held his drink aloft and Richard struck glasses with him.

Angus watched them both in silence. His hand did not stir. 'A woman came to see us today. Anna Treadway. She knew Richard was in the garden.'

'She's a journalist?' Henry asked.

'Doesn't seem so,' Angus said. 'Works at a theatre – The Galaxy. I rang them. They confirmed who she was. She knew the name of the … you know. The young man. She knew things about him. Where he grew up.'

Henry stared at Richard who didn't really know how to respond, except to shrug miserably. Angus chewed on the side of his lip.

'So she's a friend? Or a relative? Do you think she's a relative?' Henry asked.

'I've no idea,' Angus said. 'She's in the book. I found a name and address for her.'

'Are you thinking of going to see her?' Richard asked.

'No,' Angus said. 'Not that. I don't know.'

'I have done, gentlemen, all that I am reasonably able to do,' Henry said.

Angus nodded glumly. They sat in silence for half a minute.

'Is George coming?' Richard asked.

Henry smiled a small smile. 'George has decided to go to West Berlin. Father's got a bank branch. He'll pretend to do some work. He's … um … well … you know …'

'What happens when someone else wants to write a story?' Richard asked. 'How many favours do we get?'

Henry looked at him. 'I don't know,' he said. 'I don't know how many favours I have in me. Eventually it goes away.'

Angus nodded. 'Deny. Dismiss. Refuse.'

Richard felt his body slump under the weight of the uncertainty. 'I have no way of repaying you,' he told Henry. 'I'm trapped on the backbenches.'

Henry shot him a sad smile. 'What's the opposite of mutually assured destruction?'

'Mutually assured continuation,' Angus answered. 'You live, so I live. And he lives, so we live. And nobody dies today.'

'That – at least – is the idea,' Henry said. He held up his glass in a mock salute. 'Here's to nobody dying today.'

Sometimes I Am Slightly
Amazed That You Exist at All

Three times Merrian had removed the little bundle from the springs under the spare bed and then returned it to its place. She knew that once she opened it, whatever she discovered, it would be her, at least partly, who was in the wrong.

'Why didn't you trust me?' she could hear Richard saying to her now. She had betrayed him already. Even by thinking about searching through his things. She knew what would be in there. Or she thought she knew.

She drew the curtains – ochre-coloured light spread through the room. She turned on the bedside lamp and crawled under the bed once more. Then she lay on her back and stared at the little package. She wondered if she could leave it there another twenty years and she thought that, on balance, she probably could. But she was getting old already. Her life had speeded up. That little package – the idea of it transformed into the parcel of another twenty years – it was too great a betrayal, even for her. Not a betrayal of Richard, of course. But a betrayal of herself. She was still worth something.

She withdrew the duster-wrapped book and laid it on top of the bed. It was a leather-bound date book from 1956. And inside the front cover of the date book was a small pile of envelopes, perhaps twelve. None of them particularly bulky, most containing only a single page. There were letters from Richard to Angus and a smaller selection from Angus to Richard. Merrian wondered for a moment how Richard could have the letters after he'd sent them. Because Angus returned them, she thought. At some point, for some reason, Angus had returned his letters.

She opened the first of the pile. It was addressed to:

4 May 1951

3a, Ashmole St.
London SW8

Angus,

*I don't have a name for this. I'm not sure that there's a name
for anything that's running through my head. But you won't
talk to me and so I have to write.*

*I only want to talk to you. Would that really be so hard? I can
catch the train up to Oxford on any given Saturday. Or Didcot
or Henley or Marlow if those are more discreet. I can say I'm
going on business. Or there might be a gaudy. Or just some old
friend I need to see.*

Because there is. And I do.

*Have you applied to the American places yet? Please write to
me if you are accepted. I cannot bear to think that you might
leave for years and I simply wouldn't know. Maybe you think
we have both moved along to a new passage in our lives. Is that
it? Is that what it means to be an adult now. To build a neat
brick wall inside one's heart so that love before can stay where
it is put.*

I am sorry for my weakness. But I cannot fall out of love.

I have tried. But I have also failed.

Richard

Merrian had thought she would read the letters properly, but now she found her eyes racing ahead. She scanned the words for something, she didn't even know what, pulling letters out of envelopes, reading fragments and then casting them aside. Angus's handwriting, then Richard's – her sense of desperation equal regardless of which of them was writing.

Richard's hand: *I think of you constantly.*

Then Angus: *You are so very real and present and this rather precludes fondness. The thereness of you has killed the fondness. Stopped it ever being born.*

Angus again: *I don't know about August. I don't think I'll have much time.*

Richard: *Sometimes I am slightly amazed that you exist at all.*

Richard again: *I have a son. He's called Benjamin.*

She paused at one from Richard dated 30 April 1954. They'd been married on the twenty third.

21, Kinsale Road,
Peckham SE15

Angus,

I saw you in the church and I saw you talking to Merrian and even to my mother. But then you seemed to disappear. You're not in any of the pictures. Was it anger? I found myself wondering. Or fear? Or did you want me to see you as a kind of punishment?

Don't rewrite all that's gone before. You're not allowed to be angry. It's too cruel.

I sat there miserable at my own wedding supper, thinking about you punishing me. I don't deserve it, Angus. If you can be civil to me at work, you can treat me decently at other times. I asked you and you said yes.

I asked you.

How we go forward, I don't know. But I won't hurt Merrian. This is not her fault. Whatever happens now, we must be kind to everyone involved. And yes, Angus … Yes. That means you must be kind to me as well.

Whatever happens, we'll do it decently. I'm at the trades' union conference from the 7th. If you're there too we can go for a drink at the Imperial. I am doing the best I can. I have to believe the same of you.

Richard

Merrian felt the crushing embarrassment of seeing her own name for the first time. After pages and pages of thoughts and feelings and party business, there she was. At her own wedding. Not understanding anything.

She lay down upon the bed.

*   *   *

The phone rang in the living room of Anna's flat. Kelly never answered anything before noon, so Anna turned off the grill, abandoned her toast and picked up.

'Hello?' she said.

There was breathing on the line. She waited but no one spoke.

'Hello?' she tried again. Still breathing, still no sound of a voice. She put the receiver down in annoyance.

Five minutes later, as she was eating her toast and spilling crumbs on her copy of *The Magus*, the phone rang again.

Once again she picked up: 'Hello? Hello?'

More breathing. She wondered for a moment if it was Louis, trying to call her from Jamaica. He'd said the lines could be awful. 'Louis?' she tried. 'Is that you?'

The breathing continued. She put down the phone again.

Five minutes later, the ringing returned. Now Anna had stopped reading and was staring in puzzlement at the phone. She picked up. A man's voice on the end of the line said, 'Stop!'

'Sorry?' Anna said. 'Stop what? It's you who's calling me.'

'Just stop,' the man said. English accent, southern. She didn't recognise the voice.

'What am I meant to be stopping?' Anna asked, unable to keep annoyance out of her voice.

'Nik Christou killed that boy,' the voice said now.

'Who is this?' Anna asked.

'You can be implicated.'

'What?' Anna said. 'Implicated? What do you mean? Who are you?'

The line went dead. Anna stood for some minutes still holding the receiver. She was, at once, somewhat scared and extremely angry.

How bloody dare some man ring her up – no name – and tell her what to do. Cowards the lot of them. In their offices and their clubs, hiding behind the anonymity of scary phone calls. Of course she wasn't going to stop. She pulled herself together, scooped keys and purse into her handbag and headed out of the flat.

* * *

Merrian's mind bombarded her with memories of kind words, happiness, elation – the intense embodiment of love. She could not process the betrayal because all she could think of, in this moment, was how happy Richard had made her. How erudite he had seemed. How open-hearted. With what grace he had observed the pain of others.

They had met at Oxford University Labour Party drinks, but in those days the student party had still leaned heavily communist. A young Harrovian with a shock of red hair had got up on a chair and launched drunkenly into a soliloquy about the inspiration of Soviet endeavour, during which Merrian had caught Richard's eye and they had both smiled and then laughed – recognising their own embarrassment in the mortified face of the other. They had crept out onto a balcony, even though it was November and neither was wearing a coat, and clutched their glasses of wine and giggled like children at how out of place they found themselves. At the university. In this version of the Labour Party. In their not-quite-smart-enough smart clothes.

On their second date – in the Angel & Greyhound on a wet afternoon, drinking their cider slowly, holding hands under the table, Richard's voice still bearing soft traces of his Leicestershire accent – he had told her about afternoons with his grandfather, a man in the process of slipping into a place of old age. Richard had sat with him, alarmed by the changes he saw but doing as his father had suggested: describing all the cranes and machines he could see through the window of that house above the docks. Describing for his grandfather – for a man who would no longer look out of his own window, who did not seem to understand the geography of the house he had lived in for fifty years – the colours and the smells and the busy-ness of the world below them.

'I was at the grammar,' he told her. 'I was reading Milton and Hobbes. My grandad embarrassed me … his poverty. But then I had to do this thing. I had to try and make his life stay real. I had to explain why everything he had done was meaningful. And at first it was a lie. A kindness. I thought … I was very arrogant and I thought what he'd done didn't matter but that I could pretend it did. And the more I pretended, the more I talked to him, the more I understood my own mistake. Because he had done something entirely necessary and real for sixty years. He had built the world that the grammar rested on. And I felt ashamed at how much I had wanted to keep my distance.'

'But you can't go backwards,' Merrian told him. 'Just getting here. It changes everything.'

'For me it does,' Richard said. 'But if I just take this, if I – I don't know, become a minor civil servant … Yes, I'll have a nice house one day, but where's the meaning in it? I might as well have won this life in a lottery at a fair. I've climbed up here on all these backs, all these people and their lives so much worse than mine. Not worse … Harder. And it *does* matter. Hauling coal matters. Building houses matters. Driving trains … And yet you come here and you think: my ticket, I got the ticket! I don't have to care about barges and hods and steam engines any more. That whole world will carry on and it will serve my lovely life …'

They talked like this a lot. Richard more than Merrian. How you could rise up and yet not forget. It bothered Richard. He saw the shadow of forgetting in his future and so he talked and talked. Always about his family. About the noble poor who – Merrian noticed – grew more romantic the longer he thought about them.

And then Angus was there. Quietly at first. Joining them for drinks in the union. Rolling his eyes at the communist proclamations of Richard's chums. Finally, suggesting to him that he could be a sober head within his party. Someone who'd seen the reality of poverty. Someone without ideology, just a resolute, almost plodding desire for social reform. Angus had been Richard's political messiah.

And of course she had seen the love. She had seen the admiration. It had shone from Richard. Angus was his inspiration. Angus was his guide. Angus made Richard thrillingly ambitious. Merrian liked the Richard that Angus could inspire.

She would have married the minor civil servant. She would have married him if he'd become a teacher or worked for the council. But how much more thrilling to marry a man who might have power one day. To be the MP's wife. To lay down your ambition for the cause.

She stroked her stomach to calm herself. But she was not calm. She pulled the quilt back and crawled under it, allowing the letters to slide onto the floor.

* * *

Games time was on a Monday, Wednesday and Friday, from one until three.

This Friday, Nik and Max sat on either side of the backgammon board, moving the pieces and talking about music and families and films. Max liked *The Hill* and really anything with Sean Connery in it. Nik preferred *A Hard Day's Night*. In truth, he also had a fondness for *Mary Poppins*, despite his misgivings about the horrible parents, because he had taken Dennis to see it the year he left. He treated Max to his diatribes on the awfulness of Bond and Alfie and how Jane Fonda should have pushed her husband off that roof. Max laughed. They invented a game where they'd think of unsettling endings for films that other people loved. Eliza Doolittle turning out to be a con artist and Higgins returning from his final search for Eliza to find his beautiful London townhouse stripped bare. Tippi Hedren, in *The Birds*, discovering that Bodega Bay, its residents and the birds are all part of a delusion which she senses is not real but cannot break.

'My dad once told me there are no happy endings. We just stop watching before it all goes to shit,' Max said. 'Except he didn't say shit.'

'I think my dad believed there were happy endings,' Nik said. 'And if you only did what you were told that's where you ended up.'

'If everyone ends up dead, in the end, is a happy ending even real? Isn't it just life without the bit where you die?' Max took a row of Nik's counters with a sly smile.

Nik looked up at the steep grey walls. 'Who fucking knows?' he said.

One of the wardens appeared at Nik's shoulder and gave his chair a swift kick.

'You've got a visitor.'

'What?' Max said.

'Not you. Christou here. He's got a visitor and he's not stood outside the visitors' room so now I've had to walk the whole way up here to get the useless piece of shit.'

Nik stood and turned towards the guard, anxious not to anger him further. 'I'm sorry. I didn't think I was down for a visit. I didn't request a visit.'

But the guard was already walking away. 'Do I look like I care?' he shot over his shoulder and Nik ran to catch him up.

There were half a dozen people who ran through Nik's mind as they walked the length of the prison. Of course, he wondered if it might be his mother. But his mother didn't know where he was. He decided in the end that it was probably Garry from the flat and he'd come because he wanted his rent and the £1 Nik owed him. Damn, Nik thought. It's not as if I have any money to give to him.

He queued for a little while to be nodded through by a cluster of guards and then he was in a long, low room, painted white and full of little tables surrounded by dozens of metal chairs. He scanned the room but he didn't recognise any of the people sitting there. He started to feel a bit shaky.

'Go on!' the guard behind him called.

Nik turned. 'I don't know who it is.'

The guard looked at him with exasperation and then he too scanned the room. He pointed to a table near the fire doors, where a dark-haired woman sat on her own. 'She hasn't got anyone,' he pointed out. 'You know her?'

Nik walked slowly down the side of the room staring at the woman as he went. Her face came into view. Nik wove between the tables.

'What are you doing here?' he asked.

Anna Treadway looked up at him and smiled. 'Hello, Nik.'

'Hello,' he said and sat down opposite her. 'Has something happened to Ottmar?'

'No! No. He's fine. He's worried about you.' Anna pulled out her handbag and opened it. 'Someone told me I could bring you chocolate so I got these.' She pulled out two bars of Fruit & Nut, a Twix, a Bounty and three KitKats. 'Also, you smoke, so …' She pulled a pouch of Condor and a packet of papers out of her bag, and arranged everything neatly on the table. 'I didn't know what brand you smoked. But the tobacconist said this was nice. Sorry if it's wrong.'

Nik looked around the visiting room. 'Why are you here?' he asked.

'We've been … worried. You know – upset. By what happened. That they accused you …'

Nik reached out and took a KitKat off the table. He started to play with the foil. He was unsettled. He felt that there was something new happening here, something that he didn't understand.

'Nik?' Anna said. 'It's all a terrible mess, isn't it?'

'Did the police send you?' he asked.

'God, no! No. I was … You do know we don't believe any of this?' Anna said.

Nik used his fingernail to trace out the edges of the chocolate bar. 'Was it in the papers? Did you read about me?'

'No. I mean, I think there was something but not front page or anything like that. No. It's just that Ottmar was your … sort of … alibi. For early that evening. And I was there when the policeman came to talk to him. And, of course, I saw you too. We spoke. Do you remember?'

'Is Ottmar in trouble?' Nik tried. 'Are you? I can retract my statement.'

'No! It's all fine. Ottmar is fine. I'm fine. It's you everyone's worried about. I was … I just wanted to help. I mean … I was worried you might not … um … you know … necessarily have very much money. For solicitors.' Nik furrowed his brow. 'I actually know one of the policemen involved in this and so I went and talked to some people ...'

'What people?' Nik asked.

'At Piccadilly Circus.'

And now his stomach dropped through the floor. She was singling people out. She was stirring trouble. 'Why? Why are you talking to people?'

'Because you didn't do it.'

'But those men ...' He looked her squarely in the eye. 'They could be arrested. They could ... Why would you put people in danger like that? What policeman do you know?'

Anna leaned towards him. 'I haven't explained this well. There's nothing sinister. No one's been arrested. Only you. That's the point. Only you have been arrested and, in fact, some real person – some other person – did this awful thing.'

Nik perched on the edge of the chair. 'I know that,' he told her slowly. 'But you can't get people in trouble. You can't start naming names.'

Anna Treadway leaned back in her chair. He knew that he was probably being rude to her – rude to the only person who had visited him in prison – but if she was out there speaking to men at the circus ... when she didn't even understand the risks ...

'Can I tell you something?' Anna said. 'It's not even about you. Or the circus or anything. It's about me.'

Nik's instinct was to say no, but he knew there was something here he needed to understand.

'When I was seventeen,' Anna started, and looked away, 'I did a really dreadful thing. A completely shameful, awful thing. Wrecked my entire life. I, actually, just for a few days ... I didn't want to be alive any more. I was ... gone. Do you know what I mean by that?'

Nik sank a little further back into his seat. Despite the appearance of her, it seemed that this woman might in fact be a mess. Nik retained a sympathy for messes, especially the benign sort. He saw them as living in the same large, half-visible, chaotic London where he'd found his home.

'I believed,' Anna went on, 'that the thing I'd done was the most shameful, brutally horrible thing a person could ever do. And things didn't just go wrong once. They went wrong over and over again. Everything got worse and worse. I blew my whole life up.' Anna reached her hands out to him, trying to show him in the air the violence of what she had done. 'Destroyed everything. Family. Education. Career. All of it: gone. The only thing I didn't destroy was myself.'

Nik nodded. He asked because he had to, 'What did you do?'

Anna sat back. 'Okay,' she said. 'Just between you and me ...'

Nik looked around him pointedly. 'No one in here knows you. No one's going to care.'

'Okay. But the point of this is that you won't be here forever. That you will get out. And when you do ...'

'You want everyone to keep believing you're a nice girl.'

'Maybe,' she said. 'I mean, yes. Sort of. A bit. Sorry. Foolishness.'

Nik allowed her a very small smile. 'If you confess to garrotting pensioners I'm going to have to tell someone.'

Anna paused and stared at the table for half a minute. Then she said quite quietly. 'I had relations ... with a boy. When I was seventeen. And I got pregnant because I didn't know we were supposed to use something. My parents tried to get me a way out but the doctor wouldn't help so I had the baby. And it was a boy. And they gave him away. For adoption.' Anna stopped, took a deep breath and then went on. 'I was supposed to be taking the Oxford exam. It's an entrance paper for Oxford University ... And I was supposed to go home, after all that, and just forget about it and study and do everything that ...' Anna ground into silence.

Nik could see misery in her face. He felt bad now for asking. Why had he needed to know? What business was it of his? 'Wasn't your fault,' he said quietly and left it at that.

Anna nodded. 'So ... um ... anyway ... I ran away. Before I could take the exam. Before I even went back to school. I couldn't bear to go back ... I ran away. To Birmingham!' She laughed. 'There was a train to Birmingham and another to London. And the thought of London scared me so I chose Birmingham instead.

Because everyone said the people were nice.' Anna shook her head. 'Not that any of this matters. But it all … I did it. I did the thing I decided to do. I got away from them. And from school. And I didn't have to see anyone's face looking at me … And then I had to live it. I had to live with my decision. All of my decisions. And I think I thought that because they felt like a punishment, that that was what I deserved. I deserved the fact that my life became quite shitty.' Anna paused and looked at Nik. He sat quietly and listened to her speak.

'They've locked you up, Nik,' Anna said. 'They've charged you with murder. You should be screaming the place down and banging on the walls.'

He felt the sting of that.

'But you're not raging …' Anna continued. 'And I am genuinely afraid that you have seen what has happened to you and that you're just accepting it. Because things have gone wrong. And somewhere inside yourself you feel a failure. Even with all the talk of samurais … I think you're letting them punish you. When they don't have any right. They don't have any right to do this to you. Because nothing that you've done is really that bad. Is it?'

Nik shook his head.

'Did you do anything to deserve all this?' she asked.

Nik wondered whether she was genuinely asking him the question. Because of course he had done things wrong. He wasn't innocent in any proper sense. 'I shoplifted,' he said. 'When I was homeless. I stole biscuits and butter and tins of paste. I took coins once, from a man sleeping in the park. Eight shillings and four pence. I've ridden trains and buses and never paid. I snuck into the pictures a few times when the man who took the tickets wasn't looking. I …' Nik paused. 'I once put dog shit on the blazer of a boy who bullied me at school. And I've broken the law and known that I was breaking it and taken money for sex. Hundreds of times. Maybe a thousand.'

Anna nodded. 'But does that give them the right to lock you up?'

'I don't know any more,' he told her. 'I tried telling them the truth but nobody listened. And I'm scared that if I keep hitting back …

211

I don't know … But it can always get worse. You think it can't, you think it's got as bad as it can get, but then it proves you wrong.' He pointed at his face, at the scabs running down his forehead. 'No fucking samurai in here.'

Anna nodded. 'The thing is that there are people out there who believe that it's very wrong that you should be in here. And some of them are willing to fight … just a little bit. You know?'

Nik nodded. He knew that he was meant to be polite. That she was trying to be kind.

'The thing is,' Anna went on, 'for us to work for you or … fight for you … we need to know what happened. On that Saturday.'

Nik closed his eyes. All that he wanted was to forget.

'Please,' he heard Anna say. 'I'm not a lawyer. Or a policewoman. And I was honest, wasn't I? All I'm asking is … maybe you could be honest with me in return.'

* * *

This time, it wasn't a sergeant but an inspector. Detective Inspector Kite appeared in the door of the offices of Vice and stared steadily and silently at Hayes. Barnaby rose and walked out into the corridor, closing the door behind them.

'What's going on?' Kite asked, stone-faced.

'Sir?' Hayes tried.

'Pilling. Hench. You've asked for the list. What are you doing? What are you doing that I am not aware of? Is this coming from a superior officer?'

'No!' Hayes said. 'I am so sorry, sir. There was an overlap. The pills, found by the dead man's body. We're looking at routes of pills in and out of clubs all around Piccadilly and Trafalgar Square. Gentlemen's clubs not really our thing, sir. Not as a rule. But it came up and I thought it better to be thorough than not …'

'On whose authority are you doing this, Hayes? Why haven't I been rung? Why is no one talking to me about this?'

'It might have been my initiative, sir. I am sorry. I didn't mean to obstruct anything. I do apologise …'

'We all know what happened, Hayes. Someone suggested to me that you might be looking for a way out. Some kind of ill-thought-out cry for help. Is that it? Do you want to get yourself kicked out?'

'No, sir! Absolutely not. I'm doing my best. I really am. And … I apologise if sometimes I struggle to interpret what is needed from me. If I go too far or ask the wrong questions. But I value this, sir. I value what it means to be a policeman. It matters to me, sir, it really does.'

Kite snorted gently and leaned against the wall. 'Just leave it alone, Hayes. Stick to the places the public would want us to police. Stick to the trade. Stick to the discotheques and knocking shops. You're not in Central now. All right? Am I going to need to have this conversation with you again?'

'No, sir. Absolutely not, sir. Very, very clear.'

* * *

Merrian slept. She must have slept for hours. Because when she woke there were voices in the hall downstairs. Richard and the children. Her mother must have called him when she didn't come to get them. She looked at the light bending round the curtain and wondered what time it was.

She could hear Richard shouting at Frances to pick up her socks and shoes. Later, she heard Frances crying on the stairs. She heard doors banging, water running in the sink, the sound of brushing teeth. Richard hissing at Benjamin to keep his voice down, the lavatory flushing. She closed her eyes.

What had Richard told them? That she had a migraine? That she was ill? He hadn't even come into the room to look for her. At least she thought he hadn't. The light was starting to fail.

Merrian woke again when it was dark and lay for long minutes trying to hear if Richard was up. When she decided that he wasn't she crept downstairs, taking the bundle of letters with her, to see if there was any raisin bread.

There was and she ate a slice with butter as she ordered the letters by date and eased each one out of its envelope. Then she arranged the envelopes into the pattern of a grid, starting with the earliest letter in the top left corner of the table. On top of every envelope she laid the relevant letter, opened out so the writing was visible. When the table was covered to her satisfaction, she made a cup of tea and took the rest of the raisin bread upstairs with a scrape of butter on a plate.

In the darkness of the yellow room, Merrian slept long and deeply, as though drugged, only awaking when the sound of Frances arguing with her husband filtered through the door.

He hadn't come to see her. It was morning and he hadn't come.

They argued over brushing teeth. She heard the sounds of the kettle whistling too long on the hob. She smelled toast. Feet clattered on the tiles in the hallway.

At twenty to nine the front doorbell rang and the voice in the hall now was her mother's.

'… Headache. Migraine …'

'Oh no … Oh dear … Poor Mummy …'

The children put their shoes on and left with her mother. Five minutes later the door slammed shut again. Merrian sat up and listened for sounds of Richard. When time had passed and no sounds came, she crept, first to the top of the stairs, then halfway down them, and lastly to the kitchen. There was no one here. The house was empty. And all the letters on the table were gone.

Very Expensive Penguins

Friday, 14 July

Dear Anna,

By boat! You write to me about ambushing politicians and then you send it here by boat! It's been a week. Are you all right? Send me a letter, for goodness' sake, and pay for airmail!

Yours, in agitation, Louis xx

Sunday, 16 July

Louis,

Forgive me. I might actually have forgotten that I wrote to you at all. It's been a very strange few days. Odd and somewhat disconcerting. I've spoken to someone from the club and to the politician – and his wife. I even went and visited Nik in prison. He sort of did tell me to f—k off, or, at least, I think he wanted to. But he talked to me, Louis. I got him to talk. And now I'm hopeful. Quietly hopeful that this might all be made right somehow.

I did not mean to scare you. No more letters on boats!

Take care, my lovely man,
Your Anna xxx

Anna ate her Sunday lunch with Leonard and Benji, at the table nearest to the hatch at the Alabora. This Sunday, as with most Sundays, lunch meant lamb stew with roast potatoes and some rather flat Yorkshire puddings, Ottmar having never really mastered Yorkshire puddings but still feeling he should serve them as some sort of point about Englishness.

'We've got American producers in next week,' Leonard announced, scraping gravy from a milk jug. 'But keep that under your hat. And don't read too much into it. They always come and see things that play to ninety per cent houses for this long. I don't think anyone in New York is aching to see the revival of a country-house murder mystery.'

'I'd have thought the same about London but ...' Anna made a face.

Leonard stopped eating and gave her a long look. 'Never, Anna, never underestimate the desire of the English to be told about the sophistication of their past selves. All of those stupid jokes, all that laughter, it's covering for the great desire of the middling classes to sit in a theatre and think: aren't we good-looking, aren't we clever, aren't we good at being rich and in control.' Leonard dropped his voice. 'It's fucking propaganda disguised as jolly japes for car-owning Londoners. But on the other hand – and there is another hand – it's bringing in thousands of bloody pounds and digging the management out of the pit that *The Field of Stars* made for us. So, swings and roundabouts.'

Leonard went back to his lamb stew and Anna didn't feel that there was much to be added to this assessment, so she sneaked a very small smile at Benji and kept quiet.

'How's your young man?' Benji asked her.

'Louis? Not terribly happy given everything, I think.'

'Ahh,' Benji said. 'I actually meant Nik. But they both count, I suppose.'

'Oh.' Anna readjusted the conversation in her head. 'Well, Nik is ... you know. Pretty awful really. And I suppose that's not really surprising, but all the same ... His face is a mess. He's lost that sense of spark. There's no anger in him. And if you or I ... I think there has to come a time when one stops saying, oh well, he's a you-know-what, so of course bad things will happen to him.'

Leonard looked at her. 'We're both you-know-whats, Anna.'

'No!' Anna shot back, then, lowering her voice. 'Not homosexual. I meant because he's a prostitute. I just mean, shouldn't there be some sort of limitation on how awful things can get before people start noticing that these boys need help?'

Leonard shook his head. 'It's another world,' he said, and shrugged.

'Is it?' Anna asked.

'Yes,' Leonard said, sharply.

'No. I didn't mean that. I just meant … Oh, I'm not expressing this well.' Anna fell into silence and pushed her large, flat slice of Yorkshire pudding around on her plate. The men ate in silence for a couple of minutes, until Anna spoke again.

'I'm sorry. I know it must seem that I'm flailing around in things I don't understand. But I am actually doing my best. And it isn't my fault – it is not really my fault if I don't understand these things. I wasn't even brought up to see them in the world. I come at this – I know I do – from a place of ignorance. But I am trying. I mean, I was in St James's Park just a couple of days ago and there were these two old gents sitting together, under black umbrellas. And in their laps they had these empty packets of waxed paper, which must have held their sandwiches. And suddenly, I was looking at them and I thought: are they a couple? Am I seeing them but not really seeing? And I thought back to this promenade near my house when I was a child. All the men and women sitting on these benches, which were always flaking green paint, under the swoop of the gardens … I thought about how I could only see them as a family. Or as friends. Because I hadn't been taught to see any other way at all. And then I thought back and there must have been times when I was so stupid, when I offended people, when I misunderstood everything about a person's life. I was thinking all of this and then that evening in the dressing room Bertie said something about not knowing what it was to be a parent and I realised that I always assume that all the single men are just pining after women they can't have or who they lost when really …'

Anna glanced across the table. Leonard was saying nothing. But he was saying it very, very loudly.

'What?' Anna said. 'Bertie? No! Really? You see! I am *so* stupid.'

Leonard smiled. 'Not stupid. Men like Bertie – God knows, men like me – can't really afford to be known.'

Anna looked from Leonard to Benji but Benji discreetly stared into his glass of water.

'But …' Anna said. 'But … I know.'

'Yes. And you're my tenant. And you're junior to me on the staff. And even you … I had to feel you out a little bit. Get a sense of you before I offered you the flat. I sensed you wouldn't scream and tell and I was right. You see, you think I'm known at work. But I'm not. *You* know. The long-term staff know. Even the management sort of know after all this time. But I never bring Benji to anything. I don't announce myself to the incoming casts. If they want to guess about me, then they can feel free. But I'd never say it. Not at work. Because you see, one day the management may change or I might need another job. And at that point I may not have the option of being a homosexual. So I will have – to all intents and outer purposes – to stop being one. Do you see?'

Anna nodded.

'See, a man like Bertie,' Leonard went on, 'can't be open any more than I can. Because he isn't worth enough. He doesn't have enough capital saved up. He isn't a name. If he had a big career, if he made money in the movies, then maybe, just maybe, he could live with … a manager. An agent. And it would be tolerated. Because he was worth it. Literally worth it. Think of Gielgud. Think of all that cache and still it nearly sank him. Think' – here Leonard dropped his voice down very low – 'think of Bogarde. You know and I know but it isn't in the papers. Bogarde can throw parties and he can live with Tony Forwood and it can be an almost open secret. But it isn't really open, now, is it? And you have to be Dirk bloody Bogarde even to have that level of acceptance. Dirk bloody Bogarde who can make Warner Brothers and United Artists a million pounds just by starring in their films. The moment Bertie became known, that would be that. Half the directors in the country wouldn't want to work with a queer.

There're a good few leading men who would turn down productions if they had to act opposite one. Even though …' Leonard put a hand up because he could see Anna starting to open her mouth. 'Yes, I know! Even though they're already surrounded by us. But that's the thing, isn't it? If we never say we are, they can pretend we aren't. They can know that they'll never have to meet "a boyfriend". They can calm their fears that we're going to touch their thigh in the notes session. They don't have to think about us, or what to do with us or get over any internal wrinkle they have. Because they just pretend that we aren't there.'

Leonard stopped and looked at Benji.

'Bloody hell,' Anna said. 'Apart from everything else, it's just so complicated.'

'Try living it,' Benji said softly and attempted to saw his Yorkshire pudding in half.

'It's all very well,' Leonard went on, 'you wanting to help Nik. God knows, London is full of boys like him who need a million helping hands. But you don't really know what you're dealing with, do you? You don't know this world. You don't know prisons and pubs and clubs and what they do to boys like Nik when they have them in the cells. The intent is all very well. But you haven't got power enough to lift the lid.'

Anna started to nod, but then she stopped herself. She was tired of acquiescing. 'Actually,' she said, 'he told me something. About that Saturday night.'

Leonard looked at her quizzically.

'It isn't over,' Anna said. 'It isn't nearly over at all.'

*　*　*

At six o'clock, Anna walked down through the quiet market and crossed the river. She met Barnaby Hayes, who was standing in Waterloo station in his white shirt and off-duty chinos, looking self-conscious, which is how he often looked.

'Maybe try to look less like a policeman,' Anna said, as they went to queue for their tickets.

'I don't think I do look like a policeman,' Hayes said, looking down at himself.

'Yes,' Anna said. 'I know you don't.'

They caught the 6.45 slow train from Waterloo to Twickenham, and rode the stuffy carriage through densely packed warehouse districts and housing estates.

The main drag at Twickenham was thronged with curtain shops and cafes, hairdressers and ironmongers, every one of them closed on this warm Sunday evening. Something about suburbia made Anna smile. It was all so terribly beige and clean and unthreatening. The streets were swept and the litter bins could hold their contents. The air did not smell like hot waste but only something odd that she could not define, but that after walking for some minutes and cutting down a leafy alleyway she began to suspect was 'clean air'.

'I have to tell you something,' Hayes said, as they walked the quiet alleyway. 'Kite came to see me on Friday.' He looked nervously across at her. 'Obviously, I'm not telling you any of this,' he pointed out. 'Nor am I actually here.'

'Right,' Anna said. 'I mean … how completely are you not here? Should I even be talking to you? Should I start walking ten paces ahead?'

Hayes smiled tersely. 'It's been made clear to me that my continued … delving … is being seen as a provocation. I was asked – and I do think they were serious when they said this – I was asked if I was trying to get myself the sack. If I'd had enough. Was trying to leave the job.'

Anna made a face. 'That's not good.'

'No,' Hayes said slowly. 'That isn't good. Really. All things considered. So, when you said that you'd like someone to back you up … I hope this is okay, but I decided that I would come – of course – but that I'd come as Barnaby. Not as a policeman. Do you see?'

They walked on for a few seconds, then Anna paused.

'Someone started calling me,' she told him. 'At first they didn't speak. And then, the third time they called they told me Nik killed the boy. Just like that. And I had to stop.'

'But who is it?' Hayes asked.

'I've no idea. It didn't sound like anyone I know. Just a very normal accent. Middle class, I'd say. English. Three times they called on Friday. And then on Saturday morning, another one but completely silent. And again this morning. Honestly, I don't know what to think. I haven't even told anyone up to now. Am I meant to be scared? I mean, I am a bit. But mostly I'm just furious.'

'Right,' Hayes said. 'Hm. That's also ... not very good.'

'I know,' said Anna. 'And I don't know how I feel about it at all.'

They walked on in silence. The riverbank spread itself before them with long dirt paths leading to left and right beneath a canopy of trees. There was a slipway for small vessels and a few rowing boats lay upside down in front of a pub with a large fenced patio, upon which affluent-looking, middle-aged men drank pints of beer and stared out at the river.

Anna paused again. 'You can go home,' she said. 'I don't think you should feel indebted in any way. I'll be fine.' She tried to make this sound breezy, but inside she was cringing a little. She didn't want to go on her own; or, rather, she didn't want to confront this man on her own. Not without anyone even knowing that she was there.

'I'm just ...' Barnaby was descending into a kind of elongated stammer. 'Not really ... It will need to be you who speaks to him. If he's a witness, he can't recognise me in any of this ...'

'Right,' Anna said, getting brisker as the uselessness of Hayes unfolded before her. 'Okay. Not to worry. Let's just get on.' And she turned and marched towards a high, slim bridge which sloped up into the air and then down into thickets of bushes on what Anna imagined must be Eel Pie Island.

The island was thick with every kind of tree: oaks and weeping willows, cherries and spruces and white birch. So densely did the trees grow along its edges that it was very hard to discern if there were any streets, and where one house began and another ended. They joined a cluster of young people funnelling slowly onto the bridge to Eel Pie Island. As they reached the other side, a lady in a yellow twinset was taking four pence from every newcomer. Hayes paid for both of them and Anna let him, still rather annoyed to find that he was tagging along without any intention of getting his hands dirty. The crowd they moved in flowed on past the bridge and down a lane that wound its way through the middle of the island and then widened out to a green space studded with signs for the Eel Pie Hotel.

They were informed by a bouncer that the club was members only, but they needed only give a name and address and they could go in. Anna gave her real name, and then, rather regretting this, she gave an old address in Forest Hill. She did not see what Hayes wrote. The bouncer carefully stamped the veined insides of their wrists with a sign like a phoenix and then they crossed the threshold.

The sound of guitar and drums rang loudly off the white-painted walls and echoed above in the high wooden beams of the filthy ceiling. The hall they found themselves in was full of alcoves, doors and corridors leading to other places. On the columns and at the corners large, cartoonish figures had been painted in thick black lines. Women with great bushes of curly hair, wide lips and large, round glasses. Men with beards, the collars of their jackets turned up, broad smiles upon their watching faces. Soldiers in uniform, their chests heavy with crazy-looking medals. At the far side of the hall a low stage stood before a larger alcove, this one covered in a jumble of coloured faces – a crazy scene of tumbling characters and dancing, fretting figures. Filling the room, bodies moved and twirled and swayed and carried glasses and kissed and touched each other. It had, in many ways, all the markers of a club on Carnaby Street, but the atmosphere was less commercial, more ragtag and student common room. Anna felt as if she'd walked in on a sixth-form dance, except that the air was thick with the smell of marijuana, and the floor sticky with beer and all the sweet liqueurs that lined the shelves behind the little bar. There was something sweet and suburban about the whole enterprise: the dancers less good-looking than their central London counterparts; the clothes less fashionable; the crumbling place breathing good intentions and low finances.

'Try not to smell everything that shouldn't be here,' Anna said to Hayes.

'It's fine. I'm just going to ignore it all,' he told her.

They crossed to the bar and Hayes ordered Anna a Coke and himself a tonic and lime from a diminutive girl in brown corduroy whose head and shoulders, but little else, could be seen above the counter.

'Gin?' she asked Hayes, when he made his order.

'Sorry?' he shouted above the noise.

'Gin or vodka in the tonic!' she shouted back at him.

'No!' Hayes called to her in some alarm. 'Just tonic! No alcohol!'

The girl laughed and walked to the back of the bar to fetch the bottle of lime. 'Vicar or policeman?' she shouted and both Anna and Hayes turned sharply in her direction before realising that this was not a discreet way to behave. The girl turned back to them and grinned, her teeth a snaggle of varied directions and colours.

'He's an alcoholic,' Anna called back. Hayes started a little but so did the girl behind the bar.

'Jesus!' she said to Hayes. 'I'm sorry. I didn't mean to be a twat.' She handed him the glass of tonic and momentarily patted his hand. 'Good for you,' she said enthusiastically.

Anna gave her a big smile. 'Nelligan playing tonight?' Anna asked and the girl nodded. 'It's just I thought I might have missed them.'

'They haven't been on yet. I think there's seven of them on the list tonight, so they might not get on until ten. I'm Marlene, by the way.'

Anna was slightly put out by the un-English forwardness of the introduction, but she decided it was probably politest to go along with it. 'Anna. This is Barnaby.'

'Brennan!' Hayes said.

Marlene stared at him and then smiled slyly.

'She calls me Barnaby when she's making fun of me. Because she thinks it sounds posh. I'm Brennan,' Hayes said, very definitely.

'Okay …' Marlene said slowly. 'You both been here before? Because you struck me as sort of new.'

'Embarrassingly new,' Anna said. 'We've been meaning to come forever. And then I liked Nelligan when I saw them at Mason's Yard and I said I'd take Brennan.' She carefully enunciated the new name. 'This place is wild … the walls, I mean. And the whole stylish … wreck thing.'

Marlene grinned at her. 'I like it. They didn't even pay me the first few months. I just came and worked here for the love of it. But then Arthur said he had to pay me something. 'Cause he's like that ...'

Anna looked around them but Marlene seemed as good a person to feel out as anyone else. Certainly she was eager to talk.

'We live a bit more centrally than this,' Anna shouted, over what she felt were some unnecessarily loud guitar chords, 'but I thought it'd be good to escape the whole Carnaby Street scene. You know. For once.'

Marlene made a face. 'Oh my God, yes. Aren't they all idiots up there, anyway?' Hayes laughed and Marlene rolled her eyes at him. 'Yeah,' she said, 'in their stupid clothes. All that bloody black and white and red. My nan calls them "the very expensive penguins" when she sees them in the paper. "Oh, look, Marlene!" she'll scream. "The expensive penguins are waddling up and down the streets again. Never bloody going anywhere, are they? No bloody jobs. It's all swagger swagger up the bloody street and waddle waddle down the bloody street. Look at my clothes! Look at my clothes! Thirteen quid these boots cost me and my feet aren't bleeding yet!"' Marlene nodded at Hayes' white shirt. 'You look quite normal for a London type.'

'Thank you!' Hayes shouted back. 'Normal was what I was aiming for.'

A group of girls came to the bar and Marlene busied herself opening bottles of beer for them. Hayes shuffled closer to Anna.

'Brennan?' Anna whispered in his ear.

'I can't be me,' he loudly whispered back. 'I'm not here!'

Anna laughed and rolled her eyes. 'Okay. I'm going to need to get backstage at some point. So I might just go and figure out the lie of the land.'

Hayes nodded, his eyes rather wide, and let her leave without another word.

Clutching her drink, Anna made her way through the dancers and started to explore the edges of the dance floor where numerous doors and corridors led off into the dark. One to the right led only to the gents' toilet; another, in the far corner, led to metal fire-escape doors and a hall crammed with wooden crates. Anna tried again, weaving through the dance floor. She tried a half-open door on the far side of the room but the shaft of light showed only crates of beer and a stack of newspaper and kindling. Anna turned and her eyes met those of Marlene, twenty feet away, at the bar, watching her stepping out of the store cupboard. Anna smiled in embarrassment and crossed back to where Hayes cradled his tonic and lime.

'You lost?' Marlene asked.

Anna exchanged a quick glance with Hayes, who at least had the nerve to save her from this conversation.

'Marlene was telling me all about Arthur Chisnall,' Hayes told her. 'He runs this place. Takes an interest in waifs and strays. Gets them back onto the good path.'

'I was telling your boyfriend, if he ever found himself in trouble 'cause of …' Marlene pointed in a pantomime gesture at the bottles of gin. 'Arthur would help him out. That's what the money goes on. It's why we're such a wreck. All the money to fix this place up goes on rescuing people.'

Anna smiled. 'Really?'

Marlene nodded intensely. 'Really. My little brother got himself in all kinds of trouble at school. He was taking stuff. Then they said he was dealing. Anyway, someone told Mum about Arthur and she sent us both down here to see if he could … you know … give Patrick something else to do.'

'You mean a job?'

'No! I mean study,' Marlene shouted to them both over the sound of a song that seemed to be entirely composed of thrashing drums and bass guitar. 'See … Patrick was really good at sciences. So, I brought him across to meet Arthur. Which is as weird as it sounds. 'Cause there's me all of seventeen and there's this old bloke with a pipe playing records in a hall. And I'm thinking, "This is bloody dodgy", right? Like, what's he want with lads? So, then I stick to Patrick like glue. 'Cause I'm not having anyone touching up my little brother. But there's none of that. Arthur just talks to him and lets him come to music classes where they all listen to stuff. Anything, really. Just the stuff they like. And then he gets him into classes at

Richmond Adult Ed., so of course I have to go there too. Three evenings a week. Two terms I did with him before I finally decided they weren't kiddy fiddlers. Bloody boring it was too. Anyway, on he goes – Patrick, that is. And he gets his Os and then he gets his As. They never let him back into school, of course. But it didn't matter. Every time we got stuck, we just went and saw Arthur. And he'd be all jolly and get it sorted. In the end he sent Patrick off to Harlech. In Wales. To a college. He's doing combined sciences. We're not even paying for him.'

'Bloody hell,' Anna said. 'That's sort of amazing.'

'Is it a Christian sort of thing?' Hayes asked.

Marlene looked at him, puzzled. 'I think he just does it because he's a nice person. Anyway … They say they're going to shut it down.' Marlene pointed up at the broken beams in the ceiling, at the walls pitted with missing plaster and brickwork. 'It's falling to pieces. And no one has the money to mend it.'

The music had fallen quiet. People were clapping. There was a general movement towards the bar.

'That's really sad,' Anna said, before Marlene disappeared to work. 'I'm really sorry. That's crap.'

Marlene laughed, a short, violent shout of pleasure. 'I love it when posh birds swear,' she said.

* * *

Merrian had gone out without telling Richard where. She had been out most of Saturday and now most of Sunday, coming home so late that everyone was in bed and she could go directly to the spare room. Richard sat in the kitchen and watched the clock move. He wondered if she was preparing to leave him. But then she didn't seem to be involving the children at all, and if there was one thing he knew, it was that if Merrian left she was taking the children with her. Nine o'clock came and went. Then ten. There were no sounds now from Frances's or Ben's room above his head. He went to the hall and carried the phone into the living room as far as it would go. He closed the living-room door.

'Hello?' the strange voice said. 'Hampstead 4895 – or whatever we're saying these days.'

'Is that Stuart?' Richard asked. 'Angus gave me this number for weekends. It's Richard. Wallis.' He wasn't sure how far his explanation should go.

'Oh. Right. Well, he's here.' Richard could hear Stuart calling Angus's name. Richard sat patiently and waited.

'What is it?' Angus asked.

'I'm sorry to call at the weekend,' Richard said.

'What's happened?'

'It's probably nothing. Merrian found letters and now she keeps … disappearing on me. We haven't spoken in two days. She's just out. All the time.'

'What letters?'

'The ones you gave me back.'

'Richard! Jesus! Why?'

'I'm sorry. I was sentimental. I couldn't just burn them.'

'Would she go to the papers?'

'What?' Richard hadn't even imagined this suggestion and was now a little shocked to have it thrown into the list of possibilities.

Angus's voice grew louder in the earpiece. 'Would she go to the papers?'

'No! Merrian? God, no. Of course not.'

'Really? How are you certain?'

'Because she'd never hurt the children. Would she? No. No! Not for a second. It wouldn't even occur to her.' Richard felt slightly wounded on Merrian's behalf. 'She's not vindictive. Or cruel.'

Angus was silent on the other end of the phone. Richard felt the reproach in what wasn't being said.

'We don't need this,' Angus said quietly. 'There's enough to deal with as things are.'

'I know. I'm sorry. Mind you, I haven't heard anything more from that Treadway woman.'

Angus was silent.

'Have you?' Richard asked.

'I've warned her off.'

'You've warned her off?'

'I got Stuart to call her. Put a bit of pressure on.'

Richard held the receiver further away from him. His chest felt tight.

'Richard!' Angus said. 'Come on! We have to get a handle on this. We can't just let it spread. We shut down every route, every possibility, every story. We deal with it. You know that's what we do.'

Richard pressed the receiver back into the side of his face. 'What if she traces the call? What if she finds out it's Stuart, and through Stuart, you ... God, have you told him? Have you told Stuart?'

'He's fine,' Angus said. 'He's with me. I wouldn't have told him if I couldn't trust him. Really. This thing – this stupid thing – it's been blown out of all proportion. Just wait. September. October. It'll all be over. Gone. Onto the next scandal. Someone else.'

Richard held the receiver very far away from him and sank back into the armchair he was sitting in. He couldn't do it. To be so cavalier. To threaten and to call in favours. Some days he just wanted to give up. To get a quiet job in a bank or a school. To live within the limits of his bravery. He could hear Angus talking on the end of the line but he felt too tired to join in. Instead he listened for the tread in the hall which might tell him that Merrian was home. And, at length, he hung up the phone and sat in silence.

* * *

Anna pushed her way through the throng; the band was playing 'A Night in Tunisia' now, an instrumental, and the singer was just disappearing from the stage into the far left corner of the hall. Anna followed where he went, staying at a generous distance from him, and found herself walking down one half-painted corridor after another, noting the strange cartoon figures which seemed to follow her into this part of the building. There were a couple of curtains strung across one end of the corridor and a rectangle painted on the wall filled with block words:

ARTISTS ONLY

'Come on!' Anna whispered to herself and pulled aside the curtain. But on the other side of the curtains was only another corridor, stretching 30 yards into the distance, with a door marked 'FIRE' in large letters at the other end.

Anna wondered where the singer had gone but, retracing her steps, she found only two locked doors back along her way. She knocked at each in turn but no one answered. All stage doors, she thought, open onto the outside of the building somewhere. She hurried back into the main hall – glancing only momentarily at Hayes, though cursing him inwardly for standing and watching the music that he did not understand while she did all the work – and then out towards the bouncers and the entrance, waving the phoenix on her wrist as she went.

Outside, the night was cool, and beyond a short line of young men sitting together on a fence sharing a spliff, the lanes around the Eel Pie Hotel were quiet and dark. Anna slipped quietly around the edges of the hotel and explored the darker corners of the garden. She found a couple more doors marked with 'FIRE' in large letters and then a line of a dozen dark windows.

She thought she could hear the bouncers talking around the next corner and, having lost count of how many corners she had turned, she plunged onwards, thinking that she must be back at the entrance. Instead, though, her feet hit gravel and now she seemed to be in a loading area of some kind. Light bled in weak bars from a line of frosted windows at head height and she could make out what seemed to be piles of crates and kegs. She knew that the river was close because she heard the slap of the water on a jetty.

'Evening, darling,' a man's voice called out.

'Evening.'

'You after one of the boys, are you?'

'Actually … I was. I don't suppose Brian's gone on yet?'

'O'Hare?'

'Yes,' Anna spoke into the darkness and then a crackle sounded in the space between herself and the voice and a light flared. Anna heard a cigarette being lit.

'He's just getting his stuff in. Does he know you, petal?'

'Sort of. I'm a friend of the family. I was told to grab him quickly if he was over this way. Just for a minute. Nothing sinister.' Anna infused her voice with as much of a smile as she could manage.

The smoker was silent for half a minute and then, 'Brian!' The shout echoed so loudly in the quiet that it made Anna jump.

She recovered herself. 'Much obliged,' she managed, somewhat dryly.

A long column of light flowed across the gravel in front of Anna, spilling from a door which had opened in the wall to her right.

'What is it?' a man's voice called out into the darkness.

'There's a girl here says she's a friend of yours. Wants a little word with you.'

'What she called then?' the voice asked. It was tight and rather nasal.

'She's called Anna,' Anna called back. 'I'm a friend of your cousin and she told me to look you up.'

'I'm on in twenty minutes,' the voice came back. Irritated, Anna thought.

'Yeah. I'm sorry. I wanted to see you play. But my last train goes soon. Do you have one minute? Just a minute. I'd be ever so grateful.'

The man in question, Brian, who was dressed in a long, slim turquoise suit and T-shirt, swung a keg against the door to prop it open. He stepped out into the loading area and peered through the darkness.

Anna briefly took in a large man in shirtsleeves, smoking and watching.

Anna walked towards the lighted patch of gravel and nodded her head towards the jetty at the water's edge.

'Quiet word. Just quick, I promise.'

Brian looked her up and down and then strode down towards the sound of the water.

'What cousin?' he asked as soon as she joined him.

Anna spoke quickly and quietly. 'On Saturday the first, you played a gig at Mason's Yard and that same night you bought a boy called Nik Christou. After you'd been with him—'

'Jesus,' Brian spat the word out fast as a bullet and started to run back towards the square of light as if he was being chased.

'You're going to want to hear this, Brian,' Anna called loudly across the space, as the smoker stood and watched it play out.

Brian paused as he neared the door into the hotel. 'Fuck off,' he shouted back at her.

Anna shouted louder. 'The police, Brian!' Brian stopped, just inside the hallway. Anna paused. 'The girl was underage, you know.'

Brian looked back, first towards the smoking man and then to Anna.

'What do you want?' he asked.

'I don't want to shout this, Brian. But you're going to want to talk to me and not the police.'

Brian stepped back outside the building.

'You're welcome to invite a witness if you don't trust me.' Anna nodded towards the smoker.

Brian walked slowly back and down to the riverbank.

'What do you want?' he asked her softly.

'You bought a boy called Nik Christou. He ended up trapped backstage. When you found him, when you and your friends found him, you beat seven bells out of him and threw him into the street.'

'What of it?'

'While Nik was lying in St James's Square recovering, a young man called Charlie was being murdered just off Pall Mall. And, right now, Nik is sitting in Wormwood Scrubs because the police think he's guilty of Charlie's murder. Up to this point Nik hasn't named you. But this is Sunday. And Nik has a fresh interview on Monday. And he's got nothing left to give them. Except your name.'

Anna paused and allowed the silence to grow around her. She could hear Brian breathing. She tried to quiet her own breath. She thought she could hear her blood rushing. She felt almost as if she were high. She wondered if this man would hit her. And, if he did, what the man with the cigarette would do to stop him.

Brian's voice, when it came at last, was very quiet. 'What do you want?' he asked.

Anna took a long breath and then she spoke to him almost as if she was talking to a child. 'Nik can name you. He can describe everything you did to him. He can describe the gents' toilet you did it in and the manager's office he was forced to hide in. He can describe every intimate detail of you if he really has to, and … and just like that you'll get taken in for questioning. Or, if you prefer, you can go to the police tomorrow, and you can tell them that you caught Nik attempting to pick pockets at Mason's Yard. And that you gave him a hiding after you came offstage. Say, at about half eleven. Yes? You can tell them you're the reason for the bruises they found on him. You can tell them that there was a £20 note missing, but you couldn't find it. You can tell them that you're coming forward because you read he'd been charged with Charlie's murder except that when Charlie died Nik was in an alley, being thrashed by you. Nik gets charged with petty theft. He declines to press charges for the assault. And we all go back to our lives.' Her throat was closing. She swallowed. The water slapped against the jetty.

The Music Box, the
Huntsman and the Scene

In the days afterwards, Anna waited to hear from Hayes that Brian had confessed. She felt the weight of the threat she had made against the singer as if somehow it had been made to her. She woke at night, in a panic that she had done something terribly wrong. And so she looked for ways to assuage her unease. She wondered if, like her empathetic actresses and socialist friends, she was simply more comfortable with victims than with perpetrators. Or whether the constant baiting of these men was turning her into something that she really could not admire. She felt herself drifting towards stasis, so she chose another path – something uncontroversial that would salve her sense of self.

Hayes had told her that he would have liked to have tracked down Charlie's parents, but that he couldn't risk the ring-round of police stations. Anna thought briefly of ringing police stations in his stead but she felt that this would require more subterfuge than she was comfortable with in the context of the police. So, instead, she did what seemed the next best thing and rang churches. She copied numbers from the telephone books in Westminster Reference Library and set about ringing every church that seemed to be in Wiltshire. St Mary's; St Thomas's; All Saints; St Katharine's. Where someone picked up, they listened to her patiently. 'A Charlie?' they would ask. 'Missing for a year?' No – none of them had heard of him, though here and there a message was taken. Anna rang on, filling her morning and then her afternoon with phone calls, and trying not to think about the phone bill. Holy Trinity; The Priory; Penknapp; St Laurence; St Margaret's; St John's. It was just as Anna was making herself a comforting plate of almost-ploughman's lunch that someone finally called her back.

'Miss Treadway?' a man's voice asked. 'Asking about a Charles?'

'I am. I was,' Anna told him, trying to swallow the end of a pickled onion as quietly as possible and nearly choking.

'I'm the vicar here at Holy Trinity in Dilton Marsh. We had a young man go missing. Charles Burgess. There was a notice up in the porch of the church for nearly a year about him. But I don't think he ever came home. Do you think it might be him?'

'I don't know,' Anna said. 'How old was your Charles?'

'Sixteen, seventeen. Something like that. I didn't know him, though I think I might have baptised him. He never came but his mother did. She does our flowers occasionally when my wife's away. Family ran stables, I think. And she knits hats for Africa. Good woman. Nice woman.'

'Charlie was mid to late teens. They're actually not sure.'

'Was?'

'He … I'm very sorry. Charlie died. And there's no one to come and pick him up. You know. When the police let him go. We didn't even know his last name.'

'That …' the man started and then he stopped. 'That all sounds rather sad, Miss Treadway. Was it an accident?'

'No. I'm afraid it wasn't. It was something horrible,' Anna said. Because, really, how could one go into anything else with a vicar one didn't even know. 'Do you … Is it bad of me if I ask that you tell his mother? Only I don't know her. And you do.'

The vicar laughed a humourless laugh. 'It isn't bad, Miss Treadway. It's my job.'

When Anna put the phone down she felt exhausted. Charlie Burgess. Whose mother knitted hats for Africa and went to the church of Holy Trinity in Dilton Marsh. Whose notice of disappearance had hung in the porch of the church for a year. Who had sandy hair and wanted to ride horses.

* * *

234

Sunday, 16 July

Darling A,

I went for a walk today. Up past the fields to the east of the town and then round. The sun was splendid – a very un-English sun – and I took off my jacket and rolled up my sleeves and I was as warm as anyone has ever been in his life.

And the further I walked from the town the freer I knew myself to be. And I thought about anything and nothing.

There was a band playing somewhere as I got back and I stopped at the edge of a field, behind a fence and listened to the music. I didn't even know where they were or where I was. I could have been anywhere.

I sat in the dust and I closed my eyes and I imagined – very clearly – that my mother was sitting next to me. Not speaking but just completely there. So I sat with her for a whole hour. Just she and I. Sitting very peacefully. Listening to music.

I need to come home. I'm so tired, my darling.

Your Aloysius

* * *

The call came again on Tuesday morning. Breathing on the line.

'What is it?' Anna shouted into the receiver. 'What do you want?' The breathing slowed.

'Piss off!' she shouted. She slammed the telephone down and went into her room to cry for a minute. Though she didn't entirely know what she was crying about.

In the end it took nearly a week. For Brian to give his statement, to talk to the police, to talk to lawyers, to take it to the CPS. Hayes asked and stuck his nose in where he could, but he couldn't be directly involved. They asked the guitarist if he or the venue wished to press charges on Nik for theft. Brian graciously declined: the man, he told them, had been through enough. Maybe even learned an important lesson.

At eight on Thursday morning, Ottmar and Anna took the bus to East Acton to welcome Nik out of Wormwood Scrubs. He was finally released at quarter to ten, and they watched him step outside the building, blinking a little in the bright sun of morning.

He seemed almost embarrassed to see them both. He shook his head.

'You didn't have to.'

You don't have anybody else, Anna wanted to say, but she didn't think it was kind or helpful to point this out. Nik drew the pouch of tobacco she had gifted him out from his pocket and started to roll a cigarette.

'Whose sofa would you like to sleep on?' Anna asked. 'We think you should come somewhere quiet, at least until the weekend. Ottmar's sofa is comfier but my flat's quieter. We don't mind who you pick.'

Nik looked at both of them, his face pale and inexpressive. 'I don't know,' he told them. 'I just want to go somewhere quiet and sit down.'

They caught the 7 back into town, sitting in a line at the back of the lower deck; Nik and then Anna and then Ottmar. Anna gazed past Nik's face at Ladbroke Grove – the coloured houses and shabby antique dealers. As they drew near Paddington she felt something in her palm and realised that Nik, without turning to look at her, had slipped his hand into hers. They sat like that for a minute, then he let her go and they went on, still in silence.

Back on Neal Street, they fed Nik eggs on toast in the cafe and then set him up on Anna's sofa with a blanket and a cup of tea. By the middle of the afternoon, he was fast asleep.

Anna had been avoiding calls from Merrian. It had been more than a week since they'd met in the 101. So far, Merrian had left two messages at the stage door of the theatre and phoned Penny more often than that. Every time Anna turned up in Penny's dressing room, Penny would make a deathly face at her and Anna would tell her: 'I know, I know – but I don't actually know anything yet.'

Nik was out, that was the important thing – at least to Anna's way of thinking. But the problem of Charlie's death would rumble on. She sympathised with Merrian, you couldn't fail to sympathise with a woman in her position, but that didn't mean Richard Wallis was ever going to be her first concern. The world he existed inside of, she wasn't even sure if it was a world of privilege, or a world of politics or a world of homosexual men, but whatever it was he seemed to be sealed inside it. And Anna could not truly say that she knew whether she believed him guilty or innocent of hurting anyone.

She contemplated ringing Merrian and then she thought better of it and rang Hayes instead.

'I heard Christou was getting out today,' Hayes told her. 'Are you going to see him?'

'He's asleep on my sofa. We picked him up this morning, Ottmar and I. We thought he could do with somewhere safe to stay.'

Anna heard the pause on the other end of the line. Hayes biting back judgement.

'I wanted to ask …' Anna went on. 'I don't really know if I want to go further with this. I feel as if Nik's out and I don't really know who else to talk to. The porter knew a bit but not that much. No one else saw Charlie, apart from the boy in the cafe and then he only saw the other man for a minute. I'm taking your advice on this one. I'm not police. I'm getting out.'

'Of course,' Hayes said, sympathetically. 'Probably for the best. I mean, short of digging up the rough sleeper … I don't really know …'

'Oh, him,' Anna said. 'I thought nobody could find him.'

'Not according to PC Pilling. They looked for him but he'd shifted himself. Probably terrified by the whole thing. He saw them … but maybe he just saw Charlie. It wasn't clear. And the homeless … it's not the easiest of worlds. I mean, short of traversing all the parks and the bridges and the underpasses and the doorsteps … Well …'

'Yes,' Anna agreed. 'Probably too much. Too large a city.'

'It always is,' Hayes told her. 'Always too large a city.' She heard him smile on the other end of the line.

With a slightly sinking heart, Anna bid Hayes farewell and braced herself to phone Merrian.

The woman picked up after only two rings. 'Wallis residence.'

'Merrian? It's Anna.'

'Oh my goodness. I …' Merrian fell into silence.

'It's okay,' Anna said. 'I know. I've been concentrating on my friend. The boy they accused. And he's out.'

'He's out?' Anna could hear deep alarm in Merrian's voice.

'Yes. The charges were dropped yesterday. He got out this morning. I found him an alibi. And … well, it's tricky getting people to alibi him given the circumstances, but we found a way around it.'

'I see. Okay. Well, good. Poor lad …'

'I'm not sure that I've really found anything that's helpful to you,' Anna told her. 'I spoke to a porter from the Hellenic. He was there that night. And Richard was in the garden with his friends. But the porter – József – he doesn't remember anyone breaking away from the group. They were there and that's about all we can say. It's all got a little bit … dead-endy …' Anna twisted the phone cord between her fingers. 'Sorry.'

'Oh,' Merrian said. 'I see …'

There was a long and terrible silence.

'I really am sorry,' Anna tried again.

'Yes. I know,' Merrian said, seemingly unwilling to help Anna out and move the conversation on.

'How are you?' Anna asked. 'In yourself?'

'Not great,' Merrian said, matter-of-factly. 'Not that good at all.'

They lapsed into silence.

'Is there really nothing else?' Merrian asked, unable to conceal the distress in her voice.

'I don't know. I mean, have you heard anything more from the newspapers?' Anna asked.

'No. Nothing.'

'Right.' Anna scanned the room about her, wondering how she could possibly end this call. Goodness, but she was being ungrateful. Hadn't Merrian rescued her when she needed someone? 'I mean, Hayes, the policeman, he said that if the homeless man could be found …' Anna hesitated. 'But I really don't know where anyone starts with that. The city is full of homeless. He could be anywhere. He might even have moved on …'

There was a long silence on the other end of the phone. And then, in a voice which sounded considerably lighter than it had up to this point: 'Well, I'm not doing anything tomorrow …'

Which was how Anna came to be sitting with Nik the next morning, sharing a plate of buttered toast and trying to explain why she was taking Merrian Wallis on a manhunt in the city's parks and underpasses.

Nik listened to Anna's explanation with a smile that only grew the more Anna tried to rationalise what they were going to do.

'I mean, if it comes to it … I'm not doing anything today either,' Nik pointed out.

Anna looked at him in alarm. 'I don't think you should come,' she said, rather bluntly.

Nik fixed her with a long look. 'You ever slept rough in a park?' he asked her. "Specially good at knowing the streets where people sleep?'

Anna crunched her toast. 'Okay,' she said. 'Fine. Everyone can come on this ridiculous day out. What does it matter? It's not as if we're going to find him …'

* * *

St James's Park was a veritable mass of bodies. Boys in shorts and T-shirts lay on the grass, which grew in scarce patches and revealed a lot of earth. A couple of people were trying and failing to fly a kite. There were toddlers and babies staggering around like drunks or being clutched and played with and rolled around on the ground. There was a slovenliness to the atmosphere, a hot breath of distemper and secretions. A group of teenage boys walked together by the water, one wheeling a bicycle, a transistor radio strapped to the back emitting metallic sounds – something which might have been the Kinks.

Nik and Anna walked towards the bandstand to meet Merrian at just past noon. Ottmar had given them £10 to buy Nik something new to wear, since his old clothes still bore traces of the blood from the Saturday night when he'd been beaten. They dropped into a clothing store at the beginning of the Strand and Nik chose black jeans and three black and grey T-shirts with an assortment of festival and band names on them. Nik had refused to give up his trench coat, but Anna persuaded him to let her wash it in the bath. Anna could not gauge at all what was going on inside of him. One moment he seemed fine and the next he'd fall silent or a kind of fury would fill his features and Anna would back away and give him space. She questioned the wisdom of bringing Nik and Merrian together, but since neither seemed to have any antipathetic views towards the other, she doubted that it would become openly combative. All the same …

Merrian waited for them on the steps of the bandstand, in a billowing sundress covered in a print of blue and white seagulls and a pair of blue wedge-heeled espadrilles. Anna eyed this outfit with a certain degree of horror and then exchanged a quick, doubtful glance with Nik. She looked like she was off to sports day at a minor public school.

They drew close and Anna realised too late that Merrian had picked up on their eye-rolling.

'What?' she asked, her lips pursing into a little ring of annoyance.

'Nothing,' Anna lied.

'That's quite a flamboyant dress,' Nik pointed out, ignoring Anna's attempt at deceitful politeness. 'I mean, I thought we were on a quiet recce.'

Merrian stared with annoyance down at her dress. 'Well,' she said. 'Fuck.'

And that made them all laugh.

'So ... this is Merrian,' Anna told Nik. 'And this is ...' Anna couldn't remember if she'd ever told Merrian the name of the man she'd been trying to exonerate. She didn't think she had. She'd been careful to hold it back. 'This is my friend, Nik. He knew about Charlie through his work. And he offered to help. Which was nice of him,' Anna said lightly. 'Shall we start up on Waterloo Place?'

Without further conversation they walked up to the gardens and Anna showed them both the railings behind which Charlie had been found. Nik walked off into the shadows for a couple of minutes and Anna told him to take his time. Then she showed Merrian where Hayes thought the vagrant had been planning to sleep that night, at the top of the steps, just across from the statue of the Duke of York.

There was nobody camped up there right now, so they headed down the steps and back towards the park. All along the north side of the Mall sat cream-coloured classical buildings with little dark windows and many, many half columns spread along each front. Between each column, the buildings were set back and Merrian and Anna started to trawl along the recessed spaces, looking for newspapers or blankets signalling a sleeping place. As they neared Admiralty Arch they found a heap of newspapers, all spread out in the shadow of a column. A ragged red jumper had been rolled into a ball and half tucked beneath them. They looked about for an owner and as they did so, Nik caught them up.

'Someone's sleeping here,' Anna said.

'Yeah, but it's sunny. They'll be in the park maybe or begging. You can't really beg here. The police get upset ... By the closeness to ...' Nik nodded his head over his shoulder and towards Buckingham Palace, almost out of sight behind the trees. 'You could leave them a note ...'

Anna looked at him, a little startled.

Nik gave her a pitying look. 'Yeah, that was a joke.'

They crossed the Mall and started to walk the verge which ran between the road and St James's Park. They found a dirty shirt spread out under a tree, more newspaper under some bushes. All around them were signs of where people had sat or slept, but no sign of the actual people themselves. They walked down towards Horse Guards Road and back into the park itself.

Anna scanned the bodies all around them for anyone who looked out of place, dishevelled or overdressed. Down by the water's edge, just north of Duck Island, two skinny, middle-aged men sat on coats. Their faces were thick with hair and their cheeks and hands were brown from the sun. Anna nodded and Merrian strode purposefully forward.

'Hello,' she began, bending down to talk to them. 'Sorry to bother you. We're looking for a chap often sleeps up near the Mall Galleries. He saw something rather upsetting a couple of weeks ago and we need to talk to him about it.'

Both men peered up at Merrian.

'Hello, love!' one of them said.

'Hello,' she said again. 'Do you know who I might be meaning?'

Anna and Nik joined Merrian.

'Bloody hell,' said the second man. 'How many of you are there?'

'We're it,' Nik said. 'Just the three of us.'

The men looked from Merrian to Anna to Nik.

'What's he done?' the first man asked.

'Nothing,' Anna pointed out. 'He saw something. He got scared. He ran. Completely understandable. Except that we'd like him to talk to us. Not the police. Just us. I don't suppose … The policeman on the night thought he was over fifty. Bearded. Slim. About five foot six. Dark and greying hair. Does that ring any bells?'

The second man shrugged his shoulders. 'That's fifty people, isn't it? I don't know. No one said anything to us … Have they?' he asked his friend. His friend shrugged.

'Thank you so much for your time,' Merrian said and for a moment Anna wondered if she was going to ask them to vote for her husband. But she was being unkind. They carried on around the pond.

'So, where do people go?' Anna asked Nik. 'In the daytime?'

'Churches. Other parks. Some people go and sit in galleries. In cafes if they can afford a cup of tea. I mean …' He threw his arms up in the air to signal the impossibility of pinning these things down.

'Do you work with the homeless, then?' Merrian asked Nik.

Nik thought about this. 'Yes. Yes, I suppose I do.'

'It's very important work,' Merrian told him and placed a hand on his arm for a moment.

'Thanks,' Nik said. 'We try to fill a gap in the market.'

At the west end of the park, they paused. Nik looked up at the palace above them but Anna looked back to the trees and the bushes, believing that there must be someone out here in the sun who was sleeping rough.

Beside them a family of tourists were looking at birds, an American father and his two teenage girls.

'Look at that big white duck!' the younger girl said.

'That's a pelican,' her father pointed out.

'Aren't they basically just all ducks?' the daughter said and walked away in disgust. Merrian smiled at Anna. Then she looked up at the palace and looked away again.

'What about them?' Anna asked, pointing to a scrawny young woman and the toddler on her lap.

'Would they be sleeping rough?' Merrian asked.

'Look at her. Look at her hair. And the kid. He's wearing too many layers. And a coat. Like he's been asleep somewhere cold. We'll just swing by. Try to be casual,' Anna warned.

Merrian said nothing.

The three of them picked their way through the sunbathers and sandwich-eaters. As they neared the young woman she stopped what she was doing and pulled the little boy closer to her. She looked down at the grass even as Anna tried to make eye contact.

'Hi. I'm really sorry to bother you. This isn't anything about you, okay …' Anna started and the young woman glanced up at her for a second. 'We're actually looking for an older man. I don't know how well you know this park, but sometimes there's a man who sleeps up there, at the top of the steps between the gallery and the column with the soldier on the top. Does that ring any bells?'

The young woman looked at all three of them and then went back to looking at her son.

'I'm not a dosser,' she said. 'I don't know who sleeps out here. I work.'

'Yes,' Anna said. 'I'm sorry. I didn't mean anything by it. We're asking lots of people.'

'What's he done then?' the woman asked. 'It's not kids, is it?'

'No!' Anna said. 'No. He didn't do anything. He witnessed a crime two weeks ago. Very scary for him. And he didn't want to speak to the police. Which is fine. But a poor young man was killed and we're just trying to find out what might have happened. Or what people might have seen.'

The young woman looked up at her now. 'He was rent,' she said.

'Yes, he was,' Nik replied, a very slight air of warning in his voice.

'That was that murder outside the clubs. I heard about that.'

'Did you?' Merrian said. 'Did the man who saw things … the homeless man … Did he speak to anyone round here? Did you hear what he saw?'

The young woman shook her head. 'I don't know who that is. Only that people were talking about it because it was really scary. But they got the boy who did it – someone told me. They arrested him.'

'Mmm,' Nik said. 'Thing is, he didn't actually do it. And they had to let him go.'

'Oh,' the young woman said and bounced the child on her thighs. 'Oh. Sorry. I thought they got him. You know who you should talk to?'

'No,' Anna said. 'Who should we talk to?'

'The boys that hang out round the back of the cafe. They turn up here at least once a week. Here for hours. Drinking, mostly. And they're … you know.' She did a little whistle to explain herself.

'I see,' Anna said. 'Well, that is very helpful. And we're much obliged. Round the back of the cafe? Thank you. We'll try there.'

And flashing Nik a pointed look, Anna turned and led the way across the bridge to the tea house.

There were sunbathers and picnickers spread thickly on the lawns all about the tea house and it wasn't immediately obvious who they should be looking for.

'Everyone on the lookout for somebody a bit …?' Nik impersonated the woman's whistle. Anna kept discreetly silent and instead tried asking Merrian something that she'd been meaning to bring up for a long time now.

'Your husband,' she began. 'Richard. Does he ever drink brandy? Is that something that he likes?'

Merrian looked at her with raised eyebrows. 'Mostly he drinks Scotch,' she said. 'Angus drank Scotch so Richard did as well. He picked it up at university. A little piece of grown-up Dickie to throw into the mix. Scotch, except at meals and then just wine. I mean, I'm not saying he wouldn't drink brandy. He might … Why?'

Anna shook her head. 'Just a stupid detail about that night. Something that's been bothering me. But if he wouldn't have been drinking brandy perhaps it doesn't matter.'

And then a call came from across the grass. 'Nik!' And they each turned in different directions for the noises in the park deceived you and it wasn't immediately obvious from where the sound was coming.

'Nik!' they heard again and now a young man in a blue shirt and faded jeans was standing up at the top of the bank and waving in their direction.

'Oh my God,' Nik said and walked towards the man without further explanation. Anna and Merrian followed him towards a group of young men who sat on jackets or the shirts they had removed, under the shade of a large, pale green oak. Nik went immediately to the man calling him, embraced him quickly and then they both sank down upon the grass. Merrian and Anna stood on the edge of the little group and watched Nik and his friend. They seemed utterly lost in conversation. And then a young man sitting at Anna's feet said to her, 'We have beer, you know. If you're staying …'

Anna thanked him and she and Merrian sank down on the grass on the edge of the little crowd of men, who blended into the wider crowd so that Anna could not quite see where they ended and all the others began.

The young man nearest her held out a bottle of beer, unopened, but Anna shook her head.

'Bit early for me,' she told him. 'Do you know Nik?'

'Him? No. But Miles does. You been out having a picnic?' he asked, nodding at Merrian's dress.

Merrian laughed an embarrassed laugh. 'Not really. We're meant to be on business … It's just I got the dress code wrong.'

The young man laughed and held out his hand to Merrian. 'I'm Will,' he told her. Anna and Merrian shook hands with him.

Will pulled a plastic bag from his pocket and started to unpack a pouch of tobacco, papers and a little bag of something dark brown which looked like peat.

'D'you mind?' he asked the women and they shook their heads, though Anna wondered if Merrian knew quite what it was he'd asked them. When the spliff was rolled, Will offered it to Anna first.

'I won't,' she told him. 'I have to go to work in an hour or so.'

Will nodded and lit up. He seemed to know not to bother offering anything to Merrian. Anna watched Nik and Miles from a distance, deep in conversation, laughing, and she wondered if Nik remembered what it was that they were trying to do.

Merrian had fallen into conversation now with Will and a tall, thin man who sat next to him and was regaling them both with some sort of crazy history lesson, involving female lepers raising hogs in St James's Park as a kind of constructive quarantine. The time seemed ripe for Anna to make a move across the group. She moved around what seemed to be the outer circle of men and deposited herself about six feet away from Nik and Miles, not so close that they had to acknowledge her, but close enough that she could hear what they were saying.

As it happened, Nik and Miles seemed wholly unconcerned that Anna had come to sit near them. Instead they ploughed on with their intense exchange of information, running through a litany of places and people of whom Anna had never heard. Anna could hear the map that seemed to be spread out between the two men, but she could not see it. Most of the names meant nothing to her, though she could hear the significance they held within the world she eavesdropped on. The Eagle and the Londoner's; Take Five and Kismet; the Music Box, the Huntsman and the Scene; the Alibi; the Red Room; the Carousel, the White Bear and Le Duce. Ronan O'Rahilly, Ken Leech, Bill Bryant, Mr Death and John Michael Ingram.

'But she was furious,' Miles was saying. 'And she went in the next night, full slap, and within an hour she's shouting the odds to anyone who's coming in: "Where's Jonathan Falkes? Where the fuck is he?" 'Cause he's had the lot from behind the bar. He's had the takings and he's had her lock box and he's had the jewellery she kept up at the flat on a shelf. So eventually Bernard comes in and he's half-cut already, 'cause it's nine o'clock and he's never sober past five, and he tells her that Johnny Falkes has been known round Soho for two years now for robbing boys of their watches and their takings, and he wouldn't touch him with yours and all of that. And Queenie's raving now – "Why did none of you fuckers tell me who this fucking Falkes was?" – and the bar is starting to empty out because no one's seen her like that before. And the mascara is going and the lipstick's up her face and she's leaning over the bar and screaming so hard there's spit flecking off everyone's face who passes. And the bar is getting emptier and emptier and Queenie's getting angrier and angrier and then she picks up a whisky glass and – smash! – it's firing in pieces off the bar-room door and poor bloody Gordon Heigh – do you ever know Gordon? He's seventy. Queen in tweeds, likes to listen to the talk? – well, Gordon gets a forehead full of splinters and then everybody's screaming. And someone calls the police – bitch – and someone calls the ambulance and then the police come and randomly arrest three of us for soliciting because someone's invited them into a queer pub and they reckon it would be rude not to … And Heigh's gone off to hospital, no idea what's happening … And I'm only in there because this Stephen had given me a £10 for all night so I'm stuck, aren't I? And that was the last time I went in there … 'Cause a night like that, you sort of think: time's up.'

'Bloody hell,' Nik said. 'I'm barely going into half the bars now. I'm flat and supper and four hours at the Dilly and that's me done. I'm tired.'

'You should come down,' Miles told him. 'It's better out of the centre.'

'Isn't it a bit thin? Money-wise.'

'The rent's cheaper once you're outside Blackheath. And it's slower. But everyone's high all the time round here. It makes people stupid. I don't want to deal with someone on meth. I don't want to spend four hours listening to some twat on speed.'

Nik laughed. 'I know. But all the same, there's life.'

Miles put a hand on Nik's leg. 'I heard what happened.'

'Yeah.'

'Didn't even know you were out. Glad you're out.'

'Yeah. I know.' Nik glanced across at Anna and raised his bottle of beer to her. 'I'm grateful.'

Miles studied Anna, a little warily. 'You his lawyer?'

Anna laughed. 'No. Just a friend. I poked around. I asked some questions. I talked to the police.'

'She got me out,' Nik said.

Miles reached for a bottle from a pile of bottles in the midst of all the men. He held it out to her. 'Have a beer,' he said.

Anna smiled. 'Okay then. Just one. I have to be at work by seven.'

Miles raised an eyebrow.

'Theatre,' Nik said. 'She works in theatre.'

'Fancy,' Miles said and kept looking at her. Anna dragged herself closer to them across the grass. 'You got a horse in this race? You think you know who did it?' he asked.

'I don't know,' Anna said. Then realised that wasn't quite true. 'There's an MP called Richard Wallis ...'

Miles laughed. 'Oh, we all know about Richard Wallis ...'

Anna looked across at Merrian but she was too far away and couldn't hear.

'Sorry?' Anna said. 'What do you know?'

'Ask Vincent,' Miles said. 'He'll tell you all about Mr Wallis and his parties. Hey, Vincent!' he shouted across the group.

At this, the tall young man who was talking with Merrian and Will looked over. 'What?' he shouted back.

'Tell Anna here all about Richard Wallis and his parties.'

Anna watched Merrian's face change. She watched the surfaces of her face, so expressive one moment, become flat.

Vincent rolled his eyes at Miles. 'Thought we'd had enough of that.'

Anna watched Merrian reach out and place tentative fingers on Vincent's knee.

'Excuse me,' Merrian said. 'I'm so sorry. But you're not Vincent Mar?'

Vincent looked at her and smiled. 'Yeah. Why?'

Merrian looked at Anna and then she looked at Nik. For a moment, no one spoke.

Then Merrian said, her voice shaking very slightly, 'I'm Merrian Wallis. My husband was accused of hurting you. And … I'm so sorry … I …' She stopped, her mouth open, unable to continue.

'Jesus,' Vincent said. Then, softly, 'Fuck.'

'I'm so sorry,' Merrian said again.

Vincent shook his head. 'You don't have to be sorry,' he said. But he looked anxious.

Merrian looked at Anna.

'Vincent,' Anna said. 'Look, you can say no if you want, but could myself and Nik and Merrian talk to you? Just for a couple of minutes? Could we maybe just go the other side of the path? Have a quiet word? A friendly, quiet word?'

Vincent's face looked as if he wanted to say no, but he got up, without a word, and followed Anna to the darker side of the path, beneath a line of trees. Nik and Merrian followed them and so did Miles, moving to stand with Vincent, a hand briefly placed upon his arm.

'What is it?' Vincent asked, crossing his arms in front of himself.

'I …' Merrian started. 'I need to ask … And you can be completely honest with me. I need to ask if you think … if you know that my husband hurt you.'

Vincent stared through them, not speaking for many moments. Anna reached out and took Merrian's hand and squeezed it hard.

Vincent blinked. 'Um,' he cleared his throat. 'The night it happened I was at your husband's flat. He lived there on and off with Angus. I don't know if you knew that ...'

Merrian nodded. 'I know bits.'

'I'd been hired for the evening, along with another two. We each got £15 to go off with guests if that's what they wanted. I think ... It was Angus's birthday. Or an anniversary. Or something. There were lots of people taking things. Mostly speed, I think. Meth wasn't really such a thing a couple of years ago. So it was just pills. And there was a guy dealing. He was always there. Um ... I did ... I went with a couple of the people there. Not with your husband. Or Angus. Around midnight they got a complaint, from a neighbour, about the noise. So the music got turned down and people started to drift off. They ... I think it was Angus ... they said I could go. They'd already paid me. On the way down the stairs, I met the dealer who was coming back up and raging because someone'd stolen a bag of something. And he pushed me, hard, screamed in my face. Thought I'd stolen his bag. He tried to go through my pockets and I had to fight him off. It was really nasty. Really ... not good. No one else there. And there were people – neighbours, I guess – shouting at us from the higher floors to shut up, but no one came down. So I pushed him off me and I ran down into the square ... And I walked over to this dark bit, under the trees, just to pull myself together ... you know ... And that's when it happened.'

'But did you see them?' Anna asked.

Vincent shook his head and then he bent down and allowed his hair to fall forward and pointed to large, jagged scars which ran from the top of his neck all the way up the back of his head, almost to the crown. After a moment, Vincent straightened. 'When I woke up in hospital, I had bits missing out of my head. But I didn't remember. They kept asking me, but I didn't know. I told them who I thought it was.'

'Who was that?' Merrian asked.

'The dealer. I thought he must have come back for me. He was a scary man. After I got out of hospital, I went back to work and I asked about him. He'd had people beaten, with metal bars, for failure to pay. He wasn't much on the streets, that wasn't his thing, but when he was, you didn't want to mess with him.'

'Do you know his name?' Anna asked.

Vincent shook his head. 'He was posh. Posh voice. Posh clothes. Tall. Pale-ish. Dark red hair.'

Anna sucked the air in hard. 'Oh,' she said. The events of that Sunday night reeled back and then sped forward in Anna's memory. She remembered sharing the spliff with him, taking the pill; the odd intimacy of the whole experience. Could it be the same man? She remembered the violence of the way he'd driven her out of the party. The way that the anger had exploded within him. Nothing – and then fury. It unnerved her.

'Did you tell them about him?' Nik asked. 'The police?'

Vincent made a face. 'I did. I was trying not to name names. You know … the men who were there.' He looked at Nik.

Nik nodded. 'Trying not to take everyone down with you.'

'I was doing my best. But I told them about the dealer. I told them about how he'd pushed me on the stairs. How angry he'd been. And they wrote it down. I think one of them even seemed to know who he was. And then …'

'Nothing.' Nik said.

Vincent nodded. 'They wrote it down but nothing happened. No one came back to me. When I asked someone months later, they just said there was nowhere else to go with the investigation. So, I don't know. Sometimes I think, well, there weren't any witnesses. And sometimes I think they got a bit burnt going after Mr Wallis. And then someone else told me the dealer was well connected. And maybe they didn't touch him because of that.'

'Vincent?' Merrian asked. 'Could it have been my husband?'

Vincent shook his head. 'He was still up in the flat. I mean … maybe … But I don't think the timing works. The lights were still on up there when I went into the garden. And … I … I mean, why? Why would he have done that? He wasn't angry at me. We hadn't had a row. He never seemed violent or anything like that. It would have been so odd …' He looked apologetically at Merrian.

'Thank you,' she told him. 'It's very brave of you to be so honest.'

251

Merrian and Vincent both seemed a little bruised by the encounter, so Anna thanked Miles and Vincent and suggested that she and Nik and Merrian retire to the tea house to think about what should come next.

Merrian bought them all cups of tea and Anna secured them a table by the window. Nik sat himself on one side of the table, the women sat down on the other. After the tea had been brought over, milk poured and sugar distributed, Anna searched her mind for something to say that would not stray into any unfortunate areas. She needn't have bothered.

'Have you ever met my husband?' Merrian asked Nik, politely and directly. 'Or slept with him?'

Nik paused before he answered. 'Not that I'm aware.'

'Do you know about him, though? Do people talk about him?'

Nik smiled and shook his head. 'I know there are MPs who go with boys. But there's a fair few of them and I couldn't tell you names. That world isn't so small that I can tell you everybody's height and weight. There are a lot of us, you know.'

Merrian nodded and drank some tea. 'I just wondered. I'm just trying to ... figure it all out.'

'Have you asked him?' Nik said.

'Have I asked him what?'

'Who he goes with? If he's seeing someone?'

Merrian looked bemused. 'Of course not. No. I mean, officially, he isn't seeing anyone. Apart from me. I suppose ...'

They drank their tea in silence. Anna watched a pair of secretaries swing by in pencil skirts and yellow blouses. There was such freedom in looking in on other people's lives for a second and thinking: no, that's not for me. She caught the smugness in her thinking. And then she thought of Gill's comment about never bothering to see the world through other people's eyes. Was it possible to stay certain of who one was and still curious about all the other ways of seeing things? She hoped so. For otherwise how would one ever find oneself sitting with a Nik or a Merrian and what would one make of the things that came out of their mouths?

'I wish there were an underground society for women,' Merrian said. 'Where's our bloody underground society, that's what I want to know.'

Nik smiled out of the window. 'I think they're called convents.'

Anna laughed politely.

'Is that it then?' Merrian asked. 'Is that what we get?'

'Yes,' Anna told her, 'I think it is.'

Nik studied their faces for a second. 'Why would anyone want to be hidden?'

'It's not the hiding I want,' Merrian said. 'It's just not to feel alone.'

Nik raised an eyebrow but he said nothing more.

It was after five now and a steady stream of men in dark suits flowed along the paths around the lake. Anna thought she spotted the Home Secretary flanked by three young men with folders, but they moved so swiftly, and the young men hugged the older man so closely, that she couldn't really tell.

It was time for Anna to go to work. Nik offered to take Merrian to the Alabora for supper and she accepted. They agreed to meet back at the monument to the Duke of York at around eleven, and make one more push to speak to the homeless after dark.

The Lights at Night

After supper, Nik walked the dark streets between the Royal Society, the British Academy and the clubs, scanning the edges of the railed gardens, looking for sleeping spots. He had left Merrian tracing her own path on the Mall, peering between the trees and underneath the arches. Nik tried not to look over the railings or to think about Charlie and how scared he might have been. He spoke to a man lying under newspaper who could not understand what he was being asked.

I am balanced, Nik thought, halfway between a place under newspaper and the warmth of a regular flat. In three months I may have gone one way or I may have gone the other.

* * *

The show had run long tonight. The audience had dawdled at their interval drinks, were slow to retake their seats. Anna unpeeled Bertie's wig in silence. Bertie at his crossword puzzle, Anna at her work. She had to go out again and she hadn't even eaten. There was no time to get back to the Alabora.

'Bertie?' she asked. 'Can I be really cheeky and take one of your apples? I'll replace it tomorrow.'

Bertie looked bemused – a thousand miles away, she thought – but he nodded at her. 'Of course,' he told her. 'Eat all of them. Please.'

Anna thanked him and took an apple and a banana, eating them in giant bites as she packed up her things and prepared to walk down to Pall Mall.

* * *

Merrian leant against the column on which the Duke of York posed. She looked across the park. Up towards the palace, down towards Horse Guards Parade. In St James's Park spots of faint light illuminated the trees and paths, the kicked-up, churned-up grass. Along the Mall, the Union flags hung limply from their posts. Very far in the distance, mostly obscured by trees, Buckingham Palace glowed myriad shades of cream and brown and grey.

Nik appeared at her shoulder. 'There's a man curled up by the steps of the Carlton Club said he thinks he knows the man we mean. And he knows it because he's taken his old spot. Says his name's Mark. And he's ex-navy. Beard – brown going grey, he thinks. Heavy drinker.'

Merrian nodded at him. 'Okay,' she said. 'Good. It's a name.'

'You okay?' he asked her.

Merrian thought about this. 'It's hard to know how to answer that some days,' she said.

'Yeah. Fair enough. I'm not really okay either.'

* * *

Anna found Merrian and Nik at twenty to twelve. 'Sorry,' she said. 'Came as quickly as I could. Where are we going?'

'Nik's got a name. Mark. There was a man sleeping by the Carlton Club thinks that's the man we're after. So ...'

'Any idea where he is though?' Anna asked.

Nik shrugged. 'I was wondering about trying the river. There's a load of them sleep under the Hungerford Bridge ... Waterloo Bridge ... Plenty of bodies, most nights.'

'I'm just worried about how many places we might be looking. Is there a cleverer way of doing this?' Anna asked. 'Who else knows the homeless? Other than the homeless?'

'Shelters?' Nik said.

'Yes. Shelters. Churches. Sally Army.'

'There's St Martin's,' Nik said. 'That's got a shelter by it. They might know him. Also the Sally Army place down on Embankment.'

They tried the shelter by St Martin-in-the-Fields, but it was closed already for the night, so they cut across the Strand and down to the Embankment, where a group of Salvation Army ladies sometimes stood at night. As they were passing through Embankment tube station, Anna noticed one of them, her cap off, her little stand of pamphlets under her arm, just buying a ticket at the last lit window.

'Excuse me!' Anna called and the lady turned. 'Are there any more of you left on the riverbank? I don't want you to miss your train home.'

The lady smiled at her. 'Just me.'

'We're looking for a homeless man ... Older but maybe not elderly. He has a beard. He drinks. Ex-navy. He used to sleep around the Carlton Club and the Royal Academy but then he witnessed a crime a couple of weeks ago. I don't suppose any of this means anything to you?'

The lady stared over their heads for a minute. 'There are two or three come to mind. I'm sorry. I'm digging this out from the back of a very tired mind.'

'We think he's called Mark,' Merrian put in. 'Mark who used to be in the navy. Did you ever speak to anyone like that?'

The Salvation Army lady smiled. 'There's someone it could be. We used to feed him a lot but he's sleeping on the other side of the river now. At least that's what one of our regulars told me.'

'Since when?' Nik asked.

'A couple of weeks. Two or three, I think. I'm sorry. I wish I could remember but it does all blur after a while.' She shot them an embarrassed look.

'No. It's fine,' Anna said. 'Don't feel bad – this is helpful. South of the river ... Where would that be?'

'Gardens at Lambeth Palace or Battersea Park, I'd say,' the lady told them. 'If you're looking, that's where I'd start. That's where people get fed.'

Merrian smiled at her. 'Thank you. We're very grateful. You should go and get your train.'

The Salvation Army lady turned. 'Good luck!' she called as she went down the stairs towards the platforms.

They crossed the river at Westminster, many of the windows in the House of Commons still aglow.

'Will your husband be worried about you?' Anna asked Merrian.

'Well, that's the question, isn't it?' Merrian strode on ahead, across the bridge and towards the south side of the river and St Thomas's. Anna and Nik shared a sheepishly amused glance. As they rounded the corner of the hospital, Merrian glanced at Nik and slowed her pace a little to fall in line with him.

'When I asked before … if you worked with the homeless … I didn't mean to be stupid. I just misunderstood.'

'That's okay,' Nik told her. 'No harm done.'

'Do you have somewhere … If you don't mind me asking? Do you have a home?'

'I'm with Anna. And before … I had a sublet in south London. I'm a little way off park benches.'

'Oh,' Merrian said. 'Good. I'm glad. I wouldn't want to think of you …' She waved her hand in the expanse of darkness.

The gardens at Lambeth Palace were not as large as Anna had imagined. They were somewhere between being a front garden for the palace and a public park, and they were sandwiched between a number of roads leading off in all directions.

'Shall we check the benches?' she asked as they drew near.

'I'll walk the south side,' Merrian offered. 'But if I find anyone, I'm calling you over first. I don't know what to say …'

She left them and Anna walked along with Nik, on the north side of the park. In as much as they could see anything, with half the lamps put out and the benches under the shadow of the trees, there didn't seem to be anyone in the park tonight.

'Can I tell you something?' Anna asked.

'Go on,' Nik said.

'I keep thinking about that man – Brian – the one who didn't want to alibi you. I keep thinking about how I basically blackmailed him … Just like … you know.'

Nik stopped walking, so Anna did as well.

'I did the thing that anyone can do,' Anna said in a hushed voice.

'Newspapers and policemen and horrible neighbours. I knew that it was cruel and I did it anyway.'

Nik frowned. 'We all drink a bit of the poison, don't we? It can't be helped.' And he looked at her for a long half-minute.

'There isn't anyone,' Merrian called, striding towards them across the dark grass. 'Not on the benches. No one at all.'

'Battersea?' Nik suggested.

Battersea, they agreed. They made the walk in near silence. As they neared the park, the road led them away from the river. Through the trees Anna thought she could see the dim lights of a fairground. Strings of colours, white and red and yellow, shining in the distance, on the other side of a dark expanse of ground.

'Let's start by the fair,' Nik said. 'We can do without my matches if there's lights.'

They stumbled a little, over tree roots and into divots in the ground, the way in front of them unlit until they reached the fairground. The lights which illuminated the rides had been turned off. But the perimeter was still marked by the glowing strings of bulbs and, in the distance, Anna could see a man on a step ladder working with a splutter of flame at a broken chain on the chair swing ride. Beside it was a brightly painted merry-go-round and a dragon of a roller coaster, its back arching as high as the tops of the trees. Anna smiled to herself in the darkness and thought of Aloysius. He would like this. Just now, as it was. No people shrieking, or kids cramming candy-floss into their mouths. In the quiet of the night he would look at it and see the Vauxhall Pleasure Gardens.

'I'm going to do the benches around the fairground first,' Nik said. 'But I'm telling you, an hour from now I'm going to need to be heading home to bed.'

'It's okay,' Anna said. 'Me as well. Don't worry. We'll try here and then we'll go on home.'

Anna and Merrian walked in the opposite direction. Merrian had been quiet a long while, all through the walk on the Embankment, but now she spoke. 'You know that marriage is a gamble. And you make the decision with too little information. You'll do it too, Anna, when the time comes. I hope that doesn't sound condescending.

It probably does. But we're none of us gods. I just needed him to be good.'

Anna smiled and nodded but she kept her thoughts to herself. So they walked on across the grass until they caught the ripple of a man's voice calling in the distance.

'Is that Nik?' Merrian asked.

'I think so,' Anna said and they moved towards the sound.

It was Nik's voice. It came ringing across the grass. 'I have him here. He's here!'

The women came running now and found Nik standing over a bench where a hunched figure stared up at them.

Nik lit one of his matches and now Anna could see Mark, his face dark but little lined, almost boyish beneath the beard and whiskers. He might have been any age, she thought. Not really old. Just poor.

Merrian produced a £5 note. 'It's the best I can do,' she said. 'Would you like it?'

'I don't want to see the police,' he told them, staring nervously at the money.

'You don't have to,' Anna said, and wondered immediately if this was a lie.

'I don't want to go to court,' he told them.

'I know,' Anna said.

'I don't want to get locked up,' Mark said softly.

'We're not the enemy,' Anna said. 'We're not out to trap you, or anything like that. A friend of ours was accused and then let go. But, in the meantime, no one's really looking for the man who did it. And you saw them … didn't you?'

'I saw the men climb into the garden. I got the police …' Mark sounded defensive, but then fell into a silence.

'Can you tell us anything about the men you saw climbing the railings?' Anna asked. 'Were they young, old, thin, fat? Was it easy getting over? Did they struggle?'

'The one I saw best, he climbed straight up. He was young and thin. Strong, I guess. T-shirt and jeans. Pale face, I'd say, but I only saw it for a second. I started moving as soon as I saw them. I didn't want to be involved. I thought they were … I thought maybe they

259

were going to hurt someone. I started to move my stuff and then I looked back, just for a minute. It was dark and I could only see him from behind. A man. Bigger than the first one. He struggled on the railings a bit.'

'Was there anything else, though?' Anna asked. 'What he wore? Or his hair? Or his height?'

'Tallish, I suppose. I don't think he was huge. Not fat. Just a big man all round. He made me think of a soldier. As if he was wearing a uniform …'

'A uniform?' Anna asked.

'Like those soldiers from the war films … Or an explorer. In the desert.' Mark stared intently down at his hands, which moved around each other as he tried to conjure the words. 'Those coats … Those jackets with the big pockets on the bottom. All belted around the middle.'

'A safari jacket?' Anna asked.

Mark looked up and smiled. 'Yes. Big pockets and a belt. That's what I remember. Because it made such an odd shape on him. This man, all dressed up like an explorer, struggling to climb the fence.'

The Potency of What
You Have to Give

Anna woke in the morning and felt the knowledge like a kind of doom which no one else yet shared. She made Nik some buttered toast and tea and went out after breakfast, walking the streets of Soho in a confusion of thought until it was time to go to the theatre and prepare for the matinee.

She greeted Susan in the wardrobe and scooped up the handful of costumes that needed to be taken to the dressing rooms. Anna worked without a word, finding each rail that the costumes hung upon. Tucking the boots and shoes neatly into place beneath the rails. She made a cup of lemon tea for Penny without being asked. She made a cup of coffee for Bertie and put it on his dressing table ready.

She was standing at the little window, looking down at the alley that ran alongside the theatre when Bertie came in and deposited his things. Anna moved quietly and shut the door. Bertie greeted her and sat down at the dressing table to arrange his make-up.

Anna went and leaned on the wall behind his dressing table, so that she could see his face in the mirror.

'It's been so hot,' she said.

'It never ends ...' Bertie agreed.

'And all through last winter you never wore a vest under your clothes. You always said the shirt and the suit, that was enough. You boiled under those lights.'

Bertie smiled. 'I do.'

'But then you started to wear it. In the middle of all this heat. You haven't been out of it. Not once. Not in the dressing room. Not at Angels.'

Bertie looked at her, his face open and puzzled. 'Sorry?'

'And you stopped wearing your jacket,' Anna said. 'The safari jacket. The one you always wore. You just stopped.'

'Anna,' Bertie said. 'What are you talking about?'

'You left the same time as Richard Wallis that night. I just assumed you went home.'

Bertie's face crumpled up in annoyance. 'I *did* go home.'

'Did you?' Anna asked, for genuinely there was a part of her that still wondered. That could not imagine Bertie committing violence.

Bertie's voice came low and cracked. 'What is this about?'

'I have a friend. You wouldn't know him – his name's Nik. On that Saturday night a man in a band beat him up, at a club in St James's. And as he was trying to go home, the police ... they'd found that boy, dead, in Waterloo Gardens. And they arrested Nik. They charged him. On the slimmest of evidence.' Anna was watching Bertie very carefully.

Bertie nodded. 'That's terrible,' he said, softly.

'Nik had twenty pounds in his pocket because the man who'd bought him earlier, he'd paid over the odds for him. Probably thought it would keep him silent. And it did. In a way. Because Nik protects people. He's very careful not to let other men get hurt. If you know what I mean.'

Bertie started to arrange his powder and his panstick, taking the lids off things and spreading them out on the tea towel he used to keep the table clean.

'They arrested Nik,' Anna continued, knowing now how she had to proceed. 'Without a confession. Without a motive. Without any witnesses. And charged him ... with murder.'

Bertie carried on preparing his make-up and started to cover the red patches around his nose and on his forehead.

'If he's found guilty by a jury he may spend his whole life in prison. And, you see, I know Nik. He's nineteen years old. He hasn't even really begun to live his life yet. Still making mistakes and figuring out who he wants to be.'

Bertie didn't speak. He was mixing his foundation now and dotting it around his chin and cheeks.

'There was a homeless man in the street,' Anna went on. 'He saw you trying to get over the railings. He remembered the safari jacket and the way you struggled to get into the garden.'

Bertie sat very still now. His eyes met Anna's, just for a second, in the mirror.

*   *   *

'Detective Sergeant Hayes. Vice squad. How can I help?'

It was Anna Treadway's voice on the other end of the line but she spoke very quietly. 'I think I've found the person.'

'Hello, Anna …' Hayes said, somewhat bemused. 'What person?'

'I think I found the man. The other man. From the tube station. And the garden. I think he would agree to speak to someone but he's scared.'

'Goodness,' Hayes said. 'Right. Well, we should take him over to CID. I can go with him …'

'The thing is … I don't know. Could we come to you first? No arrest. No fuss. Could we come and speak to you? And then, if I'm right, you can take it from there.'

Hayes met Anna and Bertie in the foyer of the station and led them back to his office with the minimum of fuss. Bertie was a plump man, Hayes noticed, with flushed cheeks and a dishevelled appearance. Strands of hair stuck to the side of his face, one of the buttons low down on his shirt was open, and his eyebrows seemed to have been drawn on with a kind of crayon. Hayes fetched them all glasses of cold water and a packet of Rich Tea biscuits, which he opened and put on the desk beside Bertie.

'Would you like to smoke?' he asked.

Bertie shook his head.

Hayes sat back in his chair and looked from Anna to Bertie. 'How can I help?' he asked.

Bertie rubbed at his cheeks and then stared at the make-up on his hands, seeming to have forgotten that he was half made up for a performance. Hayes handed him a tissue from a box on his desk.

'Thank you,' Bertie said.

They sat in silence for nearly a minute, Hayes attempting to have a conversation with Anna using only his eyes. Neither of them made it very far in that endeavour.

'Bertie?' Anna said at last. 'Barnaby and I have known each other for some years, and I think it's worth saying that Barnaby is a nice and understanding sort of a policeman. And maybe you could just tell him what happened, on the Saturday night. Because I think you know you need to tell someone …'

Bertie looked at Hayes. 'Am I under arrest?' he asked.

Hayes smiled and shook his head. 'Not a bit of it. You're having a chat with me. Though I am a police officer. And I won't pretend that I'm not. And I would like to know what happened to the young man …' Like Anna, Hayes allowed himself to trail off, ending on the lightest of notes, as if he was just wondering whether the sandwiches on the plate were cucumber or salmon.

'There …' Bertie started and his voice was very low. 'There was nothing deliberate—' He broke off.

Anna nodded enthusiastically at him. 'Of course there wasn't,' she agreed.

'I've never hurt anyone …' Bertie said.

Hayes leaned towards Bertie. 'Of course you haven't.'

'Nothing would have happened, only we were being chased …'

'I see,' Hayes said, putting on his most concerned face.

'I was on the steps of the tube. I wasn't *doing* anything. I think I might have seen him, the young man, but we hadn't done anything,' Bertie said. 'And then there were police … Absolutely everywhere. Running at people. Men. Regardless of what they were doing. So I ran away. Across Piccadilly and down Lower Regent Street. There was a man in front of me – I didn't recognise him at first, and then I realised he was the young man from the tube. I thought he might be more together than I was. So I followed him. He crossed the road by the clubs, past all those statues, and then he ran towards the park. I thought we were running to the park; I should have run there. But he turned right, into this dark street. Behind the clubs. And I followed him. And he stopped. And he stared over these railings for a moment, and then suddenly he was up on them and he'd gone right over. I tried to follow him. I thought he knew that it was a good hiding spot, a known hiding spot. But I haven't ever climbed a lot of railings. Not since I was a kid. I struggled, and I fell a couple of times. But then I found my footing and I made it over.'

Bertie glanced up at Anna. She forced herself to give him a smile.

'There was music in the garden, lots of voices. I'd thought we were climbing into a back garden or a gated park. It was happening so fast. But then I realised there were people standing close to us. Beyond the bushes and the trees. This lit-up lawn and all these men. Honestly, I think I was in shock.'

Bertie stopped and took a long drink of water, spilling some of it down his shirtfront.

'Sorry,' he said.

Hayes smiled at him.

'The young man,' Bertie went on, 'I couldn't see him for a moment and then he stood up. Still between the trees, half in light. I could see the colours of his clothes, his skin, so I thought: those men will see him too. He opened his mouth ... I saw him open his mouth and for a second I thought he was going to shout. God knows, perhaps he *was* going to shout. I just don't know. So I put a hand over his mouth. I was standing behind him and I put a hand over his mouth. And then he started hitting out. I mean, out of nowhere he started going absolutely crazy. So I hung on tighter and we both went down, into the bushes. And he was on top of me, I think, for a moment, so I kicked. And then we were side by side, and then I swung a leg over. I didn't mean to hurt him. I just needed him to stop, to stay in the darkness, to keep quiet. I knew – he knew – there were police out there in the street. Other men, running and running. We didn't know what was going to happen. We just needed to get through those moments. Just to hide. And wait.'

Bertie wetted his lips. Took a second to collect himself.

'I didn't mean to hurt him. But he was still trying to push me off. So I knelt on him, just for a minute. I knelt on him in the darkness. I didn't know what was happening. But he stopped fighting. He seemed to understand, it wasn't just for me; I was protecting him as well.'

Hayes glanced across at Anna. They shared a long, miserable look.

'I thought he was fine. I thought he was angry with me, or he'd fainted. I didn't know what had happened.'

Anna nodded slowly. 'It was an accident,' she said quietly.

'It was,' Bertie said. 'I couldn't hear anyone in the street. I thought that maybe the police would come down, come looking in the gardens, but it was quiet. I just wanted to get out. I left him and I started to crawl through the bushes. But I was making noise. There was no way round it. So I ran, quiet as I could, pressed against the railings. There was another bit of the garden, all dark and too far away for any of the men to hear me. So I tried to climb out again. Except this time I made an even worse job of it than before. I got stuck on the top of the points. Gouged bits out of myself. All across my middle. I was bleeding and it took me minutes … I don't know. But I got over and I walked. Just trying to seem calm. Normal. Round the back of all these buildings. More clubs, more gardens. It was so dark. I came out on the edge of Green Park, so I walked north towards the road. And once I was on Piccadilly there was traffic again. I got a cab, and I told the driver I'd been attacked and robbed by a hooligan and could he drive me to the police station near Stamford Bridge, because I knew the officers there. And he did. Kept asking me if I was okay. Wouldn't even charge me for the ride.' Bertie took a deep breath and shook his head. 'He left me at Fulham police station and I waited for him to drive off and then I walked home.'

Bertie stopped again and looked at both of them.

'It wasn't murder,' he said softly. 'Because I didn't mean to do it. I thought I was protecting us both.'

* * *

Anna walked home from the police station numb and cold. She thought of Bertie – and of Charlie – crouched in those bushes; the party blaring right beside them; the singing and the talking and the trays of drinks. He had been so close to so many people who might have helped him and he had felt himself entirely alone.

266

Back at the flat there was a postcard, sent by airmail, waiting for her.

Darling Anna,
The flat is sold. We are splitting the
money from the sale, but Clemence
will have the larger part. Her
situation is more delicate than mine.

I have told Clemence she is mother
and father now and no one else can
tell her what to do. 'Except,' she said,
'you are actually telling me what to do
right now.' But that is Clemence all
over.

I am coming home, my darling. I
am coming home.

Louis x

Miss Anna Treadway
84b, Neal Street
London
W1

* * *

Manslaughter, the charge was, in the end. Not murder. Hayes told her it was part of an agreement because Bertie had handed himself in. Because he was willing to plead guilty to manslaughter and spare everyone – not least the Hellenic – an ugly trial. After the news of Bertie's arrest made the newspapers, the phone calls to Anna's flat stopped coming. Anna waited for them, and tried to understand what they meant, and ran over the details of them in her head. But the phone did not ring with the strange voice again.

Less than a week later, Anna took a tube and then a bus out to Heathrow airport, travelling through the terraced rows and past the stranded, brown fields of Hounslow. She waited in the arrivals hall and saw the shape of his head, the outline of his glasses bobbing slightly above the crowd. Aloysius emerged slowly from the melee with many 'Excuse me's and 'Thank you so much's. He was carrying an unfamiliar and battered large brown suitcase and, for some reason, a blue china table lamp. He found Anna's face and blinked at her.

She went and stood beside the wall in a quiet corner of the hall and waited for him. And when he reached her he put down his case, and placed the table lamp carefully on the floor beside them and then Anna put her arms around him.

Not a word was spoken. And, in time, Anna felt Aloysius's shoulders stretch themselves out, and he reached his arms farther around her back and she felt his face nestling into her neck.

She realised there were no words that could properly convey the thing he needed or the thing she offered. She only knew that she was capable. And willing. And something in her understood the potency of what she had to give.

* * *

It was supposed to have been Benjamin's sports day. But nobody was quite prepared for all the rain. The House of Commons had risen for the summer. And so Richard was at home, dressed in a pale suit and tie, ready to appear in the stands and cheer his son, when Merrian rang the school at quarter to nine and they confirmed that sports day had been cancelled.

Merrian put a pot of coffee on the stove and waited to see if Richard would make an excuse and leave. But he only sat at the kitchen table and stared at the rain falling on the garden. She had moved her things into the spare room and Richard had not questioned this. She told the children that Daddy was snoring and Mummy was full of hay fever and it was better for both of them that they slept apart.

It was nine days since she had met Vincent Mar.

She poured the coffee into little painted cups and put some cream in a jug. Slowly, she transferred everything to the kitchen table, still waiting for Richard to excuse himself.

'You're free to do whatever you want now,' she told him. 'You could go to the pictures.'

He stared at her, as if perplexed that he was not alone.

'I'm going to go through Frances's drawers and find all the things with holes in,' she continued. 'Lots of darning, no doubt. She never gives me anything that's ripped … it just all goes back.' She put a spoonful of sugar in her coffee. She still hadn't committed to sitting down with him.

'I might just stay here,' Richard said. 'Do you mind?'

Of course she did, but she could not say so. 'Whatever you want,' she told him, nursing her cup of coffee, halfway between the table and the door.

'I don't think there'll be any more … journalists,' he said, not quite looking at her.

'It does all seem to have gone quiet,' Merrian agreed.

'They arrested someone,' Richard said. 'After they let the boy go. They arrested someone else. An older man. A … client, I believe.'

Of course, Merrian knew that this was so. Anna had rung and told her. She drank her coffee and watched the back of Richard's head.

'I know you didn't do it,' she said.

Richard turned to look at her, bemused. 'Of course I didn't do it.'

'No. But … I mean, I really know.'

'Am I missing something?' he asked her.

'I went and asked some questions. Discreetly.'

Richard's face was all confusion.

'Are you still together?' she asked him. 'You and Angus.'

Richard stared at her. 'Not in the physical sense,' he said, at last. 'But he's my friend. He always was, Merrian.'

She did not speak. She only watched him. She did not owe him anything in the way of reassurance.

He opened his mouth again, and then seconds later the words came: 'I had so little ambition. I wasn't brave, Merrian. I barely had a sense of what I might do in the world. And there was this man who said that if you were bright enough and you put yourself out there, you could do anything. Nobody in my life had said that to me. We were such dwarfish people. We were so cowed. It was as if Angus handed me my life.'

'And I handed you children,' Merrian said. 'And years of my life.'
She could have gone on.

'I know,' Richard said. 'Each of you. Both of you. You made my
world bigger ...' There was silence. And then he asked, 'Did you
really think I might have killed that boy?' She could hear the devas-
tation in his voice.

Merrian shook her head. She drew herself together. 'My guess
was no.'

Richard leaned his face into one hand. 'It wasn't my fault,' he said.

'I know,' Merrian said. 'I know it wasn't.'

'I feel ... responsible. Even though we did nothing ... I ...' Richard
propped his head in his hands and peered at her through half-
opened eyes. 'I feel responsible,' he said again. 'I feel like we did
wrong.'

'We?'

'Not you! Not you. I just feel this ... We should have told someone. We should have said.'

Merrian's mind ran over the conversation with Vincent Mar. Her
husband hadn't been there. He'd been upstairs in the flat. Had he
been watching from a window?

'You saw?' she asked. 'You saw it happen?'

Richard's voice was very quiet. 'We found him. You can't tell
anyone ...'

'I don't ... Did you go downstairs and find him?'

'We were in the garden. We heard him. Henry heard him. He was
crying ... moaning, really. There was this sound. Under the music.
Gasping, I think. And the rustling of the bushes.'

'Vincent?'

'No! No. The boy in the garden. The Charlie person. We heard
him, Merrian. He was still alive.'

Merrian was silent for a minute. She tried to replay the conversation that had just taken place.

'The boy was still alive?' she asked.

Richard looked as if he might cry.

'I don't understand,' she said. 'You found him in the garden ...
But then what?'

'There was this awful group of men. This birthday party. And they'd been out there for hours in the garden. Just being loud and drunk and singing. And then Henry came and said it was ridiculous to skulk indoors and he had cigars, and myself and ...' Richard paused.

'And Angus ...' Merrian said.

'And Angus ... and George as well, we decided we'd go out and just stake out our own corner of the garden. Just to remind them that they didn't own the place. But they were bang in the middle of the lawn, so we ended up at the edge, under the trees. And then ... Henry thought he heard someone running in the bushes. We thought it was someone messing about. But Henry kept looking, just peering between the trees. We got closer and then we could hear a voice. Henry started diving down into the bushes to see. George as well.' Richard stared at Merrian. 'I never saw him properly. Only his legs. It was so dark and I was rather drunk. We'd had all that wine earlier and then Angus and I were drinking whisky. It all felt a bit unreal. Anyway, Henry and George came staggering back out. And George was white as anything. He looked sick, to be honest. Because ...' Richard made a face. 'You see ... he knew him ... He knew the boy. Recognised him because ...' Richard looked at her. Merrian nodded. 'And then Henry was telling us to get back inside the club. George and Henry, they'd left their drinks, but they couldn't go back for them. We just had to walk inside as quickly as we could. To get away from that ... boy. We hid, Merrian. We sat in the darkest corner of the library and we hid. Because we knew the police might come, and it would have been too awful to be remembered leaving all at once.'

'You left him?' Merrian said. 'When he was still alive?'

'If Golden Square taught me anything ... You cannot be too careful. We couldn't be seen out there with him. And we couldn't let the boy see George.'

Richard looked at her and she knew that she was meant to tell him that it was not his fault. But all her forgiveness was used up.

'It wasn't really our fault,' Richard said. 'Only it might look ...' He didn't finish the thought. 'George has gone to West Berlin. I think he feels ... really dreadful about it all.'

Merrian nodded.

'We all feel dreadful,' Richard said.

Merrian sat in silence and then she thought: there will be no coming back from this.

Richard's fingers were tapping on the table. They roused her from her thoughts. 'You can't tell anyone,' he said. 'You do know that, don't you?'

* * *

Hayes didn't know what to do with it all, but he wrote it down. Anna came to sit with him, one hot Saturday at the beginning of August, and they went through everything they knew and could not explain away. The strange phone calls and the warnings. The *News of the World* story that had gone away at the prompting of an editor. The brandy glasses under the bush. The defensive Mr Wallis and his friend. The tall, red-haired man called Gill who dealt drugs, seemed to know everyone concerned, and who might well have been the one who attacked Vincent. They worked together on a single-page, facts-and-nothing-but, description of it all. And then Anna copied it into a notebook to take home for safekeeping, and Hayes placed his copy in an envelope and stowed it in the drawer of his desk. Where it sat, as he tried and failed to forget about it.

* * *

It was Aloysius's idea to put a notice in the newspaper. He even paid for it himself. Of course, he had wanted to put it in *The Times*, but Anna managed to persuade him that the *Evening Standard* might prove a little more helpful in this case.

For the attention of all friends of Charlie Burgess:
Charlie's funeral will be held at the church of Holy
Trinity in Dilton Marsh, Wiltshire on Monday,
5 August at 11 a.m.

If you would like to attend and require further
details, please contact Miss Anna Treadway
on (01) 012 137.

If preferred, you may send flowers on the day.

Anna had been down to the circus a number of times since Bertie's confession. She had found Tony and Saj and told them that it had, in a way, been an accident. She thought that they might find that of some comfort. Tony told her that there was a man called Luke, someone he knew of old, who had had a bit of a thing with Charlie, and had been distraught to find out he was dead.

'Do you think he'd like to come?' Anna asked. 'His mother phoned me last week – Charlie's mother. She got my number from the vicar. She wanted to ask me to come. and she said I should invite anyone that seemed appropriate.'

Tony smiled. 'Do you think she knows what that means?'

Anna shrugged. 'I can't really tell.'

* * *

Anna went to stay in Streatham with Aloysius and Nik moved into her room above the Alabora for the rest of the summer. He had lost his room in Brixton; it had been given away to someone else. He had worked a couple of nights since he'd come out but the events of that awful Saturday had taken their toll on him. The uncertainty of darkness scared him now in a way that it hadn't in the past. He found the noises at the circus took him by surprise and confused him. He thought he heard people calling to him, shouting at him; he thought he heard his name.

Anna had arranged for him to call Arthur Chisnall at the hotel on Eel Pie Island, and the man on the end of the phone had sounded interested, asking him about himself and what he liked. There was a place for him, Arthur thought, at the adult education college in Richmond, if he could find somewhere stable to live. Nik said he would call him back.

He went to see *Bonnie and Clyde* one afternoon in a small cinema off Haymarket. The pinks and yellows of Texas lifted him, but when the bullets hit he felt a horror. His sense of himself was fragile now. All the maps redrawn. Too many fresh memories that he could not erase. If he shut his eyes he might be back in Blackpool; or in an interrogation room; or lying on the floor at Mason's Yard. For almost the first time in his life he felt old.

He thought of Max far more often than he would have imagined. Still in the Scrubs, still on remand, still without a date for a trial. In some ways Max was like so many people that Nik had come to know, his friendship intensely important for the few hours or days that he'd fallen into Nik's company. Nik wondered how long it would be before he forgot his name, or recalled his face but could not remember where they'd met. He thought about Miles telling him to come to Blackheath. He thought about ringing Arthur Chisnall back.

He bought a postcard of Trafalgar Square – this had been Anna's idea but Ottmar had egged him on – one with the black metal lions and a red bus passing by. In the space for the message he wrote:

Safe and well.

Thinking of you. A very big hug for Dennis please.

Nikos

Mr and Mrs Christou,
56, Albert Road,
St Annes on Sea,
Lancashire

He carried it around with him for nearly three months before he posted it.

* * *

They met at Paddington station at half past eight on the morning of the funeral. Anna, Aloysius and Nik; Tony and Saj; two other young men called Fred and Kyle; and a nattily dressed older man in a sports coat, who Tony introduced as Luke. Anna noted that hardly anyone seemed to be wearing black, but they were all dressed soberly enough.

'What will his mother make of us all?' Aloysius whispered in her ear.

'Absolutely no idea,' Anna said. 'I'm slightly scared.'

They sat together in a third-class compartment. Nik soon fell to talking with Saj, Fred and Kyle. They told stories in hushed voices, sometimes giggling. Just once, the subject must have turned to Charlie, for out of the corner of her eye, Anna saw Saj crying. The man called Luke, who wore a wedding ring, sat slightly apart from them and gazed out of the window. Tony made conversation with Aloysius, mostly about cricket but a little about Rilke, for whom Tony seemed to have a passion, quoting pieces of his work with great intensity.

Anna watched the edges of London pass them by. The Victorian villas reminded her of the ones she had grown up around. The tree-lined avenues; the comforts of nature laid gently on the heads of twentieth-century travellers stunned and astounded by the venality of the world. She wanted to look on these places with cynicism, but her cynicism had rather drained out of her. She found herself hungry for beauty.

She was struck with the idea that if she only wished hard enough, she could go back in time and rescue Charlie. That his life was still somehow reachable, could still be turned around. I want to save everybody, she thought. I want to bring them back.

To Anna's eye Holy Trinity looked more like a medieval fort than a church, and she did wonder, as they walked down Dilton Marsh High Street, whether Charlie had believed in God at all.

She tightened her grip on Aloysius's arm.

'Are you sure you don't mind being here?' she asked.

'I'm fine,' he told her.

'But your mum …'

'It's funny,' Aloysius said. 'It's not there all the time. Sometimes I'm okay for nearly a whole day and then boom. I'm not.' He smiled at her. 'If everything goes boom I'll just slip away.'

They walked on, Anna trying to ignore the fact that every single person on the street seemed to think it permissible to stare at Aloysius as he passed.

A vicar stood outside the church; a little group of middle-aged people beside him in dark summer suits. Behind them, a girl in her early teens was perched on the edge of a planter, staring at the ground. As they drew nearer, Anna saw a woman in a long black shift step away from the crowd and move towards them.

Anna touched her chest. 'I'm Anna,' she said.

'Peggy,' the lady said; her eyes were rather wide. 'Peggy Burgess. I think we spoke on the phone.'

Anna let go of Aloysius and approached the woman, laying a hand on her arm. 'I'm so sorry, Mrs Burgess. This is an awful thing.' She gestured to the men standing around her. 'I hope this is still okay. You said I could bring some of Charlie's friends.'

Mrs Burgess nodded and looked at the group standing behind Anna. 'It's another world, isn't it?' she said quietly.

Luke, so quiet all the way to the church, stepped forward and held out a hand to Mrs Burgess. Anna saw Charlie's mother take him in, the nice jacket and the wedding ring and the air of middle-class solidity. She seemed to take his hand gratefully.

'Mrs Burgess, my name's Luke Merlon and I knew your son when he lived in London. I would like to extend my deepest sympathies to you and your husband and Charlie's sister. He talked about you with great warmth.'

'Did he?' Mrs Burgess's voice was filled with doubt.

'He told me a bit about you. That he missed you. I think he felt …' Luke's fingers jangled in the air.

'Go on.'

'I think … that Charlie would like me to tell you that he loved you very much. I know things hadn't been perfect at home. Not before he left. But I never heard him say an angry thing. Not once. He … he was sorting himself out, Mrs Burgess. I think … if he had had more time … he would have found his way back.' Luke stopped and looked intently at the woman.

'Thank you,' Mrs Burgess said.

Luke went and said good morning to the vicar, offered Charlie's dad and his little sister his sympathies, then disappeared inside the church.

Mrs Burgess watched him until he was inside, then she turned to Anna. 'Thank you,' she said. 'For bringing them.'

Anna and Aloysius sat together in the cool church. The younger men sat together in one of the pews at the back. The vicar spoke, but his words seemed disconnected from the awfulness of what had happened. He spoke of family and love and age, but Anna couldn't find anyone or anything particular in what he said, so instead she thought about her parents. She tried not to see her own mother in Mrs Burgess, but she failed. All of the bad children in the world and I am one of them, she thought. All of us failing and failing and trying to start again.

Aloysius told her when to stand and when to sit. When they stood to sing 'Jerusalem', Anna held Aloysius's hand tight as the music swelled. And he squeezed back. And they stayed like that, their hands tightly curled together, until the last note died.

Acknowledgements

This book has taken many forms. In my mind's eye, I see it now as a 3,000-piece jigsaw which, in its first incarnation, tried to describe everything in the world that interested me and how it all related. Subsequent versions would get smaller and smaller, focusing on this character here or that incident there. Plots came and went. The characters who dominate this book – Nik and Merrian, especially – were in the earlier versions people who barely got two lines to themselves, but who seemed interesting or challenging nonetheless. I kept thinking about them and so they grew. The final version of this story is both much smaller than the original but also – I hope – somehow larger and more generous as an act of imagination. I would like to thank Helen Garnons-Williams who came on this journey with me, read every version, offered advice, told me when things were boring and when they resonated. Waited while I threw entire versions of the novel out of the window. I am profoundly grateful.

I would also like to thank my tenacious and supportive agent Caroline Hardman – who is the reason that I get to spend my days being a novelist. I would like to thank the many hardworking staff at Fourth Estate and HarperCollins who put a tremendous amount of time and effort into championing, describing and advocating for the books their authors write. And I would like to thank the community of book bloggers, vloggers and Instagrammers, the online and print-based critics and literary editors who help to facilitate the ongoing life and liveliness of the publishing, reading and writing communities. More power to you.

When you imagine and write a novel over a number of years it inevitably becomes a collaborative effort of sorts – filtered, constructed and re-imagined through thousands of conversations, articles and chance discoveries. I couldn't possibly thank everyone who has contributed to this process but I would like to mention the following contributors. I would like to thank my father Oliver Ford Davies who talked at length about the challenges, restrictions and prejudices faced by gay male actors in 1960s British theatre. I would like to thank the archivists at The Postal Museum who helped me understand delivery times between Jamaica and the United Kingdom in 1967. And I would like to thank Sarah Galasko for inspiring the use of Lytham/St Annes in the novel and in giving her thoughts on the likely location of fish and chip shops!

I would like to thank my PhD supervisors at Cardiff University – Chris Williams, Claire Gorrara, Clare Griffiths and, in particular, Kate Griffiths – for understanding and supporting the odd nature of my thesis- and novel-writing life.

I'd like to thank my husband, Chris, to whom this book is dedicated. I spent a lot of time during the writing of this book thinking about what it meant to love another person and to make a life with them: the complexity of this act but also the grace of it. The way in which partnership or marriage arises from the simple human need to be heard or seen, to have someone who will hold your hand or put an arm around you when you feel despair. The fact that for many people on this planet, the simple and human desire to love and be loved in return is still vilified and derided, legislated against and supressed comes as close to an act of evil as anything I can imagine.

I'd like to thank my children, Alice and Rosalind, for being loving and ebullient cheerleaders for their mother's career even while they aren't yet old enough to read my books. Kids, when you get this far, I hope you enjoy them.

Amongst the many works I read for this book I'd like to give special mention to Matt Houlbrook's *Queer London* and Jeremy Reed's *The Dilly*: excellent, insightful, fascinating works both. Though not by any means a work of documentary or history, this novel stands on the shoulders of the many men and women who have worked hard to document the pieces of London's intense, shocking and beautiful past that have previously been written out of history.